# TRICKSTER CLERIC

# TRICKSTER CLERIC

## THE VULARIA REINCARNATION CYCLE

### BOOK 1

## G. B. SCALLY

Podium

# TRICKSTER CLERIC

# CHAPTER 1

The cavernous room stretched impossibly far into the distance, and a forest of vast stone columns climbed toward the domed roof where they disappeared into shadow. From above, a single shaft of light pierced the gloom and illuminated the cool marble slab where Amara had awoken moments earlier.

She stared upwards as she tried to orient herself to her unfamiliar surroundings. Turning her head to the side, she saw endless rows of slabs like the one she was lying on interspersed between the soaring columns. A glance in the other direction revealed more of the same.

*Where in the world am I?* she thought to herself groggily. But when she searched her mind for how she'd gotten here, her memories were fuzzy with large gaps in them.

Amara rolled over and pushed herself up with one arm. As she did, a terrible weakness washed over her body and she nearly collapsed onto the stone slab. It took all her effort to remain sitting, and her limbs trembled with the exertion.

When she finally felt steady again, she glanced down at herself and was shocked to see her clothes had been replaced by pristine white robes. Who had changed her, and why?

The sound of hurried footsteps grabbed her attention, and she watched as a man wearing richly embroidered vestments raced in her direction. He clutched a thick tome to his chest, and a bronze medallion around his neck bounced with each footfall.

He skidded to a stop in front of her. He didn't speak for several seconds, his face deathly pale. The young man had blue eyes, a narrow nose, and wisps of a beard on his face. "This . . . this is impossible," he finally gasped. "If you're here, then it means *everything* is real."

Amara opened to her mouth to speak, but nothing emerged from her parched throat. The young man seemed to understand her predicament and handed her a wineskin with trembling hands. She popped off the cork and the powerful aroma of wine assailed her nostrils.

While she didn't normally accept drinks from strangers, her thirst won out and she lifted the spout to her lips. The first few gulps burned as they went down her throat, but as it soothed her dry mouth the bitter wine might as well have been the nectar of the gods.

"Where am I?" she whispered, voice scratchy as though from long disuse. "And who are you?"

The young man seemed to calm, and then he inclined his head. "I am Brother Otto. And I suppose I'm a servant of the god of Sirveig."

"I'm Amara," she replied, glancing around the room again. "Is there anyone else here?"

"I am the sole caretaker of this crypt, though other monks and nuns reside here," he said hesitantly. "Most rational thinkers, myself included, thought that stories of avatars being reborn here were nothing but fanciful tales. None have been reincarnated here for nearly a millennium. But then the beacon was lit, and well, here you are—"

She interrupted him, her eyes narrowing at his words. "What do you mean, *reincarnated?*"

Otto blanched slightly. "I'm only an initiate in this order. And to be honest, not an overly dedicated one. I joined this church for the steady meals and shelter. My only job is to keep this place clean and maintain a vigil should an avatar arrive. Not that one has in living memory, mind you. I . . . I must send for the Bishop Krause, who is out visiting the nearby chapter house. He is only a day's ride from here."

Amara swung her legs over the side of the marble slab, letting her feet dangle. "I'm not going to wait days for someone to come answer my question. Tell me what you meant when you said reincarnated."

The monk grew paler, and his fingers tightened around the massive book he carried. "I understand this may come as a shock, but if the scripture is to be believed, you . . . died in your world. And through the will of the gods, you've been reborn here. But if that's true, then we must be nearing another Age of Strife." He swallowed hard, his Adam's apple bobbing.

"I . . . died?" Her eyes widened. She focused on her memories, but she couldn't recall anything about her final moments. The last thing she remembered was planning her father's funeral.

The thought of her dad made her chest tighten, and she blinked rapidly to keep the tears away. She refused to cry in front of someone she'd just met.

"Do you know how I died?" she asked, her voice raspy.

Otto shook his head. "That knowledge is never imparted to the servants of Sirveig. However, it is written that only those who died heroic deaths earn another chance at life."

"I see." Amara couldn't believe she'd done *anything* worthy of reincarnation. For as long as she could remember, she'd looked after herself and her sick father. While her friends went off to university, she'd resorted to petty crime to keep food on the table and a roof over their heads as her father languished in bed.

She dropped down from the stone altar and staggered as her knees buckled. The monk lunged forward and caught her arm with his free hand before she fell. "Thank you," she said, giving him a lopsided grin. "So, what's next?"

"Do you not wish to rest?" His face twisted with confusion. "I assume the process of reincarnation must be taxing. And should anything happen to you, Bishop Krause will have my hide."

Amara shrugged. "I'm not exactly going to miss my old life." And there wasn't anyone she'd miss, either. She hadn't had many friends, and her mother had left when her father fell ill. Truth be told, she felt vaguely excited at a new chance at life.

"Good, good," Otto said, unconvincingly. "Now, if you would just allow me to examine you."

She reached up to cover herself. "You're not touching me unless you want to lose that hand of yours."

"I apologize," he said, his face flushing crimson. "I only meant to scan your class and stats."

Her eyebrow rose. "Like in a video game?"

"I don't know how it relates to games. However, if you wish, you can take a moment to examine yourself first. In order to do so, simply think about your class and it should appear."

She followed his instructions, feeling skeptical, but a moment later writing appeared in her vision.

| Amara Solace (Unranked Adventurer) | Trickster Cleric, Level 1 |
| --- | --- |
| Stats | |
| Strength | 2 |
| Dexterity | 3 |
| Constitution | 2 |
| Intelligence | 4 |
| Wisdom | 6 |
| Charisma | 1 |
| Vitality | 1 |
| Luck | 10 |
| | |

| Weapon Proficiencies | |
| --- | --- |
| Staff | Novice |
| Darts | Novice |
| | |
| Skills | |
| *First Aid* | Apprentice |
| *Herbalism* | Apprentice |
| *Alchemy* | Apprentice |
| | |
| Martial Abilities | |
| None | |
| | |
| Spells | |
| *Cloak of Shadows* | 1st Circle |
| *Charm Person* | 1st Circle |
| *Heal Wounds* | 1st Circle |
| *Avatar of Melischar* | Inactive |

She read over the chart, wincing at how low some of her stats were, and then paused when she reached Luck. After the last few years, she would have expected Luck to be her lowest stat—not her highest.

With a shake of her head, Amara continued reading through what appeared to be her character sheet. The skills were likely derived from caring for her father over the last few years. However, the listed Weapon Proficiencies and spells seemed to be linked to her class, not her lived experiences.

Also, she had no idea why the last spell was grayed out and described as "inactive." When she tried to mentally select it, nothing happened. Maybe she could puzzle out its meaning later.

After a few moments of silence, Brother Otto asked, "May I?"

"Fine." She pressed her lips together and crossed her arms. "Might as well get it over with."

Otto furrowed his brow and then his eyes darted from side to side. After a second, he frowned deeply. "This is most . . . unusual."

"Is there something wrong?" she asked, his gaze spreading unpleasant prickles across her skin. Maybe something had gone wrong with the reincarnation process.

"It's . . . it's just not what I expected." He placed the tome down on the stone altar and cracked it open. As he flipped through the book, the sheets of parchment rustled gently. Finally, he stopped and ran his finger down a page.

Amara craned her head to try to see what he was reading, but all she saw was unfamiliar writing and fantastical illuminations. While she could apparently communicate with people in this world, she wasn't able to read their language.

"This is very bad," Otto muttered. "Very bad indeed."

"What's going on?" she asked, exasperated. "Is there something wrong with me?"

Otto shook his head. "I must fetch someone who knows more about these things."

"Not until you tell me what's happening." She let him wilt under the weight of her glare. "I'm not going to have you make all of those disapproving sounds and then run off without telling me what's wrong."

Otto looked like a rabbit ready to bolt, but he shut the book. "Clerics are quite rare in this world, and a specialized cleric is even rarer. But you are . . . aligned with a deity in great disfavor. Melischar is known as the Trickster Goddess. She is the patron of thieves, gamblers, rebels, and many other undesirables."

Amara blew a strand of her red hair away from her mouth as she let his words sink in. Of course, she'd arrived in a new world, and she had immediately been branded as an undesirable. While she'd allowed hope to kindle that she could have a new life here—free from her past—it turned out she was just the same old Amara: the one constantly in trouble with the law and looked down upon by all those around her.

"I . . . I think I should detain you," Brother Otto said, his voice quavering. "If you have been granted such a class, it speaks to your moral character. I don't believe you should be loosed on the world until I can contact the bishop."

She wasn't about to let anyone detain her, and if spells worked here like she expected, then she might have a chance to escape. Amara pulled up her character sheet again and scanned the page until she spotted what she was looking for: *Cloak of Shadows.*

She mentally selected *Cloak of Shadows*, and almost immediately, as if a shroud had descended over her eyes, the world turned gray. When she lifted her hand, she only saw its fuzzy outline.

Brother Otto let out a yelp and stumbled back, a look of shock on his face. "Please, you must remain here," he cried out. "If you don't, then there is no telling what may happen."

Amara circled around the distressed monk and then set off in the direction from where he'd arrived. While she couldn't see an exit, there must be *something* that way.

Her legs burned as she walked, and soon a thin sheen of sweat beaded on her brow. She still felt weak, though some of the strength was returning to her limbs. But with each step, a gnawing hunger grew.

*After I escape from here, I need to find some food,* she thought.

While the concealment spell was active, Amara felt as though she was burning through some sort of energy in her chest. And with every moment that passed, her reserves shrank. She doubted she could keep this spell up much longer.

She increased her pace, her legs feeling rubbery underneath her. Finally, she spotted a wall with a wooden door in the distance. She hurried forward, passing through the opening and into an unadorned stone hallway beyond.

By the time she reached the end of the corridor, Amara's spell guttered like a spent candle. The hallway opened into a room filled with tables and glowing orbs. At each table sat a person bent over an enormous manuscript, their quills scratching as they wrote on the parchment.

As she stood at the entrance to the room, the last of her energy waned and *Cloak of Shadows* dropped. At her sudden appearance, several of the monks gasped, half of them rising to their feet.

Amara didn't want to give them a chance to react, so she bolted toward the door on the opposite side of the room. Before the shock of her arrival had worn off, she reached the doorway and ducked through it to find herself in another long hallway. Amara hurried past numerous rooms as she searched for an exit. Finally, she spotted a huge, ornate door with sunlight streaming through its stained-glass windows. Amara reached the end of the passage and burst through the door into the blinding sunlight. She squinted as her eyes adjusted, and then she saw an open gate across an immaculately landscaped garden.

She picked her way through the plants and flowers before stopping at the unguarded archway. This monastery—or whatever it was—was perched atop a hill overlooking a city on an island.

Amara couldn't help but gasp at the sight. Every building shimmered with a rainbow of colors that merged to create a tapestry of incomprehensible beauty. Vast bridges spanned the fast-flowing river that encircled the city, and towers of the purest white reached toward the heavens. A thick wall snaked around the island, and at the center, a squat, ominous fortress stood guard.

She only hesitated a moment before setting off toward the nearby city. The rocks on the path dug into her bare feet, and her white robes billowed with each gust of wind. She felt unprepared for heading into the unknown dressed in little more than a nightgown, but anything beat being locked up in a monastery.

And, if her new stats were accurate, she might finally experience some good luck.

With that hopeful thought, she headed off to explore this new world.

# CHAPTER 2

Amara arrived at the city gates with weary limbs, a parched throat, and a gnawing hunger that grew sharper with every step. She'd expected some form of pursuit from the monks, but none had materialized during her brief journey to the city. Either they hadn't thought she was worth the effort, or they were afraid that she was dangerous. Brother Otto had seemed unnerved when he discovered her class.

The thought of anyone being afraid of her made a ghost of a smile flicker across her lips. Right now, she probably couldn't beat a butterfly in a fight.

As she approached the gates, the roads became clogged with oxen-drawn wagons, riders, and others on foot like herself. Many of them appeared to be soldiers, while others wore little more than rags. She waited in a queue leading toward the city gates.

Her white robes and bare feet drew several stares, and when a richly dressed man focused his incredulous attentions on her, she felt an unpleasant prickling sensation.

She didn't know what the sensation signified, but Amara didn't like it.

The line shuffled forward until she arrived at the gates, where bored-looking guards questioned each new arrival. When she finally reached the front of the line, she felt pins and needles across her exposed skin again. Then the guards lowered their halberds menacingly.

She stepped back in alarm and bumped into the mass of bodies behind her. Someone shoved her forward, and she nearly impaled herself on the sharp tip of the nearest guard's weapon.

"We don't want no thieves here," the guard snarled, any trace of boredom gone. "Get out of here before we run you through."

Amara fought down the anger rising in her chest at the guard's baseless accusation. The one thing she'd learned living in her old neighbourhood was to never talk back to someone holding a weapon. Even though she didn't *always* follow her own rule, in this moment Amara swallowed her retort.

She glanced back at the crowd, where dark mutters were spreading like wild-fire. The guards showed no sign of relenting. With a huff, she brushed a strand of loose hair behind her ear, and then turned and marched away while biting her tongue.

Thankfully, merchants hawked their wares outside the wall, so hopefully she could find what provisions she needed without entering. The first thing she had to do was to find some food and water. And then she wanted to buy some cloth-ing more substantial than her flimsy robes.

Avoiding puddles and piles of manure swarming with flies, she wandered through the narrow streets until she spotted a man pushing a pie cart. The freshly baked pastries gave off the delicious aroma of cooked meat. There was no one else nearby, so she approached him hesitantly.

The merchant looked her up and down, and then scowled. "I don't see a coin purse on you," he said. "And I don't give out alms to the poor. So, you'd best be moving on if you don't want a knock on the head." From behind the cart, he lifted a club and smacked it against his palm threateningly.

She resisted the urge to hurl an acerbic retort that would have combined her thoughts on his bulbous stomach, terrible comb-over, and stinking breath. Through gritted teeth, she said, "I'm a healer. Maybe I could trade you some healing for one of your pies?"

The man gestured at himself. "Do I look like I need healing? I'm a prime specimen, in nearly perfect health. Now, if you don't have coin, move along, little girl."

"Are you sure you don't want me to cure whatever devastating condition is afflicting your face?" she asked sweetly. "You look like something a child would scribble on a building."

"What did you say to me?" he roared, a vein throbbing on his forehead. "I'll make you pay for that."

With surprising speed for someone of his size, he waddled around the cart and came at her, his club raised to strike her.

Amara backpedaled furiously, cursing herself for losing control of her temper. Her father had always told her that someday her mouth would get her in trouble. She slowed her retreat, however, as it dawned on her that she wasn't weak and helpless like back in her world. Here, in this place, she was a cleric with spells at her disposal.

She briefly considered using *Cloak of Shadows* to slip away from the mer-chant, but instead decided to test out *Charm Person*. If it didn't work, she could always use her other spell to escape.

Amara cast *Charm Person*. It took several seconds to weave together the strands of the spell in her mind. After the casting was complete, she expected to see impressive visual effects—almost like in a video game. The only sign of her success came when the merchant slowed. He then looked around with unfocused eyes. Finally, his gaze landed on Amara, and he grinned broadly.

"If it isn't my favorite customer!" he exclaimed, the club tumbling from his fingers. "What will you have today? Maybe one of my finest meat pies? I also have this egg I bought from that gaudy elvish merchant. He says one out of every thousand is a dragon. Wouldn't that be amazing to get such a pet? My family would finally respect me if I had one of those beasts at my beck and call."

Amara watched him warily, looking for any sign that this was all a deception to lull her into false sense of security. But the man continued to gaze lovingly at her like a big, dumb puppy.

"I'll take one of your pies," she said slowly. "Oh, and all the money you have on you. Also, why don't you give me that egg?"

The merchant nodded and handed over a pie. Then he grabbed the purse off his belt and upended it over Amara's palm; a stream of glittering copper and silver coins poured onto her hand. Finally, he reached under the cart and lifted out a metal bound lockbox. From inside, he took out a scaled egg and several more silver coins. "I was saving this money to send my daughter to a private school in the hopes of giving her a better life than I had. But it's better that my best friend takes it."

Amara swallowed, her parched mouth even dryer as he extended the money toward her hand. What was she doing? She had a chance to make a new life for herself here—one where she didn't have to lie, cheat, and steal. And while she had no love for this man, if she took his money, then she'd be stealing his daughter's chance at a better life. And she knew what it was like to have your future snatched away.

"You know what," she said, wincing slightly, "on second thought, I just realized that I don't need any coin. Why don't you keep it for your daughter?"

"Are you certain?" He almost looked like he was going to cry at learning she wouldn't take his money. "I don't want you going away empty handed. What sort of poor friend would that make me?"

Her face burned as she spoke. "It's fine." Then she handed back the remaining coin. She hesitated with the pie and then tucked it under her arm. The man *had* tried to attack her. The least he could do was to give her a pie as an apology.

And she'd been hungry enough in the past to know that you didn't give up free food—no matter your morals. It might be a long time before she found anything to eat again.

Plus, she could always pay him back when she learned how to make some money in this world. She wasn't stealing the pie, so much as borrowing it from him.

Satisfied with her logic, she waved farewell to the merchant—who still looked crestfallen that he couldn't give her his life savings—and then hurried away down the muddy street.

Amara didn't stop until she reached a canal that led toward the river where she sat down heavily on a barrel. A gust of wind sent a chill up her spine. She placed the pie beside her and then pulled up her legs before wrapping her arms around them. As she rested her chin on her knees, she gazed across the murky water and wondered what she should do next.

"You're lucky you gave that money back," a deep voice said from behind her. "Otherwise, I would have been forced to report you to the guards."

She glanced over and saw a young man standing nearby. He didn't appear to be much older than her and wore leather armor with a pair of daggers sheathed on his belt. His hair was sandy and hung down past his ears. But it was his sharp blue eyes and their firm resolve that immediately drew her attention. As she examined him, he grimaced, his jaw tightening.

"Are you the town watch or something?" she asked. "Or whatever they call it here?"

"I am Jonas of House Stein, seventeenth in the line of succession, and a noble of the Kingdom of Mansfeld," he said, drawing himself to his full height. "And I witnessed the black magic you cast on that poor man."

"Wow, seventeenth in the line of succession? So, you're somewhere behind the family dog and the maid? And that *poor man* was about to bash my brains out with that club of his."

"Seventeenth is nothing to scoff at," he said, frowning. "And I didn't witness the first part you described, though I promise I would have stopped him had he attacked you unprovoked."

"It wasn't *exactly* unprovoked," she said wearily. "But I didn't take anything, so just leave me alone."

He raised his brow. "What about that pie at your side? I didn't see any coin change hands back there."

"Are you going to arrest me for taking a pastry?"

Jonas rubbed his chin and then frowned. "No. I will go remunerate the merchant for what you stole. However, this is your one warning: I won't allow you to commit any heinous crimes under my watch."

"I didn't have any coin and I'm hungry. If this is the most *heinous* crime you have around here, then you're lucky you never lived in my neighbourhood. Plus, I figured that the merchant owed me for wanting to club me over the head." Amara raised her eyebrow as she stared down this young man from the House of Stein. "If you're not going to arrest me, leave me alone."

He coughed uncomfortably. "Don't say you haven't been warned."

Jonas, seventeenth in line of succession, turned smartly on his heel and marched away. Amara returned her attention to the water. Was she going to meet anyone in this world who was actually friendly?

"I know how to get coin," a tiny voice said from nearby.

She lifted her head again and scanned the area, but she didn't see anyone. A moment later, a painfully skinny girl emerged from behind a stack of broken crates.

Dressed in filthy rags and gaunt to the point of emaciation, the new arrival's face was mostly obscured by dirt, and her greasy hair stuck out in every direction. She sniffled and wiped her nose with the sleeve of her ragged dress. "But it's going to cost you."

"How much?"

The girl raised her chin defiantly. "Half of any food you have. And I won't take any less."

"Deal," Amara said quickly. If this girl knew how to get coin, then she would gladly give up half of her pie—she looked like she needed it more anyway. "What's your name?"

"It's Salamander," the girl replied. "Like the dangerous kind that live in fire."

"I know what a Salamander is," Amara replied. "So, about that coin?"

"There's one of those board things for quests close by," Salamander said. "And I saw what you did to that jerk pie seller. You'd beat up some rats, no problem."

"All I have to do is kill a few rats to earn some money?" Not that she liked rats, but if there was a bounty here for killing them, she'd happily hunt a few down.

Salamander nodded with wide eyes. "They're pretty scary, though."

*How scary can a rat be?* Amara thought to herself. *I'd fight a dragon right about now for some clothes and sturdy boots.*

"Alright, come on." Amara stood up. "Show me where it is."

Together, they strode through the muddy streets until they reached a board shimmering with magical energy. She stood underneath it and looked up at the shifting text. "What do I do?" she whispered to Salamander. "Do I touch it or something?"

"Put me in your group." Salamander said solemnly. "I'm an adventurer, too."

Amara pressed her lips together as she tried to figure out how to create a group. Then she decided to try to just do it the way she had accessed her character sheet. She thought about creating a group, and then off to the side of her vision, a little icon with Salamander's face appeared. The image showed what appeared to be health and mana bars beneath it. Hovering above the icon was the name "Persephone."

She glanced down at the young girl. The more she was around her, the more she realized that she wasn't as young as she'd first thought—just malnourished. She might be eleven or twelve. The only way to tell for sure would be to scrub off the layers of dirt, but Amara had no plans to do that. "Are you Persephone?"

The moment she uttered the name, Salamander's face screwed up in a scowl. "Don't call me that. I hate that stupid name."

"Alright, Salamander it is," Amara continued. "Now what?"

Salamander stood on her tippytoes and shifted the clumped-up writing on the board until an image of a rat appeared. Then she pressed her fingers against it and the image dissolved.

Writing immediately appeared in Amara's vision.

***Slay the Rat!***
***A foul rat with wicked intent has made its den in the basement of the Dancing Gnome Inn. Brave adventurer, set out to banish this evil from the world.***
***Reward: 2 Copper Pieces***

She skimmed the quest text and then grimaced at the reward. If even a humble pie merchant had a purse full of copper and silver, then Amara wasn't likely to get far on the money offered for defeating the rat. But at least it might buy her enough food to last the evening.

"I don't suppose you know where the Dancing Gnome Inn is, do you?" Amara asked Salamander.

Salamander giggled and covered her mouth. "It's right behind you."

Amara turned around to face the ramshackle two-story building looming over them. Tiles were missing from the roof, and what little paint remained on the outside was peeling. A one-legged man had fallen asleep leaning against the wall near the entrance, a jug held limply in one hand. The inn didn't look very inviting.

"Alright, let's get this over with," she said as she marched across the deeply rutted street. "I want to do this as quickly as possible so I can buy some clothing." But she stopped when Salamander didn't follow. When she turned around, the girl was standing in the middle of the street with her arms crossed.

"I'm not going anywhere until I get some food."

Amara was about to argue but then changed her mind and broke off a piece from the meat pie. She was starving herself and should probably eat before facing the rat. The soft crust crumbled in her hand as she walked over to hand the wedge of pastry to Salamander. Once they'd both finished with their portions, they could dispose of the vermin in the inn's basement.

After all, how hard could it be to kill a rat?

# CHAPTER 3

Amara stopped a few paces away from the inn, realizing she needed a weapon if she was going to slay a rat. With Salamander in tow, she veered toward the nearest alleyway. When she reached the opening between the two buildings, she peered down its dim length. She didn't see what she was looking for, so she headed toward another lane across the street. This one was strewn with trash, and after gingerly picking her way through it, Amara found a length of wood that resembled a staff. She still didn't quite understand how this world worked, but the rules seemed to mimic a roleplaying game. And since she only had "Staff" and "Darts" listed as her Weapon Proficiencies, she didn't want to risk going into combat with anything else.

Her makeshift staff in hand, she returned to the Dancing Gnome Inn. When she reached the front door, she tried the handle, but it rattled against a latch. Were they closed in the middle of the day?

She lifted her hand and rapped on the wood. As she did, a stream of dust drifted down from the overhanging roof. Amara was still busy coughing and waving her hand to clear the air when the door opened a crack.

An old woman with wiry gray hair tumbling out of a shawl poked her head out. She looked Amara up and down. "We're closed. Come back when we're done with renovations."

When the woman tried to slam the door shut, Amara shoved her foot inside to block it. The impact against her battered feet made her wince, but she ignored the pain and said, "I'm here to deal with the rat problem."

Once again, the woman looked her up and down and then chuckled. The deep lines on her face twisted up into a ghastly smile. "It's *your* funeral."

"I think I can handle a little rat."

This only made the woman laugh until she wheezed, which turned into a hacking cough that rattled her old bones. After she'd finally caught her breath, the innkeeper opened the door wide and allowed Amara inside. But as Salamander moved to follow, the old woman held out an arm to stop her. The woman's smile faded.

"If she wants to throw her life away, that's her business. But I can't abide letting a girl go face that monster in the cellar."

"I've seen twelve winters, and I'm a mage," Salamander said indignantly.

"Fine," the woman said, dropping her arm. "The gods know I tried to stop you. We'll have to take down the barricade to let you through. And it's going back up the moment you're down those stairs, so don't try running to us for help."

*A barricade?* Amara thought to herself with alarm. *I don't think this is going to be as easy as I thought.*

"What haven't you told me?" she hissed to Salamander. "Why do they have a barricade to keep out a little rat?"

"It's . . . not so little," Salamander replied. She stretched her arms out until they were wide enough to fit a large dog between them. "They're about . . . this big, usually."

"Why in the world are the rats so big here?" Amara exclaimed in a hushed tone. "How can something like that even exist?"

As they moved between the long tables filling the ground level—the straw on the floor whispering under their feet—several men emerged from the back and dismantled the barrier made of lumber and heavy barrels. By the time the ladies had arrived, a breach had been opened that led down into darkness.

Amara stopped at the top of the stairs, having second thoughts about the quest. *Maybe I could find an easier way to make money. Surely, there has to be someone out there who would pay for healing services.*

But before she could change her mind, the old woman shoved Amara through the opening, and Salamander stumbled in a moment later. Then pieces of the barricade slid back into place, cutting off what little light there was in the staircase.

"Good luck," the old woman called out from behind the barrier. "You're going to need it."

Amara fought down the urge to hammer on the wood until they let her out and instead turned to peer down into the dark cellar. Now that she knew the size of the rat, her spells and makeshift weapon felt terribly inadequate. But she desperately needed the money.

"New plan," Amara said. "You stay here where it's safe and I'll go fight this stupid rat of unusual size."

"I can fight," Salamander protested. She raised her hand and it was immediately wreathed in tongues of flame. The fire gave off a soft glow and made the shadows dance. "See?"

"Alright," Amara said, grateful for the light. "Keep doing that and don't move. I think I have an idea. Wait a few seconds and then make the flames as bright as you can. But don't get involved in the fight."

Amara placed the leftovers of precious pie down on the stairs, and then hefted her staff as she cast *Cloak of Shadows.* Once again, the world shifted, and her vision turned gray. She crept down the steps, taking care to make as little noise as possible, and then stopped at the bottom.

Constructed of round field stones, the cellar shared the same footprint as the building above. One side of the room was filled with enormous wooden casks. The barrels nearly reached the ceiling, and Amara suspected they held alcohol. The other wall housed stacks of crates and clay jars. Something had chewed through many of the containers, and their contents were scattered across the floor.

It had only been moments since she cast *Cloak of Shadows,* but already Amara could tell her mana—or whatever they called it in this world—was running low. She wondered if there was some trick to regaining it, but she knew now wasn't the time to ponder the inner workings of her magic.

As her eyes adjusted to the gloaming, Amara saw a shape separate from the dense layer of shadows surrounding the casks. The creature that slunk into the flickering firelight of Salamander's spell was so much worse than she'd expected.

Beady, dark eyes swept the room, locking onto Salamander's burning hand like a hyena spotting an injured antelope. It opened its mouth and long strands of saliva oozed out. The mangy gray fur covering its body rippled as powerful muscles launched it toward the light on the stairs.

Salamander cried out, taking a step back. "It's coming! Where are you?"

Amara didn't dare answer lest she give away her position. Praying the rat wouldn't sense her before she attacked, she waited at the bottom of the steps, staff raised and ready to strike the approaching beast.

She held her breath as the rat bounded forward, and the moment it came into range she brought down the staff with all her might. The heavy wood cracked against the rat's skull. The beast stumbled before slamming face-first into the earthen floor, where it skidded for a few paces before coming to a stop.

A cry of triumph died on Amara's lips as the beast shook its head and then staggered to its feet. Lifting its head, it sniffed the air and spun around. Eyes glinting, focused on the spot where Amara hid, the rat lunged.

*It can smell me,* she realized with panic before hurling herself to the side.

Amara wasn't fast enough, and the rat crashed into her hip. The force of the impact sent her tumbling to the floor, where her legs became entangled with her staff.

The rat sensed her nearby and snapped its dripping maw at the empty air until it found her leg. Letting out a squeal of rage, the rat's jaws clamped down hard. Teeth pierced her skin and blood sprayed forth, the crimson liquid coating the beast's muzzle.

Amara screamed with the pain and lashed out with her other foot. She connected with the rat's face, and for a moment its grip loosened. With a fierce tug, she ripped her leg free and tried to ignore the throbbing agony that followed. She didn't dare look down at the wound, but she knew it was bad.

A shout from the stairs drew her attention to Salamander rushing into the fray, both hands ablaze. The rat tried to skitter away from the fire', but Salamander pressed her burning fingertips into the tangle of fur at its flank.

Fur ablaze, the rat shrieked. The pain-maddened beast bucked wildly, striking Salamander and knocking her back onto the stairs. As she fell, the flames dancing about her hands extinguished like a candle being snuffed out.

Amara dropped *Cloak of Shadows* in an attempt to draw the rat's attention away from Salamander. "Over here!" she shouted, waving her hands as she staggered up to her knees. "Attack me, you big dumb rodent!"

The beast rounded on her, its fur smoldering, eyes filled with murderous rage.

*Not bad enough fighting a giant rat, now I'm fighting one that's on fire,* she thought sourly. *What god did I piss off in this world?*

Amara lifted her arms and braced for the rat's charge. The beast slammed into her forearm. Struggling to hold it back, she accidentally thrust her hand into its burning fur. Agony lanced through Amara's fingers, the pain loosening her grip. Exploiting the moment, the rat sprang forward and sank its slavering mouth into her shoulder.

Working its jaws, the rat tore open her flesh while its clawed feet scratched at her stomach.

She groped desperately for her weapon on the nearby floor. When her fingers grazed the wooden staff, she clutched it tightly. Her position on the ground combined with the staff's length complicated matters, but she swung the unwieldy weapon and bashed it against the rat's head. Amara continued to strike the rat until it finally stiffened and keeled over.

With the last of her strength, she pushed the limp rat's body off her chest. Then she took a moment to pat out all the glowing embers on her robes. After taking a minute to regain her breath and wits, she crawled over to check on Salamander. The girl was sitting at the base of the stairs, looking dazed.

As she edged forward, writing appeared in her vision.

*Congratulations, Adventurer!*
*Through skill and bravery, you have driven off the heinous beast, freeing the inn from its rat infestation.*
*Collect the quest reward from the proprietor of the Dancing Gnome Inn.*

Amara dismissed the notification with a thought and then sank down next to Salamander. Still avoiding a look at her gushing wounds, Amara vaguely understood that she had lost a lot of blood. She was rocked by a wave of dizziness and nausea—which, she noted, was probably not a good sign. "Are you alright?"

"That was amazing," Salamander exclaimed, roused from her stupor. "You killed a giant rat all on your own!"

Relieved that her young companion wasn't injured, she flopped onto her back and brought up her character sheet. She wasn't sure if she had enough mana left, but she needed to try to cast a healing spell on herself.

She mentally selected the spell, and after she wove the threads of power together in her mind, a brilliant white light enveloped her body. Motes like glowing stars drifted down onto her open wounds. She watched with awe as the flesh knitted shut and scabbed over. A dull ache remained, but at least she wasn't losing any more blood.

Amara pushed herself up, using her staff as a walking stick, and then hobbled up the first few stairs. She stopped and stared in horror at the remains of her pie on the floor. During the fight, Salamander must have knocked the scraps of pastry over and they were scattered all over the stairs. She let out a long sigh. She'd planned to finish it off after fighting the rat. "Let's go collect our reward. And I hope food isn't too expensive around here."

Salamander nodded and then limped over to join her, rubbing her side. "That stupid rat really hurt me. Do you have another one of those spells for me?"

Amara tried to cast her healing spell again—even though the girl's wounds seemed minor—but then grimaced as she had the feeling of trying to draw water from a dry well. "Sorry, but it looks like I can't cast one at the moment. If you're still hurting later, I'll try again."

"That's not fair," Salamander pouted. "How come you got a healing spell, but I didn't?"

"Maybe because I was on the verge of death?"

"I've seen adventurers with way worse wounds just walk them off," Salamander continued. "This one time I saw a wyvern bite a woman in half, and she was fine by lunchtime."

Amara arched her eyebrow. "I find that hard to believe." But then she thought about how her wounds had been miraculously healed by her spell. With magic, who knew what was possible?

They slowly ascended the stairs in silence until they reached the barricade. She rapped on the wood. "The rat is dead," she called out. "You can let us out now."

"Did you really slay the rat?" the innkeeper's muffled voice replied. "Are you certain?"

"I'm pretty sure," Amara called back. "Now open up before I remember that you almost pushed me down the stairs."

The old woman's face appeared as the barrels were pushed aside. "No need to get testy. I just couldn't believe you two actually killed that horrible beast—even when I got the quest completion notification. I hope you understand."

"Oh, I *understand*," she said drily. "Now, about my payment?"

"Right." The woman reached into the purse hanging from her belt. "It was one copper, right? How does that sound?"

"If you try to cheat me, I'm going to go out and find another rat to put in the cellar. And I promise it's going to be bigger *and* meaner. How does *that* sound?"

The old woman grumbled and then pulled out a second copper piece. "Why are all you adventuring types so grumpy?"

Amara took the money from the woman and then paused. "How much for room and board here? And before you say the price, remember that business about almost pushing me down the stairs."

"One copper a day for both of you," the woman said. "Though I suppose with business being a little slow, I can let you stay for a half-copper."

"She's not with me," Amara said, without thinking.

Salamander's expression crumpled.

She'd just spent the last few years taking care of her father, and she wasn't ready to become *anyone's* caretaker again. But the girl looked emaciated, and Amara had been in her situation before. She wished someone had taken the time to help her back then. Plus, Salamander had known about quests, so she might be helpful in other ways.

Amara exhaled and shook her head.

"One half-copper for both of us?" she asked, ignoring the look of relief flooding Salamander's face. "If so, I'll take a room for the night."

Amara suspected she could find a better deal elsewhere. But right now, she was injured, exhausted, and starving. She didn't have the energy to wander around the outskirts of the city.

She pressed a copper piece into the woman's hand. "I don't suppose you have a bath available for guests?"

The old woman scowled. "That's extra."

"Of course it is." She looked longingly toward the kitchen. "Do you have anything I can eat right now? My meat pie met an unfortunate end in your cellar."

"I'm sure I can rustle something up for the rat slayer." The old woman tugged on her shawl. "And my name is Frieda. I thought you should know if you'll be staying here. I'll have one of my sons dispose of the rat."

Salamander pushed herself forward and lifted her chin to stare up at Frieda. "Don't you dare touch it. That's ours!"

Amara glanced down at her diminutive companion. If Salamander wanted to keep the carcass, then there must be some value to it.

"What she said." Amara crossed her arms. "Now about that food . . ."

# CHAPTER 4

mara luxuriated in the waters of the bath as her fingertips toyed with the bubbles floating on the surface. She could only partially stretch out in the narrow bronze tub, and the water was tepid at best. But it still felt wonderful.

As she sank into the water up to her chin, she pulled up her character sheet. She'd only noticed after the fight, but she'd gained a level from completing the quest.

| Amara Solace (Unranked Adventurer) | Trickster Cleric, Level 2 |
|---|---|
| Stats | |
| Strength | 2 |
| Dexterity | 3 |
| Constitution | 2 |
| Intelligence | 4 |
| Wisdom | 6 |
| Charisma | 1 |
| Vitality | 1 |
| Luck | 10 |
| New Stat Points | 3 |
| | |
| Weapon Proficiencies | |
| Staff | Novice |
| Darts | Novice |
| | |

| Skills | |
| --- | --- |
| *First Aid* | Apprentice |
| *Herbalism* | Apprentice |
| *Alchemy* | Apprentice |
| | |
| **Martial Abilities** | |
| **None** | |
| | |
| **Spells** | |
| *Cloak of Shadows* | 1st Circle |
| *Charm Person* | 1st Circle |
| *Heal Wounds* | 1st Circle |
| *Avatar of Melischar* | Inactive |
| | |
| **New Expertise Points** | 1 |

She'd already spent a little time considering how to allocate her allotted points for stats and expertise. Back home, she'd only played a handful of role-playing video games—her family's laptop had always been right out of the stone age—but she knew that Wisdom was one of the most important stats for priests. And a Trickster Cleric likely wasn't that different.

But that was assuming everything here worked the same as in the video games from her world. And that was a big assumption. Still, until she found someone more knowledgeable on the subject, she'd have to rely on educated guesses.

The water sloshed around the tub as she leaned forward to touch her character sheet. She allocated two points to Wisdom, and then placed the last point into Luck. With everything that had happened since her arrival, she could use a little more good fortune.

Then she moved on to her expertise point. This one was a much harder decision. She'd already tried to upgrade her *Charm Person* spell—which had proved its usefulness—but when she'd tried, the following message had appeared:

*Not enough Expertise Points to upgrade the selected spell.*

While she couldn't be sure, Amara suspected she would need at least two Expertise Points to upgrade the spell to the second Circle. Hopefully, she could find someone who could explain all of this to her in the near future. She'd asked Salamander, but the young girl had no idea how any of this worked.

Amara was left with the choice of unlocking a new Weapon Proficiency, Martial Ability, skill, or spell. She immediately dismissed the first two, as she had no weapons to speak of, and none of her skills seemed likely to help her with quests.

That only left Martial Abilities and spells.

After mulling it over for a minute, she selected Spell, and five new options appeared floating in the air in front of her.

*Select Casting School to Unlock Random Spell:*
*Healing*
*Offensive*
*Defensive*
*Support*
*Speciality: Trickster Cleric*

Since she'd performed so poorly against the giant rat, without hesitation she selected the option offering offense. If she was going to keep fighting monsters, then she needed a better plan than just hitting them with a stick and hoping for the best.

The moment she pressed it, bright colors exploded in her vision, and flaming text appeared out of nowhere. It almost reminded her of the flashy animations from *gacha* games.

*New Spell Unlocked!*
*Critical Luck Success! Level 20 Spell Granted.*
*Divine Weapon*
*A spectral weapon appears directly in front of the caster and will remain for the duration of the spell. The weapon can be commanded to attack any target within sight of the caster. If no target is chosen, the weapon will attempt to defend against any attacks or spells directed at the caster. If this spell is cast a second time, the original weapon will disappear.*
*Duration: 1 minute + 1 minute per caster level*

Amara immediately felt vindicated for allocating an extra point to Luck, as this spell was far above her current level. And it sounded like it would make questing much easier. If she cast *Divine Weapon* and then hid with *Cloak of Shadows,* she might not even have to put herself in harm's way again.

With her leveling completed, she knew it was finally time to get out of the bath. After all, she wanted to leave some warm water for Salamander.

With a sigh, she rose from the tub and shook off the water from her hands before grabbing the towel that had been provided. She wrapped it around herself and stepped out of the bath. A pool of water immediately formed under her feet as she shivered in the cool air.

She turned and pressed her lips together as she examined her dirty and singed clothing lying on the nearby chair. The idea of putting her filthy robes back on wasn't especially appealing, but she had no other options—unless she wanted to run around the streets naked like a mad woman.

And she still had no shoes for her feet. She hated the idea of going back out there barefoot. While her feet were holding up surprisingly well with only a few scrapes and minor cuts, they were still too soft from a lifetime of wearing shoes.

*I need to earn enough money to buy some clothing and sturdy boots. And fast.*

She tossed the towel aside and then reached out to grab her robe. With a grimace, she pulled the stinking rag over her head and let it fall into place. It made her look like a sack of potatoes, but beggars couldn't be choosers. After dressing and folding the towel, she left the room to find Salamander standing outside.

The girl glared at her and then crossed her arms. "I don't need a bath."

"Yes, you do," Amara replied. "Your appearance is only going to draw attention from the guards."

"I hate baths," the young girl explained. "The rain gets you nice and clean. And it rained only a few days ago."

"Go take your bath." Amara raised her eyebrow and added, "At least, if you want to eat."

"You still owe me half a pie." Salamander showed no signs of moving. "Most of it wasn't even touching the floor. I don't see why we couldn't eat it where it fell."

"Because it was disgusting, and that's how you get sick. Now go take a bath!"

Salamander grumbled on her way into the bathroom but didn't argue any further. A moment later, there was a splash, followed by sputters and shouts of discontent.

Leaving the girl to her ablutions, Amara looked around for the innkeeper and the food she'd promised. As if on cue, Freida emerged from the kitchen holding an earthenware pitcher, two wooden cups, and a plate overflowing with cheese, bread, and dried fruit. Frieda placed the bounty on a nearby table and motioned for Amara to join her.

Approaching the table, Amara's stomach produced noises which were decidedly unladylike. It felt like forever since she'd last eaten, and she could probably devour the entire platter without coming up for air. But she didn't want to eat without Salamander, so she sat down on the chair and crossed her legs.

As she waited, she drummed her fingers against the tabletop, and then finally gave in and snatched a piece of dried fruit. She popped it into her mouth and chewed slowly. It tasted like a cross between mango and apple, and while delicious, it barely took the edge off her hunger.

After a few minutes, Salamander appeared, looking like a butterfly that had emerged from its cocoon. Her dark, filthy hair had been replaced with flaxen strands, and freckles now dotted her cheeks. While she was dressed in the same ragged clothing, at least she no longer looked like a street urchin.

"So, there was a girl under all that grime, after all." Amara smiled as the girl scowled back at her. "The food arrived while you were in there."

Salamander slunk over to the table as she tried to pat down her wild hair. "I look stupid," she grumbled. "No one is going to recognize me."

"That's a good thing," Amara said. "And it means we won't draw too much undue attention." She took the pitcher and poured a dark liquid into the cups. The drink looked and smelled like cheap beer. Didn't they have something for children here?

But before she could say anything, Salamander snatched the cup and upended it into her mouth. Her face lit up with delight. "This is the best beer I've ever had."

"Do you . . . drink beer often here?"

"What else you going to drink?" the girl asked. "Water?"

Amara frowned. "Well, yes. I'd prefer to drink water over beer."

"For someone afraid of floor pie, you sure are strange. Water will kill you faster than a goblin holding a dagger to your throat."

"Good to know," she muttered. "But won't you, you know . . . get drunk?"

"You can't get drunk on short beer, silly." Salamander wiggled her cup toward Amara. "Can I get another drink?"

Amara hesitantly poured some more. She felt conflicted giving alcohol to a child, but—for now, at least—she'd have to trust Salamander's word. The thought of the girl's name urged Amara to bring up another question she'd been pondering. "Salamander is a bit of a mouthful. Do you mind if I shorten it a bit? Maybe something like Sally?"

Salamander shook her head. "No way. Who's going to be scared of someone with a stupid name like Sally? Lots of people are afraid of fire salamanders."

"If you say so." Amara sighed. "But I'm hoping that you won't need to strike fear in the heart of anyone anytime soon. Not while we have a roof over our heads, at least." Her own brief time on the streets had given her a general idea of how dangerous it was for a girl out there and she understood why an imposing name might be important to Salamander. Which meant Amara was stuck saying the girl's mouthful of a name for the foreseeable future.

As her thoughts turned to her own past on the street, she once again wondered about her death. Why couldn't she remember anything about her last moments? Was that part of the reincarnation process? Or did it mean something else?

After dwelling on it for a few moments, she returned her attention to the food on the platter. While she'd been preoccupied, Salamander had gotten a head start and she was stuffing her face like she hadn't eaten in a month. Amara smiled and then joined her. The bread was slightly stale, and the cheese was a bit too tart, but it was still the best meal she'd ever eaten.

Neither of them spoke as they devoured the meal.

Once Amara finished the last morsel, she stared at the empty platter longingly. It was doubtful they'd get any more until dinner time. She gave Freida a hopeful look, but the crone's scowl confirmed her suspicions.

Instead of pressing the issue, she leaned back and looked at Salamander. "Any ideas on what we should do next for some money? I'd like to stay in this inn for as long as possible. At least until I get my footing in this city."

"Sign up for the guild," Salamander said around a full mouth of bread. "Then get some really good quests and upgrade your skills."

"What guild?"

"What *guild?*" Salamander replied with a chuckle. "The Adventurer's Guild. You know, the one with all the guys with big swords and stuff?"

"Is that located inside the walls?"

Salamander nodded.

"Then we have a problem." Amara lowered her voice so Freida couldn't hear the next part. "Apparently, my class is only given to thieves. So, I'm not *exactly* allowed inside the gates."

Salamander twirled a loose strand of hair around her finger. "I guess we could just keep doing local quests. They barely give you any coin, though."

"Would it involve fighting more rats?" Amara shuddered at the thought of encountering the ridiculously large beasts anytime soon. The fight in the cellar had been far too close, and she resolved to never go into a battle blind again. This world was turning out to be far deadlier than she'd expected.

"Maybe?" Salamander looked thoughtful for a moment. "There's some that send you to the forest as well. But there're all kinds of scary beasts hiding in there. My mother told me . . ." Her voice trailed off and the girl looked down at her feet. After a moment, she spoke again, her voice small. "I just heard it's not safe in there."

Amara didn't press Salamander on the mention of her mother, since she didn't know her well enough to pry into her life. Not yet, at least. "Since we're done eating, why don't we go check out the quests?"

"Does that mean I can come?"

"I don't know." Amara examined the girl—who looked like she would burst with excitement—and mulled over what to do with her. She wasn't responsible for Salamander's well being, but she also didn't want to put her in danger again.

After a moment's thought, she changed the subject. "How do you normally make money around here?"

"Mostly I go through garbage to find good stuff." Salamander plucked a breadcrumb from the platter and dropped it into her mouth. "I tried begging for a while, but the guards beat you if they catch you."

"Well, I don't want you picking through garbage anymore. If you promise to stay out of danger, you can come with me."

"This will be great!" Salamander screamed in excitement. "I'm going to be an adventurer for real!"

"How does all that work, anyway? How do you become an adventurer?"

Salamander gave her a strange look. "Did you get knocked on the head or something?"

Amara craned her neck to see Freida busy with washing a table on the far side of the room and then she lowered her voice to a whisper. "Can you keep a secret?"

The girl nodded quickly.

She didn't think Salamander had anyone to share her secret with, and at some point, she'd probably figure it out on her own. After all, Amara didn't know the first thing about how this place worked, and her questions would eventually make the girl suspicious. "I'm not from this world. I woke up here this morning in some kind of church."

"There are other worlds?" Salamander gasped before clamping her hands over her mouth. "Sorry, I didn't mean to say anything."

Amara winced, but it didn't seem that Freida had overheard Salamander's little slip. "You don't know about other worlds?"

Salamander shook her head and shrugged. "It sounds like something you'd learn reading books. Pass."

Amara thought back to the monk she'd encountered when she first arrived. Maybe she'd have to find some scholars in this world to answer her questions. After all, Brother Otto—a man she suspected was highly educated—had mentioned that he and many others believed reincarnations were nothing but myth. Which meant few people would know anything about the process.

As she was lost in thought, Salamander squinched up her eyes and studied her.

Just when she was about to ask the girl what she was doing, a wave of faint prickles passed over her skin. "What was that?" Amara frowned. "What did you just do to me?"

The young girl collapsed back in her chair, breathing hard. "I'm not too good at *Inquiring Eye*. But I'm getting better, though."

"Do you want to explain exactly what you did to me? And what is *Inquiring Eye*? That didn't feel particularly pleasant."

"Sorry. My nanna used to say it was rude to do that to strangers," Salamander replied, but her grin revealed that she wasn't remorseful. "A *lot* of fights get started from someone using that. But I just had to see your class. You're a Trickster Cleric!"

"Tell me something I don't know," Amara replied. "Did that thing you just mentioned let you see my class?"

Salamander nodded, looking like a cat who had swallowed a canary. "And your level."

"That's interesting," Amara mused. It would be incredibly helpful to learn someone's class. That way, she'd know who posed a threat and who didn't. Plus, it might give her other useful information. "Do you think you could teach me how to do it?"

"Who cares about learning?" Salamander leaned forward. "We could be rich! Rich as silk merchants!"

"What are you talking about?"

"You could trick people into giving up all their gold." Salamander's eyes gleamed with excitement. "We could buy a huge house and I could get a dog. One of the little cute ones. Oh, and I could get some pretty dresses. Wouldn't you like some dresses?"

"I'm not stealing from anyone." Amara was troubled by the girl's reaction. Would everyone she met here think of her as nothing more than a thief?

*But I did steal a meat pie from that merchant,* she thought to herself sourly. *Which pretty much proves that my mother was right—I'm nothing but a delinquent.* She ruthlessly pushed down her thoughts, knowing where they would lead. She reminded herself that the sanctimonious young man she'd met had promised to pay back the merchant which—by Amara's logic—meant she technically hadn't stolen anything.

"Why wouldn't you want to steal?" Salamander asked, incredulous. "All of those rich people looking down on us here in the outer city. Did you know they lock up people who can't pay their bills?"

"They put people in prison who can't pay their debts?"

"My dad owed a lot of money." Salamander said before she trailed off, suddenly seeming very small. Then, she blinked her eyes and her face hardened. "Those rich nobles and merchants should have every last coin taken from them. Then they'd know what it was like."

Amara recognized the hurt in the girl's voice. Apparently, Salamander's parents were locked away in some form of debtor's prison—which explained how the child had ended up on the street. Now that Amara thought about it, maybe there were some people here who deserved to have their possessions liberated.

But she wouldn't go down that path until she'd exhausted all other options.

"Come on," Amara said, standing up. "Let's go look at the mission board. Then we can see about making us both some money."

# CHAPTER 5

Amara awoke to darkness in her room at the Dancing Gnome Inn. When she glanced over at the shuttered window, not a speck of light was visible through the cracks. Which meant it wasn't dawn yet. While she never rose before the sun back home, it felt like she'd had a full night's rest. And she had no desire to go back to sleep.

She took a moment to gently push Salamander's foot out of her face before swinging her legs over the side of the straw mattress. As she yawned and stretched, Amara heard grumbles coming from the girl. A moment later, Salamander's head rose and she gazed around the room blearily. Voice thick and groggy, she asked, "Is the sun up yet?"

Amara shook her head no.

Salamander plopped back on the bed, and soon snores filled the air.

Since she didn't want to wake Salamander again, Amara stood up gingerly and winced when the floorboards creaked underfoot. She needn't have worried as her snoring companion didn't stir. Amara crept over to the corner and grabbed the length of wood she had been using as a staff. Having gathered her meagre possessions, she left the room.

She padded down the stairs to find the main room of the inn already bustling with activity. The delicious scent of baking bread filled the air. Frieda hurried about the kitchen, stopping at the hearth to tend to a pan of sizzling bacon before an opening to the brick to retrieve a loaf of bread with the deft use of a wooden paddle.

Amara turned her attention back to the main room. Frieda's three sons sat on chairs around the fire. They laughed as they shared a drink together as Amara strode by. She came to a long table where a group of four had gathered.

The four of them were arrayed around the table: a huge man with a shaved head dressed in armor; a striking woman holding what looked like a miniature harp; a spindly man dressed in blue robes who clasped a thick book to his chest; and finally, a hawk-faced man who absently sheathed and unsheathed a sliver of his rapier's blade.

Their clothing and armor were stained and battered. Their faces were downcast and drawn, as though they weren't happy to be here. It looked like they'd fought a dragon and lost.

*They must be adventurers*, Amara thought.

When the woman at the table caught her staring, Amara jerked her gaze away and pretended to inspect the ceiling. *Mind your own business,* she reminded herself. It was like she'd forgotten all the lessons she'd learned back home to keep herself safe in dangerous neighbourhoods.

Frieda bustled over and placed a platter of dripping bacon and buttered bread on the table. "Good morning to you," the innkeeper said. "And just so you know, I don't serve breakfast twice. If your little friend wants some, then you'd best bring some up to the room."

"Thank you," Amara said. "I'll save some for her."

Frieda sniffed and then returned to the kitchen. A moment later, she emerged with another heaping platter. As she passed her sons, one of them tried to snatch some bacon only to be slapped away by his mother. His look of shock was greeted by raucous laughter from his brothers.

The innkeeper deposited the food on the adventurer's table, but no one moved or even looked up to acknowledge her. After a moment, she huffed and then hurried away.

Amara waved Frieda down as she passed her table. Against her better judgement, she asked, "What's wrong with them?"

Frieda shook her head. "Apparently, they lost their healer during the last dungeon run. How you mess up something that badly, I'll never know. No one will run with a group that lets their healer die."

"So, they have no healer?" Amara said thoughtfully. She had a lot of other questions about what the innkeeper had said, but she could ask Salamander. The last thing she wanted to do was expose herself as someone who knew nothing about this world. For example, what exactly was a dungeon?

"Will you be staying another night?" Frieda placed her hands on her hips. "If you want to stay past noon, then it will be another half copper."

Amara considered the price for a moment and then fished her last coin out of her robe. The room and board had cost a half copper, as had the bath—which she felt was an exorbitant price—but she'd desperately wanted to clean herself up. Which left her with exactly one copper piece to her name.

She handed the money to Frieda, who then gave her change. It was a smaller coin, with the image of a dragon stamped on it. It immediately went into the little pouch sewn inside her robe.

Setting aside portions for her companion, Amara ate her breakfast. The food didn't taste as good as yesterday when she'd been half-starved, but it was still a hearty meal. Once she'd devoured the crispy bacon and the freshly baked bread slathered in butter, Frieda brought out some sweet oat cakes.

Amara had been finished for nearly twenty minutes when Salamander finally wandered downstairs. She waited as the girl tucked into the food she'd set aside.

"Did you decide on a quest yet?" Salamander asked, her words muffled by a mouthful of food. "Snakes or bandits?"

Amara twirled a strand of hair around her finger. "Neither."

"Huh?" Salamander frowned. "I thought we needed coin."

Amara leaned forward. "I saw some other quests that are a little more suited to our skills. There's a quest to pick ten silverbell flowers, and another to gather a bundle of firewood." After performing so poorly against the giant rat, Amara wasn't in any rush to fight a monster again, even with her new spell.

Salamander licked the grease off her fingers. "But they pay almost nothing. We might as well pick through trash. At least it's safe."

"Gathering flowers in the forest sounds a little more palatable than sorting through mounds of rotting garbage," Amara replied. "And the quests will still pay enough to get us a few more nights at the inn. I don't know about you, but all I care about right now is keeping a roof over our heads."

"Then go charm some noble and take his mansion." Salamander lifted an oatcake and inspected it. "Are these sweet?"

Amara nodded at the sweet cake while pondering Salamander's suggestion. In truth, she *could* simply charm some merchant to empty his coin purse and probably steal enough to buy a house. But she didn't want to become that person again. And regardless, there would likely be repercussions in the future. *Someone* would find out what she'd done, and then probably hunt her down. For now, she wanted to earn everything legally.

"That's not an option," Amara said, firmly. "I'm not stealing from anyone unless they really deserve it."

"You're crazier than a kobold." Salamander bit into the oat cake and her eyes lit up with delight. She made little moaning sounds as she devoured the entire thing.

By the time Salamander had finished her meal, the crowd at the inn had grown thin. The innkeeper's sons had disappeared—most likely to continue drinking—and the adventurers had departed several minutes earlier.

Amara searched the room for Frieda to check what time lunch was served. But when she couldn't locate the innkeeper, she consoled herself with the fact that if she returned before midday, she shouldn't miss it.

She grabbed her staff and then led Salamander through the maze of tables toward the exit. When she reached the sturdy door, she pushed it open and strode out into the dazzling morning light.

Outside, the shrill calls of birds filled the air, and the cloudless blue sky seemed to stretch on forever. It looked like a perfect day. She might actually enjoy searching the woods for flowers and firewood.

They headed in the direction of the quest board but were forced aside by a huge wagon trundling down the street. A slender man with long blond hair, a strangely ageless face, and pointed ears snapped the reins at the horses pulling the wagon. He wore clothing that made him look like a discount wizard; his robes were gaudy and cheap looking, and his pointed cap had the images of stars sewn into it.

"Move aside for the great Galando," he shouted, his delicate eyebrows pinching together. "I'll crush you urchins to paste under my wheels if you don't stand aside, and the guards will thank me for removing impoverished filth from the street."

Amara scowled at the man's words. So much for thinking a bath would do much to change their appearances. As long as they both wore little more than rags, they'd probably only be seen as beggars by most residents of the city.

She guided Salamander by the arm to a nearby alley, and then watched as the wagon creaked past. The sides of it were painted with all manner of beasts and monsters, along with a young man holding an egg in his hands, an expression of amazement on his face.

*This must be the wagon selling those monster eggs the merchant mentioned,* she thought to herself.

It took almost a full minute for the wagon to clear the alleyway, the horse straining to pull it through the thick mud. Once it had finally moved past them, they emerged from the cramped lane. She shot one last glare back at the strange wizard and resolved to buy them both new clothing before dinner.

As she walked down the street, an overpowering urge told her to veer right. And while she didn't see any reason to do so—the muddy street looked no more passable there than anywhere else—she trusted her instincts.

Her foot caught on something buried in the mud, and she toppled forward. She windmilled her arms in an attempt to right herself, but it was no use. A moment later, she splashed into a muddy puddle.

She lay in the cold water for a second, the wind knocked out of her. Finally, she managed to draw in an agonized breath. Then she pushed herself up and wiped some dirt from her cheek. As she did, she glared at Salamander, who was laughing so hard her legs were crossed.

Glancing down, Amara saw that she'd tripped over what appeared to be an egg, the tip barely visible in the muck.

*Is that one of the monster eggs,* she thought, all her annoyance disappearing. *Did I trip over one that fell off the cart?*

Amara reached down to pull the egg free. Once loose, it fit comfortably in her palm. She gently brushed off some of the dirt, exposing a ridged, leathery surface. The merchant she'd charmed had said his cost a silver piece, which meant she could resell it for probably half that much and pay for an entire week in the inn.

Salamander's laughter cut off suddenly, her eyes widening as they fell on the object in Amara's hand. "Is that a monster egg?"

"I think so." Amara pushed herself to her feet, looking down in defeat at her robes. They were now burned, covered in mud, and had many other stains of dubious origin. No one could tell they had been as white as pristine snow the day before.

*At least it will be harder for the monks to recognize me.*

Since escaping, she hadn't really thought about the monks. Would they be searching for her? According to Brother Otto, her arrival had been something of a big deal. And once news got out about it, her reincarnation would likely cause waves among philosophers and religious figures. Maybe she should keep a low profile—just in case.

But as much as she was worried about the church hunting for her, it couldn't usurp her base needs like hunger, clothing, and shelter. Until she had those things, she didn't have the luxury of worrying about anything else.

Amara wiped the rest of the dirt off the egg, and the moment she finished, writing appeared in her vision.

*Loot Received:*
*Monster Egg: This mysterious egg contains your very own pet monster. Using arcane and powerful magics, the great wizard Galando has conditioned the monster to form a bond with whomever holds it upon hatching. Through the bond, the creature will become incapable of harming you or anyone else in your party. Some lucky buyers have even received powerful dragons. What exciting monster will you get?*
*Time Until Hatching: Three Hours*
*Good luck!*

Amara frowned at how little time remained. With only three hours until it hatched, it hardly gave her enough time to find a buyer. The only thing that made sense was to keep it herself. She certainly didn't plan on returning it to Galando.

"We should sell it," Salamander said excitedly. "Just think of the coin we'd get!"

"There's no time," Amara replied, feeling slightly guilty at convincing herself to keep it. "It's going to hatch in a few hours, and who would we sell it to? Maybe we can make money off whatever hatches."

"Oh," Salamander said, staring down at her feet. "I see."

Amara checked the timer on the egg again and then motioned for Salamander to follow her. While they waited for it to hatch, they could get started on the quests.

If they hurried, they could gather the requested items, turn them in, and be back at the inn before lunch. It was nice having things go her way for once. Amara thought she could really get used to having a high Luck stat, especially if it resulted in more fortuitous finds like lost monster eggs.

# CHAPTER 6

Amara stepped over a gnarled root and then stared up in wonder at the surrounding forest. The towering trees reminded her of a cathedral. Shafts of sunlight pierced the thick canopy like rays from the heaven, and a reverent hush consumed the area as the mossy forest floor swallowed all sound. This place felt older than time itself and gave her a sense of peace and serenity.

She knew the sensation was all a dangerous illusion. Based on the missions available on the board, there were all manner of hostile creatures dwelling in this forest and even a group of bandits. But she still felt herself relaxing for the first time since she'd arrived in this world.

"I hate this place," Salamander grumbled. "There are way too many trees."

Amara stopped at the girl's words. "Why *are* there so many trees?" she asked. "I would have thought a forest this close to the city would have been cut down for firewood long ago."

"The lord doesn't allow it." With a disgusted look on her face, Salamander pushed back a leaf-laden branch in her path. "If you try to cut down a tree, you'll end up in chains faster than a goblin pick-pocketing the king. All the rangers make sure of that."

"Good to know," Amara replied. If no one was permitted to cut down a tree, and they could only gather dead wood, her quest might be harder than she thought. The forest might already be picked clean.

Side by side, Amara and Salamander traveled down the well-worn path, keeping a wary eye out for threats. Aside from a few birds, however, there didn't seem to be anything larger than a squirrel living in these woods. As they walked, Amara picked up a few sticks, grimacing at the painfully slow pace at which they were filling the progress bar. She also kept her eye out for the silverbell flowers, praying her herbalism skill would allow her to instinctively identify them.

After hiking down the path for nearly a quarter of an hour, she knew they had to try something different. The area around the trail didn't have a scrap of firewood, and at this rate, they'd never finish in time to get back for lunch.

They'd have to head deeper into the forest.

"I think we need to leave the trail." Amara took a deep breath and then tightened her grip on her staff. The thought of heading into a dark forest unnerved her. Back home, the wildest place she'd ever visited had been a city park. She didn't have any survival skills to speak of. What if she got them lost?

"What about the flying snakes?" Salamander eyed her, looking fearful. "I really don't want to end up in a snake's belly."

"I remember them," Amara answered, an icy feeling spreading up her back. She *hated* snakes. "But everyone has taken all the firewood from here. And I haven't seen a single flower."

"Fine." Salamander brushed back a stray lock of hair and then lifted her hand. After a second, it was enveloped by flames. "I'll run if we see any snakes, though."

"I'll be right behind you," Amara muttered to herself. After all, it would be stupid to risk her life for a few flowers and a bundle of firewood.

Choosing a direction at random, the pair plunged into the forest. Before they'd gone three paces, a cry of pain rang out from the trail behind them. They exchanged glances, and then Amara whirled in the direction of the yell.

Salamander tugged at the sleeve of Amara's robe. "What're you doing?" she hissed. "My nanna always said run *away* from danger, not toward it."

"Someone could be in trouble." Amara watched the path. "We should see if they need help."

"Did you get knocked on the head again? Remember, snake bellies?"

Amara sighed. Back home, she would have followed Salamander's advice. But there, she couldn't cast powerful spells. And if she helped someone, they just might repay her kindness by showering her with coins. Especially if they needed healing.

"This could be a good way to earn some money," Amara said. "But you can stay here if you want."

"And let something happen to you?" Salamander shook her head, strands of golden hair falling over her face. "Don't forget—I'm a member of your party and a real adventurer."

Amara fought down a smile at the girl's concern. It felt good to have someone in this world who cared about her—even if, as she suspected, it was only because she was Salamander's meal ticket.

After a second to orient herself, she set out in the general direction of the scream, questioning her decision several times. What if a large group of bandits was attacking someone? Or what if something worse than flying snakes dwelled in this forest?

*I'm no hero,* Amara thought to herself. *Why am I doing this?*

She resolved to stay in cover until she discovered the source of the cries; if it looked too dangerous to intervene, she could always retreat. Salamander had mentioned rangers, so if things were beyond her skill, maybe they could find one of them to help.

Pushing through the dense undergrowth, they reached a clearing where a desperate battle raged at its center. A man dressed in leather armor lashed out with twin daggers as flying creatures assailed him from every side. Nearly six feet long with scales a verdant green, the airborne snakes resembled flying squirrels more than the winged horrors Amara had imagined. Flattening their bodies as they flew, the beasts launched themselves from branches high in the trees, struck their target, and then sailed to the other side of the glade to prepare another volley.

The bodies of dead or dying snakes lay in piles around the man, but he staggered drunkenly with each step. Blood dripped down his face, and there were several punctures visible on his armor.

Amara quickly tallied up the number of snakes attacking the man. There must be at least a dozen of them.

"We have to run," Salamander whispered, tugging on Amara's robe again. "There's too many."

Amara glanced down at the girl. She looked ready to bolt. The man's scream drew Amara's attention. Another snake landed on his shoulder, sinking its teeth into his exposed neck. If they left him, there was no question that he would be overwhelmed.

"I . . . I have to try," she said, trying to bolster her courage. "If I don't, he's going to die."

"Please, I don't want to lose you."

"I'll be fine," she said with false bravado. "Stay here. And if anything happens to me, then run for it. Don't try to help if it looks hopeless."

Salamander clung to Amara's arm, "Please, don't."

She gently peeled off the child's hand then strode on wobbly legs into the clearing. Her knees felt like jelly as she walked forward, and her chest was tight. But she needed to prove to herself that she was more than just a thief.

As she marched toward the creatures, Amara cast *Divine Weapon,* and a staggering amount of mana flowed in a torrent. Like a raging river of energy, power gushed out of her, leaving barely a drop remaining when she finally completed weaving the spell in her mind.

Noting the feeling of being utterly spent, Amara grimly mused, *I'd better make sure I don't need to heal myself.*

Slowly, a weapon took shape in front of her. As if forged from the air itself, a flaming sword nearly six feet long appeared, its blade gleaming like a beacon. The thing looked powerful enough to slay a god.

She blinked and examined it in disbelief. Was this what casting *Divine Weapon* conjured up?

Amara had no time to ponder such things as several snakes aimed their focus at her. One creature hissing as it sprang toward her. Gripping her staff tightly, she prepared herself to meet her foe's strike.

The attack never came. Amara's conjured weapon slashed out faster than her eyes could follow. The shimmering blade sliced the creature neatly in half, showering Amara and her poor beleaguered robes with blood and gore. She winced but pressed on. Only a few minutes remained until the weapon would disappear.

The man finally spotted her—the burning sword an unmistakable herald of her presence. Waving his arms sluggishly, he called out, "Retreat and save yourself, my lady."

Amara scowled when she recognized the voice. It was the same sanctimonious jerk who had accosted her near the canal after her encounter with the pie merchant. Still, she wouldn't turn back now just because she didn't like the person in trouble.

Sprinting forward, she trusted the *Divine Weapon* to keep her safe. With every footfall she took, the blade sang through the air to follow, creating carnage among the snakes that would have struck her. Like blossoms in an orchard, pieces of dismembered reptiles fell around her. When one slipped past her guardian, Amara caught a snake with her staff, knocking it from the air before crushing it to paste under her bare heel.

When she finally reached the desperate fighter—Jonas, if she recalled—Amara was breathing hard and covered from head to toe in gore. She raised her sleeve to wipe some blood from her face, but stopped when she realized the material was probably dirtier than her cheek.

At that moment, her *Divine Weapon* cracked. The towering blade disintegrated, crumbling like sand before blowing away on the wind. She starred in horror as it disappeared, while nearly a half-dozen emboldened snakes hurled themselves at her from the trees.

She swung her staff awkwardly at the nearest reptile, but it changed course and slammed into her chest. The impact knocked her from her feet and sent her sprawling to the ground. Pain blossomed in her arm as the snake sank its teeth deep into her flesh.

Amara screamed and tried to wrench the snake free. But its muscular body coiled around her arm, and its jaws latched down harder. Fiery sensations seeped into the wound, and her vision swam. *Venomous*, she confirmed to herself.

Another snake landed on her leg, but she kicked it away. As it tried to slither off, a pair of burning hands clutched its scaly hide. The snake burst into flames, twisting and coiling on itself as it blackened.

Amara waved her companion back from the fray. Then she reached up and tore the other snake off her arm. She tossed it aside before casting *Cloak of Shadows.*

Reluctantly, the mana drained out of her soul like the last dregs from a bottle, leaving her reserves almost completely dry. But finally, her vision grayed, showing that she'd successfully cast the spell and become invisible.

She stumbled forward a few paces to place herself between the snake and Salamander. Then she took a deep breath to quiet the pain rocking her then threw herself back into the battle.

She found the serpent that had bitten her slithering toward the edge of the forest. Amara crushed its skull under the butt of her staff then charged after another target, beating it clumsily with her weapon until it stopped moving.

Amara glanced over at Jonas, who had a snake impaled on his dagger. The creature writhed and snapped at him, but somehow, he avoided its deadly jaws. His face looked terribly pale, but he remained on his feet despite his myriad wounds.

She searched the clearing for another enemy only to realize they were alone. If any snakes still lived, they must have retreated. Nearly a dozen twisting corpses littered the forest floor.

Amara let the *Cloak of Shadows* drop then sank to her knees. Her very soul felt battered. The burning sensation had begun to spread from her wound, the veins in her arm turning black.

She was in rough shape.

Despite her tapped mana pool, Amara made the attempt to cast *Heal Wounds.*

"Are you alright?" Salamander called out, the worry evident in her voice. "Did one of them bite you?"

Amara didn't answer, focusing instead on weaving the strands of mana together in her mind. As she cast the healing spell, her soul shuddered as if it might tear itself apart with the effort. She knew immediately that she was trying to draw on mana that she didn't have, and she gasped in pain as the energy was ripped from her limbs.

Exhaustion descended across her body like a heavy blanket as the skin on her shoulder knitted back together. But she frowned as the burning only intensified.

The healing spell hadn't neutralized the venom.

*I knew it was a stupid idea to play hero,* she thought grimly.

The sensation of something being pressed into her hand nearly made her jump out of her skin. She looked up to see Jonas standing over her, a concerned expression on his face.

"Drink this," he said. "It's the antivenom."

She upended the small bottle into her mouth. As she swallowed, the pain blinked out almost immediately. Her vision steadied.

Jonas watched her for a short time before he flopped down in the grass. He wiped off his blades before sheathing them. "Even with the venom in my blood neutralized, I still have quite a few wounds. I don't suppose you have enough mana remaining to cast a healing spell?"

"How much will you pay for it?" she asked without thinking. Amara cringed, remembering that he'd given her a bottle of antivenom. She'd never given anything away for free back on Earth. Old habits died hard sometimes.

"I should have known you'd have a mercenary heart," he said, sounding disappointed. "Unfortunately, I don't have any coin remaining on my person, having spent my last few coppers on the bottles of antivenom before embarking on this quest."

"No, I'm sorry," Amara blurted out. "I'll heal your wounds for free. At least, I'll try to once I regain my mana."

"I'll wait while you meditate, then." He rested his arm over his eyes to shield them from the sunlight, adding, "You needn't rush. None of my wounds require immediate attention."

"I . . . uhh . . . don't know how to meditate," she admitted. "Is that how you get mana back?"

He lifted his arm so he could peer at her. "Exactly who are you?"

"It's a long story," she said. "And one I don't particularly feel like sharing."

"That is understandable," he replied. After a beat, he offered, "While I am no sage, the advice given to me as a child was to close your eyes, clear your mind, and focus on your soul. This will allow you to draw in mana from the surrounding world. However, everyone develops their own technique over time."

Once Amara had recovered enough to sit up, Salamander exclaimed, "That. Was. Amazing! That flying sword of yours was swatting the snakes down like bugs. And I bet we'll make a fortune from these things. There are teeth, and venom, and scales, and meat—"

"They're not all ours," Amara interjected. "Jonas gets at least half of them."

Motioning to the carcasses spread around the clearing, Jonas said. "Please, help yourself. I have little skill in the way of skinning or butchery. The reward from the quest is more than enough for me."

"We'll figure all this out later," she said. "Right now, I need some time to regain my mana."

Salamander nodded then set to the task of harvesting what she could from the reptilian remains.

"Be wary," Jonas called to the girl. "These beasts are known to bite for a short time after death."

Amara knelt in the soft grass. She banished any thoughts from her mind and focused on meditating. Hopefully, she'd pick the skill up quickly because she had a lot to accomplish before midday. And more than anything, she didn't want to miss lunch.

# CHAPTER 7

Amara meditated in the middle of the clearing for nearly an hour, and by the end of that time, she'd only refilled a sliver of her mana. It felt as though her soul had somehow been strained by drawing too much power from it during the fight.

*I don't think I should ever risk casting again when I'm out of mana.*

She was afraid that if she pushed her soul too hard, she might permanently damage it. But she still knew little about the rules of this world and could only guess. It was frustrating that she always had to fly blind. There was so much she didn't know, and she had found no one to answer even her most basic questions.

Maybe she could pick Jonas's brain after she finished meditating.

With that thought, she settled down and continued the slow process of refilling her soul. After nearly another hour, it felt like her mana had been fully restored. When she opened her eyes, they felt grainy from being closed for so long, and she rubbed them with her fingers. Getting to her feet, Amara gazed around the clearing.

Nearby, Salamander was in the process of cutting a dead snake's head off with a knife that she must have gotten from Jonas. The head went into a sack—which she must also have borrowed—and the body was tossed aside. It looked like she'd nearly finished butchering every snake they'd slain.

She didn't see Jonas at first, but then she spotted movement at the edge of the clearing. Even though he was injured, he'd been walking the perimeter while she meditated. She felt a strange surge of gratitude toward him—an emotion she didn't often feel back home. Quickly, she reminded herself that he wanted something from her.

Jonas noticed that she'd regained her feet before he trotted in her direction. As he did, he slammed both daggers back into their sheaths. He adjusted a bandolier of throwing knives around his chest as he stopped a few paces away from her. "Are you ready to mend my wounds?"

"I'll try my best." She focused on him and then cast *Heal Wounds*. Almost immediately, brilliant white motes descended on the swollen bites on his face. The puncture marks shrank, and then a scab formed over them.

Jonas breathed out and touched his face gingerly. "It has been a very long time since I felt the soothing touch of a healer. You have my thanks, my lady. If you would be so kind to heal the rest of my wounds?"

Amara nodded and then focused on the next injured area. Thankfully, the bloodstains and puncture marks in his armor made them easy to spot. She cast the spell three more times and then paused. "Did I get all of your injuries?"

Jonas kneaded his side before rotating his arm at the shoulder. "I believe I am mostly healed."

"Good. I have something else to take care of now." Amara reached into her pocket to check on the monster egg. If she was right, it should hatch at any moment. But when her hand found only empty air her heart skipped a beat. Had she somehow lost it during the fight? What would happen if she wasn't around when it hatched?

She scanned the ground in a panic—already in a foul mood from missing lunch—but the leathery egg was nowhere in sight. Somehow, she'd lost it. So much for her high Luck stat.

"Is something wrong?" Jonas asked, obviously noting her panicked expression. "Did you misplace something during our epic battle?"

"I . . . lost an egg. I don't suppose you've seen it?"

Jonas shook his head. "I apologize, but I saw nothing. And I circled the clearing many times while you meditated. I thought it would be rude if I allowed flying snakes to assail you while your attention was elsewhere."

"Damn it," she swore. "I really wanted to see what was inside that thing."

"By any chance, was the egg from a pompous Elven merchant?" he asked. "If so, then nothing of value has been lost. Most of the eggs contain worthless creatures that hardly rate as monsters. That merchant is well-known as a charlatan in my lands."

"It could have been a dragon," she said stubbornly. "And it might have made me rich."

"Perhaps, but more likely, it would have been a giant rat or something equally unsavory."

"What do you know?" Amara snapped with a scowl. "My high Luck stat probably would have given me something amazing."

Jonas chuckled as he adjusted his throwing knives. "And how in the name of Holy Birgitta would you have such a thing? Have you stumbled across a rare and ancient treasure to grant you Luck?"

"Why would I need that?"

"There's no way for an adventurer to gain Luck," he explained. "Which is unfortunate, as I have heard even a single point in that stat is incredibly powerful. How are you so ignorant to the ways of the world?"

Fearing that she'd given away something important, Amara slowly asked, "There . . . isn't any way to get it?"

Jonas's eyes narrowed for a split second, but then his expression smoothed over. If she hadn't been watching him, she never would have seen the near-imperceptible change. He *knew* that there was something unusual about her stats.

"Perhaps we should continue our alliance," Jonas suggested. "My class has made it difficult to find a party, and I've learned it's foolhardy for a Rogue to attempt solo quests. Had my coin purse not grown so light, I never would have attempted to hunt the flying snakes."

While his fighting aptitude and knowledge would doubtless prove themselves to be invaluable, didn't know the first thing about him. His earlier shift in demeanor still unnerved her. However, despite this and his reaction to her encounter with the pie merchant a day before, Jonas hadn't given her any reason to distrust him.

"I'll think about it."

"That is all I ask," he replied. "If you need me, I'm staying at the Drunken Minotaur Inn while my coin holds out. Though after cashing in today's quest, I imagine I'll be there for several more days, at the very least." He stopped and gazed at Salamander, who was struggling to cut off one of the snake's heads. "And your little companion may keep the knife I gave to her. While they say a rogue can never have too many knives, I currently find myself with a surplus."

"Thank you," Amara said as she crossed her arms, "but we don't need your charity."

"It's not charity," he replied. "There's an excellent chance those snakes would have overcome me today if not for your aid. Consider it a small token of my appreciation for your help."

Amara nodded as the man bowed to her. Then she watched him tromp back the way they'd come. He quickly disappeared into the dense forest.

She turned to Salamander. "We should get going on our quest."

"Why would we do that?" Salamander asked. "Merchants give good coin for these heads and skins. Why do backbreaking work when you don't have to?"

"Because I want to level up," Amara responded, though she was pleased to hear someone confirm the snake parts were valuable. She assumed the venom they contained was used to make the antidote that she'd drunk.

"No way I'm missing lunch," Salamander said. "I'm hungrier than a wasteland giant."

"We're going to finish the quests," Amara said firmly. "And anyway, there's no way we'd make it back in time."

"Fine," Salamander grumbled. "But if I'm not eating, I'm not carrying these heads and skins."

Ignoring the threat, Amara asked, "What about the snake bodies? Are those worth anything?"

"Barely," Salamander grunted. "All the meat might be worth a copper . . . maybe."

"Let's get them, then," Amara said. "I don't want to miss out on any coin."

Salamander held up her hands. "I don't want to carry around slimy meat."

Amara stopped at the girl's words. Hadn't she been picking through garbage just a few days earlier? But she didn't want to press the matter and let it drop. She'd carry the disgusting snake bodies back to town herself. After all, a copper piece could mean the difference between a full belly and going hungry.

She turned her gaze toward where the girl had tossed the carcasses to see nothing but an empty patch of bloodstained grass. No, not empty. There was a small chest sitting there, like the ones used for storing jewelry. "Where did that come from?"

"Bet your friend left it for us," Salamander said, taking a step toward it. "Think it's full of copper or something?"

"He told us he was out of coin," she said, her annoyance growing. "And I told him I didn't want any charity."

"So what?" Salamander leaned down to inspect the wooden box. "Whatever's inside might pay for a week of meals and separate rooms."

"Is there something wrong with my company?" Amara asked as she poked the chest with her toe. With fine carvings and whorls stretching the length of it, the box looked expensive.

"You snore like a badger."

"At least you don't have to deal with stinky feet in your face." Amara reached out to try the latch, but it wouldn't budge. She shook it a few times, but it remained stuck. "It won't open."

"I wonder why? It doesn't have a keyhole or anything." Salamander poked it a few times. "I say we take it back to the inn and break it open."

"But what happened to all the snakes? It's not like the chest ate them."

"Maybe what's his name took them?"

"Maybe . . ." Unconvinced, Amara let her voice trail away with her thoughts. The chest somehow felt *off*. "Let's just get out of here."

She grabbed the wooden box with both hands and lifted it up. It was surprisingly heavy, and though she didn't look forward to the long hike back carrying this thing, neither did she dare leave something so valuable in the woods.

With a grunt, she set course to head deeper into the woods. She had to adjust the chest's position several times until she finally found a comfortable way to carry it. Much to Amara's delight, the firewood gathering went faster in this area, as it appeared few adventurers left the worn path.

Before long, Amara carried a full bundle of firewood under one arm and the chest under the other. Now all she had to do was find the flowers.

But after meandering through the woods for the better part of an hour, she still had found nothing. She'd expected recognition to hit her like a thunderclap when she finally stumbled across some silverbells, but none of the flowers she saw looked familiar. It appeared that if she wanted to become an herbalist, she'd need some training first.

With only one quest completed, they set out toward the path back to town and they traversed the forest without further incident.

By the time they reached the outskirts of the town, Amara was sweating, exhausted, and covered in grime. So far, she didn't feel like much of an adventurer. And she certainly didn't look like one, based on the looks she received from passing groups.

"Do you know where to drop off the firewood?" Amara asked Salamander.

The girl nodded and pointed toward the canals. "It's about a block or two that way."

Amara nodded and, with leaden feet, followed Salamander. They reached what looked to be a woodcutter's shop. Cords of lumber were stacked up around the permitter. Their bundle delivered to a girl who was quick with a smile, the adventurers received only a quarter copper for their efforts. At least it felt like she got a bit of experience, too.

The quest fulfilled, they returned to the Dancing Gnome Inn. With the sun already well past its zenith, it was far too late for lunch, but Amara hoped they might still scrounge up some food. And if not, at least they could rest for a while before dinner.

Salamander pulled out the blade and balanced the hilt on her palm. "Now that I have a knife, I can cut up the giant rat. I've heard the fur sells pretty well. Especially with winter close."

"A little extra money wouldn't hurt," Amara said wearily. In truth, she was exhausted. However, she didn't really care about it at the moment. "Do you know any good street vendors to buy food from?"

"Not many you can trust," Salamander said. "Unless you like eating rotten food."

"Great."

She felt relief wash over her as they turned the corner and the inn came into sight. Strangely enough, the place was starting to feel like home.

When she reached the front door and stepped inside, Frieda appeared with a stricken look on her face. "You can't track that filth into my inn!"

Amara glanced down at herself, to see she was covered in a mixture of snake blood, leaves, and dirt. But she didn't want to pay for another bath if she could wrangle a free one out of the innkeeper. "Sorry, but I can't afford a bath. And I *did* rent a room here, which means I can come and go as I please . . ."

Frieda's lined brow descended. "What if I charge you half price for a bath?"

"Sorry, not enough money." She suspected it would cost more to clean the bedsheets after she stained them than a bath was worth. Plus, she had a feeling that she'd been grossly overcharged for yesterday's. Amara held her hands out helplessly and took another step inside. "You'll just have to deal with my appearance."

"Are you trying to put me in the poorhouse?" Frieda shrieked. "Couldn't you at least rinse off in a stream before coming back here?"

"Maybe next time," Amara replied. "But right now, I'm just trying to get some rest."

"What about that box under your arm? Does that have money in it?"

"It's broken," Amara said. "Feel free to try to open it." She knew it was a gamble, but she doubted that the frail older woman could open it after her own attempts had failed. Assuming the innkeeper didn't break out any heavy tools, of course.

"Give me that." Frieda snatched the chest from her, but a moment later cried out in pain. She held up a finger that was welling with blood. "I cut myself on the edge! You should have told me it was sharp."

Amara shrugged.

"A quarter copper and I'll give you the leftovers from the lunch you missed along with some food for your questing tomorrow,"

"And you launder my robes."

Frieda scowled. Which probably meant Amara had received a good deal. "I suppose I have no choice," the innkeeper relented.

Amara passed the quarter copper she'd received for the firewood to the older woman then sent Salamander up to their rooms with their loot. Frieda led her to the bathing room.

Hopefully, once they sold everything, Amara could buy herself and the girl some proper clothing. And, if she was lucky, maybe even a real weapon.

# CHAPTER 8

A knocking awoke Amara from a deep sleep. Groggily, she stared around the room as she tried to figure out the source of the noise. The door rattled as something hammered against the wood. She threw the blanket aside and sprinted to her staff propped up in the corner. Weapon in hand, she turned to face the entrance.

Why was someone knocking on the door to her room in the middle of the night? While it was of sturdy construction, she had no illusions of withstanding a determined attacker.

A flame lit the room as one of Salamander's hands ignited. She had leapt out of bed as well, and she held a knife in one hand, while her other blazed with magic. The flames illuminated her youthful face, showing her features twisted with worry.

"Who do you think it is?" Salamander whispered.

Amara shrugged only to jerk as something heavy banged against the door again. Thankfully, the lock held.

She heard a door open in the hallway, followed by an immediate slamming as it shut again. *The noise woke the other guests,* Amara thought, *but whatever is out there was enough that they immediately ducked back into their room. If most of the people staying here are adventurers, whomever is pounding must be especially dangerous.*

"The window," Amara hissed. "We need to get out of here."

Salamander nodded, rushed to the window, and threw open the shutters to expose the pitch-black night beyond.

Amara hurried to her companion's side and peered from the second story to the hard packed dirt of the courtyard below. If they jumped in this absolute darkness, it was almost certain the fall would injure them. Would her *Heal Wounds* cure sprained and broken limbs?

Another rattle of the door urged her to risk it.

She lifted her leg to climb out, but stopped short when she spotted movement below. Two armored men holding halberds emerged from the shadows and stared in her direction.

Amara ducked back inside, panic setting in.

All the exits were covered. There was no escape.

"We're going to have to fight our way out," she said to Salamander, hoping she sounded braver than she felt. "Stay behind me while I cast *Divine Weapon*."

Salamander nodded and raised her knife, some of the worry in her expression now replaced by determination.

"Open the door!" a voice shouted from the hallway. "I must speak with you, Amara!"

Something about the voice sounded familiar, and she furrowed her brow. "Who are you?" she called back. "How do I know I can trust you?"

"It's Brother Otto," he replied, his words muffled. "I greeted you when you first . . . arrived."

Amara exhaled, some of the panic draining out of her. She couldn't imagine that someone as harmless as Brother Otto meant her any harm. However, she continued weave the initial strands of *Divine Weapon* then held the spell—and her staff—poised for action. If things went poorly, she could always slice her way out of here.

"Please, I beg of you, let me in," Otto continued. "Time grows short, and the entire fate of the world may rest upon your shoulders."

"Nothing too dramatic, then," she muttered to herself. Raising her voice, she said, "I'll only let you into the room. If anyone else tries to enter, I'll consider them hostile and react accordingly."

"Yes, yes," Brother Otto called back. "But please, make haste."

Amara moved to the door and took a deep breath. Then she reached out and slid the bolt open. She opened the door a slit and peeked out. Flanked by two ominous figures, Brother Otto stood in the hallway. To one side, a man clad in armor held a longsword in his gauntleted hand, while to the other an unarmed robed companion radiated danger.

"Remember," Amara reiterated, "just you."

She opened the door wide enough for the monk to slip into the room before slamming it shut and sliding the bolt back into place. Brother Otto shifted nervously from foot to foot as she addressed him, "So, what's so important you have to almost break my door down?"

"The church is hunting you," he said, wringing his hands. "You are in great danger while you remain here." He unslung a backpack from his shoulder and shoved it in her direction. "Here, take these and get changed. We must leave for the Khaneri Monasteries immediately."

Amara lifted the flap and examined the contents of the pack. It held a pair of sturdy dresses that seemed popular among the peasant women here, a sheathed knife, and a waterskin. She closed the backpack.

"Why is the church hunting me?"

Explanations babbled forth from Brother Otto in a hurried gush. "Your arrival has upended centuries of doctrine. The Church teaches us that the gods abandoned this world after the Age of Strife. This meant the bishops had the final say on all spiritual and worldly matters, and that any prophets claiming to speak for the gods were false."

Amara tapped her foot on the floor impatiently while she waited for Otto to arrive at the point. She didn't want to hear about some boring religious dispute. "Once again, why does the Church care about *me*? And why did you have to nearly break down my door in the middle of the night?"

"Your arrival is proof that the gods are still with us! And it portends to something far more terrifying . . ." he trailed off and looked sheepish. "When I informed Bishop Krause of your reincarnation, he argued that I'd been taken as a fool by a charlatan. He wishes to try you as a heretic and prove to everyone that you are nothing more than a false prophet. But I witnessed the Beacon of Khaneri being lit the other night to herald your arrival! It would have been impossible to fake such a thing."

"They're going to put me on trial?" Icy dread crept down her spine.

If she was prosecuted by the Church, she suspected it would end badly. Mentally, Amara cursed this world. All she wanted was a fresh start, but everywhere she turned, she found obstacles. First, it had been her Trickster Cleric class that had made others wary of trusting her, and now she found herself in the middle of a theological dispute. All she wanted to do was get away from this place.

"What happens if I'm found guilty?"

"If you're found guilty, then they will burn you at the stake," he replied, sounding increasingly nervous. "But you must understand that your very existence will create a schism within the Church. Already, several clerics and paladins have broken away and vowed to keep you safe. And they're not even devotees of Melischar, your goddess!"

"What should I do, then?" She frowned. "How am I supposed to fight against an entire Church?"

"There are monasteries in the deserts far to the south where Gnostics worship in defiance of the Church. I have prepared safe passage and, should we reach them, they will grant you refuge."

Amara shook her head. "I don't want to have anything to do with either side of this. All I want to do is live my life in peace. Is that too much to ask?"

"The Harbingers will rise, which means nowhere will be safe," Otto said quietly. "I . . . have spent the last two days delving into forbidden knowledge in the monastery archives. It's difficult to even admit to such a thing after serving the Church. Had I been discovered, I likely would have been burned as a heretic myself. But I *had* to know after encountering you. The texts all agree that the arrival of an avatar marks the beginning of another Age of Strife. The Chaos Gods shall also birth champions, who will attempt to awaken the Harbingers. Should they succeed, this world will face the gods of darkness themselves."

"Gods? Harbingers? There's nothing I can do against things that powerful. I just want to be left alone."

A sound from outside made Brother Otto jump. "Please," he urged. "Accompany me south and I'll explain everything. You are far too important to risk your life by staying here."

If there were people truly hunting her, then it made little sense to remain on the outskirts of a city that would never accept her into its walls. But she didn't want to hide in some remote church with a group of religious fanatics.

"I'm not willing to go to the monastery," she said quietly, adding, "but I'll leave the city with you."

"Thank the gods," Brother Otto exhaled. "Please, get changed immediately. The robes you wear will give you away to anyone trained by the Church."

Brother Otto slipped out into the hallway. Immediately, Amara tugged her ruined robe over her head. *At least one good thing has come out of this,* she thought.

She slid into the dress. As she adjusted it, she said to Salamander, "There's one for you. Put it on."

When no answer came, she looked up to find the girl standing quietly in the corner.

"I can't go with you," the child said. "My parents . . . I can't just leave."

"I understand," Amara replied, though the thought of losing her companion hurt more than she cared to admit. In just the last two days, she'd grown fond of Salamander, but Amara couldn't expect her to flee from the only city she'd ever known in the middle of the night. And she didn't want to put the young woman in danger, either.

They'd sold off the snake parts for three coppers. Having spent her whole existence in this world scrounging, the trio of coins felt like a fortune. She'd planned on using the money to buy them some clothing, but with that need fulfilled . . .

"I'll leave you with what little coin I have," Amara promised. "It should buy you at least another week here at the inn. And maybe Otto can do more for you."

Amara let out a surprised *woof* of air as Salamander ran forward and flung her arms around her waist. She hesitated for a moment, but then returned the girl's hug with equal force. Hopefully, if there truly were gods in this world, they would watch over her friend.

"I'm going to miss you," Salamander said, sniffling. "Will you come back?"

"I promise that I'll try to return when it's safe."

"You better." Salamander stepped back and wiped her nose with her sleeve.

"I want you to wake up Frieda and change rooms as soon as I'm gone. Do you understand?"

Salamander nodded.

Amara stuffed her old robe into the backpack—she'd learned long ago to waste nothing—and then smoothed down her new dress with her hands. She opened the door, revealing Brother Otto and the two other men waiting in the hallway.

"I'm so glad you decided—" Brother Otto's words cut off as a crossbow bolt slammed into the side of his chest.

In shock, Amara reeled, searching for the missile's source. She spotted chain mail glinting in the dim light as a man clambering up the stairs. His cold eyes peered from a narrow slit on his helmet's visor. As he approached, he deftly reloaded his crossbow. Beside him, a dark-haired woman appeared wearing a veil, her hands aglow with blue light.

Otto's companion shouted, "They found us!" He hurled a bolt of electrical energy toward the stairs. The spell exploded against the wooden ceiling, raining down cinders over the attackers.

The veiled foe thrust her hands toward them, and several blue fireballs shot out from her fingertips, slamming into the wall beside Amara and setting the wood ablaze. She recoiled from the sudden searing heat just as another crossbow bolt sailed close enough for its wake to buffet her hair.

With a battle roar, Otto's armored companion raised his longsword and charged into melee. After taking a few steps, a jet of azure flames engulfed him. He staggered from side to side, screaming in agony.

Amara ducked low, holding her arm up to shield her face from the heat. She tried to tune out the screams from the burning man and reached out to grab Salamander's hand. She pulled the girl into the room and then hurried back out to drag Brother Otto to safety.

The injured monk had barely cleared the threshold when Salamander slammed the door shut. Explosions rocked the inn, and through the open window Amara could hear the clash of weapons in the courtyard below. Farther off, shouts filled the night air and torches bobbed in the distance.

"You . . . must . . . escape," Otto gasped, with each word. "Leave . . . me."

"No," Amara said, her eyes darting around the room. "Not after you came to save my life."

After another detonation outside of the door, the screams of the burning warrior ceased. Though Amara hoped the attackers had been slain as well, the creak of footsteps outside dispelled her optimism.

Amara wheezed with the exertion of hauling Brother Otto to the wall where she propped him up. Then she bit down on her lower lip and steadied herself for what she had to do next. She reached down and grabbed onto the slick bolt protruding from his chest. With one hand braced against his shoulder, she ripped it free and watched as blood poured out from the wound.

She cast *Heal Wounds,* but it did little to stanch the flow of blood. After three more iterations of the spell, the deep puncture wound finally closed, leaving Brother Otto looking terribly pale. While her would-be rescuer panted on the floor, Salamander {what?}.

The door shuddered with a heavy impact. Amara eyed the open window. The sounds of fighting below had only intensified.

Amara saw no means of escape for herself, the girl, and the wounded monk.

They were trapped.

# CHAPTER 9

Splinters spraying across the room, the door split open as an axe head burst through the wood. Another strike wrenched the boards apart. A solid kick shattered it. As the pieces of it fell away, the crossbowman ducked into the room and thrust an axe through a leather thong at his belt. The veiled woman followed a moment later.

A fresh bolt nocked, the assailant leveled his crossbow in Amara's direction. Nearby, however, the woman shook her head and pushed the weapon down. "I believe this girl is the one we are searching for," she said. "Bishop Krause wants her alive."

Amara gripped her staff with white knuckles. She'd planned on using her spells to ambush the attackers the moment they entered the room. But she'd never hurt anyone before—even in self defense. She'd been frozen with fear while they broke down the door.

*Now isn't the time to be weak,* she thought, furious with herself. *If you don't save Brother Otto and Salamander, who will?*

"If you leave now," Amara said, "I'll spare your lives."

Though she'd tried to sound haughty, the quaver in her voice betrayed the fear of a girl begging a bully for mercy. A wave of prickles passed over her skin, and she knew that one of them had examined her class.

"She's only Level 2," the man sneered. "Nothing to worry about."

The veiled spellcaster aimed her glowing hand at Amara. "Childish threats. If you could hurt us, you would have." She waved dismissively at Salamander, who still stood in the corner. "Surrender, and we'll grant your companion a painless death."

"I won't let you hurt them."

"Enough of this shit," the crossbowman said to Amara. "Get on the floor or I'll put a bolt through your leg. The bishop only said you had to be alive—not unharmed."

Amara took in a deep breath and cast *Divine Weapon*. As she weaved the spell, the blazing spectral sword materialized in front of her. The dancing flames bathed the room in ghostly green light. Mana flooded from her soul, but it didn't leave her feeling completely empty this time.

"I thought you said she was only Level 2," the veiled woman cried out, stumbling away. She raised her hands and hurled a stream of flames at the floating weapon, but her spell parted around the blade before dissipating into sapphire sparks.

"I swear to Holy Birgitta that she's only Level 2," the man shouted in retort. He threw himself to the ground to avoid a strike that would have easily decapitated him had the spectral blade struck home.

"Then how in the name of the Harbingers is she casting that spell?" the woman demanded. She directed another stream of blue flames at the weapon, but the raging magic only notched the blade.

In apparent desperation, the soldier lifted his crossbow and loosed a bolt at Amara. The spectral weapon shifted its angle to intercept, easily deflecting the missile. The bolt clattered to the floor and slid to a stop near the bed.

Amara mentally commanded the ghostly blade to attack the crossbowman before he could reload. Swinging in a high arc, it descended on him like divine judgement. It cleaved through his shoulder and didn't stop until it reached the pit of his belly.

With the spectral sword sticking out of his abdomen, he swayed, blinking dumbly. The conjured weapon tore itself free with a gout of blood. His mangled body collapsed to the floor with a wet slap.

No one moved or spoke, all eyes fixed on the corpse oozing blood.

"I swear, I thought he would dodge," Amara whispered in horror to the veiled woman. "I didn't mean to . . . kill him."

Wrenched from her stupor, the woman shrieked, "Frederick!" Her hands burst into an uncontrolled blaze, the flames coiling their way up her arms until it formed a nimbus around her body. Turning her murderous gaze upon Amara, she snarled, "Your torment will be endless as my fire consumes you!"

Amara shook her head to dispel her guilt then returned her focus to her *Divine Weapon*. As she ordered it to attack, it whirled to assume a defensive position in front of her where it blocked another spray of fireballs.

The woman screamed wildly as she launched frenzied attacks, errant flames igniting the floor and ceiling. Within moments, the temperature spiked and tongues of fire licked toward Salamander and Otto who sheltered in the corner.

Amara was forced back by the attacks, sweat trickling down her face as she searched for an opening to attack. But the woman's spells were now an inferno fueled by her rage, and pieces of the spectral weapon broke off under the assault.

With a duration of only two minutes, Amara knew it wouldn't be long before the *Divine Weapon* spell ended. She needed to try something else.

Her only option was to cast *Charm Person,* but as she weaved the spell, a firestorm struck the *Divine Weapon.* Shards of the ephemeral blade glittered in the air as they tumbled to the floor where they disintegrated into colored smoke. Dumbfounded by the display, her spell faltered, allowing the woman the opportunity to gather a massive, fiery maelstrom near the ceiling.

There was nowhere to run or dodge as the churning flames descended on her. She was going to die.

As she raised her arms in a vain attempt to shield herself, a scream rent the air and shredded the hellish storm. The flames scattered harmlessly dissipating in a wisp of smoke.

For a moment, Amara didn't dare breathe, unable to believe that she'd been granted a reprieve. With a panicked search for the spellcaster, Amara found her struggling to shake off something stuck to her foot. Closer examination revealed that she'd somehow gotten her boot tangled with Amara's jewelry chest.

Amara didn't know how this strange tableau came to exist, but she chose to chalk it up to her high Luck stat. Using the distraction to her advantage, she finished casting *Charm Person.* A gout of fire roared in her direction.

Amara threw herself to the side, but the burning orb clipped her arm. The sleeve of her dress immediately burst into flames. Pain like she'd never experienced wracked her body. Her own terrible screams filled the room as the blaze consumed her limb.

Darkness engulfed her as a blanket was thrown over her head. The flames quickly snuffed out, Amara struggled to get free. Had her spell worked? When she finally clawed her way out of the blanket, she saw Salamander standing over her. Nearby, the veiled woman gazed around the room.

"Why did I just cast *Blue Lava* at my best friend?" The woman pulled down her veil. "Oh no, did I injure you?"

She tried to take a step forward, but then stumbled with a cry of pain.

"I seem to have hurt my foot," she explained, "though it's not nearly as bad as your wounds. Allow me to tend to your arm."

Relieved that her *Charm Person* spell had worked, Amara mumbled, "I'm fine." As long as the magic held, this woman would think she was her best friend for the next few hours.

She risked a glance down at her burned arm and immediately regretted her foolishness. She gaped at the mangled flesh. Fresh waves of pain threatened to send her into a swoon, but she gritted her teeth and tightened her grip on consciousness. She cast *Heal Wounds,* and a few patches of the skin reformed.

Amara wanted to cast another healing spell, but she'd used the last of her mana. With their escape still uncertain, she didn't want to push her soul too far.

For now, she'd have to bear the pain. Once she'd meditated and regained some of her mana, she could focus on healing her burns.

"Thank you, Salamander," Amara said in a strained voice. She knew that had the girl not had the wit to smother the flames with the blanket, her injury would have been far worse.

"Your arm," Salamander whispered, her eyes wide. "I think I see bone."

"Don't look at it," Amara said, struggling to heed her own advice. "We need to get out of here. Gather your things."

She turned toward the woman she'd charmed. "What's your name?"

"I never told you my name?" The woman cupped her hands in front of her mouth and looked at Amara in horror. "I'm so sorry. My name is Selena, and I have no idea why I never told you my name. You must think that I'm a terrible person. I hope you can forgive me."

"Selena," Amara said, ignoring the woman's ramblings. "How many others are outside?"

"The bishop sent twelve casters and thirty soldiers to pacify the heretics. I thought it was overkill, and in hindsight I probably should have told him we were friends. Why would anyone want to arrest you?"

Amara's heart sank. This meant there were over forty attackers waiting for them outside. "What's your rank, Selena? Are you in charge of the group?"

"I'm only a humble nun," Selena said. "The more senior members of our chapter house remained outside to make sure there were no escapees."

Amara opened her mouth to reply, but then stumbled forward. The world tilted around her and a cold sweat broke out on her brow. She staggered over to the bed and sank down. Her stomach heaved uncomfortably, threatening to spill. When the world finally steadied itself, she realized that her injury was worse than she thought.

*I think I'm going into shock.*

Which meant she wasn't in any shape to fight a large group of skilled fighters. Frederick and this "humble nun" had been cannon fodder, leaving the more powerful forces waiting safely outside with fresh mana pools.

The situation felt hopeless.

*I won't give up,* she thought to herself fiercely. *I never have in the past, and I won't start now.*

She rose to her feet and unsteadily tottered over to Brother Otto. The monk's eyes were glazed and his breathing erratic. She knelt at his side, asking, "What should we do?"

Otto dropped his hand into the pouch on his belt and fumbled inside for a moment. Finally, he withdrew a sealed scroll. He opened and closed his mouth in several attempts to speak, but no sounds emerged. Then he handed the scroll to Amara.

As she unrolled the first inch of the parchment, unfamiliar script appeared. She sensed a great magic contained within the words.

"What am I supposed to do with this?"

Selena joined them and looked over Amara's shoulder. "That's a Scroll of Teleportation. Did he steal that from the bishop? If he did, then he'll probably be strung up by his toes. Or maybe crucified if the bishop is in a particularly bad mood."

"A Scroll of Teleportation?" Amara repeated excitedly. This would solve all their problems. "So we can teleport away from here?"

"Scrolls can only teleport one person at a time," Selena explained. "But they're really an amazing magical item. All you have to do is visualize a place, and the scroll's magic will take you there. Some will even work with just the name of the location," she continued, quickly scanning the parchment, "but this one only works by visualization."

Amara felt her hopes deflate. "Only one person?" She couldn't leave Otto and Salamander to save herself. If Selena was correct, the monk would be brutally executed. Who knew what they would do with Salamander?

If Amara was going to escape, she had to bring them with her.

As if following Amara's thoughts, Salamander solemnly said, "It's alright. I'm a good hider. They'll never find me."

"I'm not leaving you," Amara replied. "No one is being left behind."

She brushed back her hair with her uninjured hand as she tried to hatch a plan. But the pain and worsening vertigo made it hard to think.

*There* must *be a way out of here,* she insisted to herself.

Voices called out from below. Amara jerked at the sound of heavy footfalls stomping up the stairs.

They were coming.

The word *"Avatar"* flickered in her vision, but then just as quickly disappeared. Amara desperately tried to reactivate it, but nothing happened. For a second, she thought her patron goddess had granted her a way out.

She asked Selena, "Is there any way to use the scroll for two people?"

"I suppose you could hold hands, but the magic would be erratic limited to a short distance. Why bother teleporting when you could simply walk there instead?"

"That will have to do." She retrieved the jewelry box, then took Salamander's hand and led her to Brother Otto.

"Did I mention how dangerous it is to teleport more than one person?" Selena reiterated, worry etched into her features. "I can't let you—my dearest friend—risk materializing inside of a wall."

"That's a possibility?"

Selena nodded.

The sound of footsteps running down the hallway forced her hand. She didn't want to risk their lives using the Scroll of Teleportation, but neither could she see any other means of escape.

While she awkwardly unrolled the parchment using her good hand, Amara motioned for Salamander to touch Otto. Once they were all connected, she began to read the scroll.

"Wait!" Selena cried out. "It's too dangerous!"

Strangely, the unfamiliar words came to her easily, and her voice resonated as her chanting grew to a crescendo. As armored men burst into the room, Amara finished reading the spell, and the world folded around them. With a sound like the tearing of fabric, a seam appeared in the air and opened into a portal that sucked the trio into a world of darkness.

# CHAPTER 10

Amara floated in a lightless void, all sense of time fading away until it felt like eternity stretched out in front of her. Like pinpricks of light piercing through a tapestry, stars began to appear, a galaxy birthing countless solar systems before her eyes.

In this liminal space, she inspected herself. The pain from her burns had disappeared, and the skin on her hand was smooth and unscathed. Her new dress had been replaced with finely crafted silver armor. A sword hung from a belt around her waist. Her hair floated weightlessly, the strands waving lazily as though from a soft breeze. And most shocking of all, golden tendrils curled around from her back, forming arched wings.

Normally, she would have been terrified to find herself floating in an airless void, but instead, she felt a sense of tranquility suffusing her body.

After what may have been several minutes or a thousand years, a goddess approached, her ethereal beauty surpassing that of any mere mortal. With golden hair that shone like a thousand suns, she wore armor the color of the night sky. A moon and a constellation of stars floated deep within the metal. In one hand, she held a flaming sword, the blade and guard a twin to Amara's conjured *Divine Weapon*.

"Hello, my child," the goddess said, her melodic voice shaking the cosmos. "Fear not, for you are safe here."

Amara fought down the urge to avert her gaze. Every fiber of her being told her to prostrate herself in front of this being, but her desire for answers overrode her instincts. "I assume you're Melischar?"

She nodded, a slight smile flickering across her mouth. "And you are Amara Solace of Earth."

"Why did you bring me here?" She gestured at her armor and wings. "And what is all this?"

"This is your avatar form, my child." Melischar watched Amara with an amused expression, adding, "I felt you calling upon my power far too early in your development. That is why I took the great risk of summoning your spirit here. Had you succeeded in casting your avatar form, the celestial energy would have reduced you to a burned-out husk."

*It would have been nice if someone had warned me.* Amara thought to herself.

"Why did you choose me for reincarnation?" Amara asked the goddess. "And why did you throw me into this world with no help? I've almost been killed half a dozen times already."

Melischar smiled knowingly. "Yet you have found everything you required to survive. How strange. I had planned to contact you during your resurrection. However, the Forces of Chaos moved far earlier than expected. Because of this, my attention was elsewhere." Frowning, the goddess turned her gaze away from Amara. "Even here, in the Forge of Stars, they come for me."

As she spoke, a shadow crept across the galaxy, swallowing the stars one by one until all that remained was a yawning abyss and a radiating sensation of endless hunger.

Amara recoiled. "What is that?" Somehow, she knew that if it reached her, she would be erased from existence.

"Those are the Chaos Gods," Melischar intoned. "Once again, they have set their sights on Vularia. However, this time, the gods will not rise to defend the world. The Celestial Court believes their energy is best spent elsewhere."

"Vularia? Is that the world where I was reincarnated?"

Melischar inclined her head.

Amara chewed on her lower lip. She didn't want to anger Melischar, but she suspected that no world could stand against something that devoured galaxies. "What kind of gods would just let everyone die?"

"The kind who cradle infinite worlds in their arms. Not every battle can end in victory. Sometimes, a world must be sacrificed for the greater good."

"But why are you helping and not the other gods?" Amara pressed. "Surely, you could convince them to come to our aid. And what does this have to do with me? What am I supposed to do?"

Melischar smiled, flashing her perfect teeth. "I have always been the champion of the downtrodden and oppressed. I will not so easily give up on the world. As for you, and your role," she continued, "no god can directly touch a world. To do so would shatter it completely and render it worthless to the Pantheons. The Chaos Gods can only claim victory through champions of their own. An avatar such as yourself carries with them a sliver of a deity's power. Should you rally the Forces of Order on Vularia, then Chaos may be resisted."

"What if I don't want to be your avatar?" she said, her voice rising slightly. "I never asked for any of this. All I want is to live a comfortable life without having to worry about where my next meal is coming from. Is that too much to ask?"

She thought the goddess would grow angry at her words, but instead Melischar's expression filled with a deep sorrow.

"If you wish to renounce the mantle, I will do nothing to stop you. However, everyone you have met, everyone you care about, will perish when the world falls to Chaos. And once Vularia has fallen, the Chaos Gods will set their gaze on Earth next."

Amara continued to chew on her lip. The thought of Salamander dying, along with everyone else, was sobering. And while she had few attachments remaining back on Earth, she couldn't let it fall to darkness. But she also didn't think she was strong enough to carry out this goddess's crusade.

Melischar's eyes darted toward the approaching darkness. "Our time grows short, and I must impart something upon you before you return. Remember, no hero has ever saved a world while hiding in a monastery." The goddess raised her hand and a brilliant light enveloped Amara. "I have faith that you will accomplish everything needed to defend Vularia. You must complete this crusade within five years, lest all be lost to Chaos."

Writing appeared in Amara's vision.

**New Quests Received.**

Amara lifted her hands. "Wait! I still have so many questions."

Then she was falling, the stars zipping past her faster and faster, until she was forced to shut her eyes.

Amara jerked to a stop without warning, and she stumbled forward into complete darkness. The pain from her burns returned with a vengeance as she steadied herself and peered around the space, but the darkness was absolute.

Had her meeting with Melischar—an actual goddess—been real? In hindsight, it all seemed like a fever dream.

But the sight of a new quest notification in her vision confirmed her strange encounter. And she also noticed that she'd gained a level.

Warm light illuminated Salamander and a familiar interior. Wooden beams stretched toward the ceiling above, and stacks of crates and sacks obscured the fieldstone walls. The ground was hard packed dirt.

They were in the cellar of the Dancing Gnome.

"I can't believe we made it," Salamander exclaimed. "You were amazing in that fight. Your sword was all over the place."

"We didn't make it," Amara replied darkly. "We're in the basement. It's only a matter of time until they find us."

When she was casting the spell, she'd pictured the forest where they'd gathered firewood—hoping to at least teleport outside of the city—but the scroll must have defaulted to a closer location. And in doing so, it had probably doomed them.

"Oh," Salamander said, her face falling. Then she brightened. "Maybe they won't look down here? And where's that priest guy?"

At the mention of Brother Otto, Amara spotted him sprawled out on the floor nearby, not moving. For a second, she feared he was dead, but then she saw his chest rising and falling shallowly.

Relieved, Amara moved over to the stairs to listen for any sound of pursuit. She heard the scuff of boots on the floor above and then a few muffled shouts. But it didn't sound like anyone was headed toward the cellar.

"We need to get out of here," Amara said. "Our room was on fire. It's likely to spread fast, and we won't be safe down here. I need a few minutes to meditate. Will you keep watch while I do?"

Salamander nodded and then took up a position hidden under the steps.

Amara's soul was completely drained of mana, and she didn't want to risk trying to escape without at least partially refilling it. She sank down on her knees beside some crates and then tried to clear her mind of any thoughts. But the throbbing pain from her arm made it difficult.

She only managed to meditate for short stretches, and by the time she finished, she had barely refilled one quarter of her mana. Based on her previous casting, she could probably cast one *Charm Person,* and maybe a few *Heal Wounds* spells. Her *Divine Weapon* was completely out of the question, and it would take hours to get enough mana to use that again.

"There's smoke," Salamander cried out. "What should we do?"

Amara glanced over to confirm that smoke was drifting down the stairs. The fire in the bedroom must have spread throughout the inn. While she felt a pang of guilt for ruining Frieda's business, the chaos of a fire might give them a chance to escape.

She hurried over to Otto and cast *Heal Wounds* on him. While she would have preferred to use it on her ravaged arm, she needed the monk on his feet, so she repeated her spell. Finally, after her fourth cast—mana running dangerously low—he raised his head.

"What . . . what happened?" Otto muttered, his voice scratchy. "Did we escape?"

"Not exactly," she replied. "The inn is on fire, and we need to make a run for it."

"I see," he replied, his features becoming pinched. "I . . . don't know how to fight."

"Of course you don't." She reached out and helped him to his feet. "What class are you?"

"I'm a cleric," he replied. "But I have spent all my Expertise Points increasing my skills. I've reached Journeyman as both a scribe and illuminator."

"Do you have a weapon?" Amara asked, taking up her staff. "Any way you can help in a battle?"

Otto shook his head.

"Well, find one then. And you can't go out dressed in that." She gestured at his priestly robes. They would be spotted the moment they emerged onto the street.

"What will I wear?" He scrubbed a hand through his hair. "I'm not going naked."

Amara took the knife from Salamander and cut open one of the sacks. She poured out the grain inside and then cut rough arm and neck holes. Once she was done, she thrust it toward Otto.

"You expect me to wear sackcloth?" he exclaimed. "The material will probably rub me raw."

Her expression was enough to end his protests. He handed her the jewelry box as he quickly began the business of disrobing.

Amara walked over to the stairs again, the smoke becoming thicker. She remembered hearing once that most people died of smoke inhalation and not burns in a fire. And she had no desire to suffocate in this basement.

She turned back to the others. "This is what's going to happen. I'm going to use *Cloak of Shadows* on myself. No one should recognize Salamander, and hopefully Otto will only look like a beggar. If we get in trouble, I'll attack."

Neither of them said anything, which hopefully meant they were onboard with her plan.

For good measure, she knelt and grabbed a handful of dirt, and then walked over to Otto. She smeared it on his face and exposed arms. Wearing the meager costume and an expression of pure misery, the monk looked like a proper street dweller.

She made sure Otto had the jewelry box in hand, then cast *Cloak of Shadows*. The world faded gray and Amara headed up the stairs slowly, taking care to not make any noise. When she reached the main floor, she found it abandoned. While the smoke was thick, it clung to the ceiling. She saw no flames.

"The coast is clear," she hissed down the stairs. A moment later, the others emerged from the cellar.

Amara padded over to the open door and peered outside. The road in front of the inn was a beehive of activity, and throngs of people were rushing madly. A bucket brigade had formed leading toward a nearby canal, and they were tossing water onto the burning walls. On the far side of the street, Selena argued with several heavily armored men. Thankfully, none of them were looking in their direction.

"Hurry! While they're preoccupied," she whispered to the others.

She stood to the side as Salamander and Otto scurried out of the inn. A few people in the bucket brigade seemed to take note—just another pair of survivors—before returning their attention to fighting the fire.

Amara followed her companions around a nearby corner before letting her *Cloak of Shadows* drop. She was getting dangerously low on mana, and she wanted to save something to treat her burns.

As they walked through the deserted alleyway, she emptied the last of her mana casting healing spells on her arm. The pain dulled slightly, but Amara's skin remained a swollen, angry red. Her wounds, it seemed, were too severe for her low-level ability.

When they reached the river, they stumbled to a stop, and Otto addressed her. "I chartered a ship before I left. It's waiting for us at the docks and will take us as far as Sanaria. From there, we can hire a caravan for the rest of the way to the Khaneri Monasteries."

"I . . . I can't go with you," Amara said. "This might sound crazy, but a goddess gave me a list of quests to save this world."

Otto gaped at her. "You met with a goddess? What was she like? When did you meet with her? I wish I had a quill and parchment. This needs to be recorded for posterity. I always say to myself, don't go anywhere without your writing implements, Otto, but look—"

Amara interrupted his ramblings. "It's a long story." She didn't want to tell him about floating in the void of space and meeting with Melischar, as it still seemed insane to her—and she'd experienced it firsthand. "But I know that I don't have time to hide away in some monastery."

"At least take the ship with me to safety," Otto said, rubbing his hands together pensively. "While my talents don't lend themselves to martial combat, the least I can do is give you safe passage."

"It's a tempting offer, but I'd rather take some time to figure out my next step before I leave," she said. "And I think I know somewhere we can hole up for a bit."

"I will spread word that the gods have returned, then," Otto said, straightening up slightly. "By the time you have completed your divine missions, I will have heralded your presence to all true believers. I should probably write a moving tale of your arrival and deeds."

"Thank you, I guess?" She hoped that Brother Otto wouldn't make himself a target for the bishop. "Just make sure that you don't get hurt on my behalf."

She turned to Salamander. "Do you know where the Drunken Minotaur Inn is?"

Jonas had said he owed her after saving his life, and now she planned to cash in.

# CHAPTER 11

Amara rapped lightly on the door again, whispering Jonas's name through the wood. When they'd arrived at the Drunken Minotaur Inn, the windows had all been dark and it was silent within.

While chaos spread as fast as the fire at the Dancing Gnome Inn, Amara and Salamander had traveled to the riverbank opposite their burning home. No one had raised the alarm here yet, allowing them to slip through the streets unregarded. She suspected it would be difficult to fight a fire in the outer city where most of the crowded buildings were haphazardly constructed. The conditions had been ripe for a catastrophic blaze.

Bells began to toll in the distance, a chorus of shouts ringing out in answer.

Growing impatient, Amara knocked louder. The growing commotion outside would soon wake everyone at the inn, and she didn't want to be standing in this hallway when the doors opened and those guests came running out. She especially did not want to explain the broken window downstairs.

Without warning, the door swung open, and a bare chested and annoyed-looking Jonas appeared in the entrance. He glared at them, but then his expression softened as recognition flickered in his eyes.

"What in the name of Sirveig are you doing here?" He cocked his head to the side as bells continued to toll. "And what is that unholy racket out there? Is the city under siege?"

Amara shook her head. "We're not under attack, but there might be a *minor* fire near where we were staying. Do you mind if we come in? I don't want anyone to see us."

"Minor fire?" Salamander exclaimed. "You call that minor?"

Amara shushed her. She didn't want to spook him by announcing that half the outer city was probably burning down behind them. When Jonas stepped aside to grant them entry, she rushed inside.

These quarters were far more impressive than her own at the Dancing Gnome Inn. A writing desk of finely carved wood rested against one wall, and stacks of paper scattered across its surface. Several fresh candles had been placed in holders around the room, and tapestries depicting what looked like monster hunts adorned the walls. The entire place appeared lovingly cared for, and the pleasant smell of fresh lemons hung in the air.

Jonas closed the door gently behind him. From the back of a chair, he grabbed his tunic and slipped it on. "May I ask how you gained entry to this inn? I have it on good authority that this building is locked at sundown every night."

"The innkeeper might have forgotten to lock a second-story window, and my friend is quite good at climbing," she lied. If he learned of the broken window, he probably wouldn't be happy.

Salamander shot her a sideways glance. "I am?"

"Yes, you *are,*" Amara said firmly.

"I see." Jonas slung his bandolier of knives across his chest and then wrapped a belt with two sheathed daggers around his waist. "And what was so important that it couldn't wait until morning? I doubt you were so overcome with excitement to join my party that you rushed here in the dead of night to tell me the news."

Amara contemplated her next words carefully. She barely knew Jonas, and by asking for his help, she would place him in terrible danger. But aside from Otto, she had no one else to turn to in this city.

She took a deep breath before explaining. "I'm the avatar of Melischar, and the Church is hunting me. A kill squad attacked me in our room. I defeated them, but I need somewhere to lie low until I figure out what to do next."

To his credit, his brow barely twitched at her story, but she could see that he was deeply troubled. "The Church tried to murder you? Without a trial? That is deplorable conduct, especially against someone who, I imagine, has yet to reach Level 20."

"I'm actually only Level 2." She coughed, embarrassed, then remembered, "Oh wait! I leveled up during the fight."

"I'm Level 3, too!" Salamander said. Bouncing in her seat on the mattress, she added, "This is *so* much softer than our bed."

This time, Jonas couldn't conceal his surprise. "But I saw you cast *Divine Weapon.* How could you cast such a spell at level 2?"

Amara shrugged, still unsure of how much she should tell him. "I got lucky?"

"It seems you are full of surprises, Amara." He paced the length of the room and then turned toward her. "I will grant you shelter, of course, but know that I cannot fight the Church alone. Do you have a plan?"

"I don't have one yet," she admitted. "A monk offered to take me south, but the goddess implied I don't have much time to save this world. And I won't make any progress hiding in a dusty monastery. If I'm going to do what she asked, then I need to get stronger and fast."

"Then we share a common goal." He walked over to the window, where an orange glow had appeared through cracks in the shutters. "It appears that it's not a *minor* fire, as you stated."

"It was smaller when we left," she blurted out. "One caster was hurling around fireballs like a maniac before I charmed her."

Jonas turned toward her and crossed his arms. "If it's not too late, I think you should take the option offered by the monk. If you've rankled the Church, they won't leave any stone unturned in the search for you. This place won't be safe for long."

"There must be another option," she said, her heart sinking. "I know that it's the wrong decision to hide."

"I suppose there might be another way," he mused, "but the notion is fraught with peril and should only be considered out of utter desperation."

"Would this idea also give me the chance to level up?"

Jonas nodded. "The town of Oksberg has sent out a request for adventurers. It's the last remaining bastion of mankind near Galoth's Wall, and they're offering temporary membership in the Adventurer's Guild regardless of criminal history or class. And should you contribute enough to the defense, you may earn permanent membership."

"That sounds perfect." She frowned, her brow furrowing. "I think I actually have a quest for that, too." She opened her notifications and scrolled through those she'd received from Melischar. "Here it is. It says I need to drive back the Forces of Chaos in the North and restore Galoth's Wall."

Jonas chuckled, but his mirth faded when Amara responded with a puzzled expression. "Surely, you jest."

"Is there something wrong with my quest?"

"Such a task is hopeless."

"Tell me why," she said. "I don't know anything about a wall or the Forces of Chaos."

"How do you know so little of these lands?" Jonas asked, but then continued. "The Wall was constructed by the First Emperor of Man, Galoth. It stretched across the breadth of the continent, and the magic contained within repelled the Forces of Chaos for centuries. When the Wall's might weakened, all manner of monsters and foul creatures invaded the northlands. To restore it would be, as I said, an impossible task."

She doubted it was impossible if Melischar had given it to her. There must be some way to succeed. "But they're still fighting there, otherwise there wouldn't be a quest. Right?"

"They're fighting—and losing," he said, darkly. "It's why they offer such impressive rewards. Only through a never-ending stream of adventurers do the border marches cling to existence. And several have fallen this year alone."

"Do you have any other suggestions?"

"There are few options for those with an undesirable class like ourselves," he replied. "Especially if we can no longer remain here to gain levels in the forest. Not that fighting bandits and flying snakes was a long-term solution for either of us."

"What about your family?" she asked. "Could they help us?"

"I am no longer welcome in any of the lands of House Stein," he said curtly.

She wanted to press the matter, but she could see from his dour expression that he didn't want to elaborate. If their only option was to head to the Far North to fight monsters, maybe she should have gone with Brother Otto.

"What do you think we should do?" she asked. "I don't know how useful I'd be against hordes of monsters."

Jonas scrubbed a hand through his hair and then sighed. "They are always seeking mercenaries in the coastal city-states, though the work is often most unsavory. Traveling west offers wastelands with the promise of treasures and danger among the ruins of the Tohkarian Empire. However, neither of these appeals to me. At least in the North we would fight for an honorable cause."

"I suppose we could head north, then." Amara glanced at Salamander. "What do you want to do?"

"I wanted to stay here," she said, twirling a lock of hair around her finger, "but if we go north, we could get rich. And then I could pay off my parents' debt. Plus, I'd get to see giants!"

At the mention of giants, Amara raised a brow, giving Jonas a questioning glance. When he nodded softly, her eyes widened. *We're going to fight actual giants?* The more she learned about the North, the more she didn't like the idea of traveling there. But the other options sounded even worse. And this way, maybe she could complete a quest for Melischar.

"I believe a wagon leaves at first light," Jonas said. "Both of you should attempt to get some rest before then. What other quests did this so-called goddess grant you?"

She frowned. "You don't believe me?"

"No offense intended, my lady, but you'd hardly be the first person to claim to be a divine avatar." Jonas leaned back against the writing desk. "There have been at least a dozen avatars preaching in the streets since I arrived here last month. The Church arrested several of them, but they allowed some to continue spouting their nonsense. It helps to delegitimize the heretics."

Amara tried to hide her shock at his words. She'd thought that it would be relatively easy to convince people she was an avatar. But if madmen and lunatics were claiming to represent the gods regularly, then it might be harder than she imagined.

"She gave me thirteen quests," she explained, trying to quell her disappointment. As she spoke, she opened her menu to read through them.

*Current Quests:*
1. *Rally the Human Kingdoms Under One Banner*
2. *Awaken the Dragons from Their Endless Slumber*
3. *Liberate the Dwarves of Ice Spine Mountains*
4. *Defeat the Lich Queen and Free the Undead*
5. *Rally the Halflings*
6. *Find the Lost Gnome Tribes*
7. *Lead the Wasteland Horde to Their Promised Land*
8. *Heal the Great Schism*
9. *Ally with the Nephilim and Issurians*
10. *Restore the Elven Homeland*
11. *Unite the Centaur Clans*
12. *Return the Fae to this World*
13. *Restore Galoth's Wall*

Amara read the list to Jonas who only chuckled darkly in response.

"What's so funny?"

"If I didn't know any better, I'd swear that you were pulling my leg," Jonas said. "A king could accomplish none of these pursuits, never mind an individual adventurer. Furthermore, some things on your list are mysteries even to myself, and I've had extensive education. For example, exactly what are the lost gnome tribes?"

"The goddess said I only have five years," she whispered. "If I fail, then the Forces of Chaos will destroy this world."

"Well, that is certainly worrisome." Jonas said. "Regardless, you should attempt to get some rest before tomorrow. I will see what aid I can lend to those fighting the fire. Please make use of the bed in my absence."

"I couldn't take your bed—" Amara's protests became a grunt as Salamander elbowed her in the ribs. Amara shot the girl a murderous look, but she pretended not to notice.

"I insist," he replied, donning his armor. He grabbed his backpack from the corner and slung it over his shoulder. "I'll endeavor to return before dawn."

Amara didn't know if she could sleep after the night's events. She watched jealously as Salamander climbed into bed and began snoring only moments later. With a nod to Amara, Jonas slipped through the door.

Amara stretched beside Salamander, but found it difficult to get comfortable. Every movement jostled her injured arm. After what felt like an eternity, she slipped into a fitful slumber, her dreams filled with fireballs and giants.

# CHAPTER 12

Amara awoke to the sound of the door creaking open. She sat bolt upright, the covers slipping off her and Salamander. But her initial fear of the Church having found her again evaporated when she spotted Jonas in the doorway. The outside hallway flickered with candlelight behind his sturdy frame.

Jonas stepped into the room and shut the door behind him. He looked exhausted, and his clothing was blackened by soot. After dropping his backpack on the floor near the door, he staggered over to the desk, where he sat down heavily on the chair. He rubbed a hand down his face and gave her a wan smile. "Did you have a good rest, my lady?"

She still had trouble adjusting to a world without clocks. When it was dark outside, it was nearly impossible to tell the time. "What time is it?"

"It's just before dawn," he replied. "If we plan to meet the wagons before they depart for Oksberg, we should leave immediately."

"Do you . . . want to clean yourself up first?"

Jonas shook his head. "I'm sure we'll stop at a stream on our journey northward. Until then, I will simply have to remain unkempt." As he spoke, he dusted some of the ash off his leather bracers. Then he examined the rest of his armor and sighed.

Amara jostled Salamander's shoulder lightly. The girl shrugged her off and returned to snoring softly. Amara was convinced that Salamander could fall sleep through a thunderstorm while on a bucking horse. Sometimes, she wished she could drift off so easily.

"Go away," Salamander said, without opening her eyes. "I don't want to wake up yet."

"We need to leave," Amara replied gently. "The wagons will leave soon."

At the mention of the wagons, the girl blinked and then rubbed her eyes. She stretched languidly like a cat as she ran a hand through her hair. "I've never left the city before. I mean, I've gone into the forest, but never any farther than that. Do you think my parents will be alright while I'm gone?"

"I'm sure they'll be fine," Amara said. "And the sooner we leave, the sooner we can return to free them."

Salamander nodded excitedly at that and then jumped out of bed. She gathered up her meager possessions and then hurried over to the door. "Come on. What are you waiting for? I've seen faster giant snails."

Amara turned to Jonas, who still hadn't risen from the chair. "Are giant snails real?"

"If you've never encountered a giant snail, then you have most certainly lived a privileged life." He pushed himself wearily to his feet. "Have you considered what will happen if members of the Church are watching the wagons?"

She froze in the act of standing. At least a few of the people sent to the Dancing Gnome had seen her face. And the *Charm Person* spell on Selena would have worn off long ago. What if they had shared her description and the Church was monitoring all the roads out of the city?

"I . . . hadn't thought about that."

"Perhaps your young friend and I should travel to the wagons alone. And then once we have boarded the transportation, you could join us in stealth. If I remember correctly, you cast a spell with that ability in the forest. Also, since we're going to be traveling together, do you mind if I ask your class?"

She looked at him in surprise. At some point, she assumed that he'd snuck a glance at her class without her noticing. "You haven't scanned me yet?"

"I would never do anything so discourteous."

Salamander smiled knowingly. "I told you it was rude."

"I . . . a cleric," she said. "Actually, that's not completely true. I'm a Trickster Cleric. I know how that sounds, but I'm not really a bad person. While I've done a few things I'm not proud of, I did them to help my father—"

Jonas held up his hand to stop her. "I would not judge anyone based on their class. Sometimes, a person is cursed with a class not of their own choosing. I have known this pain since I was first granted my own."

"And you're a rogue, right?" she asked, pressing her lips together.

He clasped his hands in front of him. "I'm a Wraith Rogue, a class capable of unspeakably evil acts. Upon receiving it, I swore that I would never use any of my abilities."

"How do you quest then?"

"It's been difficult, but I've been concentrating on Martial Abilities to make up for my shortfalls. However, as you saw in the forest, I'm not always successful."

"I'm glad you told me."

Neither of them spoke for a moment, and the silence stretched out until it became uncomfortable.

Jonas rose to his feet. "I should settle up with the innkeeper, and then I'll return to help you pack your things." He stopped to gather some papers from the desk, and then a few of his belongings hanging on the wall; they all went into his backpack.

After Jonas had left the room, Amara glanced down at the scorched sleeve of her dress. Her wrinkled and inflamed skin was clearly visible through holes in the fabric. While the burns still ached, the pain had greatly lessened from the previous night. But she feared the scars would remain on her hand and forearm.

She took a moment to cast another healing spell—leaving enough mana for her *Cloak of Shadows*—and watched the redness fade to a dark pink. But the skin remained puckered.

*Great. I'm going to have a nasty scar. Am I going to have to start wearing a glove or something?*

Amara pushed down the worry about her disfigured arm and focused on the task at hand. She gathered up her staff and then looped her backpack over one shoulder. Then she stopped to scan the room for her jewelry box. Somehow, it had found its way over into the corner—far from where she remembered leaving it.

She stared at chest and then took a step back. The feeling of wrongness emanating from it returned tenfold. She pointed at the small wooden chest. "Where did you put that down last night, Salamander?"

"I think I put it at the foot of the bed." The girl chewed on her lower lip. "How did it get all the way over there? That's weird."

As Amara stared intently at the tiny chest, the door opened, and Jonas strode back into the room. He must have found a wash basin somewhere, as he'd scrubbed the grime off his face. He stopped when he found them both gazing at the corner. "Is something amiss?"

"We found a jewelry box in the forest, and strange things have been happening with it."

"You found a treasure chest in the forest and brought it home with you?" Throwing knives appeared in Jonas's hand, and he spun around to face the jewelry box. In one smooth motion, he hurled both blades at the chest.

Amara reached out to stop him—thinking he'd lost his mind—but then watched with shock as the jewelry box sprouted legs like a turtle and scuttled out of the way. One knife struck the top of the chest, where it stuck quivering. The other missed and bounced off the floor.

"What is that?" Amara cried out. "Is that a monster?"

"It's a mimic," Jonas said, his daggers flashing in his hands. "I'll deal with it."

"Wait," she replied, as memories of the monster egg returned to her. "I think it saved my life back at the inn."

Jonas lowered his weapons slightly and looked confused. "It's a *mimic*, a terribly dangerous monster. Why it made its abode in a forest, I'll never know. However, it must be dealt with immediately and without mercy."

"Do you remember the egg I lost?" she said quickly, trying to stop him before he attacked again. "I think this hatched out of there. And come to think of it, this little monster probably ate all the flying snake corpses."

"Then it's . . . your *pet?*" Jonas raised his brow, but he still didn't lower his weapons. He looked like a barely restrained predator.

"Something like that." She stepped forward and knelt in front of the creature. While they'd talked, it had opened its mouth to reveal rows of shark-like teeth. She watched its tongue flop out like a puppy as it panted. "Are you friendly?"

As she examined it, she felt something tugging at the edge of her consciousness. She focused on it until writing appeared in her vision.

| Lesser Mimic, Pet | Level 2 |
|---|---|
| Stats | |
| Strength | 5 |
| Dexterity | 1 |
| Constitution | 5 |
| Intelligence | 1 |
| Wisdom | 1 |
| Charisma | 1 |
| Vitality | 5 |
| | |
| Skills | |
| *Shapechanger* | Novice |
| *Adhesive* | Novice |
| | |
| Martial Abilities | |
| Pseudopod Strike | Novice |
| Grapple | Novice |

"It *is* a pet!" she exclaimed. "This must have come out of the egg I lost. What can mimics do?"

"They can devour you while you sleep," Jonas replied darkly. "And I still think it's a terrible idea to let this monster live."

"The notification says that it's my pet, though." She reached out toward it, but it scuttled back to the corner. "Did that mean man hurt you?"

The mimic bobbed its body up and down in reply.

"I'm hardly a *mean* man," Jonas groused. "I was attempting to defend you from a vicious beast."

"You're not vicious, are you?" Amara cooed. She crept forward until she could reach the knife embedded in the creature's hide. It recoiled at her first attempt to grab it, but then allowed her to grip the hilt. She pulled it out in one smooth motion. Once the blade was free, a droplet of dark blood welled up from the wound.

Without thinking, she cast *Heal Wounds* on the creature. The cut immediately sealed shut, and the creature happily bounced from side to side.

Jonas shook his head. "A pet mimic? This can only end in tragedy."

"I think he's cute," she said. "And don't be so negative."

"Perhaps you're right," Jonas replied. "Maybe he will only devour both of you, leaving me alive to avenge your deaths."

"The egg said that the pet would form a magical bond with me." She reached out to gently pet the mimic. Strangely, it had perfectly simulated the feel of lumber—or it had somehow incorporated a plank of wood into its body. "And it already saved my life last night. When the mage was about to cast some sort of firestorm, it bit her foot."

"I still think it's a bad idea," Jonas said. "However, there is no time left to argue. If we don't depart now, then we'll miss the wagons."

Amara returned her attention to the mimic. "Could you please turn back into a chest?"

The mimic withdrew its legs into its body, and the mouth sealed shut, leaving no trace of the toothy maw behind. Within a few seconds, it was indistinguishable from a real wooden jewelry box.

She reached down to scoop it up. Then she held it out for Salamander before she thought better of it. What if it *was* dangerous and attacked her friend? She decided to test if her *Cloak of Shadows* could also hide what she was holding.

After casting the spell, it only took a second for her world to turn gray as she faded into the nether. Once the spell had covered her completely, she asked, "Can anyone see the mimic?"

Jonas shook his head as he slammed his daggers back into their sheaths. "I see no trace of you or your pet monster. That spell may prove useful in the future."

It would help if she could hide other party members beneath her *Cloak of Shadows*. She reached out to touch Salamander, but the drain on her mana increased rapidly until it felt like her soul would run dry in a few seconds.

Amara dropped the spell to stanch the flow of mana. She might be able to use it to hide the others in an emergency, but she would pay a heavy price for doing so. For now, she would just have to cloak herself and her pet. For some reason, the mimic barely placed any additional strain on her mana usage.

She tucked the box under her arm and followed Jonas out of the door. Then she stopped as she heard the rustling of papers. She turned back to see Salamander stuffing sheets into a sack.

"Do you know how much these are worth?" the girl said as she grabbed a candle from the desktop. "And real candles sell for a copper each. This place is like a dream come true."

"We're not robbing them blind," Amara said, sternly. "I don't want to steal from anyone."

"You're not stealing," Salamander said, pointedly. "I am."

Amara pressed her lips together and then shook her head. Now wasn't the time to get into a fight with Salamander over her sticky fingers. She needed to concentrate on getting to the wagons safely. And starting an argument would draw unwanted attention.

She simply motioned for the girl to leave, and then cast *Cloak of Shadows* on herself. After she was hidden from sight, she headed down the stairs after Jonas.

The main room of the inn was packed, and many prosperous-looking adventurers clustered around the tables. All manner of pastries were laid out, along with bacon, eggs, loaves of white bread, and bottles of wine.

At the sight of the food, her stomach twisted painfully. But she knew she didn't have time to stop and have a leisurely breakfast.

Salamander had other ideas, and she darted up to the closest table and grabbed a platter before darting out the door. None of the preoccupied adventurers even noticed the girl absconding with part of their breakfast.

Amara followed her companions outside but froze when she spotted a monk wearing the same robes as Brother Otto; he stood on the far side of the street examining those passing by. Whirling around, she spotted a dozen armed men marching between the buildings. On their tabards, they wore the symbol of a blooming tree—the same symbol that had hung around Otto's neck.

She suddenly realized that it wasn't going to be easy to reach the wagons traveling to Oksberg. The Bishop's minions were searching for her, and even though she was hidden by *Cloak of Shadows,* she wasn't certain that it would be enough to slip through their grasp.

Amara could only hope her luck would hold out until they were safely out of the city.

# CHAPTER 13

Amara watched Jonas slow at the sight of the Church soldiers, but then he took Salamander's hand and led her down the street confidently. Amara held her breath as the two of them passed the soldiers—she feared they might be searching for her companion as well—but the armed men barely gave the pair a second look.

She exhaled as she realized no one back at the Dancing Gnome Inn had probably even noticed Salamander. The girl hadn't fought in the battle, and she still looked like a malnourished street urchin. They were most likely only searching for herself and Brother Otto.

At the thought of the monk, she wondered if he had reached the ship safely. He'd risked his life for her, and she hadn't even thanked him properly. Someday, she'd have to find him and rectify that.

But for now, she needed to slip around the Church patrols searching for her. She wasn't sure if any of them had the ability to see through stealth spells, so she held her breath again as the patrol neared where she was standing. As they tromped by, she pressed herself flat against the wall. But none of them even glanced in her direction.

Once the road was finally clear, she hurried to catch up with Jonas and Salamander. She had to weave through throngs of people to reach her companions. As she passed the crowd, she noticed many of them were covered with soot, and she caught snippets of conversation about the fire. While she didn't hear everything they were saying, it sounded like the blaze had been extinguished. She heard someone mentioning something about a water mage, which she imagined would act like a one-man fire brigade in this world.

Amara caught up with Jonas at the end of the street, and she slowed her pace as they moved through the outer city. She passed by bakeries with loaves of bread piled high on tables, and then butcher shops with whole animals hanging in the windows. Finally, she turned down a street filled with blacksmiths where smoke hung heavy in the air.

After what felt like an eternity, they reached an inn where several wagons lined up out front. She felt surprised to recognize the adventurers from the Dancing Gnome Inn sitting in one of the carts. The woman with dark hair was plucking half-heartedly at her miniature harp, while the others sat glumly staring off into the distance. After losing their healer, they must have wanted to try their luck in the North as well.

Jonas walked over to the only wagon with free spaces remaining and then helped Salamander climb inside. The driver shot the girl a look, but then shrugged as if to say it wasn't his concern.

An squat man slid over to give Salamander his spot. Nearly as wide as he was tall, he had curly red hair that spilled out from underneath a steel cap, and a thick beard that nearly reached his belt. His eyes were hidden underneath bushy eyebrows. In one hand, he gripped an axe, and in the other, a round shield hung loosely. He nodded as Jonas took a seat across from him.

Amara waited until the wagons were loaded—there were four all together—and then she crept over to the one with her companions. Her mana was running dangerously low, and she prayed it would last until she was out of the city. While there were no members of the Church keeping watch here, they may still have checkpoints on the roads.

A man holding a book moved between the wagons as he scribbled something on the pages with a quill. Once he'd finished, he climbed up next to the driver of the lead wagon and shouted something unintelligible.

This was her chance, and she clambered up the boot into the wooden bed of the wagon, causing it to rock slightly under her weight. Though the curly-haired man raised his bushy eyebrows, he said nothing.

Within a few minutes, they were underway.

The wagons trundled along the street in a line, and soon they reached the edge of the city. As she feared, there was a cordon of armed men and casters strung out across the road, all wearing the symbol of the Church.

A man wearing priestly robes walked up to the lead wagon while the armed men spread out to search the rest. But after a quick scan of the adventurers, they waved them through.

She nearly sagged with relief as her wagon rolled past the roadblock. As the city disappeared behind them, they entered golden fields of wheat where peasants worked to harvest the grain. The din of the city's forges was replaced by birdsong and the soft buzz of insects. For the first time in days, she felt her anxiety draining away.

"That's a neat trick," the squat man said as he tugged on his beard. "The things I could do with a spell like that. Needless to say, I'd be the richest man in the Ice Spine Mountains. That's for certain."

Amara flinched as the man stared directly at where she was sitting.

Jonas chuckled and leaned back. "My father always said you couldn't trick a dwarf. I believe it's safe to drop your spell now, Amara."

She hesitated for a moment, but then decided to trust Jonas. She let her *Cloak of Shadows* fade, and after a second, her vision returned to normal. "Hello," she said, waving awkwardly at the dwarf. "How did you know I was here?"

"I felt the wagon shift, didn't I?" he said, his voice like rocks grinding together. "A dwarf always senses their surroundings. Otherwise, the first time you hit an unstable wall with your pickaxe, you wouldn't know to run for your life. It's never a good idea to ignore your footing when you're a miner."

At her appearance, the wagon driver glanced over his shoulder and stared at her with a blank expression. But then he turned his attention back to the rutted road without speaking.

Jonas leaned forward. "My name is Jonas of House Stein. And these are my companions Amara and Salamander. Is that the name you wish to be known as in the North?"

Salamander nodded. "Don't try to give me a nickname like Sally or anything."

"I would never dream of such a thing," Jonas said with a smile. Then he turned back to the dwarf. "May I know your name?"

"My name? I'm Borim Bronzejaw, of Copperhold." He raked his fingers through his beard. "At least I used to be until those bastards kicked me out. Though I suppose we all have a tale like that if we're headed to the petty kingdom of Oksberg."

"Petty kingdom?" Jonas's brow rose. "I thought it was still a duchy in the Kingdom of Mansfeld."

"They declared their independence months ago," Borim continued. "After that lousy King Conrad didn't send aid during the undead siege, the duke declared himself a petty king."

"What about the Church?" Amara asked, perhaps a bit too quickly. "Are they still there?"

Borim guffawed. "So, it was you they were looking for? Don't worry, lass, your secret is safe with me. All those holy types stick in my craw. To answer you, as far as I've heard they ran off with the town's gold and relics, leaving Oksberg on their own."

"They're not looking for me," she said, though her words sounded unconvincing, even to her own ears. "I was just . . . curious."

Borim winked at her. "Sure you were." The dwarf adjusted his axe, and then rested his hands on the head. "It's probably easy to see I don't have a group. Any chance I can earn a place in yours? Oksberg is no place for solo adventurers."

Amara and Jonas exchanged looks. They really hadn't discussed what would happen when they arrived. She assumed they would group up, but what if Jonas didn't want to be in a party with her?

"We'd be happy to have you," Jonas said. "A warrior is always a valuable addition to any group."

"Excellent." Borim stomped his foot and grinned broadly. "I say we toast this with a drink!"

He pulled out a flask from his pocket and took a swig, then passed it to Amara.

She held the flask in her hand, unsure of what to do with it. While she'd had wine in the past, she'd never had hard liquor before. And she didn't want to get drunk on a bumpy wagon ride.

"Go ahead," Borim said. "It won't bite you."

She scrunched up her face and sipped from the flask. Instead of the bite of hard alcohol that she'd expected, she tasted a sugary drink that reminded her of root beer. It was one of the sweetest things she'd had since she'd arrived in this world. After she'd swallowed, she passed it to Jonas with a surprised look.

Once he'd taken a gulp, he looked almost as surprised as her. He handed it back to the dwarf without comment.

"Well, what do you think?" Borim asked. "It's my own recipe. There's too much sugar, isn't there? Well? Out with it already."

Amara shrugged. "I liked it."

"As did I," Jonas said. "It simply wasn't what I expected."

"Ah, you thought it would be whiskey." Borim sighed deeply. "A drop of that dark liquid hasn't passed my lips in years. But that's a long story that includes my banishment from Copperhold. And it's a tale best told another time."

Amara exchanged another look with Jonas. She knew that he'd been too quick to allow the dwarf into their group. Especially without consulting her first. Who knew why the dwarf had been banished? Was he a murderer or something equally heinous?

"I hope you'll still have me in your group," Borim continued. "And I swear to you, I've committed no crime recognized by the human kingdoms. Hopefully, that will be enough to settle the matter."

"That's more than adequate for me," Jonas said, warmly. "And everyone deserves a second chance. Don't you agree, Amara?"

If Oksberg was taking adventurers with no questions asked, she doubted that the dwarf would be the last person they met with a shady past. And she understood him not wanting to share his story with a group of strangers. She nodded tersely in response to Jonas's question.

"Glad to be aboard, then." Borim fixated his gaze on Jonas. "I assume you're our fearless leader?"

Jonas pointed at Amara wordlessly.

"Her?" Borim squinted his eyes at Amara. "She looks like a half-starved scullery maid. And judging by her clothing, one who's not particularly good at handling food or fire. No offense intended, lass."

"And you look like an overgrown child wearing a fake beard and his daddy's armor," Amara shot back, adding, "no offense, of course."

The dwarf roared with laughter and slapped his knee. "I like you. If you'd care to make me an official group member?"

Amara's annoyance cooled at the dwarf's reaction. After a moment, she tried to recall how she'd added Salamander to her group. She focused on adding Jonas first then received the notification that he'd accepted. Afterward, she turned her attention toward the dwarf. An icon with Borim's name and information soon appeared with the others in her vision.

Jonas had been far too ready to accept a stranger into their circle—even if the dwarf hadn't turned her into the Church. She hoped she didn't regret her decision.

After she'd updated the group, a silence descended over them. They rode for the next few hours, only talking sporadically as the caravan passed through forests, over hills, and even by a sparkling lake. Fishermen in their boats plied the waters. When a young boy on the nearest ship waved as they rolled past, Salamander excitedly returned the greeting.

The convoy stopped several times to rest and water the oxen. But since no food was provided to the passengers Amara was grateful that Salamander had "borrowed" some breakfast from The Drunken Minotaur Inn. Technically, it wasn't stolen as it was included with Jonas's room fee, which meant she could enjoy it guilt free. They offered some of their platter to the dwarf, who graciously accepted.

By the time night rolled around, the caravan had entered a tiny hamlet and stopped in front of an inn that made the Dancing Gnome look palatial. All the adventurers piled off. There were sixteen in total, and though most had formed into groups during the trip, a few stood off from the others after dismounting.

With surprising dexterity, Borim leapt over the side of the wagon. He hefted his axe and glanced over his shoulder. "Best that you enjoy your night. Tomorrow, things get dangerous. We'll be trespassing on goblin lands for the next few weeks."

"Few weeks!" Amara exclaimed. "How long does it take to travel to Oksberg?"

Jonas jumped off after the dwarf and then held out his hand to help Salamander down. "If we make good time, only about thirty days."

She reeled at the number, shocked at how long it would take to travel. While she knew wagons were slow, she'd expected a few days at most. She hoped she wasn't wasting time, as the deadline for her quests was ticking down by the minute.

For now, all she could do was stay the course. She jumped down behind the others and then stretched before she winced with pain. Her injured arm throbbed, and her eyes felt grainy from lack of sleep.

Tonight, she would enjoy the hospitality of the inn, and then tomorrow she'd pick Jonas's brain on how to best level up. She'd gained a level after the fight at the inn but still hadn't allocated her points.

Maybe Jonas would teach her everything she needed to know about this world during the ride north. At least that way she'd have something to occupy herself on the long journey.

# CHAPTER 14

The wagon train departed from the inn shortly after the sun's ray bathed the world in crimson light. Amara could have used a few more hours' rest, and for once, she was the last one out of bed. She sat bleary-eyed in the wagon, wishing desperately that this world had coffee.

"A red sun in the morning is a bad omen," Borim grunted. "Best we keep our weapons close at hand. Or whatever you call that stick of yours," he added with a meaningful look to Amara's makeshift staff.

Amara ignored the dwarf's barb and slid closer to Jonas. She lowered her voice to a whisper. "Do you mind if I ask you a few questions about classes?"

"I'd be happy to answer any questions you may have," he replied softly. "However, I must ask—why are we whispering?"

"I don't want Borim to know how little I know about classes."

"That's understandable." He rubbed his hands together. "So, what knowledge may I impart to you?"

She still hadn't leveled up after the fight at the inn, as she didn't want to make a mistake that would hurt her future advancement. Originally, she'd planned to ask Jonas for help the previous evening, but she'd been too exhausted. As it was, she had nearly fallen asleep in her stew at dinner.

"I'm not sure how to allocate my Stat and Expertise Points," she said. "Do you know much about clerics?"

"I'm quite knowledgeable about most classes," he replied. "Until . . . my life changed, I had been expected to join the Church."

"You were going to be a priest?" she asked, surprised. "You don't really strike me as the type."

"Not so much a priest as a researcher. As my mother often said, I spend far too much time with my nose buried in a book. And while I received some martial training, it was assumed I'd be granted a non-combat class."

"But why the Church," she asked. "Couldn't you have gone to work somewhere else?"

"It's quite common for landless sons to be sent off to the Church," he continued. "After all, I have ten brothers and seven uncles ahead of me in the line of succession. There was no hope that I would ever inherit any of my family's land. Think of the Church as a method for removing potential usurpers."

"I see," she replied. "And the Church wouldn't take you because you're a Wraith Rogue?"

Jonas nodded and then gazed off into the distance. "We should return to your original question. It will be quite some time before you need to worry about Expertise Points, so for now I'll focus on Stat Point distribution."

She frowned. "What are you talking about? I have a point I need to use right now."

"That is most unusual," he said, looking troubled. "Normally, they are only given every five levels."

"So far, I've received one every time I level up."

"If true, that will give you a significant advantage," he mused. "For now, let's discuss Stat Points. Early on, you will want to focus on your main attribute. For clerics, that's Wisdom. It will increase the effectiveness of your spells. However, as you gain levels, it's a good idea to allocate some points into Vitality, Constitution, and even Dexterity. Many adventurers fall into the trap of increasing their Charisma, but it's best to avoid that until much later in your advancement."

"What about Luck?" she asked. "It seems like a useful stat."

"It's impossible to place points into Luck," he continued. "Only ancient treasures can grant you points in that stat."

She chewed on her lower lip as she stared at Jonas. It still felt a bit dangerous sharing too much with someone she barely knew, but she didn't have anyone else to answer her questions. "What if. . .I can?"

He gave her a sharp look. "Are you trying to make a fool of me? I have studied numerous texts on the subject of advancement, and no class can gain Luck points."

Amara pressed her lips together. "I'm not lying, and I would never try to trick you after all you've done for me. Just assume for a moment that I can place some points into Luck—is it worth it?"

"There is little written about Luck," he explained, unconvinced, "but what is known suggests the stat is extremely powerful. Monarchs, warlords, and powerful adventurers will do almost anything to gain a treasure that grants Luck. It is said even a single point can sway a difficult fight and allow those who possess it to find unparalleled treasures. However, with it being so rare, I cannot say how much of the material I have read is accurate."

She leaned back and considered his words. If powerful individuals sought it out, then it would make sense for her to continue increasing her Luck stat. Already, she felt it had saved her life several times and had most likely contributed to her discovering the monster egg.

"This is all very helpful," she said. "What about Expertise Points?"

"That topic is a little more controversial. There are many schools of thought on the subject. Some scholars state that all points should be placed into speciality spells. While others recommend spreading them around for a more balanced build. I have personally tried to avoid my spells as I find them. . .distasteful. That being said, it's always a good idea to have at least a few Martial Abilities."

"How do those work?" Amara asked, perking up. The thought of learning how to fight was alluring after her last few encounters. Once she was out of mana, she was almost completely useless in a fight.

"Martial abilities will grant you skills which usually improve your overall ability. Although, some do provide talents that offer a significant advantage for a short period of time. Any adventurers who possess such abilities pose a serious threat and should not be underestimated."

"That's good to know." She pulled up her character sheet as they talked. "If you'll give me a minute, I'd like to level up."

| Amara Solace (Unranked Adventurer) | Trickster Cleric, Level 3 |
| --- | --- |
| Stats | |
| Strength | 2 |
| Dexterity | 3 |
| Constitution | 2 |
| Intelligence | 4 |
| Wisdom | 8 |
| Charisma | 1 |
| Vitality | 1 |
| Luck | 11 |
| New Stat Points | 3 |
| | |
| Weapon Proficiencies | |
| Staff | Novice |
| Darts | Novice |
| | |
| Skills | |

| | |
|---|---|
| *First Aid* | **Apprentice** |
| *Herbalism* | **Apprentice** |
| *Alchemy* | **Apprentice** |
| | |
| **Martial Abilities** | |
| **None** | |
| | |
| **Spells** | |
| *Cloak of Shadows* | **1st Circle** |
| *Charm Person* | **1st Circle** |
| *Heal Wounds* | **1st Circle** |
| *Divine Weapon* | **1st Circle** |
| *Avatar of Melischar* | **Inactive** |
| | |
| **New Expertise Points** | 1 |

Salamander poked Jonas in the side. "Want to help me level up, too?"

When Amara glanced over at her in surprise, the girl simply shrugged.

"It's a small wagon," Salamander said. "Did you really think we couldn't hear your whispers?"

Amara turned her gaze over toward Borim who chuckled, his eyes filled with mirth.

"Like the girl said, it's a small wagon."

The dwarf pulled a whetstone out of his pack and set about honing the edge of his axe while whistling.

Amara rolled her eyes as she realized she wouldn't have much privacy over the next few weeks. She then returned her attention to leveling up.

Since Jonas had said it was her most important stat, Amara added two points to Wisdom——and one point to Luck. No matter what, she would continue to improve her Luck. Hopefully, it would give her the edge she needed to survive in this world.

It was more difficult to choose where to place her Expertise Point. She immediately discarded the notion of gaining a new Weapon Proficiency—she had no access to weapons and would have to make do with her staff. Any idea of a new skill was similarly dismissed. So far, she had found no use for them.

Which left her with a choice between spells and Martial Abilities. Now that she had a group, would she even need to fight with a weapon? Then she recalled the adventurer group who had lost their healer. She couldn't always rely on her companions to keep her safe. She needed to know how to fight.

And since she received more Expertise Points than others, maybe it wouldn't hurt to improve her fighting skills. She could always select a new spell when she leveled up next.

She hesitated for a moment while she wrestled with her options. Then she finally clicked Martial Ability. Unlike with her spell upgrades, she wasn't given a choice of how to specialize. Instead, writing immediately appeared in her vision.

*New Martial Ability Unlocked*
*Critical Luck Success! Level 20 Ability Granted.*
*Dart Deadeye*
*Through a keen eye and practiced hand, you have become a marksman with darts. Any missile thrown has a 50% chance of a critical hit, and a 100% chance to strike if there is an open line of sight to the target.*
*Duration: 2 minutes + 1 minute per level*
*Cooldown: 24 hours*

"Darts," she exclaimed. "The stupid Expertise Point gave me an ability for the most useless ranged weapon around. But at least I'll be useful if we ever stumble across a pub on dart night."

"What skill did you receive?" Borim asked, lifting his attention from sharpening the axe. "And I'd hardly call darts useless. They are often favored by dwarven miners in the deep tunnels under the Ice Spine Mountains. Many goblins have been slain under a hail of the sharp missiles."

"How would you even hurt anyone with a dart?" she asked incredulously. "At best, you'd annoy them by inflicting tiny little wounds."

Borim opened his sack and rummaged around inside. After a moment, he pulled out something that looked like a compact arrow. It had fletching at one end, and a wicked barbed head on the other. A round metal ball in the center of the shaft looked like a weight.

It didn't resemble the darts she was thinking of at all. She raised her eyebrow. "That's a dart? That actually looks pretty deadly."

"I have a few of these things," Borim said. "Never had much of an eye for missile weapons, but they're good to have around in a pinch. Especially if you're fighting a mage. But I could give them to you if you want."

"I don't have any money," Amara said.

"No need to pay me, lass," he replied. "My father always said you should keep your healer happy. Mind you, his group's healer was my mother, and he rarely took his own advice. What did the ability give you, anyway?"

She took the offered dart and was surprised at the weight of it. "Fifty-percent chance of a critical hit, and a guaranteed strike if I can see the target. I'm not sure how good the ability is."

Borim sputtered. "How in the name of Glonin Goldhand did you get that? It sounds like a high-level ability."

"She's apparently blessed with great luck," Jonas said. "Some of her spells are quite intimidating."

"But she's only Level 3," Borim shouted, holding his hands out to the side. "What god has smiled on you, lass?"

"She's the avatar of Melischar," Salamander cut in, "and she's amazing."

Borim's eyes widened and then he let out a bellow of laughter. He continued hooting until he had to wipe a tear away from his eye. "Could you imagine? The gods return to the world and one of their avatars groups up with a banished dwarf? The stories they'd tell . . ."

Amara had initially felt alarm at her friend's words, but it seemed that no one would believe that she was an avatar.

From the front of the convoy, cries of alarm interrupted their conversation. The steady beat of drums drifted from deep within the hills, and wild cries echoed through the valleys.

Borim jumped to his feet, his axe gripped tightly in his hands, swaying slightly as the wagon lurched to a halt. "Goblins," he snarled. "I knew the orange buggers wouldn't let us pass unmolested."

Amara stood up . She spotted creatures in the distance boiling from between the trees. They stood shorter than humans, and their skin was a burnt orange color. Most wielded primitive weapons, with many carrying little more than rocks. But dozens had already appeared. With more pouring out every second, they would easily overwhelm the caravan with sheer numbers.

"Why did we stop?" she asked. "Shouldn't we try to escape?"

Jonas drew his daggers and spun them in his palms. "I'm afraid an ox-drawn cart would have no chance of outrunning goblins. Our only hope is to create enough casualties to make them rout."

"I'll do that myself," Borim growled. "Too many of my clan have fallen to goblin weapons. I'll gladly reap vengeance for them."

Amara glanced over at Salamander. Hugging herself tightly, the girl looked terrified. She placed her hand on Salamander's shoulder. "Stay close to me and we'll get through this together. I promise."

The worry on Salamander's face immediately lessened. Then she lifted her hands and flames licked down her fingers.

"I'll be brave," she whispered.

As Amara gazed out over the horde charging toward them, she only wished that she believed her own words.

# CHAPTER 15

Selena stood off to the side in the cavernous cathedral as she listened to the soft murmurs of prayer. The sound of the faithful soothed her troubled mind and, for a moment, she almost forgot her great shame. She lifted her gaze toward the tinted rays of light pouring through the windows. Many of the stained-glass works had been crafted by famous artists in ages past, their colored panes depicting scenes from the Age of Strife.

She glanced over toward the bishop's office, and seeing the door still closed, she returned to pacing the length of the pews. Since her failure to capture the false prophet, she had spent every minute here in prayer while waiting for the bishop to decide her punishment.

And today, she'd finally received his summons. She been afraid that her courage would falter, but in the end, she trudged like a zombie to the cathedral. Though she suspected the bishop would sentence her to death, Selena would face her end as a faithful follower of the Holy Church. When she'd arrived at the cathedral, a monk Selena didn't recognize shepherded her inside before leaving her outside of the bishop's office. She'd been surprised that they had not placed her in shackles upon her arrival.

After more praying and waiting, muted footsteps drew her attention to the same monk hurrying in her direction. She took a deep breath and then smoothed down her dress. Maybe she would finally learn her fate.

"Sister Selena," the man said breathlessly. "The bishop will see you now."

"Thank you, Brother."

She fought down the urge to flee and steadied herself as she walked to the entrance to the bishop's office. With a trembling hand, she lifted the latch and pushed on the heavy iron-bound door. It swung open to reveal a spartan room with tapestries hanging from the walls, and a simple wooden desk. Bishop Dieter Krause stood nearby, his hands clasped.

"Excellency Krause," she whispered as she dipped into a curtsey before the bishop.

When she straightened, she inspected him. She rarely saw the bishop outside of worship, and even then, only from a distance. While many men his age had a softness to them, Bishop Krause radiated power. At such close proximity, Selena noted a strength of purpose in his lined face and sharp jaw.

"How may I serve you?" Selena asked.

Bishop Krause walked forward and inclined his head in the smallest of movements. "I'm sorry for your loss, sister."

Startled, she replied, "My loss?"

With dread, she thought, *He knows about my relationship with Frederick.*

She tried to school her features as a chill traveled up her spine. "Brother Frederick was a loyal member of your flock," she intoned. "We all mourn his passing."

Dieter stared at her with hard eyes, boring into her very soul. "Yes, but some of us will miss him more than others? Hmm?"

"I don't know what you mean, Your Excellency." She couldn't keep the quaver from her voice.

"Do you think the gods have rendered me blind in my old age? Do you believe I don't know everything that happens within my flock?"

Selena's knees buckled. "Please forgive me, Your Excellency. My flesh was weak—"

Bishop Krause held up his hand to silence her. "You have failed your vows and failed in your duties."

"I can only beg for your forgiveness," she whispered, bowing her head. "My heart still serves the Church."

"And what will you do for redemption? Hmm?"

"Anything," she said, hope blossoming in her chest. "There is no challenge I wouldn't overcome to regain my place in the Church."

Bishop Krause continued as though he hadn't heard her words. "Do you know High Inquisitor Gunter? No, I don't imagine you do. While he is a loyal servant of the Church, he sometimes lacks imagination. He believes the heretic will travel south to hide among the Gnostics. However, I believe she will flee elsewhere."

"Please grant me the chance to make her suffer for what she did to Frederick. For what she did to me."

Selena still felt violated from being charmed. The heretic had murdered Frederick, and she—Selena—and called her *best friend*. The memory of it still made her feel sick.

"I don't want you to make her suffer," Bishop Krause said firmly. "The heretic will be killed with no fanfare. She should die without ever knowing from whence the fatal stroke came. I do not want someone who will toy with her before execution. Understood?"

"I understand, Your Excellency," she said, though vengeance still burned in her heart. "She will die quickly."

"Do you know why this one is so dangerous?" he asked softly.

Selena shook her head. There were always so-called avatars roaming the city at any given time. Some raved like madmen while dressed in rags, while others eloquently preached from street corners and called for theological reform. The only reason she cared about *this* one was because the heretic killed Frederick.

"Because, unlike the others, she has *faith*," the bishop said harshly. "The others may call themselves avatars, but they don't truly believe it in their hearts."

"I . . . I don't understand."

"The charlatan was here for only a matter of days and yet convinced several brothers and sisters to abandon our Holy Church. Brother Otto, though he lacked belief, was a staid member of the monastery, steadfast in his loyalty to the Church. And yet she convinced him—a man of reason—to believe in a fairy tale about the gods returning. *That* is what makes her dangerous."

"I see," Selena whispered. "She had unexpected abilities for her level."

The bishop waved his hand dismissively. "She merely found a trinket to mask her class and level. I imagine her true nature is far more than she lets on."

"But I'm only Level 16, Your Excellency," Selena continued, afraid of upsetting the bishop. "How will I alone defeat someone with so much more power than myself?"

The bishop walked around his desk and, reverently, lifted a worn, golden box. The cover was inlaid with jewels, and it radiated an intense power. "I have assembled a team for you to lead."

"An infinity chest?" she breathed. "I've only heard legends about them. I never expected to see one in my lifetime."

"Yes, this is one of the greatest treasures of the Church," Bishop Krause said. "And with it, I shall grant you the items required to slay the false prophet."

He opened the lid—purple light pouring out—and then reached inside. When he withdrew his hand, he held a silver ring, a pendant hanging from a chain, and a ruby pulsating with light.

He walked up to stand in front of her. Lifting the necklace over her head, he said, "This will allow you to resist any mental attacks. No *Charm* or *Dominate* spell will affect you so long as you wear this pendant." He slipped the ring over her finger. "This will grant you the ability to see through cloaking spells. If she escaped the city, then she must have some sort of stealth items or abilities."

Selena gazed at the ruby. "And what of the gem?"

"This ruby contains the power to dispel any spell under the fifth Circle." He held it up to peer into the jewel's crimson depths. "However, you must crush the ruby to activate this property, so only use it in the direst circumstances."

Selena thought back to the spectral sword that had slain her lover. She knew exactly how to use the ruby when she again faced the false prophet. She would relish in the look of surprise when the heretic's spells failed one after another.

Bishop Krause took Selena's hands into his and stared deeply into her eyes. "We must protect the Church at all costs. These heretics seek to force us back to an age when famine and plague stalked the land. A time when brother slew brother because they worshipped different gods. The age before the Church ruled over all the races. The Holy Church binds us all together in the fight against Chaos. Do you understand, sister?"

"I understand," she said fiercely. "I will protect the Church."

"Good, good," the bishop said. "I have arranged for you to travel north tomorrow morning. The others in your party will meet you at the wagons departing for Oksberg before dawn."

"North?" she asked, surprised. "Do you believe the heretic traveled to the Wall?"

"The North remains one of the few places outside of our reach, which makes it an excellent location for a heretic to hide," Bishop Krause explained. "Though I will be honest with you: I have also sent teams to the coastal city-states, and others to scour the border towns along the wasteland."

"Then . . . there are others searching for her as well?"

The thought of someone else slaying the false prophet was too terrible to contemplate. She had to be the one who burned her alive and listened to her last screams. It was the only way to avenge Frederick.

"Yes. However, I hope you are the one to find her." Bishop Krause stepped back and offered her the gem. "May Holy Birgitta watch over you."

Selena took the ruby then curtseyed again. She had been dismissed. When His Excellency nodded in return, she spun on her heel and hurried out of the room.

Her emotions roiled just under the surface, and she didn't trust herself to remain in the cathedral any longer. The same young monk awaited her in the corridor. He opened his mouth to speak, but Selena didn't hear his words. She sped past him and didn't stop until she burst out of the main doors into the plaza beyond. Fat droplets of rain splashed down on her face. She looked up to see the skies had turned leaden.

For the first time since Frederick had died, she allowed herself to cry. Her tears mixed with the rain and streaked down her cheeks. She collapsed against the stone wall and sobbed for her lost love. Thankfully, the rain had driven the usual crowds from the plaza, leaving her alone with her grief.

"I miss you, Frederick," she sniffled, gripping the ruby until the edges dug into her palm. "And I swear that I'll get vengeance for you. Even if it costs me my life."

Selena knew that if she died in service to the Church, she'd be reunited with her love among the stars. She would do anything to make that happen.

Hollow from weeping, she scrubbed her eyes then placed the ruby in the pocket of her robes.

Selena took a deep breath and then strode out into the square. She passed the towering statue depicting Birgitta as she slew one of the monstrous heralds. Many people had left offerings around the bronze sculpture hoping to receive a boon from the hero of old.

As she walked, Selena pulled up her hood and hurried toward the convent she called home. She had much to do before leaving on her journey.

She stopped briefly to send a prayer to Holy Birgitta. Hopefully, her appeal would be heard and she would find the heretic at Oksberg.

Regardless of what Bishop Krause commanded, Selena would ensure that the false prophet's death was slow and agonizing.

# CHAPTER 16

An arrow thudded into the railing of the wagon, nearly striking Amara's scarred fingers. She recoiled from the spent missile and cradled her hand to her chest in surprise. She'd thought the goblin archers were still too far away to hit them. Before they could loose again, she grabbed Salamander's hand and leapt off the side of the wagon.

Amara hit the ground hard and stumbled while her younger companion landed with the grace of a dancer. She then ducked down behind the side of the wagon as another volley of arrows peppered their position.

"Stay here," Amara urged, peeking over the wagon.

The rolling green hills surrounding the road were alive with goblins. Armed with slings and bows, a band of enemy skirmishers moved ahead of the swarm.

"I need to go help the others."

"I can fight, too," Salamander protested. "I learned a new skill and everything. Remember how good I did against the rat?"

"I want to keep you in reserve," Amara replied. "Your skills are best for close quarters fighting. If the goblins overrun our position, we'll need you then."

Salamander nodded, a determined look on her face.

Amara felt vaguely guilty about lying to the girl, but she didn't want her involved in this fight. And if the wagons *were* overrun, then she'd probably take Salamander and flee. She had no desire to make a last stand here.

She pointed at the mimic still hiding in chest form on the wagon. "Guard her until I return."

The monster wobbled back and forth, in what she assumed was a nod. With one last glance to make sure Salamander was staying put, Amara raced over to Jonas where he crouched behind the front wheel of the wagon.

He nodded at the sight of her then ducked as an arrow streaked past.

She'd never been involved in a large-scale battle before and hadn't paid much attention in history class. When faced with rows of archers, slingers, and rock throwers, her spells felt nearly useless. If she summoned her *Divine Weapon,* then the goblin could simply retreat until the spell timer ran out. And while she could charm one of their attackers, she doubted a single friendly goblin would do much to sway the battle.

She watched as a wave of impossible darkness emerged from behind a nearby wagon. The foul magic swept over the nearest goblin ranks. Though these rock-throwing attackers were reduced to charred bones, more orange bodies rushed forward to replace them.

The other adventurers sporadically returned fire with various spells and pro-jectile weapons, but none of their efforts appeared to make a dent in the goblins' numbers.

Amara glanced over at Borim, who had taken it on himself to defend the oxen. His shield moved impossibly fast as the dwarf deflected missile after missile.

*He must have used a skill,* Amara thought. *Nothing is getting past him.*

"What should I do?" Amara called.

As a stone soared past his head, Jonas ducked. "We must simply weather their missile weapons. The main body of goblins will attack soon enough."

"Do you . . . think we can win?" she asked hesitantly as she stared out across the horde of attacking creatures.

"I have faith in our group," he replied. "Once the horde's leader appears, we'll launch our counteroffensive. Goblins are notorious cowards, and if they see the strongest of their tribe slain, they will most likely retreat."

"Great," she said. "So, all we have to do is kill the biggest, meanest goblin? That doesn't sound difficult at all. Why don't we go punch a giant while we're at it?"

She watched as another wave of darkness splashed against the front lines of goblin archers, turning several more into piles of scorched bones. As the missile troops panicked, they fell back until they were safely behind the front line of the advancing goblins.

But any relief Amara felt was short lived as she watched a monstrous goblin shove its way through the mob. Nearly twice the height of the others, this crea-ture trampled its brethren, tossing their small bodies to the side with little regard. A battered helmet obscured its features, and a chain-mail hauberk hung down to its knees. In each fist, it gripped an enormous, spiked mace.

"A hobgoblin," Jonas breathed. "He's at least Level 30."

"Level 30," Amara exclaimed. "Do we even stand a chance?"

"The odds are not in our favor." Jonas took in a deep breath. "Though it was brief, I have enjoyed our time together. When I attack the hobgoblin, use the distraction to make your escape."

Amara grabbed his shoulders when he moved to step out from behind the cover of the wagon. "I'm not letting you sacrifice yourself to save us. If I'm escap-ing, then you're coming with me. Anyway, I can always leave my *Divine Weapon* behind to cover our retreat. That should give us enough time to lose the goblins in the hills."

"That might work," Jonas mused. "Would you truly rob me of the chance to make a heroic last stand? One that is sung about in taverns for generations to come. I'm not sure I want to miss that opportunity."

She stared at him incredulously until he cracked a smile. Then she slapped him on the shoulder. "That's not funny."

"I think we should try your plan . . ." His words trailed off. Something caught Jonas's attention, something that made his cocksure grin fade. "Holy Birgitta, watch over him."

Amara followed her companion's stare to see Borim sprinting toward the goblin lines, his axe raised high. The dwarf's war cry echoed through the hills and birds took flight from nearby trees.

"That maniac is going to get himself killed!" she exclaimed. "What should we do?"

"I believe we should help him." Jonas grimaced and spun his daggers around. "If he manages to defeat the goblin champion, he might win the battle for all of us."

"And if he loses?"

"Then he'll most likely end up inside a goblin cook pot by sundown."

"Well, that's a horrifying image," she said, wincing. "Thanks for putting that in my head."

"I was only answering your question."

Amara swore under her breath and then reached over the top of the wagon. She grabbed Borim's bag and dumped it out on the ground. All manner of tools tumbled onto the earth along with several uncut gems. What she wanted, however, were the darts. She managed to find three in the pile of gear. It would have to be enough.

While she'd only just met Borim, he'd joined her group. Amara wasn't willing to let a member of her group die. Furthermore, she didn't have much faith in her escape plan; these hills were the goblins' home. If Amara and her friends fled, the horde would likely hunt them down before nightfall.

"Let's go save a suicidal dwarf," she said.

Jonas nodded as he spun his daggers around.

She dashed out from behind the wagon and sprinted after Borim, activating *Dart Deadeye.* When Amara cast a spell, she needed to weave the power together to form it in her mind. However, the Martial Ability simply took effect. She felt her senses sharpen. Skidding to a stop twenty paces from the hobgoblin, she hurled her first dart.

The missile flew unerringly toward her target and plunged through the eye slit of the hobgoblin's helmet. The creature howled with fury, plucked the dart out of its face and tossed it aside.

Before she could fling another barb, Borim crashed into the hobgoblin. Frustrated that Borim had blocked her line of sight, she hurled the next attack at a goblin trying to outflank her dwarven friend. The dart tore through its target's neck, sending the creature toppling to the ground choking on its own blood.

She launched her last dart. This one caught a goblin with its mouth open and the barbed tip burst through the back of its skull in a fountain of blood. The goblin collapsed, the feathered shaft protruding from its gaping maw.

Scanning the battlefield, Amara found Borim being battered like a ship in a squall. While he managed to block every blow from the hobgoblin with his shield, the force of the strikes was nearly knocking him off his feet. And his round shield had cracked, with the rim hanging off.

The dwarf wouldn't last much longer.

A throwing knife dinged off the hobgoblin's helmet, making it recoil. The creature roared a challenge as Jonas raced into the fight.

She watched with amazement as he evaded hurled stones and weapons swings from nearly a dozen goblins. It was as though he could see things before they happened. As he flowed through the goblin ranks—evading swinging clubs and soaring stone——the rogue's blades slashed and tore. He spun and sent another two daggers flying at the hobgoblin.

Borim took the opportunity provided by Jonas to pull back and shake the shattered shield from his arm. Blood poured from a wound on his scalp, and he limped his retreat. But he still held up his axe defiantly.

If they had any hope of winning, Amara decided, this was the time to commit with all her spells. Intending for Borim to finish off the dazed creature, she cast *Charm Person* on the hobgoblin.

The hulking hobgoblin didn't react.

Had the spell failed?

Jonas appeared in front of her, his twin daggers slashing open a goblin's throat as it charged in her direction. His foot snapped out, kicking another attacker back. Then he spun around and hurled a knife at a goblin aiming a bow at her. The hilt of his weapon seemed to sprout from its eye socket. The goblin collapsed to the ground, twitching.

Amara didn't have time to stand around and figure out what had gone wrong. She knew Jonas couldn't keep the goblins off her for much longer. As she ducked a rock that whizzed past her head, she decided to try the more direct approach. She cast *Divine Weapon,* and the imposing, burning sword slowly took shape in front of the goblin ranks. Several of the creatures shied away, but the hobgoblin shoved them forward with a snarl.

"Kill them all," she commanded the blade.

The blade swept through the front ranks of the goblins, slicing three of them in half before reversing its thrust and taking the head off another . Like wheat before a scythe, the goblins fell, and soon the tiny warriors struggled to flee. They clawed and scratched at each other, even trampling their own underfoot as they clambered for escape.

The hobgoblin, however, didn't retreat. Instead, the creature met the spectral blade's powerful strike with crossed maces. The force of the blow sent the hobgoblin's feet sliding back in the dark earth, but the creature kept its stance.

The hobgoblin unleashed a flurry of attacks upon the *Divine Weapon,* each strike breaking chunks off the ethereal foe. Amara knew from the Dancing Gnome Inn experience that the ghostly sword wouldn't last long under such punishment.

For the first time, she realized the huge disparity in power between higher and lower levels. With her mana running dangerously low, she cast *Cloak of Shadows.*

As her vision changed, she watched Borim stagger to his feet and rejoin the battle. With the hobgoblin pinned by the relentless attacks of Amara's *Divine Weapon,* the dwarf and Jonas had an opening they could exploit. But their advantage, she realized, would only last as long as her weapon. Even if it hadn't taken a great deal of damage, the spell's allotted duration was nearly complete.

*We need to end this,* Amara thought. *Now.*

Hidden from sight by her spell, Amara picked her way through the goblin corpses until she reached the one with her dart sticking out of its mouth. She ripped it free in a disgusting spray of gore then she hefted the missile to throw. *Dart Deadeye* had run out. She could take her chances throwing, but if she wanted to guarantee damage to the hobgoblin, Amara would have to get up close and personal. Dart in hand, she sprinted into the scrum.

As she reached the hobgoblin, her foot slid on the blood-soaked earth. As she fell, the hulking creature swung its mace to keep Jonas at bay, and the weapon whistled past her invisible face. With a cold shock, Amara realized that she would have run headlong into that brutal smack if she hadn't slipped.

Amara picked herself up from the ground—once again grateful for her high Luck stat—then stumbled behind the hulking creature. With all the force she could muster, she buried the barbed tip of her dart into the back of the brute's unarmored knee.

The hobgoblin bellowed with pain, its leg crumpling under its own massive weight. Borim surged forward, axe high. With a mighty bellow, he swung his weapon down with both hands. The blow dented the hobgoblin's helmet. A second strike caved it in, and the creature flopped to the ground with a groan.

Amara had to avert her gaze as the dwarf continued to hack at the creature's neck. She'd seen a lot of grisly sights and a beheading was too much for her.

She let her *Cloak of Shadows* fall, and then turned to face the remaining goblins. While the caravan's counterattacks had been effective, there were still at least a hundred goblins remaining. Would they run like Jonas had predicted?

She breathed out in relief as the trickle of fleeing goblins turned into a torrent. Soon, only injured and dead goblins remained on the road.

"I don't suppose you have a healing spell?" Borim gasped from nearby. "That hobgoblin was a bit tougher that I expected."

She opened her mouth to reply, but then stared in shock as Jonas raised his dagger above an injured goblin. "What are you doing?" she shrieked. "The battle is over!"

"I'm going to give him the mercy of a swift death," Jonas replied, looking puzzled. "Would you have me let him bleed out slowly?"

"I'd prefer if you didn't kill him at all," she said hotly. "I won't have anyone in my group murdering injured enemies."

"But it's free Experience," Borim replied in a pained voice. "You'd expect us to give it up?"

"Yes," she said, sharply. "And I don't know if I even want you in my group after that stunt."

"I had to challenge the champion." Borim rubbed a hand down his face. "Though I had expected you to take the chance to turn tail—like the other adventurers did. I guess my groupmates are made of sterner stuff. Like fine dwarven steel you are, lass."

At the dwarfs' words, Amara noted that the wagons had been abandoned. Not a single driver or adventurer remained, and Salamander was alone by the wagons. She'd wondered why they hadn't received any help during the battle. At least the oxen appeared unharmed.

*I guess they used the diversion we created to make a run for it.*

Borim attempted to place weight on his injured leg and then winced with pain, leaning hard on his axe for support. "It's not like anyone would miss a dwarf without home or kin. My death could have meant something here."

Amara shut her eyes and rubbed her temples. "We'll talk about this later." Then she pointed at Jonas. "And you—no mercy killings unless I say so."

Jonas hesitated, but then bent down to clean his daggers on a fallen goblin's clothing. He shoved both weapons back into their sheaths before he sauntered back toward the wagons.

Amara returned her attention to the injured dwarf. She weaved together the strands of mana to cast *Heal Wounds* on Borim and then watched as the white motes spun around his body. Most of the bright specks concentrated around his knee. She then used the last of her mana to cast the healing spell again.

"That's all I can do for now," she said to the dwarf. "Are you able to walk?"

"I think I can make it back to the wagon." He tugged on his beard. "And that was some fine spellcasting, if I do say so myself. Your friend there meant it when he said you were impressive. Most impressive indeed."

She was still mad at the dwarf for charging off alone, but she understood why he'd done it. Apparently, her group was composed of people whose sole goal in life was to die a heroic death. She'd have to fix that—and soon. With a smile, Amara said, "I wasn't the one who stood toe-to-toe with a hobgoblin."

"True." Borim grinned at her, his teeth red with blood. "We got an impressive Title out of it."

"We did?"

She noticed a little flashing icon in the side of her vision.

"So we did," she confirmed.

Amara moved to Borim's side and took his arm. Once she'd helped him back to the wagons, then she'd return to see if she could do anything for the injured goblins.

And then she'd find out what "Title" meant.

# CHAPTER 17

ehind her, a wounded goblin let out a scream that abruptly cut off with a gurgle. She scanned the hills and spotted others moving among the downed creatures. the Dancing Gnome InnAs she watched, the bald warrior—the man with the downtrodden party Amara had encountered at the Dancing Gnome Inn—plunged his spear into a goblin's chest.

"What are you doing?" Amara cried out. "Those goblins aren't a threat to anyone."

"Unless they heal up," the warrior called back, pulling his spear free in a spray of blood. "Then they'll jump on the next caravan that passes through here.

Amara made sure Borim was steady on his feet before she stormed back to the site of the battle. By the time she reached the adventurers, it was too late—they had already finished off the last of the wounded goblins. "I was going to heal them!"

From nearby, the warrior's companion let her harp fall to her side as she asked, "Why would you do something so incredibly stupid? Goblins worship the Gods of Chaos. They're irredeemably evil."

"No one is irredeemable," she nearly shouted. For most of her life, Amara heard similar words used to describe her. "Aren't adventurers supposed to do more than murder helpless goblins?"

The hawk-faced member of their party strode forward, rapier sheathed at his side, and placed a hand on his companion's shoulder. Examining Amara with sharp eyes, he said, "I apologize if our actions upset you, but by slaying these wounded goblins, we may have saved many future lives."

She opened her mouth to speak, but then closed it. While she didn't believe anyone was irredeemable, the goblins *had* attacked them unprovoked. And if she had healed them, what would stop them from ambushing the next wagon train that passed through here? And would the goblins have shown any mercy if they were in her place?

"It just doesn't feel right," she said stubbornly.

"Once you become an adventurer like us," he continued, "you may see things differently. Allow me to introduce myself. I am Ackley; duelist extraordinaire, and leader of this motley band." Gesturing to the woman, he added, "This is Kymber; expert lyrist, and our group's bard. And that big bald fellow is our warrior, Eldred."

From nearby, a robed, spindly man complained, "Why do you always forget to introduce me?" Clutching his oversized book to his chest, he faced Amara. "I am Landon, the group's mage."

"I'd say it was a pleasure to meet you, but I'd be lying," she said tartly. "Where were you during the battle when my friends and I were risking our lives?"

Kymber's eyes flared with anger, but Ackley shook his head.

Resting a hand on the hilt of his rapier, the duelist stepped forward. "We didn't expect your group to rout the goblins so thoroughly. While you kept them occupied, we circled around to flank them. You defeated the hobgoblin before we could launch our attack."

Amara narrowed her eyes, unsure if she should believe them. But then again, they *had* emerged from behind the goblins. Maybe they were telling the truth. "Well, I still don't like what you did to the wounded."

"As is your right," Ackley said smoothly. "I'm impressed at how you kept your group alive during such a frenzied assault. Is there any way we could retain your services once we reach Oksberg?"

"I don't think so," she replied. "I heard what happened to your last healer."

"Why you little—" Whatever insult Kymber had been about to sling died as Ackley raised his hand.

"Our last healer was a fool and thought he could solo a dungeon boss," Ackley said. "However, should you change your mind, you'll be richly rewarded for your skills. From what I've heard, healers are in incredibly short supply in the North. If you accompany my group, I'll grant you half of any loot we receive."

Amara pressed her lips together. "I'll think about it."

"That's all I ask." Ackley walked forward and presented Amara with a satchel made of worn leather. "Here are some supplies—bandages, medicines and the like—for your companions. I imagine you expended most of your mana during the battle, and they appear to have wounds that need tending."

"Thanks . . ." Unsure of what else to say, she slung the bag over her shoulder. While the rest of his group's reactions ranged from indifference to outright hostility, Ackley seemed sincere in his intent. "I'll make sure they get these."

She turned on her heel and then strode back to Borim. When she reached the dwarf, he looked thoroughly annoyed. When he opened his mouth to speak, Amara shot him a withering glare.

"I'd choose your next words carefully," she warned, adding, "especially if you're about to complain about not getting the chance to slaughter helpless goblins."

Borim held up his finger as though he was going to reply, but then shut his mouth with an irritated grunt.

Amara sighed. "I'm sorry. I shouldn't take my frustrations out on you. It just bothers me they were probably right about the goblins. If I had saved them, they most likely would have attacked the next group to travel through here. And . . . I'm also having a tough time with all of this," she added with a floppy gesture to the battlefield.

"Killings not an easy thing to do," Borim said softly. "Was this your first pitched battle?"

Amara nodded and pressed her lips together. The skirmish at the Dancing Gnome Inn had been bad enough, but the carnage that surrounded her was something else entirely.

"I see," Borim replied as he stroked his beard. "It makes sense now why you'd balk at mercy killings."

"Come on." Amara held out her arm for the dwarf. The last thing she wanted to do was discuss this further. "Let's get you back to the wagon where I can fix you up."

"My people tried to make peace with the goblins for centuries," Borim said as he took her arm and hobbled along at her side. "But they seemed keener on the idea of putting us in cook pots than wasting any time with talking. Sometimes you just need to realize an enemy can't be reasoned with."

Amara nodded again, unsure of what to think. Were all the goblins of this world nothing more than murderous savages? She hoped that wasn't true.

She helped steady Borim several times on their trip back to the wagon. With each step, the bag of medical supplies bumped against her hip. By the time they reached their wagon, Amara was completely exhausted.

Salamander raced out from her hiding place. "You were amazing, Amara! The way you took down that scary hobgoblin was unbelievable."

"I believe I took him down," Borim said gruffly. "After all, it was my axe that struck the final blow."

Jonas appeared from behind the wagon. "Is it the first hundred axe strikes or the last that fells a tree?"

"Without the last, the tree wouldn't fall," Borim rumbled. "And why are we talking about trees? We need to celebrate our glorious victory. And our new Title. No more than a dozen dwarves in my old town had a Title to their name—and most of those were bought rather than earned. Imagine their faces if they could see me now!" Amara glanced over at the notification blinking off to the side of her vision. She noted that she'd also gained a level. She could deal with that later. For now, she focused on her new Title, and writing appeared in front of her.

*New Title: Titan Slayer (Rank 1)*
*Defeat an Enemy at Least 20 Levels Higher Than You.*
*+1 Expertise Point, +5 Strength, +5 Constitution, +5 Vitality*
*Like the Halfling and the Giant of ancient lore, you have defeated an oppo-*
*nent far more powerful than yourself. This Title grants a permanent increase*
*to your stats.*

She frowned at seeing what the Title gave her. While she didn't mind having a bit more Strength, it wouldn't do much to help her class. Then she watched Jonas's face brighten. Borim whooped with joy.

"An Expertise Point," Jonas breathed with a broad smile. "Such a generous gift from the gods."

"What a boon it was to join your group," the dwarf hollered. "When we arrive at the next inn, I'll buy you a feast you'll never forget, lass."

"I'm going to get a new spell," Salamander exclaimed a moment later than the others.

Since Amara received an Expertise Point with every level, it hadn't seemed like much of a reward. But the others were limited to one point doled out every five levels, and they were nearly delirious with happiness at receiving one.

Amara ignored the celebration around her and focused on her new stats. She lifted her staff and attempted to bend it. Surprisingly, the wood bowed slightly in her grip, and she had to hastily let it go before it snapped. While the additional Strength hadn't turned her into a powerhouse, she *felt* stronger.

After a few minutes, the mirth died down, and Jonas turned to scan the hills. "There's still no sign of the other adventurers, nor our guides."

"Do you think they fled?" Amara asked, "or did something else happen . . . ?"

Her words hung in the air, and no one answered for a moment.

Finally, Borim spoke softly. "Deep in the tunnels under the Ice Spine Mountains, bands of goblins often picked off lone miners and adventurers. There could have been more of the orange bastards hiding in the hills, waiting for us to break ranks and flee. If that's the case, then nothing good happened to the others. We should take our wagon and go about our business."

"We can't just leave them behind," Amara said, "If we do, we'll sign their death warrants."

"I'm afraid our dwarf friend is right," Jonas said. "To stay here would be folly. The goblins may rally around another champion and return. And we're still painfully outnumbered."

"Let's at least give them an hour," she said. "Then we'll leave."

"I suppose we could do that." The dwarf plopped down heavily in the wagon. As he did, he rubbed his knee and grunted. "But by waiting, we're sticking our necks out for them."

Amara hefted the satchel she'd received from Ackley and opened the flap. Inside were a few jars, rolls of bandages, and a bundle of dried herbs she didn't recognize. Ackley must be serious about wanting her to act as his group's healer—the contents of this bag probably cost a mountain of copper pieces.

"Lay back," she commanded the dwarf. "I'm going to tend to your knee."

"I'll just wait until you have a healing spell ready," he replied. "Then you can fix me good as new."

"I don't think my spell is powerful enough to repair joints yet," she replied. "It seems only capable of healing minor wounds."

"Well, if that isn't a fly in your beer," Borim said. "I'd appreciate some doctoring, then."

Once the dwarf was prone, she rolled up his pants to reveal a forest of ginger hairs coiling their way up his leg. As she stared at his injury, she felt vague thoughts enter her mind about treatment. Somehow, she knew she needed to wrap the injured knee tightly and then elevate it.

Was this her *First Aid* skill finally showing itself? Maybe it was a half-remembered memory from treating her father after one of his many falls? Regardless, Amara used the knowledge to tend to the dwarf. She wrapped the bandages snuggly around his knee and then fastened it. "How does that feel?"

"It's a bit tight," he grumbled. "But it should do."

She grabbed Jonas's backpack and slid it under Borim's leg. "Keep it elevated until we leave."

The dwarf glanced around the wagon. "Oh no. Where did my bag go? And did that chest of yours disappear? Don't tell me the other adventurers robbed us blind before tearin' off like a pack of kobolds."

The memory of her dumping out Borim's bag returned, and she smiled guiltily. "I think your bag fell over the side during the battle. If you give me a minute, I'll go find it."

"And your chest?"

Amara scanned the area around the wagon until she spotted her pet mimic scuttling toward the goblin corpses. She grimaced with disgust as she realized it was going to feed on them. Thankfully, Ackley and his companions had returned to their wagon, so at least they shouldn't spot her pet monster.

"I'm sure it's around here somewhere," she said. "Once I finish gathering your things, I'll go search for it."

Amara stood up and then hopped off the end of the wagon. When she landed, she realized Salamander must have overheard their discussion; the girl had nearly finished picking up Borim's belongings. Amara bent down to help her, and together, they quickly refilled the dwarf's bag.

With nothing else to do, she sat down in the grass and pulled up her character sheet. As she did, the other adventurers rolled up beside her in their own wagon.

Ackley sat in the driver's seat next to Kymber, while the big warrior and mage reclined in the back. The duelist leaned over to speak to Amara. "My group is traveling to the next hamlet. Will you accompany us?"

"We're going to wait to see if any of the others return before we leave," Amara replied.

"Don't tarry too long," Ackley said. "The goblins will eventually find their courage."

With his chilling message hanging in the air, he snapped the reins, and the wagon trundled off. Once they had disappeared around a bend in the road ahead, she turned her attention back to her character sheet.

| Amara Solace (Unranked Adventurer) | Trickster Cleric, Level 4 |
| --- | --- |
| **Stats** | |
| **Strength** | 7 |
| **Dexterity** | 3 |
| **Constitution** | 7 |
| **Intelligence** | 4 |
| **Wisdom** | 10 |
| **Charisma** | 1 |
| **Vitality** | 6 |
| **Luck** | 12 |
| **New Stat Points** | 3 |
| | |
| **Titles** | Titan Slayer (Rank 1) |
| | |
| **Weapon Proficiencies** | |
| **Staff** | Novice |
| **Darts** | Novice |
| | |
| **Skills** | |
| *First Aid* | Apprentice |
| *Herbalism* | Apprentice |
| *Alchemy* | Apprentice |
| | |
| **Martial Abilities** | |
| *Dart Deadeye* | Novice |

| Spells | |
| --- | --- |
| *Cloak of Shadows* | 1<sup>st</sup> Circle |
| *Charm Person* | 1<sup>st</sup> Circle |
| *Heal Wounds* | 1<sup>st</sup> Circle |
| *Divine Weapon* | 1<sup>St</sup> Circle |
| *Avatar of Melischar* | Inactive |
| | |
| **New Expertise Points** | **2** |

She immediately noticed a new listing for "Titles" on her character sheet. It seemed likely that she could earn more, and even upgrade the one she had. She'd have to ask Jonas about that later.

For her stats, she stuck with her routine of adding two points to Wisdom, and then one point to Luck. Her decision was made easier by the fact her new Title had rounded out her other attributes.

Then she stared at her Expertise Points. Maybe it was time to upgrade her Weapon Proficiencies? Since she had two points available, she could probably advance to the next stage after Novice. But did it make sense when she hardly used weapons?

She found her gaze returning to her spells. In every battle', her casting had proven decisive. With her Expertise Points, she could either get two new spells, or advance one of her existing ones to the next circle.

After considering her options, she decided to advance her *Heal Wounds* spell to the second Circle. So far, it had proved wholly inadequate for the injuries needed to deal with. She lifted her scarred hand and flexed her stiff fingers. Hopefully, an upgraded spell would also heal her lingering burn.

She selected *Heal Wounds* from the list of options. At first nothing happened, but then the world around her darkened. When the light returned, she found herself floating in the middle of what looked like a simple peasant's hut. Dried herbs hung from the wall and worn reed mats covered the dirt floor.

A terribly pale boy lay on a nearby cot, his arm twisted at an unnatural angle, and bloody bandages covered his stomach. Tears stained his cheeks, but he made no sound as a woman dressed in white robes bent over him.

Somehow, Amara knew this was a vision from ages past. And she also understood that she was here to learn something.

The woman touched the boy's shoulder comfortingly. She had deep smile lines on her face and her curly dark hair was streaked with gray. She lifted her hand and, as she gathered a staggering amount of power, a soothing glow suffused the room.

Amara carefully watched how the woman wove every strand of mana together into an intricate pattern. It was far more complex than the one she used for the first Circle of *Heal Wounds,* and she had a feeling it would take a lot of practice to copy it herself.

As the casting finished, a radiant light washed over the cot, and the boy's injured arm straightened out and twisted back into place. Then the blood faded and turned brown on the bandage. When the healer lifted the dressing to inspect the wound, the skin underneath was unbroken with no trace of an injury.

She then faced Amara and spoke in a warm, motherly tone. "Now that you have seen my weaving technique, carry on my legacy and help all those you find in need."

Amara froze with shock. Could she interact with this healer? But before she could ask, the vision faded, and Amara found herself sitting back at the wagons.

When she checked her character sheet, she found with some disappointment that her spell hadn't been upgraded. But she felt she'd been imparted with important knowledge. The vision had given her a way to advance her the technique to the next circle—she just needed to figure out how to weave it.

# CHAPTER 18

Amara and her companions waited for well over an hour, but none of the missing members of their caravan returned. If any of them had survived, then they had most likely fled deeper into the hills. When goblin scouts began to reappear among the trees, Amara knew it was time to leave.

As they hadn't wanted to leave anything valuable behind, they'd hitched the animals from the other wagons to their own. She didn't know how to drive a wagon, so she let Jonas take the reins. Taking up a seat on the bench next to him, Amara asked him to show her everything he did. If this world was her new home, then she needed to learn basic things.

Jonas spoke a command, and the oxen lurched forward.

With trepidation, Amara watched the goblins creeping down the hill. Many clasped bows in their hands or carried slings loosely at their side. And while they'd defeated the goblin champion with no losses, there was no telling if Amara and her friends would be so lucky a second time.

Thankfully, the goblins had no more stomach for another fight than she, content to shadow the wagon as they trundled away.

Only once they'd left the hills behind did Amara finally let herself relax. For the next few hours, she kept watch intently, though she saw nothing more threatening than a herd of deer.

They caught up with Ackley and his party at the next hamlet along the road. After spending the night, they sold the extra oxen to a local farmer. They only received ten copper pieces for the four animals—far less than they were worth, according to Jonas—but it still made Amara feel rich.

After concluding their business, the wagon train—much reduced from its former bulk—departed to continue their trek north with Ackley's party.

The endless monotony blurred the weeks that followed. The late summer rains reduced many of the roads to a morass, and they spent countless hours pushing the wagons out of the mud. When they were lucky, they would reach a walled village before dusk and rent a room at an inn. Too many nights, however, were spent under the stars, with empty stomachs.

Several times on their journey, the travelers spotted groups of humanoids in the distance, though the strangers never came close enough to be identified. Regularly, their group came across the wreckage of other caravans or burned-out farmsteads, but they didn't encounter any more goblin tribes.

After weeks on the road, the convoy finally reached the outskirts of Oksberg. Amara was bone weary. She fantasized about renting the most luxurious room in the city, but as it was, they barely had enough to buy food, so they'd probably have to spend another night sleeping rough.

As they crested a hill overlooking the city of Oksberg, her breath caught in her throat. A forest of spikes spread across the plains below. Impaled upon each lance was a rotting corpse.

*There must be thousands of them*, Amara thought.

Even from this distance, she could smell the decay. What sort of tyrant ruled over the kingdom?

Beyond the impaled bodies, the city was barely visible through a thick haze of wood smoke. Oksberg had been built on a peninsula where a river emptied into a vast lake. Two sets of walls snaked around the perimeter with hundreds of round towers standing sentinel. And the color of the buildings was dull and gray, with none of the beauty of the previous city. Now that she thought it, she didn't even know it's name. She'd have to ask Jonas about it later.

"Not much to look at, is it?" Borim asked. "But as long as they have a soft bed, I'll be happy."

"I doubt we have enough money for that," Amara replied. "We're down to a few half coppers."

"I still have the candles and stuff," Salamander said as she chewed on her fingernail. "Maybe I could sell them?"

"Maybe," Amara replied. She didn't particularly want to use the money gained from thieving, but they may have no choice. Hopefully, the city provided accommodations to arriving adventurers.

The group was silent as the wagon trundled among the impaled bodies. Much to her surprise, they still writhed on their stakes—they were all undead. Someone had severed their limbs and then left them here to suffer. Was it some sort of warning to the other undead?

As their wagon approached, several guards emerged from a gatehouse. One of them, an older man, strode forward to meet them.

The guard wore a weathered face, with a jagged scar traveling up his cheek to a milky-white eye. He raised his halberd and pointed the tip at them. "State yer business."

"We're adventurers answering the call," Jonas said. "The city of Oksberg must be defended from the Forces of Chaos."

The guard inspected the wagon. "Where's the clerk, then?"

"The clerk?" Amara asked.

"Yeah, the one among you lot who's supposed to have all your names and stuff."

"He . . . met an untimely end at the hands of a fierce tribe of goblins," Jonas continued. "However, after his heroic demise, we pressed on to lend you aid."

The guard spat to the side. "Hans was a fool. Told him the roads were too dangerous, didn't I?"

He pointed at the other wagon filled with Ackley's party. They had fallen behind on the approach to the city. "They with ya, too?"

Amara nodded. "They were part of our group."

"They gonna tell me the same story?" the guard asked, eyeing them. "Did ya slit the clerk's throat and sell off the oxen?"

"They'll say the same thing," Amara said, her voice rising. "And I don't enjoy being treated like this."

"I don't care," the guard replied. "Yer all nothing more than meat for the grinder, aren't ya? Line up to give me a look."

Amara raised her eyebrows, but the others piled off the wagon to stand along its side. Then she shrugged and jumped off to take up a position next to Jonas.

The guard moved down the line and, when he reached her, Amara felt the telltale pins-and-needles prickle she'd come to recognize as someone examining her class.

When he lumbered up to Salamander, the guard shook his head mournfully. "I've never seen a more worthless lot of adventurers in my life. Don't have no use for ya here."

"Are you saying you won't let us into the city?" Amara asked in a dangerously low tone.

"Have to be mad to, wouldn't I?" The guard spat another mass at their feet. "A soul-eating rogue, a thieving cleric, a mage barely off her mother's tit, and a heretic rift warrior."

"Listen," Amara said, crossing her arms. "I have spent weeks on the road, battled hordes of goblins, nearly starved to death, and I did it all without any caffeine! If you don't let me inside the city, I'm going to charm you, and then watch with great pleasure as you dunk your head into the nearest latrine. Do you understand me?"

"I'd like to see ya try." He jerked his thumb, drawing the party's collected attention up the wall to a ballista. The massive bolt in its chamber was aimed at them. "If I start acting strange, they'll shoot ya dead. Understand *me*?"

Amara gritted her jaw and clenched her unburned fist until her fingernails dug into her palm. It did little to quell her mounting rage.

Before she could do something stupid, Jonas interjected, placing himself between the guard and Amara. "Surely, there must be something you can do," Jonas sang smoothly. "Perhaps there is someone we can speak with?"

The guard shook his head. "Leave now or we'll fill ya with holes. Last warning."

"Where are we supposed to go?" Amara asked, through clenched teeth.

"Beggars are free to try their luck at Stout Oak Keep. It's about a week's walk north of here. If it still stands, they might be desperate enough to take in a sorry lot such as yerselves. Oh, ye'll be leaving the wagon and oxen. They're property of Oksberg."

Above them on the walls, archers waited, arrows nocked. She couldn't know what level the guards were. Anything Amara could try, any spell she could cast, would likely trigger a slaughter. Amara took a deep breath and then pushed down her anger.

"Would you be so kind as to give us directions?" Jonas asked.

"Follow the road," the guard grunted, indicating a hill. "Ye'll know you've arrived when you lay eyes on either a keep or a smoking ruin."

With that, he backed away, taking up a position among his fellow soldiers.

"Let's go," Amara said.

Borim's bushy brows knitted together with concern. "Just like that, lass? Don't think it's all that fair—"

"There's nothing we can do," Amara announced firmly. "Maybe we'll have more luck at Stout Oak Keep."

Jonas rubbed his chin but made no move to leave. "Perhaps we should consider turning back. Oksberg, as a prospect, was dangerous enough, but a border fortress like the keep? For a group of our level, such a destination would be tantamount to suicide."

As Jonas rambled on, Amara watched Ackley and his group approach the gates only to receive a similar reception. *So much for Oksberg taking in* anyone, Amara thought darkly. *Apparently, beggars* can *be choosers.*

"What do you think?" Jonas asked.

Amara blinked. "Sorry, what?"

"What do you think of my suggestion of heading to the coastal cities?" Jonas repeated. "Were you even listening? As I said, a group such as ourselves would receive good coin for work there, perhaps avoiding the more unsavory quests."

"And how would we get there?" She crossed her arms. "The trip here took weeks, and that was with the benefit of a wagon and beasts to draw it. Do you want to spend the next few months walking back all that way? We came here to advance our classes, and that's what we're going to do."

Borim rested his axe on his shoulder. "I set out to quest in the North, so I say we continue on. My vote is for Stout Oak Keep."

"Are you sure," Salamander whispered to Amara. "It sounds scary."

Amara softened. "We'll be fine. Besides, I still need to learn more about my *other* quests," she said with conspiratorial emphasis.

"What quests would those be?" Borim asked. "Are you holding out on me?"

"It's not something I'd like to share at the moment," she replied, "but it has to do with Galoth's Wall."

"Now that sounds mysterious."

As his party approached on foot, Ackley shot a glare over his shoulder toward the gate. "I assume they didn't allow you entry either?" he said.

Amara nodded.

Eldred rubbed a behemoth hand along the stubble on his head. It had been quite some time since he'd shaved it. "I should shove my spear up that guard's backside."

Ackley patted the warrior on his meaty shoulder then turned his attention back to Amara. "Is your group planning to travel to the embattled fortress?"

"What do you mean, *embattled?*"

"Did the ever-so-friendly guard not inform you?" Ackley asked with some surprise. "Several enemy factions have laid siege to the area. Apparently, there are impressive quests available if you defeat any of the commanders."

"That's interesting," she mused. "How impressive are the rewards?"

"He didn't go into detail, but any lord in such a situation would likely offer rare and magical items to adventurers who drove off the invaders."

As she listened to Ackley, the prospect of walking for a few more days suddenly didn't sound so bad. And while there may be more risk, it came with the chance for far greater rewards. Plus, there was no way she was walking all the way to the coast—wherever that was.

"If everyone agrees, then we'll leave for Stout Oak Keep immediately."

She shared a long, intense stare with each member of her group in turn. Though Jonas appeared uneasy at the prospect, he said nothing, choosing instead to simply avert his gaze. *Once we start gaining levels and rewards,* she thought, *he'll warm to the idea. Maybe we'll even earn another Title.*

Without objections from her party members, she said, "It's settled. We're heading to Stout Oak Keep."

"Excellent!" Ackley clapped his hands together. "I hope you'll still consider acting as my group's healer when needed."

"Like I said, I'll think about it."

Placing her staff over one shoulder, Amara repositioned the mimic under her other arm. The walk to Stout Oak Keep would be a long one, so it was best to get started. After a few steps, she heard the others fall in behind her.

Hopefully, those at the keep would be better hosts than Oksberg, because, if another guard tried to deny her entry, she had a feeling bad things would happen to them.

# CHAPTER 19

Amara stood protectively in front of the mimic on the road as she wove the strands of mana to summon her *Cloak of Shadows*. If she couldn't talk them down, she decided, Amara would slip into stealth to help her pet escape.

"For the last time, it won't hurt you," she said, with a dangerous edge to her voice.

While Ackley's group had been unfriendly before the revelation of her pet, they were downright hostile now. They stood arrayed in a semicircle around her with their weapons drawn.

"Are you thick in the head," Eldred shouted. "That thing will probably chew off our toes while we sleep."

"Toes?" Kymber regarded her teammate with a raised brow. "A monster that size could probably gobble us down with one bite. We must slay the creature."

Borim stepped forward and raised his axe. "No one is hurting that thing." While his eyes had nearly popped out of his head at the sight of the mimic, he'd quickly recovered and come to Amara's defense. "Step back before I have to crack a few skulls."

Kymber plucked on the strings of her lyre with a cold expression on her face. As she did, notes of power wafted through the air. "I won't associate with anyone who keeps a monster as a pet."

Jonas stepped between the two groups and raised his hands. "Have none of you heard of the Great Galando? The Elven merchant who travels from town to town selling monster eggs?"

Ackley frowned. Of all of them, only he hadn't drawn his weapon. After a moment's thought, he motioned for his companions to stand back. "I heard he sells little more than low-level creatures. A mimic is . . . something else entirely."

"Yes, but you see the reason of it: a purveyor of magical eggs would want to sell the occasional powerful beast. Tales would spread and entice others to spend their hard-earned coin on the mere chance to gain a rare find for themselves."

Jonas pointed at Amara. "She's known for her Luck, and she received one of the few eggs with a real monster inside."

"And you say the mimic isn't dangerous?" Ackley continued warily. "What assurances do we have?"

Amara let her cloaking spell dissipate as the others lowered their weapons. "It's been sleeping next to you for weeks and it hasn't eaten anyone yet. Not that some of you don't deserve it."

"I recall seeing you with the chest several times, though it wasn't quite so large." Ackley waved his group back. "You say that the mimic is friendly, I'll trust your word. I apologize that our reactions became so . . . heated."

"I guess your group has short memories, since I just saved most of their lives," she shot back. "And this isn't a great way to say thank you. Do you draw your weapons on someone after they bring you a mug of ale, too?"

"I'd hardly say that's comparable," Ackley replied. "The appearance of such a dangerous monster simply caught us off guard. Next time, please warn us, and this can all be avoided."

Amara nodded slightly. She knew she hadn't handled the situation well. Her original plan had been to tell everyone about the mimic and then show them. But her mimic, gorged on the bodies of the slain goblin, had apparently decided it was the perfect time for a stroll. Next time, she'd have to give it careful instructions to stay put.

"Keep that thing away from me," Kymber hissed. "And I don't ever want you as part of our group."

"You're welcome for healing your arm," Amara muttered.

Ackley put his back to the mimic and strode northward. As his companions fell in step behind him, he called over his shoulder, "We should continue our journey if we want to make the keep by nightfall."

Kymber shot one last glance at the mimic before disappearing over the next hill with her party.

With the others out of earshot, Borim rounded on Amara with pinched eyebrows. "Anything else you'd like to tell me? Do you have a dragon in your pocket? Or maybe a Chaos God in your backpack?"

"I'm sorry I didn't tell you—"

Borim raised his finger. "We're group mates, and you don't keep stuff like that from each other. What else are you hiding from me?"

Amara shrugged. "I'm an avatar of the goddess Melischar? And I've been reincarnated from another world?"

The dwarf tugged angrily on his beard. "Do you think now is the time for jokes? Maybe I should find a group that respects me."

He shouldered his axe and then stomped after Ackley's party.

"I imagine he'll come around," Jonas said softly. "The dwarf is fonder of you than he lets on."

"He's right. I should have told him before now. But I was afraid he would react like the others."

Jonas adjusted the straps of his backpack. "We should listen to Ackley's words. I have no wish to spend another night out in the wilderness. If we make haste, I believe we may reach Stout Oak Keep before sundown."

Amara sighed then shouldered her own pack. They left the devastated patch of forest behind. Despite worrying that the mimic wouldn't be able to keep up, Amara was pleased to see that her pet gamboled along with a steady, if awkward, gait. Salamander fell in at her side, marvelling at everything they saw on the road.

*I don't know how she retains such a sense of wonder after everything she's been through.*

Amara listened with a smile as Salamander pointed out types of trees she'd never seen before and the different bushes. When she pointed at one flower, recognition flared in Amara's mind.

She veered off the road and knelt in front of the white flower. The petals formed tiny little bell shapes, each the size of a fingernail. She snapped off half of the blooms on the bush—leaving the rest so the plant could recover—then placed them in her bag. If her sudden insight was correct, these could be used to making healing pills and potions.

"What do you have there?" Jonas asked, sidling up beside her. "Ah, a silverbell plant. Those are quite rare back in Leissen."

"These are silverbells?" she exclaimed. On the trip northward, Jonas had informed her the city where she'd found herself was called Leissen. "I searched the forest for an entire morning and never saw a single one!"

Jonas nodded sadly. "The alchemists, in their greed, harvested every single one they could find around the city. It's a shame. Their scarcity has driven up the prices of healing potions to unaffordable heights."

"At least they haven't done that here yet," she said, feeling guilty for taking so many blossoms.

"Or the local alchemists dare not leave the safe confines of the keep," Jonas said before adding, "if any of them still live."

Amara stood and wiped the dirt from her knees. "If you see any more of the flowers, please let me know."

"Do you plan to sell them?"

"No, I'm going to try to make some potions."

"I wasn't aware you had skills in *Alchemy*," he said, surprised. "What other skills do you possess?"

"I have *Herbalism* and *Alchemy*," she replied. "Oh, and *First Aid*."

"I have to admit, that is a powerful combination of skills for a healer." Jonas ran a hand through his hair. "If you wish, we could set up a profitable business in the coastal cities with no adventuring required."

She paused at his words. The prospect of living a comfortable life without any danger was certainly appealing. And if she earned enough money, she could simply pay adventurers to collect the ingredients for her potions and pills. But that life belonged to someone who hadn't been summoned by a goddess. If Amara gave in to the temptation of the simpler path, she would doom this world, and possibly others.

"Maybe I can make some money for us here," she said. Their supply of coin was nearly exhausted, and if they wanted to eat, then they needed to find some way to earn money. "I also need something called karo root."

"I'm very familiar with that plant, as I used to collect it for my mother." Jonas nodded. "The root has many uses, including aiding indigestion."

When they set out again, all three of them ranged along the side of the road searching for the plants. Every few steps, Salamander pointed at a different flower or bush, asking if it was what they were looking for. Finally, Amara had to task the girl with watching over the mimic.

They'd traveled several miles when Jonas stopped at the side of the road. He bent down and pulled up a plant by the roots; the muted-purple leaves led down dark stalks to a thick tuber.

"This," Jonas announced, "is karo root."

The tuber went into Amara's backpack, and, over the next several hours, the trio managed to collect two more roots another dozen blossoms. As the shadows began to lengthen, the group ended their search and picked up their pace.

Just when she feared they wouldn't reach the keep before nightfall, the forest thinned out around them before transitioning into cleared lands. Cresting a hill, Amara and her companions took in the sight of Stout Oak Keep.

Like Leissen, the settlement was situated on an island in the middle of a river twisting through a valley. The weathered fortifications seemed as ancient and immovable as mountains. Amara also felt a sense of power emanating from its thick walls. Guarded by square towers squatting at either end, a wooden bridge stretched across the water to reach the keep.

A village sat on the nearby shore, a wooden palisade protecting it. Beyond the barriers, Amara could see thatch roofs, smoke curling up from the chimneys. Animal pens dotted the outskirts of the garrison, and neat rows of crops stretched the length of the valley.

When Jonas and Salamander reached her side, Amara pointed at the mimic. "What are we going to do with my pet?"

"I suppose we could carry it," Jonas said. "However, a group of adventurers showing up with a large treasure chest may draw unwanted attention."

Salamander twirled a strand of hair around her finger. "We'd probably be stabbed and robbed right away."

Amara turned to her mimic. "Can you take on other forms?"

The mimic bobbed up and down to indicate the affirmative.

"Could you please change, then? Maybe something a little less conspicuous?"

The mimic shuddered and then, without warning, a gelatinous form burst free from the confines of the chest. The gelid mass oozed out, subsuming the wood and absorbing it until the creature looked like a giant amoeba. Then, it spread as it continued to transform.

When it was finished, the mimic stood before them in the guise of a door.

"This is just great," Amara muttered. "I guess we're out hiking with a door?"

"It's better than a treasure chest," Salamander commented.

"Except for the fact we'll look insane for lugging a door through a dangerous wilderness," Amara replied. She faced her pet again. "Could you change again?"

The newly form door shivered with a negative response.

*It must take a lot of energy to change forms*, Amara noted.

Jonas bent down to lift one end of the door. "It should not be overly difficult to carry your pet in this shape."

"How do we explain having a door?" Amara asked, exasperated.

"Maybe we found one in the forest?" Salamander offered.

Jonas stroked his chin. "Our warrior lost his shield in the battle against the goblins. Perhaps we could claim we have been using this door as cover until he purchases a new one."

"I guess we'll go with that." She walked around to the front of the door and lifted her end off the ground. "Let's get going, then."

Jonas picked up the other end, and once they both had a hold of the mimic, the trio made their way down into the river valley.

*Hopefully*, Amara mused, *we'll be sitting in front of a roaring fire and eating a hot meal before nightfall.*

# CHAPTER 20

Amara strode up to the lone guard at the gates and tried to hide her nervousness. If she and her group were denied entry because of their classes, they would have no choice but to travel to the coastal city-states. And she knew any further delay in her quests would almost certainly doom this world.

She glanced over at Borim, who stood nearby, a sour expression stamped on his face. He'd been waiting for them at the gates, and there was no sign of Ackley and his party. Maybe the other group of adventurers had already gained entry into the *castle*.

Turning her attention to the guard, she guessed he wasn't much older than her, but the lad was in a sorry state. His dark hair spilled out from his open-faced helmet, partially obscuring the patchwork of bandages that covered him, nearly, from head to toe. What drew Amara's attention, however, was the dressing on his arm drew where a worrisome black stain spread across the cloth.

Staggering to greet them, the soldier wobbled on his feet and steadied himself with his spear. He regarded them over a crooked nose and then shook his head. "No one is allowed inside the castle."

"We were told that Stout Oak Keep was besieged," Amara explained, "and we want to help."

"There's barely a single person *left* to help," the guard replied. "I'm one of the last ones standing."

"Are you telling me we walked all this way for nothing?" she said, her voice dropping dangerously low. "You won't let us help against the invasions?"

He shrugged helplessly. "That's above my pay grade, but I guess I can examine you in case I find someone with the authority to let you in. Line up, I suppose?"

Amara motioned for the others to join her on the bridge. Jonas arrived first, followed by Salamander, who took a moment to peer over the railing into the fast-flowing waters.

"I think I saw a fish," Salamander called out as she stretched her arms wide. "It was huge!"

"That's great," Amara said. "We'll talk about it later."

Borim was the last to join them, and he grudgingly stomped up to the guard. "Don't have much a defense here, do you? A few crippled kobolds could probably overrun this fortress."

"We had more swords before the last ogre attack," the guard said stiffly.

"Ah, sorry about that." The dwarf scratched his head. "We've had a long walk and all."

The guard noticed the door resting on the nearby shore. "Why, in the name of Holy Birgitta, did you bring a *door* with you?"

"Let's just get on with the examination," Amara said.

The guard shook his head and, continuing to use his spear for support, limped over to stand in front of Jonas. Bored, he lurched to Borim, then finally reached out to Amara with the familiar inspection. The guard's eyes widened. Gasping, he wobbled uneasily.

*Now what?* she thought. *Do they have something against Trickster Clerics here, too?*

"Thank the gods! You're a healer," he cried out. As he spoke, he pulled down the bandage on his arm to reveal the weeping wound beneath. "I know that you're only Level 4, but do you think you could look at my arm? Does it look infected? Will I lose it?"

She cringed at the sight of his festering wound. "It might be a little bit. . ."

"Do you think it's bad?" he asked. "My parents have been saving up for a health potion since the goblin arrow was removed, but they're naught but poor farmers and haven't made much progress—"

Amara held up her hand to interrupt him. "It would help if you're quiet."

The young man nodded. Amara took his arm into her hands. When she gingerly prodded the blackened skin of his arm, the soldier jerked and winced in pain.

Amara ignored the guard as she wove the strands of mana together to cast *Heal Wounds.* As the layers of power formed the intricate pattern required for the second Circle spell, the soft glow of holy light filled the air and seeped into the guard's. The radiance intensified until her eyes watered. Her mana flowed out of her in a torrent as she completed the work. Shocked, Amara realized more severe wounds required a greater outlay of power; her soul had been almost completely drained.

The searing light left ghostly afterimages floating in her vision and she had to blink several times to clear them. When she could finally see again, Amara noted with relief that the guard's arm had been completely healed; no trace of the infection remained. She watched as he pulled his other bandages off, revealing unblemished skin underneath.

The guard gasped. "How? You're only Level 4."

"Our leader is renowned for her healing skills," Jonas said smoothly. "Your lord would do well to employ our group's services."

"The lord is dead, and his lady is likely to meet him before the week is out." Then the guard perked up as a look of hope spread across his face. "Do you think you could heal the lady of the castle?"

While her new spell was impressive, there were still limitations to it, some of which Amara had yet to fully comprehend. It had taken everything she had to heal the guard. Had his injuries been any worse, she suspected her spell would have failed.

"What happened to her?" Amara asked.

The guard took off his helmet and tousled his hair. "I heard she was run through by a goblin while helping to evacuate a village a few weeks ago. Apparently, she's got a nasty infection. Our priestess says it's beyond her means, that Lady Ingrid knocks at death's door.

*A priestess,* Amara thought with a jolt. *Here?* Amara fought to hide her concern, taking comfort in the knowledge the bishop's reach couldn't possibly extend this far.

The guard interrupted her thoughts. "My name is Jurgen, by the way. I was a squire here until a few days ago, so I don't know everything going on."

Amara stared at him while she waited for him to continue. But he made no move to speak. "So, Jurgen, if you want me to tend to the Lady, do you think you could let us in?"

"Oh no," Jurgen said quickly, "I don't have the authority to let anyone in. Only Lady Ingrid can approve new arrivals, and she lies in a coma."

"So, there's no one else?"

"Stefan could . . ."

Amara brightened.

"But he died fighting the ogres."

Amara ran a hand down her face, her good humor quickly fading. "Why don't you go find someone to ask, then?"

"I can't leave my post," Jurgen replied simply. "Someone might get in! They'd string me up for sure."

"So, what you're telling me is that even though Lady Ingrid needs healing desperately, you won't let us in?"

Jurgen nodded, offering, "Maybe I can fetch the priestess once my shift ends in a few hours."

Amara toyed with the idea of casting *Charm Person* on Jurgen—assuming she had enough mana left. Instead, she took a deep breath to calm herself. "Is there anywhere we can stay until then?"

Jurgen pointed at the nearby village. "There's an inn renting out rooms. It's called the Winking Dwarven Lass."

"That's a bit offensive," Borim muttered darkly. "Dwarven women are known for their modesty."

Jonas stepped forward, concern etched into his features. "Surely, if your baroness is in danger, you would not deny us entry."

Jurgen scratched his head. "I'm not allowed to let anyone in, and I'm not allowed to leave my post. What am I supposed to do?"

Jonas threw up his hands. "I suppose we'll wait for word at the local inn."

Amara nudged Jurgen. "You won't forget, will you?"

Jurgen scrunched up his forehead. "Forget what?"

"About telling them we're here?" Amara replied.

"Right. And no."

Amara blinked at him for a moment, noting to herself that things must be truly dire here if such a thick-headed boy was the best they could find. With an unconcealed expression of disbelief at Jurgen, she turned and stalked across the bridge.

Once she and Jonas had collected the door, their party headed toward the village.

She watched Borim out of the corner of her eye, noting he still looked furious. She decided to say something. "I'm sorry that I didn't tell you about the mimic. It was wrong to keep it from you."

"I guess I see what you were worried about," Borim grumbled. "My first thought was to take my axe to it as well. But I can see there's something different about this one. It *might* be handy in a fight." He brightened. "If you buy me a meal at the inn, then all is forgotten."

"Deal," Amara said with a grin. She was glad that she could smooth things over so easily with the dwarf.

They arrived at the wooden barricades that marked the village entrance. Once again, Amara's party was met with a watchman. In contrast to Jurgen's fresh-faced youth, this one—with his stooped shoulders and craggy features—looked too decrepit to keep so much as a temperamental squirrel out of the village.

"State your business," the watchman said.

Amara kept her response brief. "We're here to book a room at the inn."

"Why do you have a door?" His wizened eyes narrowed. "Did you steal that from the castle?"

"Why would we steal a door?"

"Why do you have a door, then?"

Jonas lowered the mimic to the ground with a grunt. "On our tiresome journey, we had the misfortune to encounter a particularly nasty band of goblin archers. My companions and I have been using this door as a sort of *pavise*. Such shields have provided excellent cover against the hail of goblin arrows for centuries."

The man touched his temple. "Huh . . . never thought of doing that. But then, I've never been hit in the head, unlike you adventuring types." He shuffled to one side of the gate, waving his hand limply. "You're welcome to come in, but no stealing doors. Understood?"

"I'll try to restrain myself," Amara replied drily.

She walked through the gates and was immediately accosted by the foul smell. Animal dung and human waste mixed in fetid puddles on the street, and heaping mounds of garbage squatted along the gutters. The charred husks of buildings dotted the street, shabby tents sprouting like weeds in their shadows. Most of the people they passed wore bloody bandages over gaunt frames. The few villagers who met her gaze did so with haunted eyes.

"It appears that the battle does not go well here," Jonas whispered to her. "Perhaps we should reconsider the coast."

"I want to see the quests first," she replied.

"What about eating?" Salamander said. "I'm starving."

Amara paused and then looked over her bedraggled group. They all looked exhausted, and most of them had lost weight on the long trek north. She decided to relent. "Alright, why don't we see if we can afford a meal at the inn, and then we'll check out the quests tomorrow."

The relieved smiles of her group members told her she'd made the right decision, and she changed course to head toward the only two-story building in town. Based on her previous experiences in this world, that would be the inn.

They arrived to find Ackley and his group standing near the entrance. She helped Jonas prop the mimic up against the wall and then turned to face Ackley.

"I'm afraid the inn is not an option," the hawk-faced duelist said, resting his hand on the hilt of his rapier.

"Are all the rooms full?" Amara asked.

"The innkeeper is demanding a silver piece a night for room and board."

"A silver piece," Jonas exclaimed. "That's highway robbery!"

"Agreed." Ackley nodded his head.

Amara sighed and glanced up at the darkening sky. It looked like they were spending another night under the stars. If Jurgen remembered to inform someone of her arrival, she might be able to parlay her healing into better accommodations. However, she didn't hold out much hope.

# CHAPTER 21

Amara had draped her stained, tattered robe over herself and Salamander to give them some protection from the cold weather. The girl snuggled in closer as another gust of wind coursed between the buildings. As they'd traveled north, the nights had become progressively colder. And now that they'd reached Stout Oak Keep, it felt close to freezing outside.

"Here, please, take mine," Jonas said as he offered them his thick woolen blanket. "I currently find myself too warm."

"Do you honestly expect me to believe you're too warm?" She raised her eyebrow. "And if I take your blanket, what will you use?"

"I'm sure a brisk walk will be enough to warm my blood."

"So, are you just going to stroll around all night?" She pushed the blanket back toward him. "I'm not stealing the only thing keeping you warm."

They had been unable to afford a room in any of the remaining buildings in the village. Instead, they'd been forced to shelter in one of the burned-out huts. Most of the walls had fallen, and only a few charred beams remained of the roof, but it was moderately better than sleeping in the streets.

"My stomach hurts," Salamander murmured. "I'm too hungry to sleep."

Amara frowned at the girl's words. Her own stomach twisted painfully at the thought of a meal. She'd tried to purchase rations from the innkeeper, but he'd demanded exorbitant prices; the man had wanted a silver piece for a single loaf of bread. To make matters worse, the quest board was located inside of the castle, so none of them could earn any coin.

"Will you stroke my hair?" Salamander asked in a little voice. "When I was little, my mother used to do that when I couldn't fall asleep."

Amara hesitated for a moment as painful memories of her own childhood returned; her mother had often done the same thing every night before bedtime. She shook her head to dismiss the thoughts and then lifted her hand to pat Salamander's flaxen hair. After a few minutes, she heard the girl begin to snore.

Once she was certain Salamander wouldn't stir, she gently disentangled herself and stood up. As she did, she draped her tattered robe back over the girl.

"I'm not going to let her starve," she said in a hushed tone to Jonas. "The innkeeper is gouging everyone, and I won't let it stand."

"I imagine it's expensive to transport food on goblin infested roads," Jonas whispered back. "And he doesn't lack in patrons as his inn is almost completely full. However, once the crops have been harvested, I believe it will be easier to purchase rations."

"I'm not waiting that long." She reached down and grabbed her staff. "Salamander shouldn't have to go to bed hungry because someone is hoarding enough food to feed an army."

Jonas's hand shot out and caught the hem of her dress. "I suspect I know what you're planning, and I must discourage it."

Amara's expression darkened. "Would you make her go hungry when I could feed us all?"

"No matter the justification, thieving is always wrong."

"Well, my goddess would probably disagree with you," Amara replied angrily. "She's the patron of the downtrodden and oppressed. And anyone letting people starve when they have a cellar full of food is definitely someone she would want to see punished."

"And what of you?" he asked softly. "Would you become the thief you claim not to be?"

"I *am* a thief," she said, her voice falling. "There's no use in denying it anymore. Back when my dad was sick, I stole anything I could get my hands on. And I'd happily do it again to keep Salamander from suffering. She couldn't even fall asleep tonight because her stomach hurt too much!"

"And I am weak with hunger as well," Jonas said. "However, I won't betray my principles when there are other alternatives."

"And what exactly are those?"

"I have faith the guard will return," Jonas said. "And once you heal the lady of the manor, she will provide for us."

"Well, I wish I had your faith." She ripped her dress free from his grasp. "Now I'm going to go find food for our group. But if your *principles* are enough for you, then you don't need to eat anything I return with."

Jonas frowned, but said nothing as he leaned back against the blackened wall. He looked disappointed before he averted his gaze.

Amara brushed back a strand of her hair in annoyance then stepped over Borim where he had fallen asleep across the threshold. She made her way out into the street, and everywhere she looked, she saw makeshift shelters constructed of nothing more than blankets and scraps of wood. She'd heard many of the people here had lost their home to the invasions while others from neighbouring villages had come here seeking refuge.

As she approached the inn, she cast *Cloak of Shadows*. Hired by the inn-keeper—presumably—a handful of local toughs guarded the Winking Dwarven Lass's entrances and patrolled the perimeter with torches. With her spells aiding Amara's vast experiences, this was going to be the easiest heist of her life.

She stopped across the street from the inn, hidden by her spell. At the back of her mind, guilt gnawed at her. This wasn't the life she wanted anymore. She wanted a fresh start in this new world. But things were different in this new world. If she couldn't keep those around her safe with her new powers, then what was the point of them?

*This is hardly my first time stealing from someone,* she argued with herself. *And Melischar would probably be proud of me for liberating food for the hungry.*

After the patrol disappeared around to the other side of the inn, Amara darted across the road. She tried the front door and was surprised to find it swung open easily.

*Why have guards if they were going to leave the doors unlocked?*

Inside she found four more guards sitting near the door. The quartet leapt to their feet sending their chairs clattering to the floor. A bald thug with a web of scars across his face scanned the room, but his gaze passed right through her.

"There's no way that was the wind" he said. Hooking a thumb toward the men next to him, he added, "You two, check outside. We'll keep an eye on the main floor."

Deftly evading the men as they lumbered past her, Amara hurried to the stairs. The sounds of the guards' conversation faded as she descended into the basement, keeping her steps light to prevent the steps from creaking.

The cellar of the Winking Dwarven Lass was practically bursting at the seams. Crates, barrels, and bulging sacks were piled up to the ceiling with barely enough room for one person to fit between them.

Though she tried to hurry, Amara lurched to a stop as her sleeve caught on a nail protruding from a crate. She cursed softly under her breath, but froze as a shadow appeared right in front of her.

*If not for the nail,* she thought, *I would have walked right into him.*

A boy who looked to be of an age with Salamander peered around the room apprehensively. He had straw-like hair poking out at all angles and a splash of freckles across his cheeks.

"Who's . . . who's there?" he said haltingly. Lifting a rusty kitchen knife, he added, "I . . . I . . . have a weapon. So, you better get out of here."

Amara didn't move a muscle as the young man scanned the cellar. When he finally moved on, his lantern held high, she reached out and gently unhooked her snagged sleeve.

Then she froze where she hunched in the narrow passage between the crates and kegs. Back in her other life, shopkeepers might just spot a skinny girl running away. Some didn't even realize they'd been robbed. Here, with her spells, she could slip in like a ghost and take anything she wanted.

*What would happen to the young man guarding the cellar if she stole some supplies?* It's not like anyone would believe him if he claimed an invisible spell caster had robbed the inn. He might face accusations of theft himself—and she knew most medieval societies back on Earth punished stealing harshly.

It dawned on Amara that her newfound stealth—which meant easier scores for her—might mean punishment for others. If the innkeeper noticed a few loaves missing, would the lad with his kitchen knife take the fall? Would succumbing to temptation this time make it easier to steal the next time they were hungry or running low on money? Would she take the easy path every time she ran into hardship?

Amara's father had often said, "Following the path of least resistance leads to crooked rivers and crooked men." It had horrified him that she'd been reduced to stealing as he languished in bed. He'd begged her to stop. At the time, it had seemed like the only way to keep them both fed. But in hindsight, she'd simply chosen the easiest path.

*I don't want to go back to who I was,* she thought to herself. *I really didn't like that person.*

Before her resolve could evaporate, Amara turned and crept back the way she'd come toward the stairs. Behind her, the boy circled the room and continued to interject tough words with a reedy voice. When he was on the opposite side of the room, Amara scurried up the steps with little regard for the sounds of her footfalls or creaking wood. When she reached the main level, she sprinted across the space between herself and the door. The sound of her footsteps caught the guards' attention. Once again, the inn's hired muscles shot up from their seats, but they were too slow. Amara burst through the door, and as she fled down the street, the shouts of the guards faded behind her.

When her sides ached from running, Amara ducked into an alleyway to catch her breath.

She waited, watching for any sign of pursuit. When she concluded that no one followed her, she dropped her *Cloak of Shadows* then made her way to the ruined building where her group sheltered.

As she approached the entrance, the mimic—still in its guise of a door— wiggled excitedly. She gave her pet a crooked smile, stroking it lightly as she passed. Borim and Salamander, she found, were exactly as she left them; snoring soundly, oblivious to the world around them.

"I see you have returned empty handed," Jonas said from the shadows. "Did you reconsider your actions?"

"Couldn't get in," she lied testily. "Door was locked. Too many guards."

Jonas raised his eyebrow as he stared at her.

She scowled at him. "Alright, fine. You were right. I couldn't bring myself to do it. I hope you're happy since we're probably all going to starve to death now."

"I have faith one of us will come up with a plan."

She brushed back her hair, intent on solving their problem before closing her eyes for the night. While trying to summon a brilliant plan, Amara let her gaze wander the night sky. With great gaps of darkness between the twinkling pinpricks, the stars looked foreign to her. The edges of the heavens shimmered a brilliant blue, its slow undulations reminding her of the Northern Lights. She briefly wondered if the glow was a natural phenomenon—as it was on Earth—or if, here, it had something to do with magic.

Her thoughts shifted to their problem gaining entry into the keep. If the guard wasn't going to come fetch them for an audience with Lady Ingrid, then maybe she needed to go introduce herself.

She retrieved her staff and backpack and then strode toward the exit.

"Where are you going now?" Jonas asked.

"I'm going to sneak into the castle and find Lady Ingrid," she said. "And if I can heal her injuries, then it will solve all our problems. In the worst-case scenario, we'll at least get to access the quest board."

"I believe you're slightly too optimistic about the worst that can happen," Jonas said. "I understand your reluctance to continue traveling, but there's no need to commit such rash acts. If necessary, Amara, we can live off the land until we find a legitimate way to earn our coin. What happens to you if you're captured?"

"I'll just have to trust in luck." She gave the mimic a meaningful look. "And I'm not going alone."

# CHAPTER 22

Amara approached the gates to Stout Oak Keep with her pet mimic. The monster had reverted to its wooden chest form. With stubby legs sprouting from the bottom, it scurried along beside her. She glanced over and watched as it split down the middle to reveal a toothy maw.

At the gate, the guard spotted the mimic and desperately flailed to alert her to its presence. "Behind you! There's a mimic!"

She didn't respond.

In armor far too large for him, the guard readied his halberd. His helmet slid down, obscuring his eyes. To Amara, he looked barely old enough to shave. Pushing his helm out of the way, the young soldier continued to call out warnings.

Her plan was simple: magically charm the guard and ask him to escort her to Lady Ingrid's chambers. On the off chance that she was discovered, she could use *Cloak of Shadows* to disappear.

Increasing her pace, Amara cast *Charm Person*. A necklace about the watchman's neck flared with light, but otherwise he remained in his panicked mind.

*Why isn't my spell working?*

She tried her spell again, and once again the necklace provided the only response.

Before setting out, she had ordered her pet not to harm anyone, which she was grateful for, since now she'd have to rely on it to incapacitate the guard.

"Would you mind dealing with him?" she asked her pet.

A elongated tongue shot out from the mimic and latched onto the young man's halberd. With a flick, the monster tossed the weapon over the side of the bridge where it splashed into the dark waters.

The young guard gaped at his empty hands in disbelief. Spinning away from Amara, he sprinted for the safety of the fortress. The mimic's tongue shot out again, this time slapping wetly against the guard's armored leg. He toppled, his chin smacking the hard earth. As her pet dragged him toward its eager mouth, the guard clawed at the bridge.

Amara held up her hand. She then strolled up to the guard. "I promise, no one is going to hurt you. What is that necklace you're wearing?"

"Please, don't let it eat me," he cried out. "I'll give you anything you want, just don't let it eat me!"

The guard fumbled with his armor. A moment later, he tossed a small handful of copper coins at her. As his salvation fell through the cracks of the bridge, landing in the river below with a small chorus of *plunks*, his boyish face blanched in the moonlight. "Here. . .take my family's heirloom."

He tugged the necklace over his head and offered it to her with trembling hands.

She sighed. "I don't want your money. The necklace," she repeated. "What does it do?"

"It . . . it protects against low-level charm spells," he stammered. "At least that's what I've heard. No one has ever tried to charm me in the past. Least not that I would know."

*So, my guess about the necklace was right,* she thought. *Maybe I can do this without magic.* "I only want to speak to the lady of the manor," she said. "Will you escort me to her room?"

He lifted his chin defiantly. "I won't let you hurt her." He deflated when the mimic tugged with its tongue, dragging him inches closer to its mouth.

If the mimic grew too excited and accidentally ate her captive, her plan would fail. Amara shook her head at her pet then regarded the boy. "What's your name?"

"My name?" He paused for a moment. "It's Uwe."

"Uwe, I give you my word that I won't harm Lady Ingrid."

"I'm sorry, but I can't grant entry to anyone." With the mimic's tongue still wrapped around his shin, he awkwardly pushed himself into a sitting position. "Maybe if you come back tomorrow . . ."

Amara rolled her eyes. Snatching the necklace, she cast *Charm Person*.

Uwe's expression transformed from one of distrust to puppy love.

Once she was certain her spell had worked, she stood up and motioned at the mimic. "You can let him go now." Something occurred to her in that moment. "I'm going to have to give you a name, aren't I?"

The mimic bounced up and down in response. Its tongue recoiled into its mouth with a slurpy *smack*.

On the ground before her, Uwe rubbed his leg.

Gently, Amara asked, "Will you please escort me to Lady Ingrid?"

"Anything for you." He pushed himself to his feet. "But first, would you like to meet my mother?"

"Your mother?" she repeated, taken aback by the question. "Why would I want to do that?"

"Because you are the most beautiful woman I have ever seen," he replied, his cheeks flushing pink. "And I want to announce my intentions for you."

Amara choked. She'd cast *Charm Person* quite a few times, but no one had ever fallen in love with her. And the guard was practically a child. Choosing her words carefully, she said, "I . . . I'm flattered, but can we go see Lady Ingrid first?"

"I'd be happy to bring you to her," Uwe said, gazing at her longingly. "Maybe she could marry us—"

"Nope! We're not even discussing that."

Amara was grateful that none of the others had come. If they could see her current predicament, their laughter would follow her all the way to Jonas's beloved coast.

She pointed at the gates. "How do we get in there?"

Uwe led her away from the portcullis of the main gate to a door at the base of a tower. After searching through a jingling ring of keys from his pocket, he slid one into the lock, gave it a turn, then swung the door inward. A glowing gem set in a sconce bathed the area with a harsh white light.

Startled by their entry, another guard jerked and staggered to his feet . While Uwe barely looked old enough to hold a weapon, this guard—with cavernous wrinkles, and a smile like a broken fence—appeared twenty years past his prime.

"Who in the name of Holy Birgitta is that?" the man called out.

Amara worked quickly to cast Charm Person. As she watched, the man's willpower crumbled and his eyes swam out of focus.

When he opened his mouth to speak, she held up her hand to stop him. She didn't want anyone else professing their love.

"What . . . what happened?" Uwe, beside her, blinked rapidly.

Amara froze as she realized her *Charm Person* spell no longer affected Uwe.

*It must be limited to one person,* she noted.

Without hesitating, she grabbed the keys from the confused youth and shoved him outside. She slammed the door shut and locked it before he could come to his senses and try to force his way back inside.

As Uwe pounded on the door, she turned her focus to the old man. "Escort me to Lady Ingrid's room right away."

She winced as she heard the muffled shouts growing more frantic. Amara hoped that the fortress was so understaffed that no one would answer the boy's alarm. But, with how badly her plan was going, she wouldn't put so much as a copper on that bet.

Thankfully, the older guard she'd charmed was quite compliant. He led across the open ground between the outer and inner walls of the keep. Amara and the soldier slipped into another tower. The guard fumbled around in the dark room until he activated a crystal that flooded the space with light. He then led her to another thick door.

They threaded their way between the darkened buildings. Passing some animal pens nestled up against the inner wall, Amara heard the low grunts of pigs. Her mimic broke away, trundling toward the closest pen.

"There's no time for a snack," she snapped in a low voice. "Get back over here."

Reluctantly, her pet rejoined them as they neared another door. Though they had encountered no one so far, Amara wasn't sure how much longer her luck would hold out. While she waited, the guard struggled to move the heavy door.

After he'd pried it open a crack, Amara slid through the narrow opening. She was in yet another open expanse. Unlike the previous courtyards, however, this one hosted a cluster of torch-bearing guards forming a barrier in front of the next set of gates.

Amara asked her escort, "Is there another way to get inside?"

The wizened soldier nodded then led her to pool of shadows that concealed a recessed door. This door swung open easily, revealing a corridor with straw scattered on the floor. The moment she shut the door behind them, a bell began to toll.

She'd been discovered.

"We need to hurry," she whispered urgently to the guard.

The old man limped down the corridor, obviously favoring one leg. She felt a pang of guilt for forcing a rush on an old man and his infirmities, but she was almost out of time.

But her dash through the keep came to a sudden end as a door swung open and slammed into her face with a crunch of wood against nose. Tears filled her eyes, and stars burst in her vision as Amara staggered backward. When she could see, she spotted a woman in a servant's outfit peering around the door apprehensively.

A thousand angry curses died on her tongue as Amara heard the heavy tromp of boots. Ahead of her, soldiers rushed down the hallway, many of them still struggling to fasten their armor. They jostled one another, urging their cohorts around a corner and down a path.

None of them noticed Amara.

The door had opened just in time, in just such a way that it shielded her and her pet from view.

As the sounds of the guards faded, she wiped blood from her nose.

To Melischar, Amara thought, *I appreciate the Luck, but more dignified ways to escape danger?* Still, she didn't want to look a gift horse in the mouth.

The threads of *Heal Wounds* formed in her mind, but when the servant woman spotted the mimic, Amara let the spell unravel. The servant opened her mouth to scream but froze when Amara swung her staff around to point the tip at her throat.

"Go back into the room," Amara commanded in a harsh tone, "and don't say a word about seeing me."

The woman nodded then retreated to safety, closing the door. Amara heard the sound of a latch sliding into place, followed by the patter of frantic footsteps.

Uncertain if the servant had used another way out of the room, Amara doubled her pace. Her limping escort led her to the end of the hallway to a winding staircase. As they climbed, ignoring several floors, Amara and her companions narrowly missed another group of armed men, many of whom were noticeably injured.

When they finally arrived at the topmost level of the keep, Amara unshouldered her bag and retrieved her darts.

Certain that a noblewoman's chambers would never be left unguarded, Amara readied her Martial Ability.

When she emerged from the stairs, an empty hallway stretched out in front of her. Tapestries decorated the walls, depicting warriors battling what looked like horned demons. Empty suits of armor flanked a pair of intricately-detailed double doors.

"That is Lady Ingrid's room," the charmed guard said. "May I do anything else for you? Are you hungry or thirsty?"

"I'm fine," she replied. "So, the lady is just through there?"

The doors opened to reveal a towering man in resplendent white armor. As he stepped into the passage, a woman wearing the robes of the Church followed him.

The pair stopped in the act of closing the door.

For a moment, the two parties just stared at each other.

The armored man drew his sword from his scabbard with a hiss then charged at Amara with a war cry. The priestess aimed her raised hands in her direction, weaving a terrifying amount of mana to cast a spell.

Amara shoved the guard away. "Run for your life," she shouted, "And don't stop until you're safe!"

Amara darted forward as a column of golden light smashed into the reed mats where she'd been standing. With one hand on her pet, she cast *Cloak of Shadows*. The gray veil of the spell shrouded them.

As they disappeared from sight, the warrior faltered. With the mimic galloping at her side, Amara moved down the hallway as fast as she dared. Crouched low, she should be clear if the man took any desperate swings with that sword.

By the time she reached the doors to Lady Ingrid's chambers, Amara was breathless. Her quickly swelling nose ached with each attempt at a hushed breath. Once inside, she decided, she would use the mimic to block the entrance while she healed the baroness.

"Guardians!" the priestess commanded. "Protect the lady!"

Mana swirled around the suits of armor, pouring through the openings between the plates. Burning blue lights blinked into existence within the helmets. With the screech of metal, the guardians lifted their great two-handed swords and marched forward to block the entrance. Shoulder to shoulder, they formed a steel bulwark before the double doors. They lowered the tips of their weapons, presenting a bristling wall of steel.

Amara stood trapped between the holy warrior and the living armor. She realized she needed to change tactics if she was going to avoid a full-scale battle. Dropping *Cloak of Shadows,* Amara held up her hands.

"Wait! I'm here to help Lady Ingrid!"

# CHAPTER 23

Preparing another deadly swing, the hulking warrior shouted, "Do you think I'll fall for your tricks, foul servant of Malcheron! Emmaline, protect the Baroness. I'll handle this intruder."

The situation was escalating out of control, but if she could just explain herself, they might lower their weapons.

"I'm not an intruder," Amara called out. "I'm a healer, and I'm just here to help Lady Ingrid."

The man grunted in response, stalking toward her menacingly.

"Stay your hand, Noah," Emmaline purred. She approached him and laid a gentle touch on his arm. Turning her piercing gaze toward Amara, she asked, "A healer, you say?"

Amara nodded rapidly.

"And you believed the best way to help Lady Ingrid," Emmaline continued, "was to invade our castle? You are a either a fool or a liar."

"I told one of the guards." Amara's face clenched as she tried to recall the young man's name. "I think he was called Jurgen. When I told him I was here to heal Lady Ingrid, he said he didn't have the authority to let me in. Refused to leave his post to ask anyone."

Emmaline sighed and shook her head. "I warned them it was a mistake to use someone who was kicked in the head by a mule as a child."

The priestess stared at her intently. Soon, Amara's skin rippled with the familiar tingle of being magically examined.

Emmaline raised her eyebrow. "A Trickster Cleric? And only Level 4? Have you loaded your pockets with all the valuables in our keep?"

Amara scowled. "I haven't stolen anything. Do you want my help or not?" It seemed no matter where she went, people would judge her based on her class.

"We certainly won't allow a *Trickster Cleric* accompanied by a monster anywhere near the baroness. Besides, your low-level spells will do nothing to aid our lady."

Emmaline gestured to the armored golems and they advanced on Amara.

"I healed Jurgen," she cried out desperately. The last thing she wanted to do was announce her arrival with a battle outside of the lady's chambers. "And my spell has advanced to the second Circle, which cured his infection completely."

"Truly?" Emmaline eyed her carefully. "And what of the mimic? Why do you travel with such a dangerous beast if you're not aligned with the Forces of Chaos?"

Amara shrugged. "I received it from a monster egg I purchased from a merchant. But it's friendly and won't hurt anyone unless I command it."

"Much like the lady's wyvern, then," Emmaline mused. The priestess pressed her lips together. "Do you have any proof you healed Jurgen?"

"Send for him. He'll tell you."

"I won't leave you alone with a monster this close to the lady of the castle." Emmaline crossed her arms. "If I allow you entry to the room, will you agree to surrender your weapons?

Noah eyed Emmaline incredulously. "You don't honestly believe this serpent-tongued girl? She is clearly working with the Issurian prince. What healer invades a castle under stealth? And what of the monster at her side?" he added, aiming his sword at the mimic.

Amara's pet waited like a coiled predator.

Emmaline shrugged. "What do we have to lose at this point? Lady Ingrid will not survive the week without healing. Should she perish, all hope is lost. Regardless, if the Trickster Cleric tries anything, we have the armored golems and ourselves to protect the lady."

"I won't allow her to enter the lady's chamber," Noah said stubbornly. "She should be taken to the dungeon for questioning, and the mimic slain. Immediately," he added.

As Amara listened to them argue, she prepared to cast *Charm Person*. If Noah renewed his attacks, the spell would make him friendly long enough for her to beat a hasty retreat.

Emmaline continued, "And if the lady dies in the meantime? Would you have that on your head?"

"I won't hasten her death, by allowing this foolish idea." Noah replied.

"It's clear she attempted to announce her arrival. And while I disagree with her methods, I won't turn away a healer with a second circle spell in our most desperate hour."

Noah asked, "How do you know she even possesses such a spell?"

"If she doesn't then we will kill her. Swiftly."

Noah grunted. Glaring at Amara, he lowered his weapon. "I will watch you like a hawk regards its prey. If I sense you're trying to harm the lady, I'll run you through. Understood?"

Amara fought down a retort and then nodded.

"I will also require you to leave your . . . beast in the hallway, where it can be watched by the armored golems. Your weapons, please," Emmaline said, hand outstretched.

Amara hesitated before handing over her staff. With greater reluctance, she placed her darts in Emmaline's palm. She knew it was a risk to give up her weapons, but she was willing to take the chance. And with her spells, she could probably fight her way out of here if it came to it.

"Do not attempt to cast anything other than a healing spell," Emmaline warned, "or you will be dealt with severely."

While Noah glowered like a furious bull, the priestess turned to lead Amara to the lady's chambers. The sounds of footsteps ascending the stairs stopped them. As one, the three of them—Amara, Emmaline and Noah—watched as Borim emerged from the stairwell, Salamander trailing behind.

"Ah, there you are," Borim said, breathing hard. "We've been trying to catch up to you since the gate." At the sight of the priestess and warrior, the dwarf tightened his grip around his axe.

Gaze fixed on Amara's weapons in Emmaline's hands, Salamander clutched her hands to her chest and asked, "Who are they?" A glowing ball of flames appeared between her palms. "Are you their prisoner?"

"What are you doing here?" Amara asked, shocked at the sight of her group members. She held up her hand to Emmaline, who had begun to weave a spell. "They're with me."

Emmaline narrowed her eyes then let her spell fizzle out. "How many others have invaded our castle this evening? Thank goodness the Forces of Chaos didn't choose tonight to conquer us. It seems the fortress is ripe for the plucking."

A moment later, Jonas appeared from the stairs with the guard Uwe at his side. He patted the young man on the shoulder and then pointed at the side of the hallway. He coolly regarded the two castle defenders flanking Amara. "Have they harmed you?"

"I'm fine," Amara said quickly. She hadn't expected Jonas to accompany the others with the way he'd reacted to her plan. "Why are you here?"

"There are people starving out there, and I couldn't allow their suffering to continue," he said. "A noble has a duty to protect their people, and until Lady Ingrid is healed, the peasants' misery will continue. While I disagreed with your decision to storm the castle—"

"Infiltrate," Amara interrupted to correct him.

"Yes. And while I disagreed with your decision to *infiltrate* the castle, I could not rest. Not when I might be of use to these people. I will not stand by and do nothing."

"How did you get in here?" Amara asked.

"Yes," Noah rumbled. "How *did* you get in here? If you've hurt anyone . . ."

"The boy you locked outside? We convinced him that we were here to help you mend the lady's wounds," Jonas said. "Apparently, Jurgen showed him what you'd done when he relieved him of guard duty. And while I generally avoid using it, one of my skills is lock-picking. Once we'd gained entry into the tower, it was a simple matter to avoid the few guards standing watch. To be honest, I don't think I've ever seen a castle this under-manned before."

Emmaline arched her eyebrow at Uwe. "Is it true that Jurgen has been healed?"

The youth nodded his head, looking like a rabbit who wanted to bolt. "There's no trace of the rot left, priestess."

"Then you were telling the truth," Emmaline whispered softly. "Everyone will remain in the hallway until the healing is completed. Then we will decide what to do with you all."

"I don't think so," Borim replied gruffly. "We're not leaving our friend alone."

Emmaline shrugged. "I won't allow anyone else inside."

"I'll be fine," Amara said. "I promise." She felt if it came down to it, she could deal with Emmaline and Noah. Most of the people she'd encountered in this world had grossly underestimated her based on her level. And though she was still learning how to accurately assess someone's power, neither of her escorts seemed particularly powerful.

"I don't like this . . ." Borim trailed off and then glanced over at Jonas.

"Nor do I," Jonas agreed. "If you harm so much as a hair on her head . . ."

"Yes, yes," Emmaline said with a roll of her eyes, "I'm sure you'll swear vengeance and then hunt me down in a noble quest. Now, if you're done with your idle threats, we should tend to the lady immediately. Shall we, Trickster Cleric?"

With Noah at her side, the priestess walked toward the end of the hall.

Amara moved to follow Emmaline, but stopped when her mimic raced up to her. She patted her pet on the top. "You'll have to stay here for now."

The mimic whined and skittered back and forth, clearly unhappy at her command. But when Amara started to walk again, it remained with her group.

After she'd passed the living armor, the golems took up guard positions to prevent access to the room. She glanced back over her shoulder to see her companions' worried expressions and her mimic bouncing from side to side. She could only hope she was making the right decision.

Amara waited as Emmaline pushed open the great doors to reveal an opulent room beyond. The far wall appeared to be made of liquid amber. As she watched, the surface pulsed and undulated to create a stylized image of her. Rich purple curtains cascaded from a canopy bed in the center of the room, obscuring whomever my lay within.

Emmaline led Amara to the bed and pulled the curtains aside to reveal Lady

Ingrid. The cleric was surprised to note that the baroness didn't appear to be much older than herself.

Eyes shut, the woman slept, her blond hair fanning out on the pillow like a halo. She looked gaunt to the point of emaciation, and her skin was terribly pale. Her condition reminded Amara of her father during his last days.

"Seal the doors," Emmaline commanded Noah.

He grumbled something under his breath as he dropped a hefty wooden bar across the entrance. Between the thick doors and the drawbar, no help would be coming any time soon.

Amara focused her full attention on Lady Ingrid. As she gently pulled back the sheets, she exposed a bloody bandage covering the lady's midsection. Like she'd seen with Jurgen's wound, the skin around the area was festering, and a terrible stench wafted up to fill her nostrils. If her experience healing Jurgen was any indication, Lady Ingrid's wound would take an immense amount of mana to heal. With a quick mental check of her mana pool, Amara guessed that she'd likely need to meditate prior to casting her healing spell.

"Is something wrong?" Emmaline asked as she watched her expression.

"No . . . no," Amara replied, trying to appear confident. "I should be able to handle this no problem."

"That would truly be a miracle from the gods," Emmaline said.

"What have you tried?"

Emmaline shrugged. "The castle barber has been tending to the injury since she received it. We've fed her several healing potions as well as a Life magic pill recovered from a nearby dungeon. Everything we've attempted has only prolonged the inevitable. Something on the goblins blades caused an infection to rampage through the baroness."

Amara tenderly folded the sheets back over the baroness. "Before I try to heal her, I'm going to need to meditate to restore some of my mana," she said.

"See?" Noah snarled.

"Healing Jurgen's wound nearly drained my soul dry, and the lady's infection seems more severe."

But Noah thundered on. "She can't heal our lady. We should dispatch her immediately before she initiates her evil plan. And then I'll personally put down that mimic."

"We'll give her time to meditate," Emmaline said sharply, as she watched Amara. "But know we are watching your every move. Don't try anything or you'll regret it."

Kneeling beside the bed, Amara closed her mind off to the world around her. She would need to refill her soul completely, and she could only hope her spell would be strong enough to heal the lady's wounds. Otherwise, she doubted the uneasy truce would last for long.

# CHAPTER 24

By the time Amara refilled her soul completely, more than an hour had passed. While she was growing more skilled at replenishing her mana, she still needed to learn a way to do it more efficiently. Maybe once she healed Lady Ingrid, she could find someone here to teach her a more advanced meditation method.

She rose to her feet, staggering as her numb legs nearly folded underneath her; at some point, her feet had fallen asleep. She mentally added a comfortable prayer mat to the list of things she wanted to buy when she finally had some money.

Rubbing her legs to get the circulation going again, she glanced over at the door. Outside of the room, silence reigned—which was probably a good thing since she'd feared Borim would try to hack his way through the door.

She returned her attention to Lady Ingrid. In the short time Amara had turned inward, he noblewoman's breathing had grown more labored. If she waited much longer before attempting to heal her, the baroness might die. And with her, any chance of questing in the North.

"I suggest you hurry," Emmaline said. "If you are going to attempt to mend the lady's wounds, then you must do so now."

"I still think it's an unwise decision." Noah rose from the plush chair where he'd been resting.

Emmaline pressed her lips together. "Do you honestly believe she could make her condition any worse?"

"I stand by what I said."

Amara tuned out their bickering as she started to weave together the strands of her spell. Each time she cast her upgraded *Heal Wounds*, it became easier to form the intricate pattern. Soon, she should be able to accomplish it while moving or even fighting.

She concentrated, braiding the last strands together, and the room pulsed with a soft glow. Then a blizzard of motes descended on the baroness like a shining snowstorm. Where each glowing speck landed, Lady Ingrid's sickly pallor flushed to healthy pink.

Amara rocked with the force of her mana leaving her body. She steadied herself against a bedpost, her soul depleted. Before her eyes, the infection slowly receded from the baroness.

With this spell, she could have easily healed her father's disease. At the memory of him, she felt a sudden pang of sadness. *I would have given anything for this power back on Earth,* she thought to herself.

When the soft glow filling the room finally faded, she had exhausted the last drop of her mana. But she could tell from the baroness's improved pallor that the healing spell had been successful. And when she lifted the bandages on the woman's midsection with trembling fingers, she revealed unblemished skin underneath.

She'd saved Lady Ingrid.

"So, you truly could heal her," Emmaline murmured from beside Amara. The priestess regarded her with a calculating gaze as though trying to uncover her secrets. "Something tells me you are no ordinary Trickster Cleric."

"This must be a trick," Noah shouted, his expression darkening. "Such a thing is impossible."

Amara returned her attention to Lady Ingrid where she stirred in the bed. "Can you hear me?"

The baroness's eyelids fluttered and then opened. She stared at Amara uncomprehendingly for a moment before she spoke. "Where—?" She coughed into her hand, choking on her disused voice. Ingrid struggled to rise, but then collapsed back on the bed, gasping for air. "Water."

From a nearby silver pitcher, Emmaline filled a gaudy silver cup to the brim. She returned to the bed and lifted the cup to the baroness's lips. Lady Ingrid gulped greedily, and after draining it completely, she turned her head to face Amara.

"Where am I?" Ingrid asked, her voice growing stronger. While a healing spell could work miracles, apparently it couldn't completely counteract days—or even weeks—of languishing in a bed with a serious illness.

"You're in your quarters in the keep," Amara replied. "I heard you were brought here after a battle with ogres."

"Ah, I'm in my husband's room. I try to avoid this place as much as is humanly possible." Ingrid struggled into a sitting position. "Who are you? Why is the door barricaded? Have the Issurians breached the outer walls? And why are there initiates in my room? What is going on here?"

Amara helplessly looked over at Emmaline. She couldn't possibly answer all the baroness's questions.

"This Trickster Cleric arrived at the keep yesterday," the priestess answered. "After being turned away, she attempted to infiltrate the castle with her group.

Noah and I stopped them before they could reach your chambers, and upon detaining her, the cleric claimed she only took such dire measures so that she might heal you. With few other options, we allowed the attempt. Which was apparently the right decision, as she appears to have healed your wound completely."

Noah approached the bed. "My lady, this vermin attacked the castle unprovoked! She must be dealt with immediately."

Lady Ingrid held up a finger to silence the big warrior. "Remember your place, initiate. If she healed me, then she deserves our gratitude. Though I question how a Trickster Cleric managed such as thing, as their skill set generally lends itself to other pursuits. What is your name, girl?"

Amara felt vaguely put off being addressed as, "girl," especially since she wasn't much younger than Lady Ingrid. Despite veiled slight against those of her class, this was the friendliest greeting Amara had received in this world so far. "I'm Amara, my lady."

"You have my thanks, Amara," Lady Ingrid said. "If there is anything I can give you, then you need only ask. I'm curious how a motley band of adventurers forced their way into my family's fortress. How ever did you bypass the guards?"

"There's not many people *left* guarding the fortress, your ladyship," Emmaline explained.

"What of my husband?" Ingrid asked, finally finding the strength to push herself up into a sitting position. "And the master-of-arms, Stefan? And what of your mistress, Emmaline?"

"All dead," Emmaline replied, as though she were discussing the weather. "After the skirmish with the ogres, Issurians ambushed Lord Lukas as he tried to retake the village of Ahrenshoop in the South. No one returned from the battle."

Lady Ingrid looked stricken. "How . . . how many remain?"

"Uninjured?" Emmaline glanced over at Noah meaningfully. "The people in this room, my lady. Oh, and this cleric healed one of our guards. Despite being on his feet, I question the boy's usefulness."

Noah grunted from nearby, "He's got a pretty hard head. We could probably launch him from a catapult."

"How much of the land do we still hold?" Ingrid whispered.

"Nothing beyond the walls of the keep," Emmaline replied. "Unless you count the village of Fussen on the shore."

"Then Stout Oak Keep is lost." Ingrid directed her gaze at Amara. "It would have been more merciful to allow me to die from my wounds." Her eyes became unfocused as she stared off at nothing.

Amara looked at the baroness in shock. After everything she had gone through to reach Stout Oak Keep, the baroness just wanted to give up?

"Listen," Amara said, "I know you lost a lot of people you care about. But I spent weeks traveling here and fought through hordes of goblins to help you."

She left out the part where they had originally been heading for Oksberg. "And you just want to lie down and die? If you're not going to fight for your home, then at least let me."

"While I hate to agree with a Trickster Cleric," Emmaline said, "my father often stated as long as there is life, there is still hope."

Ingrid stared at them blankly. Wrapping the sheets around herself, she swung her feet over the side of the bed. "You are right, of course. With the death of my husband, I have a duty to the people here. I must defend the castle to the last drop of my blood—no matter how bleak matters may appear."

With great difficultly Ingrid pushed herself up and tottered over to one of the dressers. She swung open the lacquered door then withdrew a tunic and a pair of breeches. With a glance to those gathered in the room, she said. "If you would be so kind as to give me some privacy."

"Of course." Amara brushed her hair back with one hand. Then she glanced over at Noah to see if he would unbar the door.

After a moment, the warrior stomped over to the entrance and lifted the beam, and pushed open the doors. Out in the hallway, the tense standoff outside hadn't changed.

"Would you mind dealing with these walking pots and pans?" Borim asked, stabbing his finger at the armored golems still blocking the hallway. "I don't like them pointing their weapons at me."

"Yes, I suppose there is no need for them now." Emmaline waved at the armor, and through some unspoken command, they returned to their original positions against the wall. Her group still watched the armored golems while the guardians blocked the hallway.

As Amara emerged from the room, a smile lit up Borim's face, quickly followed by Salamander. Her mimic bounced so high at the sight of her, she was worried it would hurt itself. Only Jonas showed no emotion at her appearance.

"I assume you were successful?" he called out.

Amara nodded in reply.

Once the three of them entered the hallway, Noah shut the doors behind them then took up a position to the right of the entrance, glaring at Amara's party.

A few minutes later, the baroness emerged from the room completely transformed. Her hair was pulled up in a loose bun, golden strands framing her heart-shaped face. Wearing loose riding pants, a tunic far too big for her, and boots that reached just above her knees. As she stood in the doorway, the baroness strapped a longsword to her belt. "Emmaline, send for my maids. I will need them to change the bedding and air out the room."

"Most of your staff has fled," the priestess replied. "But I'll see if I can find any that remain."

The baroness frowned at the news and then faced the adventurers. Her eyes widened slightly at the sight of the mimic. "I'd like you to accompany me while I assess the state of the fortress. And I'd very much like to hear your story—which apparently includes an explanation of how you come to travel with a monster in your party."

"I don't suppose you'd mind stopping for a meal first?" Salamander piped in. "I'm starving."

Borim combed his fingers through his beard. "I could go for a bit of grub, too."

Ingrid examined the group one by one—her gaze lingering on the mimic—and then nodded tersely. "And I admit that I'm famished as well. Let us have a meal. Assuming my kitchen staff haven't fled, of course. The inspection can wait until morning."

"Before we eat, I have to tell you there are people starving in the village," Amara said. "They will need food as well."

"I will see that bread is distributed first thing in the morning. Is there anything else I should know?"

The thought of a meal did much to brighten Amara's mood. Hopefully, the coming hours would sate more than her hunger.

"There's something else," Amara said, chewing on her lip. She had decided to tell the baroness about her quest to restore Galoth's Wall. After all, who better to provide her information than someone who had most likely lived in the North their entire life? "I'd prefer to discuss that with you in private."

Ingrid's eyebrow rose slightly. "My, you're a mysterious one, aren't you? After we eat, I will grant you a private audience."

She strode off. When Emmaline and Noah fell into step behind the baroness, Amara offered her party a shrug and followed.

# CHAPTER 25

Agonized screams of a woman drifted through the dark camp, followed by the raucous laughter of ogres. Malcheron watched a group of the towering creatures tie a human woman to a spit and slowly turn her over a roaring fire. Normally, he wouldn't allow such barbarism in his war camp, but relations between the different races were already strained . He had grudgingly allowed the ogres to have their fun.

From beside Malcheron, Storgom Steelbrow muttered, "Bloody savages. Don't know why we ally with such monsters."

"Because aside from their predilection for cruelty, they are an indispensable part of my army," Malcheron replied.

Ogres had broken the humans lines in the battle for Ahrenshoop, and their leader Brap'toc had slain the lord of Stout Oak Keep in personal combat. Few could stand against the power of an ogre.

But the humans had acquitted themselves well at the battle of Ahrenshoop—even in the face of overwhelming odds. The captured survivors didn't deserve this treatment.

With a passing thought, Malcheron wove together a few strands of anima into a black spike of power which he used to skewer the prisoner's brain. As she went limp, the laughter of the ogres turned to cries of disappointment.

Malcheron didn't spare a second look in their direction. He doubted any of the ogres were skilled enough to sense his miniscule use of anima. The brutes would likely believe their prisoner had simply expired from the smoke and flames.

"I appreciate that," Storgom said softly. "I'm not sure I could have listened to much more of her caterwauling."

Malcheron inclined his head slightly to the dark dwarf. While Storgom and his clan hadn't engaged in any fighting yet, they would be instrumental in the final siege of Stout Oak Keep. The Dark Dwarves were the most skilled engineers in the North, and they would build the war machines needed to tear down the ancient walls.

"How long do you think before we get the quest?" Storgom asked. "I'm getting tired of sitting on my behind all day drinking beer."

The corners of Malcheron's lips twitched up into a smile. "What dwarf wouldn't want to be paid mountains of gold for doing nothing but drinking?"

"True," Storgom grunted, "but I want to see some action. Maybe we could ambush some of the adventurers coming north? You could give the goblins a break for a bit. Especially after that disaster the other day."

"We both know your clan is far too important to risk."

As they passed one of the kobold commanders, the diminutive, lizard-like creature straightened and saluted. Malcheron nodded.

"The quest to conquer the fortress will appear soon enough," Malcheron assured the dwarf. "If we continue to hold all objectives outside of Stout Oak Keep, it shouldn't take more than a few weeks for it to appear on the augur board."

"It's taking its bloody time." Storgom replied. "I say we move immediately and take the fortress."

"And give up the rewards provided by the augur? That would be a terrible waste."

Storgom narrowed his eyes. "Just why do you think the rewards will be so impressive?"

"Stout Oak Keep is no ordinary fortress," Malcheron continued. "If the fools knew what was deep under the castle, they would mobilize all the kingdoms and republics to defend it. Thankfully, the Church has done much of our work for us by discouraging the defense of the North. Soon, Galoth's Wall will be no more."

"Maybe we should carve out a kingdom for ourselves first. If the Wall falls, I'll be a landless bastard again," Storgom said. "And, from our previous talks, I gather you won't be much better off."

Malcheron paused, pensively tracing a finger down the horn curling around the side of his face. While they—he and Storgom—would be rewarded for their victory here, the dwarf was correct about their situation: once they completed their mission, he would be nothing more than a unlanded prince far down in the line of succession.

But he didn't dare disobey his mother, Abiloch. She had consumed a dragon's hoard worth of treasures to momentarily weaken the wall, which had allowed him and several high-level commanders to cross over safely. Betraying such a formidable woman—and after she'd expended such a vast amount of wealth— would ensure that his screams were the last sounds to ring out in the universe before its destruction. He already had a sister trapped in a volcano for a failure many centuries ago, and he didn't want to share her fate.

Shaking himself free of his thoughts, Malcheron at last responded, "No. We must trust we'll be rewarded once we complete our mission."

"I hope so." Storgom chuckled. "I've grown accustomed to a life of leisure lately."

"This quest will probably grant us an epic chest, and that will significantly strengthen our position once the Wall has fallen."

He quickened his pace as he heard shouts and spotted a pair of kobolds dragging a human. The man was young, with short dark hair and stubble on his face. He was dressed in the unmistakable robes of the Church.

"Malcheron!" the young man called out. "I must speak with you!"

A third kobold approached, striking him across the face. The man sagged in their arms.

"Enough!" Malcheron commanded. "What is going on here?"

"We caught this *human*," the kobold hissed, struggling to form the words of the Issurian language. "It was trying to sneak into our camp."

"Release him immediately," Malcheron ordered. "You know I have a standing order that any members of the Church are to be brought to me at once."

"We apologize," the kobold said, shrinking. "We didn't know."

"Report to your commander for punishment," Malcheron said. "Tell her I want you both placed on hard labor for the next week."

The kobolds bobbed their heads, and then let the prisoner slip from their grasp. The priest slumped to the ground as though all his bones had been removed. The kobolds raced away in an ungainly, all-fours gait.

The dwarf knelt, checking the slack human. "A bit lenient, weren't you?" Storgom asked.

"While Abiloch believes in slaughtering her underlings, I do not," Malcheron replied. "Fear is useful, but it's not the only useful tool in the arsenal of an effective commander."

"They were only kobolds." Storgom stood up and brushed off his knees. Indicating the priest, he added, "This one should come to in a second. I don't think they did any permanent harm."

As if on cue, the man's eyelids fluttered, and he sat up with a start. "What . . . what happened?"

Malcheron ignored the question and squatted in front of him. He stared with blazing eyes. "Relay your message, human."

"I am Brother Karl, and the bishop sends you greetings," the man said, his voice quavering. "And . . . he sends a . . . a warning."

Storgom chuckled. "He's sitting on his ass in luxury far to the south. What warning could he possibly send?"

"The . . . the gods have returned," he replied, "and an avatar travels to Oksberg. She could undo all of the Church's plans."

"Do you expect me to believe that?" Malcheron barked with laughter and gestured toward the night sky. "Do you see any of the stars of the Celestial Court shining up there? I do not."

"It's true," Brother Karl cried out. "The Bishop has used powerful scrying magic to confirm it. The Church is attempting to deal with the problem, but you must move now to find her before word of the gods' return spreads."

It sounded like a fanciful tale, most likely the product of a bishop having second thoughts about their deal. The powers granted by weaving chaos anima—including longer life—were enjoyed by many members of the church. But now that the Forces of Chaos were poised to breach the wall, the Church was likely balking at the terrible toll the invasion would take. Anyone in the path of Malcheron's force would be killed or enslaved. With all of humanity's allies scattered or defeated, they would stand no chance against the combined forces encamped on the other side of Galoth's Wall.

"There is no avatar," Malcheron said in a tone that would brook no dissent among his underlings. But the human missed the implied threat that any freshly weaned goblin would have picked up on.

"Listen to me," Brother Karl demanded. "The avatar will destroy everything we have worked for!"

Malcheron's expression darkened.

"My apologies, my lord. I shouldn't have raised my voice to you."

Malcheron gestured at Storgom. "As I recall, the ogres just lost a plaything, did they not? Perhaps we should provide them a replacement."

"Are you sure?" Storgom tugged on his beard. "I don't relish hearing those sounds again."

On his knees, Karl shuffled forward, hands held up in supplication. "Please," he begged, "forgive me. Allow me to return to the bishop carrying any message you wish."

Malcheron silenced him with the flick of a clawed finger. "Inform the bishop I do not believe his lies. In due course, my army will tear down Stout Oak Keep, and then—with the Wall finally destroyed—the Forces of Order will be eradicated from this world. The promised end draws nigh. But, even with his pathetic falsehoods, he will still receive his due rewards. Queen Abiloch, after all, is a woman of her word."

Karl bobbed his head up and down and then rose to his feet. "Yes, anything you say. I would be honored to relay your words. Please . . . don't give me to the ogres."

Malcheron drew Storgom's attention with a jab of his finger. "See that he is given a Scroll of Teleportation and safely escorted from the camp. I don't want any further misunderstandings to occur."

Elbowing Brother Karl in the ribs, Storgom added, "Sounds better than being an ogre's plaything, doesn't it?"

The priest nodded again, a sheen of sweat glistening on his brow.

Leaving his lieutenant to deal with the visitor, Malcheron veered toward his tent in the center of the eclectic camp. While the ogres made no attempt to shelter from the elements, the other races were more varied and creative in their definitions of makeshift housing. The felt yurts of his fellow Issurians mingled with the tusk-and-hide piles that goblins used as tents. Mounds of turned soil revealed the areas kobolds had used to dig their underground dens. Nearby, the Dark Dwarves kept to cozy, portable houses equipped with iron stoves.

As his eyes moved about his assembled forces, many faces cast envious stares in Malcheron's direction. He knew, however, that none would dare move against him while Abiloch ruled. If anything befell him, the queen would eradicate the responsible house, blotting out their line from the eldest down to the last nursing babe.

Passing a group of goblins busily sharpening weapons and fletching arrows, Malcheron nodded then entered his pavilion.

"My lord," Tecala said in her throaty voice as she appeared at his side. Her skin was nearly alabaster white, a far cry from his own blood red coloring. Her horns were black as onyx, which matched her cascading locks of hair. She regarded him with hourglass eyes. "It's not safe for you to travel alone at night. I should always be at your side."

Malcheron waved his hand dismissively. "Storgom was with me until moments ago. He is currently escorting a messenger from the Church out of the camp."

Tecala arched her eyebrow. "A messenger? What news did they bring?"

"Nothing of importance."

"I find that hard to believe," she replied. "No human would risk their life traveling here if the message wasn't dire."

Though the false warning probably wasn't worth mentioning, he decided to tell her, anyway. "According to this fool, the gods—having abandoned the world millennia ago—have apparently chosen to return. And at the moment of our triumph, no less. It is nothing more than a ploy from the leaders of the church to buy more time in their comfortable lives."

"And what if it is the truth?"

"The timing is impossible," he replied, his irritation growing. "They choose *now* to return? To thwart our plans?"

Tecala peered at him with concerned eyes. "What better time?"

"There are no stars of the pantheon shining up there," Malcheron argued, "therefore, none of the gods have returned. I'll not speak any further on the matter."

"As you wish."

It was obvious from her tone that she feared an avatar had emerged.

Malcheron grimaced with annoyance and changed the topic.

"What of the goblins? Any more failures?"

"They have successfully closed the road again," she replied. "Their chief promises no further adventurers will reach Stout Oak Keep."

Of all the forces under his command, the goblins had been the most troublesome. He'd already had to relieve several successive leaders for their constant bungling. "That is good news," he said, flexing his claws. "I would hate to have to appoint yet another chief. And what of the port?"

"The kobolds hold Ahrenshoop, cutting off the avenue for reinforcements or supplies to reach the castle by sea."

"Excellent."

"And before you ask, our people hold the other villages, while the ogres have control of the mills and the mine." Her plump lips curled up into a smile. "After we receive the final quest, we will be ready to move on the keep."

"Good," Malcheron said. "And once we destroy the last of Galoth's cores, the Wall will come down."

"And the world will be ours," she said, her wicked grin spreading.

"Yes," he replied. "With the Forces of Order eliminated, Chaos will reign for eternity."

# CHAPTER 26

Amara leaned back and folded her hands in her lap, the chair creaking beneath her. In front of her, the crumbs of her meal served as a monument to satiety. When Lady Ingrid had offered a meal, Amara and her crew were led to a long table in a dining hall. Tables stretched the length of the room, and the cavernous space could easily seat hundreds of people. It felt terribly empty, with only six of them clustered around the main table. Soon, servants provided plates laden with smoked meats, cheeses, bread, and salted fish. Once Amara had picked her platter clean, another tray of fruit, pastries, and pudding was placed before her.

As they took their late repast, silence reigned at the table. The only sound came from the crackling of the nearby fire.

Amara had eaten until she couldn't possibly swallow another morsel, and she was so stuffed she could barely move. For the first time in weeks, she felt *truly* full.

Beside her, Salamander made little contented noises as she nibbled on a pastry. She didn't know where Salamander stored all the food, yet somehow, the girl had eaten even more than Amara.

As Salamander finished her pastry, her hand darted out to grab for a cup of wine, only for Amara to slide it out of her reach. Since downing one cupful, her cheeks had gone ruddy and her words slurred.

Salamander shot a dirty look in her direction, but Amara instead gave her attention to Borim. Rising to his feet, the dwarf glanced over at the mimic slumbering by the fire, then faced Lady Ingrid. "I want to thank the lady of the manor for such a wonderful meal." He waited, allowing the baroness to respond with a dainty dip of her chin before he continued. "And now to address a matter of grave importance that we've let go unspoken for far too long. Something that should have been dealt with a long time ago."

Amara leaned forward, unsure of where the dwarf's words were leading.

"Amara, when are you going to name that stupid walking box of yours" Borim asked, cracking a broad smile. "I'll have you know, the runt and I concocted a heapin' list of great names. Got 'em up in my noggin. For example, I thought perhaps Stoutbox, in honor of our host?"

"I say we call him Nom Nom," Salamander said. Then, descending into a fit of giggles, she offered, "Or maybe Chesty."

Jonas grinned. "The only name worthy of your brave pet, I think, is Trunks."

Amara smiled, pleased to see everyone happy again. It was amazing what a full belly could do to improve one's mood.

"Actually, I already have a name picked out for her," Amara said. "I've been thinking about it for a while now."

"It's a she?" Borim exclaimed. "How could you tell? I guess there aren't any dangly bits . . ."

"Don't be so crass," Amara said, laughing despite herself. "I'm going to call her Miriam. Mimi, for short."

Borim shook his head, his shaggy beard swaying back and forth. "Mimi the Mimic? Absolutely not. I won't stand for such a silly name."

"I quite like it," Jonas commented as he plucked a piece of cheese off his plate.

Salamander swayed on her chair and hiccupped. "Me, too."

Despite Borim's groaning protest, Amara wrapped on the table. "Then it's decided."

At the head of the table, Lady Ingrid stood and raised her silver chalice. "Now that such important matters have been settled, I would like to take this chance to thank my saviors. You are most welcome in my home, and this meal is the least I can do to show my gratitude. If I can provide anything more, you need only ask. Now, let's drink to your health and good fortune."

Already buzzed from her first serving, Amara raised her simple wooden cup and drank deeply of the wine. However, she resolved that would be her last bit of alcohol for the time being. She needed her wits when she and Lady Ingrid held their agreed upon audience.

Borim lifted his drinking horn. "And to your health!" He had passed on the wine and had instead asked for water.

"May your house stand for a thousand generations," Jonas added, rising from his seat and raising his cup.

Emmaline, her cheeks pink with intoxication, followed Jonas's example "May those worthless, absentee gods watch over us all."

"Emmaline," the baroness barked sharply. "I will not hear such talk about the gods."

Amara perked up. Other than Brother Otto in Leissen, Amara hadn't heard anyone speak of any deity. She tried to remember what the monks had called the people of the North. Gnostics? Was Lady Ingrid a Gnostic, or whatever the monk had called them?

The priestess frowned. "Apologies, my lady. I meant nothing by it."

Ingrid sighed. "I apologize for her words. Since the Church all but abandoned us to our fate generations ago, all are welcome in my fief."

Amara mulled over her next words carefully, then took a tentative risk. "Our group isn't on the best terms with the Church."

Salamander giggled. "Being hunted as a heretic is way worse than being on *bad terms*."

Lady Ingrid regarded them with a calculating gaze. "Is that so? And what have you done to earn such a title?"

Amara froze, afraid that Salamander had given away too much. Lady Ingrid's position regarding the Church was still opaque. She might just tolerate those who worshipped the gods, but was still a loyal follower herself.

"I'll have you know," Salamander slurred, her grin sloppy, "she's the *avatar* of Melischar."

Around the table, the reactions to this statement varied greatly. Amara let out a horrified gasp and launched to her feet, while Borim watched the baroness.

Lady Ingrid sharpened her gaze on Amara.

A lance of pain like a firestorm ravaged her soul. Amara let out a cry of agony. She felt as if an unseen warrior had driven a flaming pike through her chest. The pain twisted and coiled, stealing her breath. Paralyzed, the edges of her vision darkened. Finally, she sucked in a ragged breath.

"What have you done to her?" Jonas demanded, as his daggers hissed free of their sheaths.

At the sight of bared steel, the laughter abruptly cut off around the table.

Borim's bushy eyebrows rose as he grabbed for his axe. "Are we really doing this again? I haven't even finished eating yet!"

"It's . . . it's impossible," Lady Ingrid gasped, her face terribly pale. Knocking over her chair, she staggered away from the table, eyes locked on Amara. "I . . . don't believe it."

Jonas glanced over in Amara's direction. "Are you well, Amara? Please, speak to me."

Amara rubbed her chest as the pain rapidly dissipated. She drew in another deep breath and then exhaled slowly. "I . . . think I'm alright. It felt like she stabbed me in the soul."

Jonas lowered his weapons slightly, his gaze trained on the baroness. "While I am no expert," he said, "it appears our host possesses a high rank of *Inquiring Eye*. However, it is a grave insult to use such an ability on a guest, Lady Ingrid, and I must demand that you explain yourself at once."

"She . . ." Lady Ingrid shook her head. "It cannot be."

Wondering if she should summon Mimi, Amara shot a glance over at her pet where she rested near the fire. Amara took a half-step toward her where here staff leaned against a nearby wall. She still wasn't sure if they would have to fight their way out of here.

*I finally found someone who didn't care that I was a Trickster Cleric, and then Salamander had to let* that *slip.*

With a rasp of metal, Ingrid drew her blade free from its scabbard. The steel shone in the flickering firelight as the baroness took a step forward, her face an emotionless mask.

As the baroness lifted her sword, Amara desperately wove together the first strands of *Divine Weapon.* There was no question about Ingrid's intentions now.

Borim jumped onto the table. His heavy boot sending plates and cups flying, the dwarf stampeded down the length of the table, and landed heavily between the baroness and Amara. Axe at the ready, he snarled. "Best rethink whatever you're planning, my lady."

Joining Borim at Amara's defense, Jonas held up his hands to stop the approaching noble. "This is all a misunderstanding, my lady. She simply calls herself an avatar to protect herself from the intolerance and fear she faces because of her class, you see. She—"

Lady Ingrid, Baroness of Stout Oak Keep, knelt. Bowing her head, she offered the hilt of her weapon to Amara.

"I am your loyal servant, avatar of Melischar," Ingrid intoned. Looking up at Amara with awe, the baroness continued, "I swear unto you my steadfast loyalty and devotion. For the rest of my days, I shall bend my will to the completion of your goals and quests."

Amara couldn't have been more surprised if a dragon burst through the ceiling and offered her a cup of tea. She eyed the baroness then turned her gaze to Emmaline as the priestess glanced around.

"My lady," Emmaline protested, "this is heresy! If the Church finds out—"

"Hold your tongue, Emmaline," Ingrid ordered harshly. To Amara, she bowed her head and humbly added, "I apologize for her lack of faith, Avatar."

Amara still felt off balance from the sudden turn of events. What had Ingrid seen when she'd used *Inquiring Eye* on her?

Sheathing his daggers, Jonas took a tentative step toward the baroness. "As I said, my lady, this is nothing more than a misunderstanding. I assure you she's not an avatar. Furthermore—and, most important to our discussions—if such a claim ever got out, it would put Amara's life in the gravest danger. And I'm sure no one here would want such a thing to occur."

"She is most certainly an avatar," Ingrid said fervently. "The gods have returned to save us in our hour of greatest need." She pulled out a medallion with an engraving that depicted a cluster of stars. Then she lifted it over her head and dropped it around her neck.

"The sign of the gods?" Jonas asked, surprise in his voice. "Then you are Gnostics here?"

Emmaline cried out. "My lady! You must not expose yourself! They will mount a crusade to expel you from your lands."

Jonas shook his head. To Lady Ingrid he said, "Your beliefs are your own, but what possible reason do you have to believe she is an avatar? Everyone knows such individuals are nothing more than a myth from an age before logic."

Though Salamander believed Amara faithfully, only Brother Otto had shared that certainty. And, according to his own account, he'd based his faith on the timely lighting of an ancient beacon, not on Amara's words or actions. What made Lady Ingrid so certain?

"She has a Luck stat of thirteen," Ingrid wailed. "She also possesses spells which are far too high for her level."

*She could see my stats,* Amara thought. *Did she see my avatar ability as well?*

Amara had left the baroness kneeling for too long, so she stepped forward and took the sword. She didn't know what to say, so she kept it simple. "Rise and serve the gods."

To Amara, the words sounded silly even as they came out, but the baroness beamed with renewed fervor.

"You have a luck stat of thirteen?" Jonas gasped, but then quickly recovered. "While such a thing is most unusual, it's hardly conclusive of her being an avatar."

Emmaline smoothed down her vestments as she joined Jonas at the baroness's side. "He speaks the truth, my lady. There could be a hundred reasons for such an unusually high stat."

"No," the baroness said firmly, still kneeling. "The gods have come to save us, and I will entertain no other explanation. This will rally the North and give us a chance to hold the fortress."

"So, you weren't joking before, lass," Borim mused. "Hah! It should be fun fighting with an avatar at my side. Maybe you could even help me with my homeland."

In her hand, the noblewoman's sword grew heavier. Without fanfare, she passed the weapon to Lady Ingrid. If there was some sort of ceremony for returning a weapon after someone had sworn fealty to you, Amara didn't know it. Lady Ingrid still shone with awe, which Amara took as a good sign that she hadn't made any major missteps.

Looking suddenly unsure of herself, Lady Ingrid asked, "Would you grace us with the reason you've come?" Quickly, she added, "Though I know I have no right to expect an answer from an avatar."

"I have received thirteen quests from Melischar to rally the Forces of Order, and one of those is to restore Galoth's Wall."

"Thank the gods," Ingrid breathed. "Though we don't know why, the magic of the Wall grows weaker every day. Perhaps the Broken Brotherhood does, but they are ensconced in their mountain fortress."

When no one else indicated confusion, Amara asked, "Who are they?"

"They are the last remnants of the Knights Tarsillan, the defenders of Galoth's wall," she said. "Centuries ago, the Church condemned them as heretics, and a vast crusade drove their numbers from the fifteen fortresses guarding the Wall. Once the knights—our defenders—scattered to the winds, the Church abandoned the North, allowing hordes of Chaos creatures to stream across our border as the magic of the Wall failed. It's why we here in the North don't hold the Church in high esteem."

"Is the Wall far from here?"

"It's only about a day's ride," Ingrid replied. "If my lands weren't infested with Malcheron's army, I would escort you there myself."

"What do we need to do to secure you lands? And who is Malcheron?"

"The foul prince of the Issurians. His army of thousands has invaded my lands." Ingrid stepped toward the door and gestured for Amara to follow. "As for securing my holdings, if you would follow me to the quest board, I will show you what is required."

Amara took a step forward but was stopped by a hand on her shoulder. Jonas regarded her, his features twisted with worry.

"I wish to speak to you in private once this is done," he said. "You've embarked on a rather dangerous path."

"This is what I came here for." She smiled at him. "But, Jonas, though I appreciate your concern, how much danger can I be in with my party watching my back?"

"A great deal indeed," Jonas said darkly.

Amara reached up to squeeze his hand comfortingly. "We'll talk later."

His expression relaxed slightly. Together, they fell in step behind the baroness, following her through the winding corridors of the fortress. Emerging from the keep into the chilly night air, they marched into one of the many courtyards to a mission board similar to the one Amara had seen in Leissen. Its surface glowed with a soft light. As she approached, the board's illumination brightened. With a gentle touch, a list of quests appeared in Amara's vision, but one stood out prominently from the others.

*Defend Stout Oak Keep (Area Quest)*
*The ancient stronghold of Stout Oak Keep has been attacked by the foul Armies of Chaos. As the last bastion of Galoth's Wall, it must be held at any cost. Drive back the invaders and retake the conquered land.*
*Objectives (0/6 Completed)*
- *Kill, Capture, or Drive off Malcheron*
- *Defeat the Issurian Army*
- *Defeat the Ogre Army*
- *Defeat the Dark Dwarf Army*
- *Defeat the Kobold Army*
- *Defeat the Goblin Army*

*Reward: Epic Chest*
*Bonus Objectives (0/3 Completed)*
- *Control the 4 Villages surrounding Stout Oak Keep (0/4)*
- *Control the Mills (0/2)*
- *Control the Mine (0/1)*

*Reward: Rare Chest*

Amara felt a surge of relief. Finally, some guidance on how to restore the wall. She had a starting point.

If Lady Ingrid could help her secure the aid of the others in the North, Amara thought that she might have a real chance of success.

# CHAPTER 27

A light rapping on the door jarred Amara out of a fitful sleep. She shut her eyes and desperately willed whoever it was to leave her alone, but the knocking continued a minute later. She pulled her pillow over her head, and then shouted, "Go away!"

"I must speak with you, Amara," Jonas called through the door.

Amara groaned and then sat up in bed. She swung her legs over the side and then tried to pat down her wild hair. Once she looked somewhat presentable, she walked over to the door and flung it open. Outside stood Jonas, already looking impeccably groomed. He'd obviously used the amenities of the castle to shave, wash himself, and comb his hair.

*Of course, he wasn't up all night healing the injured guards.*

"I'm exhausted, Jonas," she said. "Couldn't this have waited until later?"

"I have a quest to find a missing pig," he stated. "And I'd like you to accompany me."

"A missing pig?" She turned around and headed back to her comfy mattress. "I'm going back to sleep."

"It's already past midday." He stepped over the mimic sleeping by the hearth then walked to the narrow window. "I thought you wouldn't want to while away the day in bed."

"It's past noon already?" This surprised Amara. It felt like she'd just closed her eyes. She yawned and stretched. "Does this mean you don't want to leave anymore?"

Jonas didn't reply for a moment. "There are people here who need our help. And while the coastal cities would be safer for all of us, I can't leave innocents to die at the hands of the Forces of Chaos. There is meaning to be found here in a heroic last stand."

Amara didn't like his sudden switch to maudlin, so she changed the subject. "So why do you want to go save a pig?"

While she waited for his answer, she walked over to the desk to see that Lady Ingrid's maid had laid out fresh clothing for her. She'd even received a black leather glove to hide her scarred hand. The maid had repeatedly offered to burn Amara's old garments, treating her clothing as if it had come from a leper. She pulled the new dress over her head. Around her waist, she tied a supple leather belt equipped with several pouches. She placed her sleeping robes aside—also generously given to her by Ingrid—and stepped into new leather boots. Finally, she wrapped herself in a thick woolen cloak.

As she dressed and gathered her things, Amara marveled at the luxury of the room. It wasn't much larger than the quarters she'd rented back at the Dancing Gnome Inn, but it had a comfortable bed, a finely constructed wooden armoire, a writing desk with a chair, and wooden pegs on the wall for her equipment. It was one of the nicest places she'd ever stayed.

"I thought it would be best if we talked privately," Jonas said before continuing in a lower tone. "Somewhere beyond the prying eyes of the castle. And a missing pig should be a relatively easy quest to complete. If we're going to stay here, then we need to advance our levels as quickly as possible. Which means completing every quest available."

Amara was becoming more adept at sensing her advancement, and healing the injured guards last night had granted her a significant amount of experience. She felt that she was on the cusp of the next level. Maybe Jonas was right about focusing on the simple quests first. She was also curious about what he wanted to talk about.

*Probably my luck stat,* she thought. *He's likely wondering how I raised it so high.*

"I need a bit of time before we leave," she said, hefting her backpack onto the writing desk. She pulled back the flap and carefully laid out the blossoms and tubers she'd gathered on their journey. Next, she opened a package the maid had fetched for her last night.

Before turning in for the night, Amara had asked Lady Ingrid to provide alchemy supplies. As she rooted through the package, she noted that she should have everything needed to create a pill; though the knowledge was vague in her mind.

Examining each piece of equipment as she pulled it out of the kit, Jonas asked, "Are you going to craft some potions?"

"I'm just going to make some pills for now," she said. "Unfortunately, I don't have everything needed for a potion."

"I see." He leaned against the wall, resting his hands on his dagger's hilts. "It will be interesting to watch an alchemist at work again."

"Again?" Amara dropped one petal in the mortar and then began to grind it with a pestle.

"My mother was a noted alchemist," he replied. "She had wanted me to follow in her footsteps . . . before she passed."

"I didn't know you lost your mother," she said, raising her eyebrow. "Why didn't you say anything?"

"The . . . manner in which she passed is how I received my class," he replied in a strained voice. "I don't wish to speak any further on the subject."

Amara chewed on her lower lip as she added some of the karo root. A few of the pieces of the puzzle that was Jonas were starting to fall into place. Something terrible must have happened to his mother, which somehow gave him the Wraith Rogue class. Maybe she could get him to open up about it, eventually.

"Why not do this when we return?" he asked. "I don't want to lose the daylight."

"Because I've learned there is no such thing as an easy quest in this world. And I want each of us to have at least one healing pill."

"Fair point."

He pushed himself away from the wall with one foot.

She poured in a little honey and added another root into the mixture. For some reason, Amara knew it was required to bind the medicine together.

"Perhaps the missing pig will be beyond our skill. It's best to not assume this is some simple banditry or predation by an animal, after all. While I had wished to speak with you alone, there may be some merit to bringing along Salamander and Borim. I shall go fetch them while you work."

After Jonas departed, Amara continued to mix the ingredients, and as she ground them together with the stone pestle, she felt magic flowing out through her veins into the concoction. When she finished, the mixture glowed and pulsed with power.

She poured the contents of her mortar onto the desk and rolled it flat, before cutting it into individual pills that still shone with a faint radiance. As she lifted one to examine it, she wondered if the glow would ever fade.

A knock on the door made her turn. "Come in."

Borim poked his shaggy head inside. "Morning, Avatar. Glad to see even servants of the gods struggle with their hair."

Amara blushed at the dwarf's words and wiped her hands off before attempting to pat her hair down again. She finally gave up and then decided she would send the maid to fetch a comb. Maybe together they could tame her tresses.

Until then, she could tie her hair back with a strip of fabric. A ponytail would work better for questing, anyway.

"At least it doesn't look as bad as your beard," she belatedly shot back. "How many birds do you have nesting in that thing?"

"There's the fire I miss," Borim chuckled. "And I hear we're hunting wild boars? I've never slain one myself, but I hear they're fierce creatures and a worthy adversary for a dwarf."

"I'm pretty sure we're just searching for a lost pig," Amara said. "Jonas didn't say anything about hunting boars."

"That dirty, rotten nobleman," Borim fumed. "He told me we were hunting a boar!"

"Jonas doesn't strike me as someone who would ever lie. What did he actually tell you?"

"The rogue said we were traveling to the forest to find a boar. But how was I supposed to know he really meant searching for a lost little pig? What sort of quest is that?"

"Hopefully, it's an easy one," Amara replied, "but in case it's not, take these." She handed him two of the faintly shining healing pills. "If you become injured, swallow one of them. I haven't had time to test these out, but they should heal any minor wounds you have."

"A healing pill?" He surveyed the equipment on the desk. "Are you an alchemist, as well? Because if so, I have a proposal about a drink I created—"

The dwarf stopped talking as Salamander and Jonas appeared in the doorway.

"So," Borim said, stabbing a meaty finger in the rogue's direction, "you expect me to search for a piglet like some sort of . . . pig farmer?"

"I expect you to help me escort our group leader and healer," Jonas replied. "And this is the third pig that's gone missing from this farm. A predator may be responsible."

"I suppose that makes the quest a bit more interesting," Borim groused.

Salamander flopped on the bed. "I'm tired and my head hurts. Can we just stay inside today? Maybe go find more of those pastries from last night?"

Amara stood up and handed two of the pills to Jonas. "If we're going to survive here, then we need to level up quickly. And if that means taking simple quests in the area surrounding the village, then we need to do that."

"What if we run into that army thingy?" Salamander asked, her voice muffled by the bedclothes.

"Then, we retreat," Amara answered. "Lady Ingrid said that, aside from a raid on the village of Fussen, they haven't approached the castle yet. She thinks they're waiting for a quest to appear. Now that I think of it, how does that work, anyway? Who's giving quests to a hostile army here?"

Jonas frowned, his brow pinching. "No one is certain how the system works, though I've read accounts of mages studying the phenomenon. Most scholars believe it's a remnant from the Age of Strife, when quests would appear to push the Forces of Order and Chaos into conflict."

"And what of the rewards? How do you receive them, then?"

Jonas shrugged. "The promised items will simply appear near your location after completing the quest. I read an interesting treatise on how the magic may work. There was a mage several centuries ago who conducted fascinating experiments on these quests. If you have a few moments—"

Borim made a loud snoring noise to interrupt Jonas. He then sputtered, pretending to wake up. "I'm sorry, but you almost put me in a coma there."

"Thank you!" Salamander exclaimed, still facedown on the bed.

Jonas scowled and then crossed his arms.

Amara smiled at him. "You can tell me later. I want to learn everything I can."

"At least some people appreciate knowledge."

Borim tugged on his beard. "So, are we going to sit around all day or are we going to go hunt the predator?"

Amara walked over to Salamander and wait until the girl sat up to hand her the healing pills. She then placed the last two into a pouch on her belt. Slinging her backpack over one shoulder, Amara studied her party. "Shall we?"

Mimi the Mimic rushing to be at her side, Amara led her party out of the room, down the stairs to a doorway leading into the outer courtyard. Her group hadn't been granted quarters in the keep itself, but instead were staying in a two-story building built against the outer wall. Lady Ingrid had assured them that more suitable rooms would be made available for them to use, but Amara was perfectly content with their current lot.

When they reached the main gate and spotted Uwe standing guard, Amara balked slightly. The youth glared at her, obviously still angry about his encounter with Mimi. He said nothing as they passed, aggressively avoiding eye contact.

*I'll apologize to him later,* she thought. *Maybe I can give him a present to smooth things over.*

They proceeded across the bridge then traversed the heavily farmed valley. As they passed the village, her eyes narrowed at the sight of the inn towering over the other buildings. She would have to inform Lady Ingrid of the price gouging going on there. Maybe she could even get the innkeeper thrown in jail.

"If you're concerned about the starving masses in the village," Jonas said, "know they have been fed. I helped Lady Ingrid distribute bread first thing this morning, and she has assigned several of her carpenters to construct new buildings to house the refugees."

"That's good news," she said absently as they neared the forest.

From among the trees, the sound of axes striking wood rang out, and she spotted a group of guards watching over woodcutters as they harvested timber. She recognized most of the guards as those she'd healed just hours ago in the castle's infirmary. By the time she'd finished, nearly a dozen guards and adventurers had been returned to duty.

Several of the armed men and women waved at her passing party, while the laborers stared agog at the mimic.

Jonas took the lead and skirted around the edge of the forest until they reached the far end of the valley. He pointed at a simple hut nearby made of daub and wattle. A pen beside it was filled with squealing pigs, and their scent hung heavy in the air.

Borim wrinkled his nose. "How does something that smells so bad taste so good?"

"It's one of life's greatest mysteries," Amara said with a laugh.

Jonas pointed at the ground. "I spoke to the farmer this morning, and he said there were tracks leading this way."

Amara stepped in front of Mimi as her pet scuttled sideways toward the pen. "Oh no you don't. The lady gave you an entire cow leg last night, which should be more than enough for you. And I don't want you to grow to be the size of a house."

"I wouldn't worry about that," Borim replied. "The tunnels of my homeland are infested with mimics, but after a quick growth spurt when they're young, their growth slows way down. Of course, there are some legends of monstrous mimics dwelling in the depths who devour entire tribes of goblins. Now that I think about it, maybe it wouldn't be a bad idea to have a house-sized mimic."

"I like her just the size she is," Amara said, scratching Mimi's head. "Isn't that right?"

Mimi waggled her rear in response.

Jonas shook his head and then plunged into the forest. Amara followed him a moment later, and then Borim. Finally, Salamander joined them, muttering under her breath.

With only a handful of the sun's rays penetrating the dense canopy, the forest was locked in perpetual twilight. Little grew among the gnarled roots, and a dense layer of leaves covered the trail. Dead silence reigned, and their footsteps were swallowed up by the ancient woodland.

"What sort of tracks did the farmer see?" Amara whispered, afraid to disturb the ominous silence.

"Apparently, they appeared to be a woman's footprints."

Borim frowned. "Then we're tracking down a simple thief?"

"Perhaps," Jonas replied. "Perhaps not."

Amara followed Jonas deeper into the forest until he picked up fresh tracks. They increased their speed but slowed when they heard a woman's anguished cries echoing through the moss-draped trees. Amara hurried forward at the sound of distress, worried there was injured ahead, but Jonas grabbed her arm in an iron grip.

She tried to shake him off. "What are you doing?"

He raised a finger to his lips to shush her. Then he pointed off into the distance.

At first, she didn't see anything, but then she spotted an impossibly tall woman shuffling through the trees. The strange creature wore a red dress that resembled a kimono, and her frizzy, dark hair hung to the ground. As Amara watched, she realized the woman's movements were disjointed and just *wrong* in some way.

"A Weeping Woman," Jonas breathed. "A truly dangerous opponent."

Borim hefted his axe. "What are we waiting for, then? Let's go knock her teeth in."

"Amara, do you wish to withdraw," Jonas asked. "This is no simple quest, and she hasn't spotted our group yet."

"No," Amara replied. "But, I don't want to be surprised again. Tell me everything you know about Weeping Women before we run in there. And then," she added, a half-smile curling her lips, "we'll go with Borim's plan."

# CHAPTER 28

Amara stood behind Borim with her darts at the ready. Off to the side, Salamander was hidden among a thicket of trees, while Jonas had disappeared into the dense forest to lure the Weeping Woman back to their position. Amara bounced the dart in one hand, wondering if the monster was as terrifying as Jonas claimed.

"I feel ridiculous," Borim groused. "The first thing I'm going to do when we get paid for this quest is to buy a new shield."

"But just imagine if this works," Amara replied, hiding her smile. "It could revolutionize dwarven warfare."

"I still don't like it," he replied stubbornly.

Amara scanned the forest for Jonas again. Their plan for taking down the Weeping Woman was simple: she and Salamander would pelt the creature with their ranged attacks, then Borim would hold it in place while Jonas attacked from the rear.

Movement among the trees snapped her out of her thoughts, and she readied her first dart. She spotted Jonas dashing around tree trunks and ducking under branches. The Weeping Woman lumbered after him, somehow gaining ground even with her clumsy gait.

Amara activated *Dart Deadeye* and felt her eyesight sharpen. The moment the monster rounded a tree, she hurled her first missile at it. The dart plunged into the monster's stomach, but the Weeping Woman's shambling steps didn't slow.

She frowned then launched her next missile. This one struck the Weeping Woman's knee, but once again, the creature didn't react to the wound.

*What is this thing?* Amara wondered. *Why aren't my darts slowing it down?*

In front of Amara, Borim braced the angled bottom edge of his unwieldy shield against the ground in preparation for the monster's charge.

"It's not a Weeping Woman," Jonas shouted as he pumped his arms to put some distance between him and his pursuer. He slid through a narrow opening of jagged branches. Without missing a beat, he was back on his feet, yelling, "It's a karaxi!"

"By Glonin Goldhand's beard," Borim muttered. "That's some bad news."

Amara threw her last dart, cursing as it once again fruitlessly struck the monster. *Is it somehow immune to missile weapons?* Amara hoped that Salamander and her fire would have more success.

"What's a karaxi?" Amara asked Borim.

"Cast your big sword now, lass," Borim grunted. "We're in a fair bit of trouble here."

"Are you going to tell me what we're facing?"

"Karaxi are monstrous. Pretend to be nice little humans," the dwarf replied. "But they're really insatiable dwarf-eating monsters."

A stream of fire lashed out from Salamander's position, igniting the shambling woman's hair. As it staggered, terrible, inhuman screams emanated from the monster's stiff face. The cries intensifying, the creature raised its hands to tear at its hair.

Jonas skidded to a stop in front of his party, pelting Borim's shield with dirt. He sheathed a throwing knife and then drew both his daggers. His face had a dark expression. "We invited a lion to dinner and ended up with a dragon. Have you ever faced one of these creatures, Borim?"

The dwarf nodded. "One of them wandered into the tunnels near my home when I was a lad. It . . . took a lot to put down."

With clawed hands, the karaxi ripped off its hair, tossing aside the burning tangle before reaching up to shred a fleshy mask away from its face. As it loosed a series of clicking sounds, its dress billowed outwards to expose a tightly compressed insectoid body beneath. With an inhuman scream of rage, it stretched out its segmented body until its pointed head nearly reached the forest canopy.

"That is *not* an easy quest objective," Amara whispered to herself as she looked up in horror She could see her darts protruding from the creature's exoskeleton, and now she understood why they hadn't injured the monster; it was like throwing needles at a giant.

As Amara wove the strands of mana to call upon her *Divine Weapon*, another stream of fire struck the monster. Its thorax blackened and leaking clear fluid, the karaxi thrashed.

"Keep doing that!" Amara shouted to Salamander.

The flaming spectral form of her *Divine Weapon* took shape in front of her. Immediately, Amara sent her blade soaring at the karaxi. As the creature turned its attention toward the thicket where Salamander crouched, the blade smashed into the thing's face, knocking it off balance.

Jonas touched her shoulder and pointed at the staggering monster. "The exoskeleton of a karaxi has resistance to magical effects. Your sword won't penetrate it, but I have another idea."

True to his word, the impact of her *Divine Weapon* had driven the enormous insectoid creature back but hadn't inflicted any noticeable damage.

The karaxi, angry and injured from the fire spells, stampeded toward the party.

"Hurry up and talk, then," Amara shouted.

Borim braced to meet the charge, and when the monster brought down its front leg against his shield, there was a *crack*.

A *crunch*.

The karaxi chittered with pain. As it reared back, the end of its limb missing, clear fluid gushed from the stump. The insect's head swiveled, compound eyes glittering in the low light as it regarded the shield.

Amara couldn't help but smile as Mimi—in her Shield form—chewed merrily on the insect's severed limb. She'd had the idea to use Mimi for protection earlier in the day. If anyone tried to strike the dwarf, then they'd have to get through her hungry pet first.

*I guess my mimic can eat creatures with magical protection.*

Jonas pointed up into the trees. "I believe the spectral weapon should easily cut through those branches. If one of those was to fall on our assailant—"

Amara sent her *Divine Weapon* into the forest canopy. The sword gone, the karaxi focused its ire on the party.

"I don't think we're going to fool that overgrown praying mantis twice," Borim hollered as he prepared for another blow.

With a swing of its uninjured leg, the karaxi swept Borim and Mimi tumbling end over end into the thick underbrush.

With her protectors gone, Amara froze as the insect's eyes trained on her. She took a step back and raised her pitiful staff.

Jonas leapt to her defense, launching a flurry of blows against the overgrown insect before it could strike. None of the dagger thrusts injured the creature, but his sheer ferocity kept it off balance.

Amara glanced up at the trees, praying that her ghostly sword would work faster. When another gout of flames doused the creature's back, she backpedaled.

With a shriek, the karaxi unfolded its wings, the thin membranes being consumed by Salamander's liquid flames. The monster darted forward, impossibly fast for its size. As it trampled him under its massive legs, Jonas disappeared, his scream ending abruptly.

Amara hurled herself into the fight. As she raced forward, she cast *Cloak of Shadows*. The lush color leeched from the forest until only tones of gray remained.

Invisible, Amara dodged a wild swipe from the karaxi then rolled as it drove the pointed tip of its leg into the earth where she'd been standing. The soil exploded from the impact, launching dirt and leaves flying into the air. She picked herself up and then spotted Jonas under the karaxi. His face was covered in blood, and one arm hung limply at his side, but he was still alive.

The crack of breaking wood drew her attention to the canopy just in time to see a thick branch on its perilous descent. The limb smashed into the insect's abdomen, hammering it to the ground. Her spectral sword had finally cut through the wood—but it had done so while Jonas was underneath the monster.

She screamed the rogue's name, stumbling forward. Something slammed into her with the force of a speeding truck. Amara cartwheeled along the forest floor, the world upending before a tree trunk provided a jarring stop to her tumbling. With the impact, she felt something in her chest crack. The breath flew out of her and set off a quick report of coughs. With each hack, Amara saw colorless blood spray across the bark of the tree. Even as the spasms subsided, she struggled to draw air.

*I've broken a rib,* she thought, *and punctured a lung.* Then, *How did I know that?*

She quickly cast *Heal Wounds* on herself. The mana poured out of her soul, leaving her with precious little for whatever remained of this battle.

Taking in the situation, she noted that the karaxi had been crushed by the fallen branch. Many unidentifiable organs protruded from between the plates of its bulbous abdomen. But while its back segment was destroyed, its front half was still flailing about.

Amara heaved herself to her feet and mentally ordered the spectral sword to finish the creature. With a storm of falling leaves, the weapon descended from the canopy to bury itself in a section of cracked exoskeleton.

Borim, the mimic in shield form at his side, launched at the dying monster, and together they tore into it. While Mimi ripped off chunks with its teeth, the dwarf's axe cleaved through the chitinous plates. His ruddy face beamed with unbridled joy as he hacked the insect to pieces.

She stumbled forward, her *Cloak of Shadows* fading, and motes of light dancing around her as she healed. As Amara approached, her conjured weapon tore itself free from its foe, showering the area with a fountain of gore. The karaxi's frantic movements slowed, though Amara had to dodge a clumsy swipe of its crippled legs on her way to the monster's flank.

Jonas came into view.

The sight of the rogue standing there pushed a cry of relief from her lips.

While Mimi and Borim continued their gruesome work, Amara and Jonas staggered to a copse of trees. Behind her, the karaxi let out a final chittering gurgle then collapsed to the ground.

A notification appeared in her vision.

*Congratulations, Adventurer!*
*Through skill and bravery, you have defeated the heinous pig snatcher, leaving all the remaining swine safe.*
*Collect the quest reward from the owner of the Canning Farm.*

She ignored the quest completion notification, and even though Jonas was coated in unspeakably foul things, she still threw her arms around him. "I thought I lost you for a second."

Jonas stiffened, but then softened in her embrace. His hoarse voice was warm near her ear. "If it helps, I know where the baths are in the castle."

She laughed. Using the last of her mana, Amara cast *Heal Wounds* on Jonas. As the lacerations sealed and his dislocated shoulder slipped into place, the rigid creases on his face relaxed.

Borim sauntered up to them. Dripping with viscera and goo, the dwarf touched his bloody forehead. "I wouldn't mind one of those healing spells when you get a chance."

"Don't tell me something finally hurt your hard head?" Amara replied. "And here I thought it was made of granite."

"Even I have limitations, lass," Borim replied defensively. "I *was* fighting a giant magical insect, after all."

"I'm out of mana right now," she said, "but now's a good time to test one of the pills I gave you."

With a hearty nod, Borim fished around in his pocket with meaty fingers. After fetching the pill, he popped it into his mouth.

Amara watched with keen interest.

His beard bobbed as he swallowed. After a second, fleshy tendrils reached across the gash, stretching to meet one another and seal the wound.

As Amara had expected, the pill was intended for aid with minor injuries, and it seemed Borim's head required more care. While she could increase its efficacy by raising her skill level in the future, for now the pills would work in a pinch.

Borim stalked to the corpse and nudged it with the tip of his boot. "So, what vast treasures do we get from taking down this here creepy crawly? I'm thinking we deserve gold. A lot of gold."

Jonas shook some gunk off his hand. "The farmer has offered us some bacon when he culls the herd for winter."

"Bacon? I risked my life for bacon?" Borim roared. "Remind me to never, ever let you choose a quest again lest our next reward come in the form of a bouquet of mushrooms."

"Is that really all we'll receive for this?" Amara asked. "It seems a bit cheap."

Jonas shrugged. "They're a poor farming family in a war-ravaged community. It's what they can provide. However, the shell of a karaxi can be crafted into armor. That alone should earn us some silver."

"Why didn't you say so," Borim grumbled. "Let's get to work pulling it off."

"Before you go," Jonas said to Amara, "I wish to speak with you."

Amara stopped as she remembered that they still hadn't had their private talk. "What's on your mind?"

"I wasn't . . . completely honest last night," he said quietly. "When we found you? I told you that I joined the others in their efforts to storm the fortress so that I might . . . be a hero of the innocents that I would surely find cowering in your wake. But that's . . . that's not why. I didn't do it to save the people."

"You didn't?"

"No," he replied. " After we talked . . . I couldn't . . . I was beside myself with worry at the thought that something terrible might befall *you*. I . . . It was you. I did it for you," Jonas repeated.

She gave him a lopsided smile. "I had a feeling."

"And furthermore . . ." His words trailed off. He took a moment to study his boots. Without looking at her, he continued, "I just wanted to say . . . I believe you. It's hard to comprehend, of course, and flies in the face of sane belief, but . . . well, much of the evidence points to you being an avatar. I will support you in meeting your goals."

Amara felt a surge of warmth spread through her. She knew it hadn't been easy for him to be so vulnerable. To admit so much after his earlier protests.

"However, I wanted to speak to you away from the castle. It regards Lady Ingrid," he continued. "Her situation is dire and she is, understandably, desperate. Desperation is dangerous. A drowning man will often drag down those who mean to save him. I fear the baroness will do the same to you."

"I don't think she would do anything to hurt me."

"Perhaps not intentionally," Jonas countered, "but I feel that her judgement is compromised. I urge you not to do anything on your own without us."

"I promise. I'll be careful, and I'll run everything past our group first."

Amara glanced over at Borim, who was struggling to pry off a plate of exoskeleton from the karaxi.

She said, "We really should help him with that thing."

Jonas nodded.

After they harvested the karaxi carcass of anything useful, the quartet trudged back to the castle. When they emerged from the forest, Emmaline and Noah awaited them.

"What do you think you're doing?" the priestess demanded. "The baroness didn't give you permission to go cavorting about the forest like a dryad."

"Probably consorting with the enemy," Noah said, words dripping with scorn. "Are you planning to help your Issurian master to invade our castle, *avatar?*"

"Best be watching your mouth," Borim growled, putting himself between his leader and Noah.

Amara touched the dwarf's shoulder. "I can handle this." To Noah she said, "I'll speak slowly so you can understand. What. Do. You. Want?"

Borim chuckled.

Noah's expression darkened further. Hand twitching for the hilt of his sword, he lurched in Amara's direction. Emmaline's hands shot out to grip the large, armored forearm of her companion. Regarding Amara with steel in her gaze, the priestess said,

"The baroness must be informed of all your movements. Do you understand?"

"We just completed a quest to help out a farmer," Amara explained. "There was a karaxi in the forest stealing livestock. We dealt with it before it could attack the village. I assumed the baroness would appreciate the aid."

Emmaline gasped, "A karaxi?" Schooling her features, she recovered her composure and continued. "Yes, and by spending your efforts on peasants' tasks, you've wasted Lady Ingrid's precious time. She is planning a breakout and has requested your help. You will accompany our forces as they ride through the goblins' lines before their push to Oksberg."

"We're abandoning the fortress?"

"Of course not," Emmaline replied, as though speaking to a toddler. "Only the messengers will continue on. Your horse is saddled."

Without another word, Emmaline put her back to the party and strode back to the castle with Noah stalking along at her side.

Amara frowned. "I think I have a problem."

"What do you mean?" Jonas asked.

"I can't ride a horse."

Jonas crossed his arms. "That truly *is* a problem."

# CHAPTER 29

ozens of horses waited in their barding as adventurers and guards swarmed the castle courtyard. At the center of the activity stood Lady Ingrid, resplendent in gleaming white armor, a sword sheathed on her belt. Her face was still drawn, but she exuded a renewed vigor as she strode about giving orders.

Amara approached one of the nearest horses and hesitantly extended her hand. Aside from an encounter at a petting zoo when she was a child, she'd never been this close to one of these huge beasts before. Even in her new boots, Amara's full height only matched the horse's shoulder.

*How could you control something so powerful?*

"And what mischief have you gotten up to already?" Lady Ingrid asked.

The baroness had waded through the throng to join Amara. The lady now studied Amara, her gaze tracing up and down the cleric's form.

"There was a karaxi stealing pigs," Amara explained. Though still shaken by how close to catastrophe the battle had brought them, she tried to sound flippant. "So, my group dealt with it."

"A karaxi?" Ingrid tilted her head to the side. "Surely, you're joking."

Amara shook her head.

"In the future, I must insist that you clear all quests with me," Ingrid said. "Those creatures are dangerous—even for a group of experienced fighters–and you faced it with your . . . motley band. Ah, that reminds me."

The baroness reached into a pouch at her hip, withdrawing a chain. As she offered it to Amara, the chain unspooled to dangle from her hand, revealing a pendant of dull metal.

"Congratulations on becoming an adventurer," Lady Ingrid said.

Any annoyance Amara felt in regard to the baroness's demands disappeared as she reverently took the necklace and examined it. The pendant was about the size of a silver dollar. Engravings of fanciful monsters decorated the edge.

Writing immediately filled her vision.

*New Rank Achieved: Pewter*
*Through earning your initial rank, you have embarked on the first step to becoming a renowned adventurer. Any Adventurer's Guild will now provide quests appropriate to your level and rank.*

Lady Ingrid continued, "As the representative of the Adventurer's Guild here, I grant you permanent membership. Pewter is the lowest level, I'm afraid, but you'll progress through the ranks automatically as you complete quests and defeat monsters."

"So, the necklace is magical?"

Ingrid nodded. "It is imbued with magic that will track your deeds, so any chapter of the guild will be able to see them. Also, and possibly most pertinent to your interests, no adventurer who wears this may be turned away by guards or watchmen. Even those who have an undesirable class like a Trickster Cleric," she added with a grin.

Amara looped the chain around her neck and clutched the pendant close to her chest. "Thank you, my lady."

"I've not yet begun to repay my debt to you." Motioning for Amara to follow her, Lady Ingrid moved toward the main gate of the keep. "Come. Before we ride out, I want you properly armored."

"About that."

Ingrid arched her eyebrow. "Yes?"

"I . . . don't know how to ride a horse."

"I see." Ingrid pressed her lips together. "Unfortunate, however, I may have a solution. Armory first."

Amara waved at her friends who were clustered nearby and then followed the baroness. Once inside, Ingrid stopped at a heavy iron-bound door and produced a key. She placed it in the lock and then twisted it with some difficulty. The door swung open to reveal a dusty space.

"At the start of the siege, this room contained all manner of magical weapons and armor," Ingrid said wistfully. "Months of battle, however, have taken their toll on our supplies."

The baroness approached the rack and gestured to the armor it held. "I believe this will suit you, Avatar."

Amara studied the finely crafted leather, running her fingers over the metal bindings to trace the artistic whorls that adorned it.

Unsure of herself of how she should respond, Amara replied simply. "It's very nice."

"The armor is crafted in the style of the First Empire," Ingrid said. "Some believe it is a remnant of a time when Galoth himself fought the Forces of Chaos here." She traced a finger along the spirals on the breastplate. "There is magic crafted into the leather, and any damage will repair itself over time. Also, it's self-cleaning, which is a very pleasant feature when on campaign."

"This is too much—"

"Nonsense," Ingrid interrupted. Hefting the breastplate from its stand, she added, "Please. Let me help you put it on."

Amara removed her stained dress and then wiggled into the armor. The breast plate fit a bit loosely, but the baroness added some padding to keep it in place. Next, Ingrid took up a skirt made up of leather strips and fastened it around Amara's waist. Amara adjusted the richly-tooled bracers on her arms. The greaves went on last and took a bit more adjusting than the other pieces of armor.

When they finished, Amara imagined that she resembled a warrior princess. Without a mirror nearby, she would have to gauge her appearance on the reactions of others.

Lady Ingrid removed a quiver from the wall and offered it to Amara. "I noticed you favor darts. This will let you carry them more easily."

When she took the quiver from Ingrid, she was surprised by its weight. With relief and gratitude, Amara noted that it held at least a dozen fletched missiles.

"Unfortunately, not many use such a primitive weapon as a staff, so we rarely keep any in the armory. However, I have commissioned a new staff for you," Ingrid continued. "Until it's ready, you'll have to keep using your . . . stick."

Amara slung the quiver over her shoulder, and then adjusted it until it felt right. "I can't thank you enough," she said. "You've been more than generous."

"This is only the beginning of the gifts I plan to lavish on you," Ingrid said. "You saved my life and now you're going to defeat the army threatening my fief. These items are mere trinkets compared to what you deserve, Avatar."

Feeling more awkward by the moment, Amara protested, "I'm thrilled with what you've already given me."

As if she'd not heard the cleric, Lady Ingrid whisked to the door, sweeping Amara up along the way. "Now that you're prepared for battle, there's someone I'd like you to meet."

"Who?"

"You'll see," Ingrid said with a mysterious smile.

The first step in her armor felt strange. As she left the room, she frowned as she had to adjust her leather skirt again. It was obvious the armor would take some getting used to.

Amara wanted to press the baroness for information, but she held her tongue. After all, Ingrid had lavished her with gifts—the dearest of which was her belief in Amara, her trust. She would let her have her fun.

Ingrid led the way through the dim corridors. When they came to the base of a tower, she opened the door and climbed the stairs two at a time. From stairs to a ladder: the baroness shimmied up the rungs and disappeared through a hatch in the ceiling.

Amara looked up through the small opening through which Lady Ingrid had vanished. *Couldn't we meet the baroness's friend on the ground floor?*

Shrugging wearily, she gripped a rung and hauled herself up. After squeezing through the hatch, she flopped unceremoniously onto the roof of the tower.

Encumbered by her new armor, she made an ungainly spectacle of getting to her knees. Looking up, she found herself staring directly into the enormous face of a dragon.

Rolling away, Amara uttered a cry of alarm and began the work of forming a spell in her mind. She froze in place, watching Lady Ingrid petting the neck of the creature.

Shimmying away, Amara whispered, "You have a pet dragon?"

"No, not a dragon." Lady Ingrid smiled, stroking the creature's head. "She is a wyvern, a much smaller cousin of the dragons. As it turns out," the baroness continued, "we have quite a bit in common, you and I."

Amara couldn't take her eyes off the scaly creature. Its body was wrapped around the top of the tower and had to be 30 feet long. "We do?"

"To strengthen the duchy, my family married me off to a much older man," Lady Ingrid said. "I was immature and showed little interest in him. To win me over, he showered me with many gifts. In particular, a certain bauble from a traveling Elven merchant."

Amara raised her brow. "The Great Galando?"

"The very same," she said. "It wasn't the first purchase my husband made from Galando. He spent mountains of silver on eggs, hoping to impress me. The castle to filled with giant rats and flying snakes; monsters any novice adventurer could dispatch with ease. It was then that the elf provided me with Nyrax's egg."

Ingrid smiled. "You're lucky, Amara. My beloved pet grew too large to sleep in my bedroom several years ago, otherwise you may have had a more difficult time infiltrating the castle."

"She's impressive," Amara stated, "but why are you showing her to me now?"

"Because you will ride her today."

Amara's eyes widened. "You want me to ride a dragon?"

"A wyvern," Lady Ingrid corrected. "I promise you'll be completely safe on her back during our breakout."

"Unless I fall off!"

Lady Ingrid pointed at the wyvern's back, indicating a series of leather straps attached to a high saddle. "Specially crafted for safe flying. Once you are secured, there is no way to fall off."

"But what if she decides to eat me?"

"Unless I'm greatly mistaken, I believe you have one of Galando's pets as well. Which means you know there is no danger from Nyrax."

The thought of riding a horse scared her, but the proposition of soaring through the air was much, much worse. However, the baroness was right; her pet wasn't inherently dangerous and should remain that way so long as Amara didn't give Lady Ingrid any reason to harm her. And the wyvern would allow Amara to accompany her group on this task. If she was honest with herself, she was just reaching for any excuse to not fly on the giant winged reptile.

Amara conceded.

"Where are we sending the messengers, anyway?"

"Even with your impressive healing skills, our few remaining defenders are insufficient to hold the castle. I'm sending messengers to all the towns and castles in the North. I apologize for not filling you in immediately, Avatar. Now that the gods have returned, they must heed our call for aid this time."

*This time?* she thought with some alarm.

"Have you . . . attempted this already?" Amara asked slowly.

"Yes, we sent out messengers when we were first besieged. Everything is different now, though."

"And what happens if they don't come?"

Lady Ingrid stared at Amara, her eyes wild with religious fervor. "You. You will happen, Avatar. I believe in you and I know that you will drive back the Forces of Chaos from my home. You will save us all."

"Yes, of course," Amara said.

Worry blossomed in her chest. Though grateful for the baroness and her trust, Amara recoiled at Lady Ingrid's absolute faith. She knew there was no chance that she alone could defeat the army of Chaos. What if she couldn't live up to her impossibly high standards? The spiritual zeal left Lady Ingrid, her demeanor returning to the even-keeled normal Amara had come to know. "Let's get you in the saddle," she said. "The sooner we depart, the sooner a relief force will arrive."

The wyvern lowered itself to the ground at the baroness's approach, and she helped Amara climb up into the high saddle. As the baroness fastened her in, she gazed out over the land from her vantage point atop the tower.

From her perch atop the wyvern, Amara gazed upon a swelling sea of trees stretching out in every direction. To the north, vast snow-capped mountains were barely visible through the haze. An endless wine-dark sea disappearing over the horizon. There was no sign of any civilization here apart from Stout Oak Keep.

With a tug on the leather straps to test the security of her work, Lady Ingrid regarded Amara with excitement. "There we go. Sit tight. When we're ready to leave, I'll call for Nyrax."

Lady Ingrid disappeared into the hatch and made her way back down the ladder. In an attempt to peer down into the courtyard below, Amara shifted and stretched in the saddle, but no matter how she craned her neck, she couldn't see past the high battlements. Amara settled in to wait and pulled up her character sheet. If she was going to be here for a while, she might as well allocate her new points from leveling up.

| Amara Solace (Pewter Ranked Adventurer) | Trickster Cleric, Level 5 |
|---|---|
| Stats | |
| Strength | 7 |
| Dexterity | 3 |
| Constitution | 7 |
| Intelligence | 4 |
| Wisdom | 12 |
| Charisma | 1 |
| Vitality | 6 |
| Luck | 13 |
| New Stat Points | 3 |
| | |
| Titles | Titan Slayer (Rank 1) |
| | |
| Weapon Proficiencies | |
| Staff | Novice |
| Darts | Novice |
| | |
| Skills | |
| First Aid | Apprentice |
| Herbalism | Apprentice |
| Alchemy | Apprentice |
| | |
| Martial Abilities | |
| Dart Dead Eye | Novice |
| | |
| Spells | |

| | |
|---|---|
| **Cloak of Shadows** | 1st Circle |
| **Charm Person** | 1st Circle |
| **Heal Wounds** | 2nd Circle |
| **Divine Weapon** | 1St Circle |
| **Avatar of Melischar** | Inactive |
| | |
| **New Expertise Points** | 1 |

# CHAPTER 30

Amara paused when her gaze reached her new rank, pleased to see she was finally an adventurer. After she'd completed her quest to restore Galoth's wall, it should make things a lot easier for her out in the world. When she had a chance later, she'd have to ask Lady Ingrid how to advance her rank. She hoped it was something simple like slaying a certain monster or completing a pre-determined number of quests.

The sound of horses whinnying below made her return her focus to her character sheet. She wanted to finish leveling up before they departed from the keep.

She briefly considered adding some points to Wisdom again, but then her gaze dropped to Constitution on her sheet. Soon, she knew she would face incredibly powerful opponents. And her ability to take hits and keep going might decide a battle.

After hesitating for a moment, she dumped two points into constitution and then her final point into luck. No matter what, she wasn't going to stop increasing her Luck. As per usual, she didn't feel any immediate difference, but hopefully she'd be sturdier in the next fight.

Her stat points dealt with, she turned her attention to her expertise point. She briefly considered saving it to upgrade another of her spells, but right now she didn't feel her class was very well rounded. She needed a wider range of spells to deal with future threats.

Amara ignored her other abilities and selected spells. Familiar writing appeared in her vision.

**Select Casting School to Unlock Random Spell:**
**Healing**
**Offensive**
**Defensive**

**Support**
**Speciality: Trickster Cleric**


She ignored Healing and Offensive, happy with her current options. She instead focused on Defensive and Support spells. While it would be nice to support the others, what she needed right now was a defensive spell when she found herself in trouble.

Amara selected Defensive and more writing scrolled through the air in front of her.


**New Spell Unlocked**
**Holy Light**
**A divine light appears in your palm and increases in intensity until it blinds everything in a 30' radius. If any creatures or humanoids who serve Chaos are struck by the spell, then they will be filled with the overwhelming urge to flee. Group members are immune to the spell's effect.**
**Duration: 1 minute + 0.5 minute per caster level**


She felt vaguely disappointed that she didn't get an upgrade this time, but she knew she couldn't always rely on her Luck stat. And the spell—while somewhat underwhelming compared to her other ones—should still serve her well.

From the courtyard below came a bellowing cry. Nyrax perked up at the sound and, using the tips of her front wings to stabilize herself, she lurched toward the battlements. She craned her sinuous neck, seeking. Waiting.

At the sight of the wyvern preparing to take off, Amara gripped the saddle tightly until her knuckles turned white. She'd never flown before and she wasn't sure what to expect. When her mount launched itself off the tower, her stomach did a flip flop as the ground fell away beneath them. She forced herself to look straight ahead, because if she didn't, she thought she might be sick.

The wyvern soared across the courtyard and then flapped out over the wall. Once outside, it circled as the castle gates disgorged the riders, with Lady Ingrid taking the lead on a pure white horse.

Judging by the mass of horses and fighters, Amara guessed that every able body in the fief had been assembled for this mission. After watching guards in Lady Ingrid's livery swarm out of the castle, she was able to spot her companions on their mounts near the back of the force. Behind them, Ackley's quartet rode among the ununiformed stragglers. Though she hadn't seen them previously, Amara assumed that the duelist and his mates had arrived while she'd been asleep.

The armed group cantered towards the forest, and several of the guards waved at the peasants who thronged the road to watch them. A handful of the farmers threw flowers as the riders passed, while others cheered at their appearance. But most of them remained silent, perhaps fearing that the lady and her guards were abandoning them to their fate.

As the wyvern soared above the valley, Amara loosened her grip on the saddle and felt her muscles begin to relax. Though she'd seen plenty of videos depicting air travel, she'd never had the chance to try it. They didn't do the real experience justice. She felt excited for the first time in a long while.

The wyvern made a dive. With a little scream of surprise, Amara clutched at her saddle and watched the ground come careening toward them. She clenched her eyes, willing away the inevitable impact. Nyrax spread her wings and with agile grace, the creature came to rest in a field next to the dirt road.

"What are you doing?" Amara yelled. "Why did you land?"

Immediately, she felt silly for asking the wyvern questions. Of course it couldn't answer her. The wyvern didn't move until Lady Ingrid reached their position.

The baroness pulled back on her horse's reins and smiled. "I see you're taking well to your new mount, Avatar."

"I don't know what happened," she said, holding her hands out helplessly. "Did I do something wrong?"

Ingrid shook her head. "With your weight on her back, Nyrax can only fly for short distances. She will have to take regular breaks as we ride."

Amara chewed on her lower lip, realizing in that moment that she felt much safer in the sky. *On the ground,* she thought, *I'm a much easier target. Hopefully, Ingrid knows what she's doing.*

Before Amara could say more, Nyrax unfurled her wings and propelled them back up into the air. With a very unladylike yelp, Amara clutched her saddle. Below, the riders and their mounts diminished until all she could see of them were dark specks in the forest. The wind buffeted her as her mount rose higher into the sky, and she felt the cold bite at her exposed legs and arms.

The wyvern rode the air currents, gliding above the treetops. From her saddle, Amara could see the radiant white of Lady Ingrid's armor glinting in the forest.

Beneath her, Nyrax rumbled with a deep growl.

Amara spotted movement. A guard in the queue below clutched his chest and tumbled from his horse. Among the trees, something stirred as the riders passed. A cloud of arrows. A flood of orange bodies.

A horde of goblins ambushed the column.

"Do not stop for anything!" Ingrid shouted from the head of the column, her voice faint on the wind. "We ride to Oksberg!"

The riders parted around the downed guard who lay unmoving in the road. Amara fought down the urge to order the wyvern to land in the hopes she could heal the man. But she needed to trust Ingrid here. If the messengers didn't get through, then no one would arrive to aid the castle. And without help, they were doomed.

Ahead of them, goblins poured onto the road, shaking their spears and blocking the riders' path forward. The wyvern let out a roar that shook the forest. Tucking her wings close to her body, Nyrax dove at the skirmish below.

The ranks of spearmen fell beneath a sweeping attack from the wyvern's dagger-like talons. As Nyrax aimed to return to the sky, Amara looked down to see that her mount had left nothing but umber piles of small corpses.

While the soldiers crashed upon the goblin blockade, Amara could only sit in her saddle and watch with frustration. Powerless to have any effect on the goings on below, she used her vantage point to scan the battlefield. The ensuing melee was furious but brief; soon, Lady Ingrid's forces routed their foes, and the remaining goblins scattered into the forest.

*No matter what, I need to learn to ride,* she thought. *I can't do anything to help up here.*

Without warning, Nyrax banked to the left. The steep curve of the wyvern's trajectory forced Amara to scrabble for a secure hold on her seat. In the sky where they had been just a heartbeat earlier, a mass of arrows tore through the air.

The goblins were shooting at her.

Below, another adventurer fell from their horse. A group of others stopped to form a circle around the injured person, Amara could only watch helplessly as the goblins crashed over them like a burnt-orange wave. She was too far away to use her darts, and not even her *Divine Weapon* could stop that many goblins. She tore her gaze away as the goblins overwhelmed the adventurers, viciously hacking and stabbing at them.

Amara searched the column until she spotted Jonas riding hard near the front. Behind him on the saddle, Salamander clung to his waist. Trundling along behind, Borim rode a pony almost as shaggy as he. Mimi, in her shield form, hung from the back of the saddle, bouncing with the mount's earnest gait.

Relief surged within Amara at the sight of her companions. Though more goblins flooded the road with every passing second, her friends were safe for the moment.

With a deft motion of the reins, Lady Ingrid sawed on her reins and wheeled her mount around. Drawing her sword, she slashed the gleaming blade through the air. A crescent of silvery light burst from the cutting edge of her weapon, flying into the line of trees nearby. Trunks exploded into splinters, leaving only jagged rows of mangled stumps.

Amara could only stare in shock at the power on display. With a single swipe of her weapon, she'd destroyed a vast swath of the forest bordering the road.

*What level is Ingrid with that sort of ability? No wonder Emmaline had said saving the keep without the baroness would be impossible.*

The goblins, apparently, shared Amara's awe. The diminutive swarm fled, leaving only corpses on the road.

The wyvern circled the scene, then came in for a landing. From atop Nyrax, Amara counted the crumpled forms lying in the road. Apart from the mass of goblins, she noted four adventurers and one guard. Though her initial hope had been to heal these people, she quickly realized that there was no point in trying; her skills—from spells to pills—would not be enough to reattach limbs and heads.

"That's quite the mount you have, lass," Borim shouted from his pony. "Where do I get one of those?"

"Quiet," Ingrid barked. "The goblins are not alone in the forest, and you are giving away our position. We continued to ride until we reach the main road to Oksberg. Do not stop for anything."

The dwarf tugged on his beard but said nothing further.

Jonas nodded a greeting to Amara. From behind him, Salamander peeked out and gave a little wave. At the sight of the wyvern, her eyes grew to the size of saucers.

Lady Ingrid nudged her horse into a trot and the column started moving again.

Amara's mind flared with a warning. *Danger. Imminent.* Nyrax took to the air, her massive wings beating hard to gain altitude. The creature must have sensed a threat because it didn't even look back as it desperately climbed.

Ingrid kicked her horse into a gallop. Soon, the whole column thundered down the trail behind her, their mounts' hooves kicking up clods of dirt.

Terrible roars filled the forest, and when she peered down through the dense foliage, her heart almost stopped in her chest. Dozens of creatures—things Amara could only describe as "demons"—slipped through the trees like wraiths. From her mount, she could see horns curling around the top of their heads. Acting as rear guard for the ranks of demons, a group of towering figures stomped through the forest

*Are those giants?*

The enemies chased the riders for a short distance, but the frantic pace of the horses increased the riders' lead. Unable to match the column's speed, the demonic attackers broke off their pursuit and melted back into the forest.

Amara could breathe again only once she saw that the riders were safe. From the wyvern's back, she couldn't have intervened, no matter how badly the battle went. Her place was at her group's side, no matter what they faced.

After a few leagues, Lady Ingrid slowed the column's pace. For the next hour or so, the horses cantered toward a crossroads. At the divergence in the path, the baroness pulled her mount to a halt and waited for the others to catch up.

As if she'd received a silent command, the wyvern swooped low to land beside Lady Ingrid. Nyrax stretched out her long neck, leaning her head in toward her keeper for a well-deserved scratch.

"Well done, my darling," Lady Ingrid cooed at her pet. "You kept her safe the entire time."

Amara blurted, "Is this why you wanted me riding Nyrax? To keep me excluded from battle?"

Ingrid nodded. "I must keep you safe at all costs."

"I won't ever do that again," she said with barely contained anger.

"As I said," the baroness said, steel reinforcing her voice, "you *will* be kept safe."

Amara frowned and bit down a retort. This was not the time to pick a fight with the baroness, but in the future, Amara would be the one to decide when and where she fought, not her benefactor.

Amara noted Uwe among the throng of guards. He still wouldn't meet her gaze.

*When he returns from delivering his message,* Amara thought, *I'll make it up to him. How do you say sorry for almost feeding someone to your pet mimic?.*

Lady Ingrid addressed the guards. "You all have your assignments. May the gods watch over you."

A dozen guards from Stout Oak Keep—the humble contingent comprised of nearly all that remained of the castle's defenders—split from the main column and headed down the road.

Once they had disappeared into the distance, Lady Ingrid gathered the lingering riders. "Come," she said. "We will return to the castle by a safer route."

Ackley nudged his horse forward. "If you had a safer method, why did we just ride through that gauntlet?"

"Do not forget your place, adventurer," Lady Ingrid said, her gaze smoldering. "In this siege, every hour counts, and I'll not squander a single minute. The alternate path is much longer, but remains as yet undiscovered by Malcheron's scouts."

Ackley gave a casual wave of his hand. "You needed only say as much, my lady."

Though he appeared repentant, his cool smile didn't continue into his eyes. A dark murmur spread through his group, with Kymber looking especially annoyed.

As Lady Ingrid guided her horse into the forest, Amara hoped the baroness decision had been worth the lives lost. She prayed to the gods of this world that the messengers would accomplish their goals and return to the keep safely. She would do everything she could to hold the keep. That was certain. *But demons? Giants?* After catching a glimpse of what awaited her, slivers of doubt wormed their way into her heart, whispering to Amara that all she could do would never be enough.

# CHAPTER 31

Flying from her perch atop the wyvern, Amara gazed across the valley as the last rays of the setting sun cast long shadows below. In the middle of the river, the castle shone like a blazing beacon. Torches dotted the walls, and a bonfire in front of the bridge sent glowing embers swirling into the air. Crowds had gathered nearby, and it looked like everyone had turned out from the nearby village.

Gathering nearby, villagers blithely milled about. To her eyes, it looked as if the whole of Fusson had turned up. At first, she feared they had taken to the keep after an attack, but the crowds were calm, and Amara couldn't see signs of any damage to the palisade. More importantly, she didn't see any demons or giants roaming the valley.

The wyvern glided in a wide arc over the courtyard before landing gently a few dozen paces from the gates. A group of guards, unbothered by the baroness's mount, continued their casual march toward the castle. However, the peasants under their escort shied away at the sight of the beast.

Safely on the ground, Amara fumbled at the saddle straps, her legs aching from sitting so long in this restrained, unnatural position. She'd almost freed herself by the time Lady Ingrid and the others reached her.

The baroness dismounted lithely and strode to Amara. After unfastening the last strap, Lady Ingrid said, "I hope you won't find it presumptuous of me, but I left orders to arrange a feast in your honor tonight. Upon your arrival, I will announce that you are Melischar's avatar."

Amara disentangled herself from the saddle and took Lady Ingrid's offered hand to dismount the wyvern. As soon as her feet touched the ground, Nyrax leapt into the air and flew toward her roost in the tower.

"Announcing me? Are you sure that's a good idea?" Amara asked as she rubbed her back. "What if some of these people support the Church?"

She also wondered if any humans served the gods of Chaos. *Could there be traitors in our midst?* She decided to ask the baroness about that when they were in private.

"Nonsense," Lady Ingrid replied. "The North remembers the gods. Your presence will inspire these people to continue to resist Malcheron and his forces. An avatar has finally returned, and it must be celebrated from the highest towers. Don't you understand? You've saved us all!"

Ingrid stared at her with unblinking eyes. Amara avoided the intense gaze and scanned the crowd. Most of them looked like simple farmers and craftsman. *As long as they aren't fanatics like the members of the Church,* she mused, *everything should be fine.*

"My maids await you inside." Lady Ingrid frowned before she continued. "Well, the ones who didn't flee, that is. They will help you attain the proper look for the feast."

"That's really not necessary—"

Lady Ingrid silenced her with a raised hand. "I must insist. Your presentation as a divine avatar will inspire the people, and I won't introduce you while wearing anything as pedestrian as leather armor. I'll brook no argument in the matter."

Amara searched for her group in the hopes they might rescue her. She spotted them near the rear of the column. Though she was able to catch Jonas's attention, the baroness whisked her into the keep before he or anyone else might come to her aid.

Through the courtyards, up the many stairs, they came to the armored golems maintained their vigil over the lady's chambers. Amara approached them warily. She almost feared they would react to her as she passed, however, neither guardian stirred from its position.

A pair of young female servants, dressed in simple robes, appeared and opened the door for them. Ingrid strode into the room first and tossed her riding gloves aside. When Amara didn't follow suit, she stared at the glove covering her hand.

"May I ask why you wear that?"

Amara rubbed her palm, pondering what she should tell the baroness. Aside from the heavy scarring and occasional stiffness, she barely noticed her burned arm anymore.

With a bit of trepidation, she pulled off her glove to reveal the wrinkled, red skin beneath. She flexed her hand. Though, for a moment, she considered rolling up her sleeve to show the rest of her injury, but then decided to leave it covered. There was no reason to reveal the extent of her burns.

"This is a small present from the Church," Amara said, lifting her hand into the light. "When they found out about me, they sent a kill squad to deal with me."

Lady Ingrid raised her brow. "And you escaped? That's no small feat for someone of your level."

"I had help," she admitted. "A monk from the city came to warn me. And I . . . killed some members of the Church."

The memory of her spectral sword carving through the crossbowman haunted her thoughts.

"If they tried to harm an avatar, then they deserved much worse," Lady Ingrid said, her voice shaking with emotion. "Should anyone try to hurt you here, they will beg for a swift death."

Amara nodded. "I just thought I should tell you the whole story."

"And I appreciate your honesty."

Lady Ingrid walked over to a door on the far side of the room and threw it open to release a wave of heat. "Now," she said, "let's get you cleaned up."

Amara stepped into the adjoining room and was surprised to see a bath—complete with complex copper piping. Steam rose from the surface of the water, and there were all manner of bottles and jars arrayed next to the tub. The drawn bath was a welcome sight. The closest thing to a proper wash Amara had managed in recent weeks was a quick dip in a frigid stream.

"Would you like some help with your bath" Ingrid asked. "I have several servants who would be happy to scrub you clean."

"I'm fine," Amara said hastily. She didn't want anyone watching her take a bath, let alone touching her.

"As you wish." Ingrid stepped back through the door and then shut it behind her gently. "Please, just call out if you need anything."

Amara reached up to take off her armor, but then realized she had no idea how to remove it. Maybe she should have taken the baroness up on her offer. At the very least, the servants could have helped her loosen the fastenings.

She worked at the buckles for several minutes, cursing as she struggled to remove the armor. Finally, she gave up and simply pulled the breastplate over her head. The other pieces came off more easily, and she placed them against the wall carefully. She didn't want to damage a gift from the baroness.

The water nearly scalded her, but she lowered herself in. She spent the next several minutes examining the many bottles and jars until she settled on a simple bar of soap. In her other life, most of the girls at her school had often talked about their extensive beauty regimes, but Amara was content with her cheaper soap and shampoo.

After she had thoroughly scrubbed herself free of any remaining trace of grime and karaxi goo, she stood up and grabbed a towel. Carefully, she stepped out of the tub. As she dried herself, she glanced over at her dirty garments. She didn't want to put them on again after bathing. Padding to the door, she called out, "Do you have any clothes I can wear?"

Lady Ingrid—who opened the door with such speed, she must have been waiting outside the room for her to finish—flung open the door and announced, "I have just the thing."

Leaving the bathroom with nothing but a towel on, Amara shrank with modesty. But, then again, she had stripped down to her small clothes in front of the baroness earlier in the armory.

As she emerged from the bathroom, Ingrid marched over to one of the many cabinets and opened the heavily lacquered door. She pulled out what looked like a ball gown from inside and then held it across her arm for Amara to see. While most of the gown was made of a green floral-pattern fabric, a deep burgundy stripe ran down the center.

On Earth, Amara wouldn't have been caught dead is something so garish.

"I . . . don't think that's for me," she said slowly, hoping to conceal her distaste. "Maybe I could just wear some breeches and a tunic like you have on?"

"Perhaps this one, then?"

Ingrid pulled out a golden sheath with a scandalously low neckline and an incredibly high hemline.

"I'd rather kiss a giant rat," Amara blurted, as her eyes widened at the sight of the gown. When the baroness disappeared back into the closet, Amara called after her, "I don't see why you want to dress me up like some prissy noblewoman."

"I have no love of wearing dresses either," Lady Ingrid said, smiling at Amara's words. "However, this will be the first time an avatar has been presented in public in over a millennium. If we are to convince my subjects that you are an avatar reborn, then we must present you as a divine woman. It's why I gifted you a suit of armor from the First Empire for your questing. Not since Galoth reigned has an avatar walked these lands."

"Then let me wear my armor to the feast. An avatar is supposed to fight, not sip tea and gossip, or whatever someone who wears *that* dress would do." She suspected anyone who would wear the gold dress had other things on their mind, but she didn't want to insult the baroness by saying it out loud.

"Please," Lady Ingrid pressed, "this is the only time I will ask you to dress for court. Afterwards, you may wear whatever you wish."

Amara mulled over the situation then, when she realized her choices were slim, she scowled. "Fine, let me try on that first one."

Lady Ingrid smiled then called out to her servants who had been waiting nearby.

With the help of the two young women, Amara struggled into the green floral monstrosity. Then she had to stand still for nearly an hour as the women made minor alterations to fit the garment to her. By the time they were done, she was almost ready to bolt. She'd rather fight a karaxi bare-handed and with no mana than go through this torment again.

"Very impressive," Ingrid murmured.

"I'd hardly call it *impressive*," she said, her irritation leaking into her voice. "Look how tight the top is on me!"

"That's the bodice," Lady Ingrid said, "and it's meant to be worn that way."

Barely able to breathe in the constricting fit, Amara tugged down on the sides of the dress. "Can we just get this over with?"

"Once we fix . . . well," the baroness wiggled her fingers at Amara's hair. "That."

"My hair is fine," Amara replied hotly. "I just want to go eat and see my friends."

"There is no point only painting half a portrait," Lady Ingrid said. "I promise it won't take long."

Amara fumed but allowed the servants to do their work. They braided her hair before coiling it around the back of her head in a crown, adorning her tresses with pins with glowing amber gems.

When the job was finished, they brought over a dull silver mirror for Amara to view their handiwork.

She was surprised at the reflection that greeted her. She looked more mature and healthier than she had back on Earth. And while she still wouldn't turn any heads, she almost looked the part of a noblewoman. She smoothed down the front of her dress, still uncomfortable with how tight it was, and then spun a bit to make it billow outwards.

*I guess I don't look terrible.*

"We better be done now," Amara said to Lady Ingrid. If the baroness tried to paint her face, she'd probably use *Cloak of Shadows* to escape. There was a limit to what she was willing to endure, and she'd long ago surpassed it.

As she took a step back to examine her, Lady Ingrid said, "I suppose this will have to do. I must admit, the jewels are a nice touch. Come, let's go join everyone in the great hall."

The baroness was still wearing her stained armor and had her longsword belted around her waist.

"Wait. Aren't you going to change, too?" Amara asked as she crossed her arms.

"I will be wearing this to the feast. It's important I present a more martial appearance to my people."

"So, I have to dress up like a silly Renaissance actor, while you get to look like a warrior princess?" Amara exclaimed. "There's no way you're making me wear a dress while you get to keep your armor."

Lady Ingrid furrowed her brow. "What is a *Renaissance actor*?" She waved her hand as if the brush away the question. "Regardless, I have chosen to wear my armor, and I will not hear any more on the subject."

"If I'm wearing a dress, then you are, too." Amara cocked her head to the side, glaring a challenge at the baroness.

Lady Ingrid met her gaze. After a tense moment, she sighed and rolled her eyes. "I suppose it's not fair, indeed." She gestured at one of her maids. "Fetch that unpleasant red dress my husband gifted to me last year."

The servant scurried away, quickly returning with a beautiful scarlet gown of a similar cut to Amara's. In minutes, the experienced maids had stripped down the baroness, and helped her into the garment. If possible, Ingrid looked even more uncomfortable in a dress than Amara.

"I don't know how anyone can breathe in these ridiculous things," Lady Ingrid said as she touched her stomach. "At least yours makes you look like a divine messenger from the gods."

As she finished speaking, she reached out and pushed a strand of Amara's hair back into place.

"You look good, too," Amara said. When Lady Ingrid took her first stiff steps toward the door, Amara burst into laughter. "I guess you don't wear dresses often?"

"This is the first time I've ever worn my late husband's gift," the baroness replied. "He always pestered me to wear it to balls, but I refused to be his prized pig. I will not miss his presence in the castle." She paused before continuing, "And before you think me a monster for not sufficiently grieving his loss, he was not a . . . gentle man."

Amara nodded, unsure of what to say. She took a deep breath and then decided to change the subject. "Shall we go eat?"

Lady Ingrid gave a little secret smile then led the way back down the stairs. The courtyard below was deserted, but a steady murmur of voices emerged from the open doors of the great hall. The baroness took Amara's arm and then guided her toward the entrance.

Strangely, Amara felt nervous at having her secret exposed to everyone at the keep. She knew she'd have to announce she was an avatar to the world eventually, but she wasn't sure how everyone would react.

*Hopefully,* she thought, *Ingrid is right, and they wouldn't immediately try to burn me at the stake.*

As Amara passed through the wide doors, she hesitated. Hundreds of people crammed into the vast hall, filling every seat at every table. Many folks lingered around the edges of the room for want of a chair. At the sight of the baroness, the murmur of conversation died down, and the assembled crowd turned to face them.

Lady Ingrid stepped forward and held up her hands. "I have wondrous news. The gods have returned and an avatar has arrived to save our lands. I present to you Amara, Avatar of Melischar!"

Dead silence greeted the baroness's words. As it stretched out uncomfortably long, Amara began to weave together the strands of mana to cast *Cloak of Shadows.*

A woman let out a cheer. It was taken up by others. As they rose to their feet, many of those gathered excitedly banged their fists and cups against the tabletops. Amara noted, however, that several folks in the great hall remained seated and stone-faced.

Amara looked over helplessly at Lady Ingrid, unsure of how to react to the deafening cheers.

The baroness smirked knowingly in response. "I told you they would accept you as their savior. Now all you have to do is defeat Malcheron and his army."

"Oh, good," Amara whispered under her breath. "I was afraid they would expect something difficult from me."

# CHAPTER 32

Amara sat on the steps leading up to the outer castle wall, letting her feet dangle over the edge of the staircase. While the baroness had said the North remembered the gods, she hadn't been prepared for the reaction she'd received. After the announcement, people had flooded around her and Lady Ingrid, many of them asking for her blessing. Meanwhile, in sharp contrast, many others had spent the event glaring at her with naked loathing. The entire ordeal had made her terribly uncomfortable.

After enduring nearly an hour of that treatment, she'd slipped out of the great hall. The feast was still in full swing below, and with the amount of beer and wine flowing, she doubted it would end anytime soon. Wanting to keep her thoughts clear, she'd avoided any drink.

She startled, nearly jumping free of her skin, as movement from behind her drew her attention. Jonas stood on the steps, a serious expression on his face.

*But then again, when doesn't he have a serious expression?*

He gestured at the spot beside her. "May I sit down?"

"You don't even have to ask." She shifted over, compressing her voluminous skirt to give him enough room to sit. "Shouldn't you be enjoying the feast?"

Jonas sat down beside her and then adjusted his bandolier of throwing knives. "It's no fun without my group leader."

"Where's everyone else?" she asked. "Is Salamander alright?"

"Our young friend is single-handedly trying to eat all the food in the castle." Jonas grinned. "The last I saw of her, she was devouring roast pig. And, she may also have—once again—imbibed a bit too much wine."

Amara shook her head at hearing about the alcohol. She'd have to check on her friend later. She didn't want Salamander stumbling back to her room alone after the feast.

"Though, I must say," Jonas continued, "Borim is giving her an impressive run for her money, so to speak. I'm starting to believe all dwarfs have a hollow leg where they store food and ale."

She smiled at that. "You should be with them."

"I'd rather be with you."

"I'm not very good company tonight."

"I would be a pretty poor friend if I wished to be in your presence only when you are in good cheer," Jonas replied. "Do you wish to talk about your reception in the great hall?"

Amara pressed her lips together. "At this point, I'm used to people fearing and judging me based on my class. But having everyone worship me that way was almost as bad. And I have no idea how to bless people. How can I be an avatar of the gods when I know almost nothing about them? Is there a holy book or something I can read?"

"There were such writings." Jonas rubbed his jaw thoughtfully. "Many sources from before the First Empire mention them, however, the Church long ago destroyed every copy they could find. The Gnostics and the Broken Brotherhood may have hidden away some trove of scriptures, but I have never seen any trace of the holy books in the South. And I spent many years in the greatest libraries there."

"Do you have any idea what the books said?" she asked hopefully. "Would they tell me how I'm supposed to act as an avatar?"

"The old sources stated good deeds and even thoughts all helped to strengthen the Gods of Order. However, the Church discouraged such things many years ago. They decreed that the only way to stamp out Chaos was to banish and ostracize those with wicked classes. Once the South was made pure, then Chaos would hold no sway there."

"Does that make any sense to you?" Amara asked, tilting her head to the side.

Jonas nodded. "I believe so. Someone with an evil class—like myself—could only ever weaken the Forces of Order. Though it was still a bitter pill to swallow, it's something I've come to accept over the years."

"You're not evil," she said fiercely. "And your class doesn't define you any more than mine defines me."

"If you knew what I could do . . ."

She found his hazel eyes in the dim light. "Then tell me."

"I . . . I can do terrible things." He took a deep breath before continuing. "My spells give me the ability to use enemies' souls to strengthen myself. How could something so heinous not be evil?

"I don't think anything is inherently bad." She bit down on her lower lip before she continued. "What if you use your spells to help people?"

"But I may destroy someone's soul in the process," he replied in a strained voice. "What could be more malevolent than the act of using someone's soul as a weapon?"

"You're not evil," she repeated firmly. "None of us would ever judge you if you used your spells."

Jonas slumped forward. "I could never do such a thing."

Amara breathed out and then patted Jonas on the leg. She knew she couldn't dispel his long-held beliefs—or the self-loathing they cultivated—with a brief conversation. Maybe someday he'd see the truth about his class. About himself. After all, she wasn't a thief by sheer dint of being a Trickster Cleric. And just because he could use souls to empower himself didn't mean he was wicked.

The sounds of footsteps interrupted them. Turning on the step, Amara saw Lady Ingrid coming up the stairs with two cups and a bottle of wine.

The baroness stopped short at the sight of Jonas and then frowned. "I apologize. Am I intruding?"

"Not at all, my lady." Jonas pushed himself up to his feet. "I was just leaving."

Amara searched for the perfect words to make him stay. He'd come to comfort her and she'd upset him by talking about his class. However, those perfect words eluded her. While she hesitated, Jonas trudged away into the darkness.

*Some friend I am,* she thought to herself angrily.

Lady Ingrid settled down on the step where the rogue had been. Tilting her head to the side to regard Amara, she asked, "Are you alright?"

"I'm fine," Amara replied, unable to convince even herself. "I just needed a bit of fresh air."

Lady Ingrid handed her a cup then held up the dusty green bottle. "This is from my personal collection. The wine was pressed in Sanaria. It is regarded as a very fine vintage. Would you like a cup?"

Amara shook her head. "I'm planning to do some quests tomorrow, so I don't want a hangover."

"About that . . ." Lady Ingrid said as she poured red wine into her cup. "After your encounter with the karaxi, I'd ask you not to engage in any further quests. If the creature had slain you, then all would have been lost. And not just for us here in the valley, but for the entire world."

"I'm not going to just sit around your castle," Amara said, her voice rising. "I need to grow stronger to face the Forces of Chaos and complete my quests."

"Yes," Ingrid continued. "And to do so, you must be alive. When a relief army arrives, then I'll send you out on quests with sufficient forces to protect you. Until then, I must ask you to remain in Stout Oak Keep."

Amara regarded the baroness with a raised eyebrow. "If you think you can keep a Trickster Cleric confined to this place, then you don't know my class very well."

Ingrid sighed and then reached out to pat Amara's thigh. "I'm only trying to keep you safe. I owe you my life, and I'll do anything to keep you out of harm's way. You are an avatar of the gods, sent here in my darkest hour to save me. The gods *want* me to protect you. How can you not see that?"

Once again meeting the immovable mountain of the baroness's will, Amara tried another tack. "What if the relief army doesn't arrive in time? I won't have gained any levels, and I'll be helpless against Malcheron and his army. I'm going to guess he's a pretty high level?"

"He's at least Level 75," Ingrid said, drawing her hand back. "My scouts have seen him use fourth Circle spells in battle, which means he has passed at least two bottlenecks. When we face the Issurian leader, you must let me deal with him."

Amara mentally filed away the term *bottleneck* to ask Jonas about it later. Right now, she needed to focus on convincing the baroness to allow her to quest. Not that Ingrid could stop her short of throwing her into a dungeon. But she didn't want to sour the only good relationship she had with anyone outside of her group.

"What if I focus on low-level quests around the village?" Amara asked, carefully watching Lady Ingrid's reaction to her proposal. "There were quite a few on the quest board in the courtyard. My party and I are keen to get started."

"I don't trust your group to keep you safe." When Amara opened her mouth to reply, Ingrid held up a hand to silence her. "It's not their intent I question, you see, but their ability. They are inexperienced and far too low-level to survive in the North."

"We did alright for ourselves on the long trip here," she shot back.

"True."

Ingrid drank deeply from her cup and then leaned back to gaze up at the sky. "My ancestors often looked up at the stars to take comfort in the sight of the Celestial Court's constellation. But then, centuries ago, they winked out one by one. No one knows why, though the Gnostics argue it was because we turned away from the gods. I wonder when Melischar's star will once again retake its place in the heavens to give us all hope?"

Amara peered up into the night sky as a swirling river of blue energy shot across the darkness. For a moment, she thought she felt a great hungering darkness. She blinked and the sensation disappeared.

"So, what about the quests?" Amara asked softly.

"I would prefer not to risk your group members either," Lady Ingrid said, giving her head a shake and returning her focus to Amara. "The dwarf is an accomplished blacksmith, and Jonas is quite the scholar. There is a library here with many works from before the time of the First Empire, and I would very much like for him to go through the scrolls and books to find information about avatars. I doubt much remains after the Great Purge, but there might be some works that provide much-needed information on your abilities."

"I need my group members by my side," Amara stated, her voice hardening. "They're my friends, and I never would have survived without them."

Lady Ingrid took a sip from her cup, her artic blue eyes regarding Amara over the rim. She was silent for a moment before she spoke again. "I have a proposition for you. There is a dungeon a short distance away from the keep. In times past, we often obtained magical items and healing treasures from defeating the monsters dwelling within. However, a band of goblins took over the area surrounding the entrance, thus cutting off our supply."

"And you want my group to take out the goblins?"

"No, I want you protected by a more experienced party," the baroness replied. "There is a band of adventurers who proved themselves on the road today. I believe the leader's name is Ackley."

Amara's expression darkened. "I've traveled with them, and let's just say we had our differences."

"Regardless of whether you enjoy their company, they are far more skilled than your motley group," Ingrid continued. "I will have Emmaline and Noah lead you to the dungeon's entrance. Once the goblin infestation has been dealt with, Ackley and his group will accompany you inside. You will likely have ample opportunity to improve your healing abilities, as well as obtain desperately needed items for the castle. I will also order Noah and Emmaline to watch over you. They will step in if necessary."

"So, you want me to pass some sort of test for you?" Amara frowned. "I thought you swore to serve me?"

"I swore to bend my will to the completion of your goals and quests." Ingrid brushed back a strand of her golden hair. "For me to do so, you must be alive."

Amara shook her head. "I'm not here to pass your trials. My group will handle the dungeon ourselves."

"I see you are . . . *resolute*." From the baroness's frown, it was clear she'd wanted to say something more strongly worded. She reached over to touch Amara's hand as she stared at her earnestly. "Please, let me keep you safe, Amara."

Amara flinched back from the baroness's touch. "I won't do anything without my group."

Looking wounded from her reaction, Lady Ingrid asked, "Will you accept a compromise?"

When Amara didn't immediately refuse, the baroness went on. "As I lay ill for many days, my duties went neglected. There are things I must attend to which will keep me busy over the next week. Though I have few people to call upon to complete the task, I still require the dungeon problem to be dealt with in that time. If you do this as a personal favor to me, I will accompany your group on a quest of your choosing. With me at your side, it will vastly speed up their leveling."

Amara thought back to the raw power the baroness had displayed facing the goblins earlier in the day. With Ingrid in their group, anything short of an ogre would be child's play.

"I'll think about it," she offered, adding, "but if he's coming along, make sure Noah understands that I'm friendly."

"He is fiercely loyal to me, and I trust him implicitly." Ingrid poured the pale ruby liquid into the wooden cup and then handed it to Amara. "I will inform him you are to be treated well."

Amara took the wine from the baroness and then took a sip. The drink tasted *very* good.

*Maybe,* she thought, *I can have one cup tonight without suffering any consequences in the morning.*

As she drank with Lady Ingrid, they both stared up into the heavens as azure lights danced above.

Tomorrow, Amara would face her first dungeon. The more she thought about it, the more trepidation she felt about her forced partners. She trusted Emmaline and Noah about as far as she could throw a dragon, and Ackley's group had lost their healer.

She just needed to come up with another plan.

# CHAPTER 33

Amara opened the door leading to the castle courtyard and winced as brilliant light flooded the hallway. She would have sworn she'd only had a few cups of wine with Lady Ingrid, but when she'd awoken, her head had felt like it was stuffed full of cotton. To quell her headache, she'd used a *Heal Wounds* spell on herself, but she still felt like she was dying.

*I'm never having wine again,* she thought. *And now I understand why Borim doesn't drink.*

She pushed back her hair with one hand, and then adjusted the new backpack straps biting into her shoulders. It had taken a bit of trial and error, but she'd finally taught Mimi how to turn into a form she could easily carry. While the mimic was heavy, Amara's improved strength made the weight tolerable.

Resting her staff on her shoulder, Amara shifted her quiverful of darts at her hip as she set out across the courtyard. She did her best to avoid the stares she received from the gawking servants and grooms going about their work. As they noticed her, it seemed half of them wanted to drop to their knees and praise her, while the others watched with barely concealed contempt.

The hood of her cloak helped to hide her face, and she kept her head low as she moved through the rings of the fortress. Without incident, she reached the main gates then crossed the bridge leading over the rushing river.

As she walked down the road, she spotted a pleasant surprise. The unmistakable, portly frame of the innkeeper had been placed in the wooden stocks outside of the village. The amassed crowd pelted his greasy face with clods of dirt.

While her memory of the previous evening was a bit hazy, she remembered telling the baroness about the innkeeper hoarding food. Apparently, Lady Ingrid had acted on her words with great alacrity.

*Maybe there is some justice in this world after all.*

Her spirits buoyed, Amara continued on with a spring in her step toward the village. As she neared the entrance, Ackley and his party emerged from the palisade gates. A moment later, Emmaline followed them out, dressed in the pristine robes of the Church.

Amara scowled at the sight of the priestess. Of all the people she was traveling with into the goblin-infested dungeon, she distrusted Emmaline the most. She claimed to serve Lady Ingrid, but Amara questioned the limits of that loyalty. If pushed, would Emmaline choose the baroness or the bishop? If anyone would betray her, it would probably be Emmaline.

"Hello and greetings," Ackley called out as he approached. "I'm glad you finally took me up on my offer to heal my group. And I believe we're only waiting on one other now."

"I'm just doing what the baroness commanded." Amara shrugged.

"We're happy to have you," Kymber said with a strained smile as she plucked at the strings of her instrument.

"You planning to loot everything?" Eldred asked with a guffaw as he lowered his shield. "That's a ridiculously large backpack."

"It's obviously her pet mimic, you fool," Landon said as he tucked his thick magical book under one arm.

Eldred scowled at the mage. "How was I supposed to know that?"

"Open your eyes, then." Landon shook his head and then nodded at Amara. "It's a pleasure to have you accompany us again. I don't believe I ever properly thanked you for healing my wounds."

"It was nothing," Amara muttered. "Can we just get going? I don't want to stand around talking all day."

"We are just waiting for Noah," Emmaline said, her tone frosty. "Ah, there he is now."

She pointed into the distance where the warrior had emerged from the forest.

They waited as he jogged along the road, holding his sword steady against his hip with one hand. He arrived out of breath, and he leaned forward to rest his hands on his knees. "I apologize for being late," he said to Emmaline, "but I wanted to scout the forest to ensure no monsters had moved into the area."

"It's fine," the priestess snapped. "We should leave immediately if we're going to complete the task given to us by Lady Ingrid."

"She's right," Ackley said, his hand resting on the hilt of his rapier. "The dungeon is renowned as a long one, and we must still fight our way through the goblins guarding its entrance. I believe we should make haste toward our destination." Facing Amara, he added, "However, before we depart, I must ask you to join our group."

Amara pressed her lips together as she glanced over at the icons of her own group members to the side of her vision. After she'd crawled out of bed, she'd gathered them together in her room to relay her plan for the day. None of them had been particularly happy with her proposal—most of all Salamander who had wanted to go back to bed—but, in the end, they'd all agreed to go along with her scheme.

First, though, she needed to join Ackley's party. After a brief pause, she left her group. A prompt appeared.

***Join Ackley's Party? (Yes/No?)***

She mentally selected "Yes" and a moment later, icons of Ackley and the others appeared in her field of view. True to Lady Ingrid's words, they were all far more advanced than her own group, their levels ranging from Level 13 to Level 18.

The hawk-faced leader of the group—and the one with the highest level—gave a grand bow to Amara complete with a flourish of his wide-brimmed hat. "As my friend, the esteemed mage, said, it's a pleasure to have your company once more."

Amara gave him a little uncomfortable smile, but then tried to step back as Noah shoved past, striking her with his shoulder. Jostled to the side, she glared daggers at him as he walked away, shocked at his childishness.

"That was most uncouth," Ackley said quietly. "I don't believe I'll enjoy my time with him."

"If something in the dungeon wants to eat him," Amara suggested, "maybe you should let it."

The ghost of a smile passed across Ackley's lips, but he quickly stifled it. He turned smartly on his heel and followed Noah toward the forest.

The priestess breezed past, sniffing at Amara before averting her gaze. With a brisk pace, she joined Noah on the road leading out of the valley.

Amara suspected that if she got into trouble out there neither Noah nor Emmaline would offer much aid. Noah had disliked her from the moment he'd discovered her, and the priestess probably wanted to burn her at the stake.

"Thank goodness I have you with me, Mimi," Amara said, stroking her pet. When the mimic waggled in response, the sudden movement nearly made her lose her footing. She let out a little laugh at Mimi's excitement, and ignored the others' questioning looks.

As they wound their way through the farms dotting the valley, Amara took up a position at the rear of the adventurers. They passed a young girl wearing little more than rags as she scattered feed for chickens. A short while later, they marched past another homestead where a woman led a cow out to pasture. Amara's reception among the peasants was much like it had been in the keep; some waved to her, while others glowered at her darkly.

*At least they probably don't hate me for being a Trickster Cleric,* she thought. *That's progress, I guess.*

As the group reached the overgrown edge of the forest, they slowed, with Eldred taking the lead. In case of an ambush, Ackley urged the party to fan out.

Eldred took up a position in front of Amara, his shield raised as he scanned the treeline.

*They* seem *to be trying to keep me safe. Maybe I've been wrong about them.*

For the better part of an hour, Noah led them deeper into the gloaming before he held up a fist at the edge of a clearing. At his signal, the other adventurers dropped to the ground. Amara glanced around in confusion.

*No one mentioned secret hand signals,* she thought.

Eldred tapped on her foot with his gauntleted hand and looked at her expectantly. Carefully, Amara lowered herself to the forest floor.

In the bushes ahead, goblins appeared wearing cloth garments and clasping an assortment of poorly maintained weapons. She counted nearly twenty of the grubby little creatures as they trudged past her hiding spot.

Noah bent low and hurried over to Ackley's group. "The entrance to the dungeon is just beyond the treeline there. I will circle around. Once your party has engaged the goblins, I will attack from the rear."

Amara hid a smile as she watched Ackley's face twist into a frown. For once, he wasn't the one who wanted to flank the enemy and stay out of harm's way. Now that the shoe was on the other foot, he looked thoroughly annoyed.

But, without objection, the duelist gave a terse nod, and then drew his rapier. The long, narrow blade glinted in the dim light. With a meaningful gesture, he instructed the members of his group to ready their weapons.

*I really need to learn these hand signals for my group.*

Amara took a moment to check on her darts then she tugged on the straps of her leather armor. Finally, she lowered her staff and gripped it tightly. She still hadn't received a new weapon from the baroness, so she was stuck with the length of wood she'd found back in Leissen. She doubted it would do much against a goblin, but it was better than nothing.

The duelist crept over to where Amara knelt and spoke in a low tone. "Since you have most likely used all your Expertise Points on Healing matters, I want you to stay safely in cover until the fight is over. Your only job is to heal us after. Understood?"

She repressed a frown at his demands. *Is he afraid of losing another healer?*

Amara flicked back her hair. "Alright. I guess I'll just stay here like a bump on a log."

"And I will remain with her," Emmaline added quickly. "To keep her out of danger, of course."

Amara raised her eyebrow but said nothing, instead scanning the forest for any sign of movement. Nothing stirred among the trees.

"As you wish." Ackley bobbed his head at the priestess. "However, please remember if anything happens to her, we have no healer for our dungeon run. As agreed, she will accompany my party after we have handled the goblin threat. Is that understood, priestess?"

"Fine," Emmaline spat. "I still think running the dungeon is a fool's errand."

With wild eyes and a twitch in her movements, the priestess, Amara noted, seemed unbalanced.

"It's what your baroness ordered us to do," Amara stated bluntly.

Emmaline wagged a finger at her. "I know you're a false avatar, and you're leading the lady down a path to nothing but death and destruction. If you cared about her at all, you'd tell her to abandon the castle and save herself. But instead, you're using her to feed your delusions of grandeur, aren't you? You want everyone to believe you're some divine avatar who will save the world. Well, I know you're nothing but a liar and a thief. And I won't let you hurt someone I care about!"

"Enough," Ackley snapped. "Do you wish to bring the entire Chaos army down on our position?" After a deep, exasperated breath, he straightened his spine. "Let's go deal with the goblin menace before this priestess ruins all of our plans."

As Ackley's party crept past her, they turned their gaze in her direction one by one. Finally, only Ackley remained, and he gave Emmaline a meaningful look before he disappeared through the thick brush.

After a moment, Amara stole over to the edge of the glade, and then knelt behind a leafy shrub. While the others expected her to stay safely hidden, she wasn't about to ignore the battle completely.

She also wasn't going to ignore the niggling feeling that something about this whole thing felt *off*.

Amara glanced over at Emmaline and noted the priestess was engrossed with a pouch on her belt. Returning to scanning the glade, her gaze alighted on an enormous wooden archway. Someone had carefully cultivated branches and trunks to create an opening in a living wall of trees. Flowering vines twisted their way up the archway, and as she watched, their blossoms shimmered like a rainbow.

*That must be the entrance to the dungeon,* she thought in awe.

But before she could examine it further, her intuition flared with a warning. Without question, she hurled herself to the side as a golden column of light annihilated the undergrowth where she'd been kneeling.

She hastily unslung the straps holding Mimi on her back and then jumped to her feet. As she did, she was already weaving together the strands of mana to summon her *Divine Weapon*. "I'm totally *shocked* by your inevitable betrayal," she said, her words dripping with sarcasm. "But you're a fool if you think I came alone."

Emmaline raised her hand to cast again, and a throwing knife pierced her wrist. Another one buried itself in her back, and she dropped to her knees with a pained cry. When the priestess grabbed her injured arm to lift it, a third blade sprouted from her shoulder.

"I'd probably stop trying to cast if I were you," Amara said, letting her own spell unravel. "Eventually, he's going to get annoyed and kill you."

Jonas and the others from her group trotted up the path toward her, the grateful pig farmer at their side. *He must have agreed to guide them to the dungeon,* Amara thought.

The rogue's hard gaze never wavered from Emmaline, a knife glinting in his fist. To Amara, he said, "Have I mentioned how much I dislike your foolhardy plans? This viper very nearly killed you with her craven attack."

"I had to at least make it look like I was going along with the baroness's orders," she replied. "Otherwise, she would have probably tried to keep me locked in that keep. And this way we get to do some quests, and not have Ingrid interfere. The fact you helped me stop Emmaline was just a bonus."

"And when news reaches the baroness that you disobeyed her?" Jonas asked.

"That's future Amara's problem." She shrugged and smiled. "Let her deal with it."

"You'll never get out of here alive!" Emmaline screamed. "This forest will be your grave."

"I think I'll muddle through," Amara replied, her eyes narrowing. "But I'm not sure if you're going to be so lucky."

# CHAPTER 34

ou're no avatar," Emmaline screeched from her knees. "And with your
death, I will save Lady Ingrid."

Amara stalked forward, closing the distance between them as Emmaline struggled to her feet. Without hesitation, Amara brought down her staff, and it struck the priestess's head with a loud *crack*. Emmaline crumpled to the ground and lay there in a heap, unmoving.

Borim lowered his axe. "Don't you think you might have hit her a bit hard there, lass?"

"She just tried to kill me when my back was turned," Amara replied tartly. "If she's still alive, it's more than she deserves."

Amara couldn't help but berate herself. She had certainly expected treachery on this venture, but she'd been foolish to believe it wouldn't happen before entering the dungeon.

*Should I expect this treatment from everyone loyal to the Church?* she wondered. *Was Brother Otto just an outlier?* But then she remembered the many others who had joined the monk's side and given their lives to save her. *Was Otto just more persuasive?*

Salamander walked up to the unconscious Emmaline and savagely kicked her in the face. Though the priestess's head snapped back, but she made no sound.

"What are you doing?" Amara exclaimed. "We're not trying to kill her."

"She tried to hurt you," Salamander said fiercely. "She deserves to die."

Borim stroked his beard. "The baroness might get a tad upset if we start killing her advisors. I say bring the priestess back to the keep and let her face justice there."

"I agree with Borim," Jonas added. "It is not our place to carry out arbitrary executions."

Amara tucked a strand of hair behind her ear as she regarded Emmaline on the ground. The kick from Salamander had done some damage, and blood gushed out of the woman's mouth and nose. Amara'd probably need to cast a healing spell on the priestess before long.

*But did I really want to save the woman who tried to murder me?* After a long, exasperated sigh, Amara thought, *I'm probably going to regret this decision.*

"We'll let Ingrid decide." Amara pointed at Jonas. "Tie her up and blindfold her. Will that be enough to prevent her from casting spells?"

Jonas nodded. "A blinded and bound magic user is more of a danger to herself than others. However, if she attempts any casting, I will do what is necessary."

"Do it then."

She stepped back as Borim and Jonas went to work. While they used a length of hempen rope to truss up the priestess like a holiday turkey, Amara crept over to the clearing. Peeking through the wall of greenery, she saw no sign of Noah, Ackley's group, or the goblins. Stranger still, she heard no sounds of battle.

"I think something has gone wrong," she whispered to her group. "I'm going to go check it out."

"Not without us," Borim said gruffly. "There's a stinking horde of goblins out there, or did you forget that?"

"I know there are goblins, but we can't risk losing Ackley's group. I don't feel comfortable running a dungeon with them, but they could help to defend the castle."

While Lady Ingrid had demanded she attempt the dungeon with Ackley's group, Amara had not seriously considered the prospect. The plan had been that her own group would meet her at the dungeon, and they would then complete the crawl together.

Jonas had mentioned some dungeons grew ornery if the parties delving through them were too large—not that Amara grasped the concept of a dungeon having the capacity to be anything other than just there— According to him, however, that risk was typical of groups with more than ten or so adventurers. By his reckoning, both groups should be able to take on the task without issue.

Calling upon her mana to heal Emmaline, Amara asked her companions, "Do you think Noah was in on her plan?"

"That seems unlikely," Jonas said. "If so, why would she attack you alone? Why squander the advantage of a paladin at your side?"

Amara shrugged. "She's been acting squirrelly since we left Fusson, honestly. Maybe she just saw an opportunity and took it."

"Fairly reasoned." Jonas rubbed his jaw. "I must admit, Amara, I'm rather impressed. How did you dodge an attack from behind? Did you sense her drawing upon mana?"

"I think it was my Luck," she replied, unsure of how to describe her strange sense for danger.

The radiance of her healing magic went to work on Emmaline, and after several seconds, the priestess's eyes snapped open.

Amara knelt, grinning at her wolfishly. "Did that go as you planned?"

"This isn't over," Emmaline said, wildly turning her head. "You'll never return to the castle alive."

Borim's heavy boot connected with the priestess's injured leg. "Bit of an ominous prediction, there. Would you care to explain what you expect to happen to us?"

Emmaline's lips spread in a zealous leer, revealing teeth stained crimson with blood. "Find out yourself, heretic."

Amara rose to her feet. "We need to learn what happened to Ackley and his party. Is there any way to take her with us?"

Borim chuckled. "I've got a bit of a crazy idea." He hefted Emmaline over his shoulder and then walked over to Mimi. Unceremoniously, he plopped the priestess on top of the mimic and then stepped back.

The monster's outer shell molded around the priestess.

"Mimics always stick to their enemies," Borim explained. "I thought I'd take a chance to see if it worked on this buffoon."

With the priestess on her back, Mimi moved more slowly through the undergrowth, but otherwise appeared unbothered by the additional weight. And it was a good way to carry the priestess without weakening their party.

Salamander poked Emmaline with her finger. "I still say we should feed her to Mimi. Why not just let her disappear? Who would find out?" Twirling a coil of hair around her finger, she paused to follow a thought. "Oh, wait. Does she spit out the clothes and stuff? Could you imagine if we got back, and Mimi upchucked a half-eaten dress in front of that stuck up baroness?"

"I don't know," Amara replied. Come to think of it, she'd never seen her pet pass any waste.

*Do mimics just digest anything they put in their mouth?*

That mystery would need to wait another day to be solved. Amara strode once more toward the clearing, pausing at the edge of the glade. Shocked, she froze, having come face to wrinkled face with a goblin.

The creature immediately let out a wail of alarm before charging headlong into the forest to menace Amara and her party. She brought up her staff just in time to parry the thrust of its shortsword thrust. Desperate to gain an advantage, she staggered back, dodging a flurry of strikes and slashes.

Unrelenting, the orange threat lunged, its weapon swiping past her guard. The blade punctured her breastplate and drove into the flesh beneath.

She let out a gasp as pain exploded in her belly. Hot blood poured down her front. She tried to conjure *Divine Weapon*, but as she gathered the mana, the goblin struck her on the hip. Though deflected by her armor, the impact's jarring force sent her stumbling. Her spell dissipated.

Another attack came for her, and as she fumbled to bring her staff up for a blocking maneuver, a dagger sprouted from the goblin's eye. With all her strength, Amara swung her weapon, smashing into the creature's mouth. Blood and teeth sprayed onto the forest floor, a prelude to the creature's own descent. With a wheezing moan, the goblin fell at her feet.

"Where did that bugger come from?" Borim roared, racing to her side.

Amara pressed a hand against her wound to stanch the bleeding. More goblins burst out of the clearing and charged in her direction. A rock sailed over her head, ricocheting off of a tree behind her and disappearing in the foliage.

Borim planted himself in front of her, his axe held high. "Bloody orange bastards!" he shouted. "I'm going to chop you into pieces and then feed you to a mimic!"

She quickly cast *Heal Wounds*. As her spell went to work on her injury, the forest around her filled with a soft white light. The wound closed, and the pain faded to a dull ache. As the last mote faded into the ether, she felt energy returning to her limbs.

Jonas raced past, his knives flashing as he carved a bloody path through the goblins. He leapt from one foe to the next, driving his blade into a creature's neck before flipping it free with a shower of dark blood. In a blur of motion and glinting steel, the rogue sent another of his weapons flying into a goblin rushing toward Amara.

Salamander appeared at her side, a burning orb swirling between her outstretched palms. She unleashed a gout of flames at a group of archers. Their diminutive bodies ignited like someone had doused them in gasoline. Engulfed in flames, the diminutive foes lurched and flailed, their agonized screams echoing through the woods.

As her companions pushed back the horde, Amara produced the towering, flaming sword of her *Divine Weapon*. She immediately ordered it to attack a knot of goblins attacking Borim where he protected her. The diminutive creatures had locked their shields together, their spears forcing the dwarf to give ground. Her flaming sword hammered the shield wall like a meteor from the heavens and sent the creatures behind sprawling.

With the goblins' defenses breached, Borim leapt forward and wreaked havoc in their remaining ranks. Whirling like a dervish, the dwarf hacked with his axe at the fallen creatures. A spearman staggered to its feet, and he punched it in the face, his fist smashing its nose flat. The creature, dazed, had no opportunity to react. The axe fell, splitting open the goblin's skull.

Amara tore her gaze away from Borim as another missile sailed past her head. The spear quivered with unexpended force where it impaled the poor tree behind her. She directed her spectral weapon toward the javelin thrower, already preparing to launch another.

Shrill war cries made Amara spin around to see another wave of goblins appear behind them. Amara and her group had been outflanked by the little buggers.

The burning orb between Salamander's hands guttered like a candle in a hurricane, then winked out. "Umm . . . are there supposed to be this many?" she asked. With a note of alarm in her small voice, she added, "I'm running a bit low on mana."

Her *Divine Weapon* tore into the skirmishers. As the blade sliced the javelin wielder cleanly down the middle, Amara winced with sympathy. Though she averted her gaze, she could still hear the sickening sounds of the goblin's body tearing and falling to the ground with a squelch.

Focusing on the tight orange clusters, Amara tried to count the remaining enemies.

Nearly two dozen goblins swarmed the area, and though the foliage concealed their numbers, she could see more orange bodies roiling in the clearing beyond.

*There were only supposed to be a handful of goblins here—someone screwed up.*

Amara assessed her own resources: a limited mana pool, and a Divine Weapon with scant minutes left before it disappeared.

"Mimi!" she called out. "Drop the priestess and help us fight the goblins!"

The mimic spit out Emmaline like the priestess was a rotten piece of fruit before scuttling to Amara's side. Her pet's tongue shot out of its maw, smacking wetly against a rushing foe. The impact knocked the creature prone where it screamed and clawed at the dirt in a vain attempt to avoid the toothy jaws.

Again, Amara looked away from the horror, but couldn't escape the loud *crunch* followed by the sound of something soggy hitting the ground. She focused her attention on Emmaline, who thrashed in the undergrowth, struggling to free herself from her bonds.

"Did you betray us to the goblins?" Amara grabbed the priestess by the collar of her robes and hoisted her into a sitting position. "Why are there so many here? Did they know we were coming?"

"I would never work with the Forces of Chaos," Emmaline spat.

With a scowl, she dropped the priestess. She couldn't explain why, but she believed Emmaline. Which, Amara posited, meant someone else had betrayed them. She scanned the forest for an answer to the riddle, but only saw more goblins darting among the trees.

As one of the creatures moved to ambush Borim, Amara sent her sword soaring into its back. The tip of the blade burst through the goblin's chest in a fountain of blood. The force of the impaling blow was enough to lift the goblin into the air. Its feet dangling, the limp corpse hung suspended from her *Divine Weapon*.

An instant later, the spell expired, its blade shattering before dissolving into colorful mist. The skewered goblin dropped to the ground.

"Fall back to my position," she called out to her group.

They would make their stand here with their backs against the trees. At least that way, the goblins would have a hard time outflanking them.

Amara hoped that Ackley and his group would return soon enough to offer aid. She prayed there weren't any more surprises lurking in the woods.

# CHAPTER 35

A stone thumped against Amara's leather armor causing her to stagger. Her eyes searched the forest until she spotted the goblin who had hurled the projectile. She watched as it loaded another stone into the cradle and then swung the sling over its head. Hurriedly, she grabbed her last dart from the quiver and reared back. With a cry of effort, she sent the missile flying.

With her Luck and *Dart Deadeye* ability, she didn't miss. The missile sank into the creature's face, the feathered end protruding from its nose. Reeling, the goblin lost control of its spinning sling, and the stone missile careened into the forehead of an archer standing nearby. Both creatures dropped to the ground, their bodies twitching.

*I just killed two with one shot,* she thought with some surprise.

The tide of goblins seemed endless, more of the small enemies pouring forth with every passing second. If they stayed in their position much longer, they'd be overwhelmed by sheer numbers. They had no choice but to try to cut their way through the mass of creatures and retreat to the keep.

Jonas darted forward, ducking beneath a clumsy spear thrust to plunge both daggers into his attacker's chest. Disengaging, he juked to the side to avoid a speeding arrow.

Most of the goblins hurling themselves at Amara's group wore little more than rags, and they were nothing like the well-equipped ones they'd encountered on the road to Stout Oak Keep. But the creatures had worked themselves into a frenzy and seemed oblivious to the surrounding carnage.

Using her sinuous tongue as a pole, Mimi vaulted into the air, landing mouth-first on a nearby goblin. With a snap, she chomped the screaming creature in half. The goblin's severed legs of the goblin's body lurched around for a second before toppling over.

She wanted to cast *Holy Light* to blind the goblins, but during the confusion of the battle, she hadn't been able to reform her group. And the spell specifically said only her group members were immune to the effects. "Everyone, join my group quickly!" she shouted to the others while she left Ackley's party.

A flurry of notifications appeared in her vision as Jonas, Salamander, and Borim joined her party. To her surprise, another name—Harold—was listed among her allies.

"Now close your eyes if you don't want to go blind!"

"Have you lost your mind?" Borim grunted as he ripped his axe free from a goblin's chest. "I'm not closing my eyes with these stinking bastards around. It sounds like a good way to end up with a spear through my gut."

"Trust me," Amara said, impatiently. She parried a goblin attack with her staff, as she reconsidered her decision to ignore melee talents. In the future, she might need to change her stance on not spending points on weapon skills.

Salamander squeezed her eyes shut and raised her chin. "I trust you."

Hurling a fan of throwing daggers at a trio of charging goblins, Jonas didn't bother to watch his weapons meet their marks as he retreated to the group's huddle. Though two of the rogue's targets fell clutching the weapons buried in their chests, the third continued rushing forward with a war cry.

Jonas shut his eyes with an expression of barely-concealed trepidation. "Whatever you are planning to do, now is the time."

"I hope you know what you're doing, lass," Borim rumbled. "If I die, I'm going to haunt you."

Amara glanced around to make sure her group had shut their eyes and then raised her hand. She wove together the mana to cast *Holy Light*, surprised at the simplicity of the spell's pattern. But she reminded herself that up until this point, she had been casting spells far above her level.

A pinprick of shining light appeared in her hand, like a miniature sun being born. The harsh illumination expanded until all the shadows in the forest had been dispelled. The brilliant light made her eyes water, and she averted her gaze as the radiance scoured the forest.

As the spell faded, the keening wails filled the air. Tears streamed down her cheeks, and ghostly afterimages danced in her vision, depicting goblins staggering, their outstretched hands groping and clawing at the air. Blind, desperate to escape, many of the feral creatures plowed headlong into tree trunks. Several others collided with each other, descending into frenzied blurs of teeth and claws like cornered rats.

From near Amara's hip, Salamander cried out, "I can't see!" The girl raised her hands in front of her face. "Oh, wait. I can, but it's all blurry."

Borim scrubbed at his watering eyes. "Are you sure that was bright enough? I feel like I've been staring into the sun all day like a slack jawed troglodyte."

"There's no time to waste," Jonas said. "We must press our advantage and slay the goblins before they recover."

From the thicket behind their position Harold poked his head out. He'd retreated into the dense growth at the start of the battle, and they'd stashed the priestess in there with him. "Is it safe to come out now?"

Jonas shook his head at the simply-dressed farmer. "Please stay hidden until we deal with the goblins. They may yet rally and pose a threat to you. And once again, you have my profuse apologies for putting you in harm's way."

The farmer examined the mass of blinded goblins blundering about. "Doesn't look like I was in all that much danger. Maybe she truly is an avatar."

"She is!" Salamander exclaimed as she drove her tiny dagger into the neck of a goblin attempting to crawl away. "And she's amazing. You wouldn't believe the other stuff she's done."

"Now's not the time, Salamander." Amara waded into the mass of sightless goblins. Even blind, the creatures posed a lethal threat. Whenever she approached one, it would flail wildly in her direction. She resorted to standing still and striking them with the end of her staff as they came into range.

The slaughter only lasted a few minutes, and when they'd finished, no living goblins remained in sight. Dozens had likely fled—possibly from the effects of the spell—but regardless, the battle was over.

Borim grunted as he touched a gash on his cheek. "Maybe cast that first next time? Not that I mind a sporting fight, but that was a bit much. Actually, on second thought, only cast it when we're outnumbered at least a hundred to one. That way, we'll give the goblins a chance."

"Forget that!" Salamander exclaimed. "Who wants a fair fight? Start every battle with your sun-in-the-palm trick, or whatever you call it. I mean, why even bother with your other spells?"

Amara shook her head as the girl and dwarf descended into a squabble.

Drawing her attention, a notification appeared to indicate that she'd leveled up during the fight. *Strangely, she noticed, I never advance during a battle. Did the notification only trigger when she was out of combat?* If she remembered, she'd have to ask Jonas about it later.

"I need to meditate," Amara announced, exhausted. "Will you watch over me while I do?"

Jonas rubbed his jaw. "Are you sure you don't wish to find a safer location?"

"I still need to find Ackley and his group," she replied. "They were all still alive when I left his party, but I'm not going to go looking for trouble until I have some mana."

"I understand." Jonas motioned at the ground. "While you meditate, I will stand sentinel."

Amara knelt on the soft leaf litter and cleared her mind. As she opened herself to the ambient energy, her mana refilled with a slow, though steady, trickle.

For nearly a quarter of an hour, she didn't move. By the end of that time, she had replenished almost half of her mana. That amount would allow her to cast several healing spells or, if necessary, her *Divine Weapon*. More than anything, she needed to learn a new method of meditation. However, it *did* feel slightly faster than in the past. Maybe she was improving her technique after all. Though she would have much preferred to wade into the unknown with a full mana pool, she didn't dare delay any longer. None of Ackley's group had returned to the area, and Amara inferred this to mean they'd run into problems of their own.

As she rose to her feet, leaves rustled under Amara. She took a moment to inspect her party. While they all sported minor wounds from their encounter, none of them were seriously injured. If she didn't need her mana to help Ackley's group, then she would heal them afterwards.

Salamander trotted over to Amara's side, her small fists bristling with a feathery bouquet of darts. "I got these for you."

Amara smiled and took the missiles. The girl had even taken the time to clean them off. Amara slid them into the quiver and counted. She had a total of ten darts. The rest must have been damaged during—or run away from—the battle.

Seated on a stump surrounded by goblin corpses, Borim noticed Amara and pushed himself up with his axe. "Time to go kick around the dungeon?"

"Do you still want to run it after all of this?" she asked, with some surprise. "I thought you'd want to return to the keep."

"I want some real loot, not just rags and rusty weapons. All these buggers gave me was experience," Borim replied, kicking a nearby carcass. "We searched them while you were taking your little nap, but all we got were a few copper pieces. Barely worth killing them if you ask me."

Amara nodded. Why not continue with their original mission?

Jonas picked his way through the bodies to approach Amara. "I believe the only course of action is to locate Ackley's group and then return to the keep. After we report to Lady Ingrid, then we can decide if a dungeon run is warranted in the future. The goblins may have reinforcements nearby. Furthermore, who will escort Harold back to his farm?"

"Reinforcements?" Borim scoffed. "Who would be stupid enough to help goblins? No one likes working with those brainless dolts."

Salamander flicked her flaxen hair. "I want to do the dungeon. Since we left, I've barely made any money for . . . well, you know. To me, it's worth the risk."

"I'm with the others," Amara said. "We're here. We should at least attempt the dungeon. Once we find Noah, he can escort Harold back to his farm. Does that work for you?"

Jonas nodded. "I will never abandon my group, but caution is warranted. And if Noah can't be located, then I'm taking Harold home."

Amara pressed her lips together. "I agree that we should be careful." She turned to her pet. "Mimi, go fetch the priestess."

The mimic immediately bounded off toward the thicket, where the pig farmer hid.

Without waiting for the others, Amara shouldered her staff and strode toward the clearing. After spending a few heartbeats scanning the area, she took a deep breath then stepped into the open.

She heard a faint shout. Squinting against the bright sunlight, Amara searched for the source of the sound. It came again and, in a jog, she set out toward the far side. She quickly reached the opposite treeline and found Ackley's group lying among the undergrowth surrounded by mounds little orange cadavers.

The duelist pushed himself into a sitting position at the sight of her. Blood trickled out of his mouth as he let out a wracking cough. "I may have underestimated your skills if you survived this deluge of goblins. Next time, I will not be so foolish as to leave you sitting on the sideline."

Amara assessed the situation.

At first, only Kymber appeared uninjured. Propped up against a tree, the bard plucked on her lyre. However, Amara quickly spotted the arrows embedded in her legs. Eldred, had a spear protruding from his gut, and his skin looked almost waxen. The mage sprawled on the forest floor. Blood poured a head wound, staining the leafy carpet.

"I'll heal Landon first." The mage looked like he was on death's door. And something in her mind told her head wounds were the most serious.

As she wove together the strands of mana to cast *Heal Wounds,* her group reached her side. Mimi arrived last, with the bound priestess stuck unceremoniously on top of her pet's head.

Amara finished casting her spell, and the forest shone with soft light. A storm of motes spiraled around the mage before splashing down on his forehead. The skin around his wound regrew, and his breathing became less labored. But he didn't stir, which she feared was a bad sign.

There was nothing more she could do for Landon, so she walked over to Eldred. When she reached his side, she wrenched the spear free with a sickening squishing sound. She hastily cast *Heal Wounds* and watched as a flurry of shining particles descended on the big man.

Without waiting to see the results of her spell, she moved over to Ackley next. His wounds didn't appear too severe, but she cast *Heal Wounds* on him, anyway. The duelist sprang to his feet before she'd even finished, confirming her suspicions.

*I should have used the mana to heal Borim instead.*

Finally, she marched over to Kymber, and with Jonas's help, she removed the arrows from her legs. Healing the bard used what remained of Amara's mana.

By the time Amara was done, her soul felt as though she'd tried to wring too much juice out of a fruit. Without a word, she settled down to meditate at the edge of the clearing.

Nearby, Emmaline thrashed within the mimic.

Amara opened her eyes and glared at the priestess, annoyed at the interruption. "If you were smart, you'd keep quiet. I'm in no mood for of your bullshit."

"Kill her!" the priestess screeched. "Do what I paid you to do!"

Amara surged to her feet and spun around to face Ackley and his party. Jonas and Borim rushed to her side, their weapons raised. As the two groups stared at one another, a deathly silence fell over the forest.

"Please," Ackley said, hands held up. "I promise I can explain everything."

"Best do it fast," Borim growled. "Because otherwise you'll be trying to do it without a head."

# CHAPTER 36

Amara held out her hand to stop Borim as he lifted his axe and stepped forward menacingly. Her soul barely had a drop of mana remaining in it, and she wanted to avoid a battle if possible. With Ackley's mage unconscious, she believed her group could win handily.

"Talk quickly," Amara said harshly.

Ackley's greasy smile spread across his face, matching the splay of his hands. "As you know, the prices of basic goods in Fusson have become rather inflated. The priestess came to us with an offer to ease our financial burden, as it were. If, she said, you were to meet an unfortunate accident inside the dungeon, then she'd pay a hefty sum of gold. She was even so kind as to pay half up front. Needless to say, we would never have seriously entertained the idea of harming the only healer in the area. I suppose, one could say, that we took the money with no intentions of completing the contract."

Amara regarded him coldly. "And yet you told no one about her plans to murder me?"

"And who would I have told?" Ackley asked. "Do you think I have the ear of the lady of the castle? No, I had planned to watch over you like a mother hen watches her chicks."

"She nearly killed me after you left. I only escaped by the skin of my teeth."

*And with a healthy dose of Luck,* she added in her mind.

"Never in my wildest dreams did I think she would act alone. I swear upon Holy Birgitta herself that I would have informed the baroness in due time."

Jonas fixed Ackley with a burning stare. "I'll see you rot in the dungeon for your actions."

Ackley drew his rapier, the blade whispering as it emerged from the sheath. "Do you think it in the power of a lowly rogue like yourself to make such a thing happen?"

"Kill her!" Emmaline shouted from atop the mimic. "Kill—"

The priestess went silent as Salamander's fist collided with her jaw. Immediately, the girl cradled her hand to her chest and cursed a stream of obscenities that made Borim blush. "I think I broke something! How do you make that look so easy, Borim?"

Amara turned her attention back to Ackley's group.

The big warrior had moved to shield his leader while Kymber held her fingers poised above the strings of her lyre. Even though the duelist spoke of peace, his companions prepared for war.

Amara considered her options.

Ackley must know the baroness would execute him for going along with Emmaline's plans, so it would be in his best interests if she and her friends didn't return. If he didn't attack now, then he'd have to create an opportunity later when their guard was down, but before returning to the keep.

*Then again*, she reasoned, *I am the only healer in the North.* If they planned on staying, his crew would eventually need her services. Maybe he wasn't lying. Perhaps their only intent really had been to simply bilk Emmaline out of her gold. Ackley and his crew all seemed the type to want easy money, after all.

"What do you propose we do now?" Amara asked, eyeing the duelist warily.

"I say we forget this entire ugly business." Ackley lowered his weapon and then fumbled around in a pouch on his belt. From inside, he withdrew a shiny gold coin. "I'd be happy to split the proceeds with you."

Amara couldn't help but salivate hungrily at the sight of the gleaming coin. The sum he held in his hand was worth more than everything she'd earned in this world so far. She couldn't imagine how Emmaline had gotten a hold of so much money.

"This is what's going to happen," Amara said, her tone indicating she would brook no dissent. "You will give us half of the gold you received, and then leave Stout Oak Keep, never to return. Understood?"

Eldred's brow descended and his face darkened. "And try our luck getting through all those Issurians and ogres on the road? No thanks."

Ackley held up his hand to silence his companion. "There is the other path the baroness showed us, which would lead us safely back to Oksberg. A pouch full of gold should warm their previously chilly reception."

Borim glared at Amara. "Have you lost your mind, lass? Mark my words, these traitors will cause trouble for us."

Jonas nodded. "I agree with Borim. Nothing good can come from letting these conspirators escape."

If she hadn't used all of her mana healing Ackley's party, she might have been willing to make the attempt to capture them. But her party was in no shape for another battle now. The best course of action was to take the gold and banish Ackley.

"It's my decision," she announced, "and I say they're free to go."

"I agree to your terms," Ackley said, his lips curling up into a smile. "This place had become boring, anyway."

Gold in hand, he made a move to step forward. A terse shake of Amara's head stopped him.

"Put the money on the ground there," she said. "I don't want you to come any closer."

Ackley knelt and piled four thick pieces of gold on the ground. Forced smile unwavering, he straightened and regarded Amara. "I do hope we cross paths again."

Jonas spun his dagger around. "If I were you, I would hope otherwise."

"I will watch for you, too, my rogue friend." Ackley turned and motioned to Landon, still prostrate on the ground. "If you would be so kind, Eldred?"

The big warrior grumbled, but stomped over to Landon. Heaving the mage's limp form like a sack of potatoes, Eldred draped him over one shoulder as though he weighed nothing.

Amara exhaled with relief at having diffused the situation. But just when she thought everything was under control, Noah blundered out of the forest.

Noah's face was covered with dark blood, and his normally pristine white armor was covered in dings and grime. He held his long sword loosely in one hand, the blade notched and scored. His eyes immediately darted over to Emmaline, tied up on top of the mimic, and his lip curled up in a snarl. "What have you done to Emmaline, heretic scum?"

"The false avatar attacked me without provocation!" Emmaline cried out, her lips bloody from Salamander's punch. "They plan to betray Lady Ingrid to the Issurians!"

"I knew you were collaborators with the Forces of Chaos," Noah shouted. "I will see you drawn and quartered for your actions!"

He raised his sword, waves of power pulsing off the blade.

Amara felt a terrible, murderous intent emerge from Noah, and she understood: her group was badly outclassed. She realized that he'd cut through the mass of goblins—on his own!—and survived with only a few scrapes. She had to appreciate that Noah was an incredibly powerful fighter.

"She's lying," Amara said quickly. "She paid this group to betray me. You can ask them yourself."

Noah's mask of rage wavered and, for a moment, he seemed torn. Finally, after what felt like an eternity, he grimaced and addressed Ackley's group. "Does she speak the truth?"

Ackley shook his head, looking downcast. "I have no idea what she's talking about. When you arrived, I was in the process of demanding she release the priestess. I believe what Emmaline says is true: the avatar plans to sell us to the

Issurians. It's a tragedy that someone the baroness trusted so completely could betray her."

Amara gritted her teeth. She guessed, with Noah on his side, the duelist felt the scales had tipped in his favor. She swore she'd find a way to make him pay for his duplicity.

"I should have known your forked tongue could speak only lies." Noah gripped his sword with both hands and raised his weapon high. "You will accompany me back to the keep where the baroness will pass judgement on you."

"No, she must die," Emmaline protested. "The false avatar is too dangerous to allow near the baroness again. She may bewitch her mind, and then all will be lost."

"Yes, you must mete out justice," Ackley interjected. Adding, "Swiftly. As the esteemed priestess said, she may cast foul magic on Lady Ingrid if you allow the Trickster Cleric to gain an audience with her. Remember, she can enchant minds and cast illusions."

"I will ensure that doesn't happen," Noah replied in a steely tone. "If she attempts anything in my presence, then I will end her life. Now, untie Emmaline, so we may return to the castle where the lady will deal with these traitors."

Harold stepped out from behind a nearby tree, his hand raised timidly to draw Noah's attention. "May I speak, sword-bearer?"

At the appearance of the farmer, Noah looked shocked. "What in the name of Holy Birgitta are you doing here, Harold?"

"Well, you see, the avatar there saved my pigs from a karaxi."

"So, she claims," Noah grumbled. "I've seen no evidence of the creature."

"It's true," Harold continued as he raised a fingernail to his mouth. "And I owe the avatar my family's lives. A monster like that wouldn't have stopped at my pigs. And . . . well . . . I heard everything that group said." He pointed at Ackley's party. "They said clear as day Emmaline paid them to murder the avatar in cold blood."

"What are you saying?" Noah demanded. "Are you implying Emmaline betrayed our lady?"

"I'm not implying—I'm stating." Harold ran a hand through his hair, looking like he'd rather be anywhere else. "They took gold from the priestess to do the foul deed."

Noah lowered his sword, looking troubled. "Is this true, Emmaline?"

Emmaline thrashed against her bonds. "The stupid pig farmer is a liar. He's been bewitched by the Trickster Cleric!"

For the first time, Noah's gaze fell upon the pile of gold sitting in the grass. His eyes narrowed. "You would go against our lady's wishes, Emmaline?" he asked softly, "and murder someone under her protection?"

"No, the fool is lying. Please, you must believe me," she pleaded.

"I must take everyone back to the keep," Noah announced. "The lady will untangle this web of lies."

"Do something or we'll hang," Emmaline screamed at Ackley.

The duelist sighed then blurred out of sight. Reappearing in front of Noah, he thrust his rapier. Somehow, the warrior lifted his weapon in time to parry the blow.

Noah growled and launched a powerful strike at Ackley. When their blades crossed, the force of it sent the smaller man sliding back across the grass.

"I'll see you drawn and quartered for your betrayal," Noah shouted.

"I'm afraid that's most unlikely," Ackley replied, saluting the warrior with his blade. "I apologize, but I must kill you now."

Amara desperately drew mana into her soul. The process was excruciatingly slow when she wasn't meditating, but if she kept at it, she *might* be able to cast a spell before the battle was over.

As she struggled, Borim and Jonas hurled themselves into the fight to help Noah. Amara took a step back, placing herself between the farmer and the raging battle. Though he'd obviously been terrified, the man had put himself in danger to save them. And she would protect him at all costs.

Eldred dumped the injured mage on the ground and then squared off against Borim. When the dwarf charged forward, the big warrior bashed him in the face with his shield.

Borim recovered quickly, knocking aside a spear thrust with his axe before burying the head of his weapon in Eldred's shield. A grunt of pain showed the steel edge had penetrated the wood and found flesh beneath.

Amara watched Jonas chase Kymber as she retreated. Noah and Ackley continued to exchange blows. The duelist was much faster than the warrior, but his rapier was useless against the warrior's thick plate armor.

Hoping she'd regained enough mana for the spell, Amara prepared to cast *Charm Person*. If she could remove just one of Ackley's group members from the fight, it should tip the battle in their favor.

A harsh feminine laugh echoed through the trees.

From the far side of the clearing, hundreds of Issurians and diminutive lizard men emerged from the dense growth ringing the glade.

Leading them was a female Issurian, her skin the color of bleached bone, with black horns curled on either side of her face. She wore plate armor and held a spinning disc of pure darkness in her hand. Her features were disconcertingly flawless. Eyes aglow with red hellfire, she smiled at them. When she finally spoke, her words were heavily accented.

"Is there discord among the Forces of Order? How fortuitous for me."

She strode forward until she stood in the center of the clearing. Aiming a gauntleted hand at the group, she said, "I am Tecala, servant of Malcheron.

Surrender the avatar to me, and the rest of you may go free. You have my word that none of you will be harmed if you agree to my terms."

Amara took stock of the army arrayed against them. Despair welled up in her heart. There was no way to escape from this situation. If she wanted her friends to survive, then she needed to give herself up. She started to take a step forward, but Borim caught her arm.

"What do you think you're doing?" the dwarf muttered under his breath.

"It's the only way," she replied in a hushed tone.

"I'd rather die fighting at your side against those bastards than give you up."

Jonas appeared on her other side. "I share our friend's sentiments. I will stand with you until the end."

Amara opened her mouth to reply, but the words died in her throat as Noah shoved her aside into Borim's arms.

He strode away from the group and into the clearing.

"I am the avatar," Noah called back to Tecala. "Do with me what you will, but let the rest go free."

# CHAPTER 37

No one moved.

Noah presented himself to the female Issurian, his claim of being the avatar still hanging heavily in the air. He held his chin up defiantly, no trace of fear in his expression as he faced the towering, demon-like creature. Alone.

Amara couldn't understand why Noah was doing this for her. He'd made his loathing for her quite clear, and Tecala offered an easy opportunity to get rid of her once and for all. *Well,* Amara thought, *Lady Ingrid did say his loyalty was beyond reproach.*

Her thoughts were interrupted as Noah let out a cry and dropped to his knees, his sword tumbling from limp fingers.

Tecala gave a throaty chuckle. "The avatar is a woman, pitiful meatsack. You are no woman and, with your pathetic stats, you are certainly no avatar." Her fiery gaze swept across the others. "This is the last time I will make my offer. Give up the avatar, and you may live."

Borim pushed Amara aside gently and took up a position in front of her. "Did your icy home freeze your brain or something? What sort of idiot would trust the word of a foul demoness?"

The Issurian woman sighed. "Then I have no choice—"

"Wait! That one there is the avatar," Ackley shouted, a finger thrust toward Amara. He continued haltingly, choosing his words with care. "Or so she claims. We wouldn't want to . . . unwittingly . . . surrender a false avatar to you. We certainly don't want you to become . . .upset."

As Amara endured Tecala's piercing gaze, she felt icy fingers tightening around her soul. The pressure continued until she thought her chest would burst. She wanted to cry out, then—

As suddenly as it began, the sensation disappeared, leaving only a deep chill.

"So, it's true," Tecala breathed. "An avatar has returned to the world." She hesitated for a moment, seeming less assured. "As I said, the rest of you are free to go, even the foolish dwarf who needs to learn his place."

Borim planted his feet and lifted his axe. "If you try to take her, I'll send you running all the way back to tundra with your tail between your legs."

Jonas stood shoulder to shoulder with the dwarf, their bodies shielding Amara from the Issurian. "I will not allow you to lay a single finger on her."

"Yeah," Salamander called out. "What they said!"

Ackley circled around Amara, giving her companions a wide berth. "They do not speak for the rest of us, Lady Tecala. Perhaps some arrangement could be worked out with my group? We're always seeking employment, and we know the layout of Stout Oak Keep. Rather intimately."

"Yes, I imagine something could be arranged." Tecala lifted her spinning disc of darkness. "However, if you wish to serve me, I would advise you to step back."

*I'm going to make that asshole pay,* Amara thought. *I never should have healed him.*

Ackley bowed and then backed away from Amara. He ushered his group toward Tecala—Eldred, stopping to pick up Landon—before they hurried past the Issurian leader.

Amara's eyes darted around the clearing, seeking a way out of their situation. A bristling wall of steel blocked every path of escape. Maybe if she had more mana, she could fight her way through the kobolds and Issurians. But right now, she doubted she could cast more than a single spell, and it wouldn't be *Divine Weapon*. She lacked the power to summon her sword.

But then her eyes alighted on the opening to the dungeon. None of the forces arrayed against them had thought to block the imposing archway. And if she cast a spell to distract Tecala, they might make it inside before the demoness could recover.

"Is there another way out of the dungeon?" she whispered to Noah as he regained his feet.

Noah nodded almost imperceptibly. "There is an exit many leagues from here if you defeat the final challenge," he muttered under his breath. "However, few groups are capable of progressing so far into the dungeon."

Amara glanced around the clearing. Once again, she reached out to her mana to cast *Charm Person*. With Tecala under her thrall, she might be able to ensure that her group could make it to the dungeon.

Noah shook his head. "Whatever you are planning will almost certainly fail against someone of her level."

"I have to try something!"

"Know I do this for the baroness," he said, "and not for you."

Noah's face hardened as he raised his sword and saluted Tecala. Then he launched himself toward the horned woman.

"Holy Birgitta, guide my blade!"

Tecala hurled her ring of whirling darkness which he deflected it with his blade. The umbral missile spun off to the side where it struck a patch of grass and exploded with a shower of dirt. Another disc appeared in the demoness's hand.

Skidding to a stop, Noah slammed the pommel of his sword against the ground. The earth broke open around him, swallowing several of the Issurians as they rushed to aid their leader. Tecala leapt agilely to a spit of solid ground.

Noah and the horned woman clashed, his shining sword dispelling the shadowy weapons she summoned. All around them, the yawning fissures spread, sending dozens of kobolds tumbling to their doom.

Jonas grabbed Amara's shoulder and spun her around. "Do not make his sacrifice for nothing."

"But why would he do this for me?" she asked, still stunned by his actions. "He hates me!"

"He serves his lady," Jonas replied simply. "And he is willing to die for her."

Amara shook her head to clear her mind. The Chaos army roared toward them. She gestured at Mimi to follow then sprinted for the dungeon. Amara slowed after a few steps, realizing that Mimi struggled to keep up with the added weight of the priestess. She considered giving Mimi the order to drop Emmaline. She knew the smart thing to do was order Mimi to leave the priestess to Chaos.

She let out a sigh and raised her hand to cast *Holy Light*. A pinprick of illumination appeared in her palm before sending shockwaves of radiance surging outwards. The light grew until it surpassed the sun and cleansed the world in pure white brilliance.

She blinked her eyes furiously as tears ran down her cheeks. When the light finally faded, relief flooded her as the outlines of the kobolds staggering around became visible. She'd feared they might be high enough level to resist her spell. But she noticed unlike the weaker goblins, none of them were attempting to flee.

Her mimic scampered past, and Amara urged the rest of her group to race for the dungeon. By the time they reached the archway, the kobolds had recovered, and crossbow bolts rained down around them. But the creature's vision was likely still off as the missiles sailed wide.

Harold staggered into the dungeon, holding his side. "Remind me to never help you folks again."

Salamander arrived next, breathing hard. "Next time I see him, I'm going to burn that jerk Ackley to a crisp."

"I'm going to do far worse," Borim promised darkly. Then he lifted his hand to shade his eyes as he peered into the dungeon. "Which way do we go?"

At first glance, it didn't appear much different from the forest outside. Instead of one path, as with the exterior, five well-traveled trails spread out in front of them. She'd been told this was a Life Aspect dungeon and that it used beasts from the forest for the challenges. Since the layout and complement of monsters constantly changed, it was impossible to know much more about what awaited them.

"Are you truly an avatar?" a quiet voice asked.

When Amara turned to answer, she saw it had been Emmaline who'd spoken. "If I were you," Amara warned, "I'd stay quiet until we return to the castle. Considering that my pet is too busy babysitting you, she won't be able to help us with whatever's in there. It would be easier for everyone if we just let the dungeon monsters have you."

"Does . . . Noah still live?" Emmaline continued.

"He was still fighting the last time I saw him," Amara replied. "I doubt he will survive against such overwhelming odds."

She'd recognized the look on Noah's face when he strode out to face Tecala—she'd seen the same expression on her father during his last days. Noah had known he was facing certain death.

Borim pushed back his helmet to scratch his head. "So, which way?"

She glanced over her shoulder to see a handful of kobolds armed with spears clustered around the dungeon entrance. For some reason, the creatures hadn't crossed the threshold. She pointed down a path on the right. "We'll go this way."

Jonas stepped out in front of her. "Please, allow me to lead the way in case there are any traps."

Amara nodded and waited as he ranged out in front of the group.

As they followed the rogue into the strange forest, the path grew narrow. When the Forces of Chaos followed them inside, their superior numbers would be stymied by the tight trails. Amara remembered something else Jonas had mentioned; that dungeon cores grew "annoyed" if too many adventurers entered at once. If the kobolds counted toward that limit, the dungeon's nature might work in her group's favor.

As she delved deeper into the dungeon, the other sounds faded away until only birdsong and the buzz of insects remained. The scents of loamy earth and fragrant flowers filled her nostrils. She felt a strange sense of peace radiating from the dungeon around her.

They walked for nearly a quarter of an hour before they reached a clearing. At the center stood what could only be described as a sentient tree. Nearly thirty feet tall, the creature stretched thick, leaf-covered limbs. Eyes like oil drops regarded them from recessed sockets in the center of the being's trunk.

Though Amara believe it saw them, the entity didn't react to their presence.

Borim stroked his beard. "There's no question this is one of the main challenge monsters. It won't make a move unless we show ourselves to be hostile, or until we try to cross the clearing. Best take some time to regain a bit of mana, lass."

"You want me to meditate *now*?" she asked, surprised at the suggestion. "There are demons right behind us."

"And we're about to tussle with a monster taller than a house," Borim said. "I'd feel a mite more comfortable if you could heal me. What if I'm squashed flat by a giant foot?"

Without meditating, Amara could only restore herself by dips and drabs. She doubted her current reserves would allow her to cast a single spell.

"I agree with Borim," Jonas said. "I would feel better if our greatest asset was prepared for the battle ahead. While you meditate, we'll lie in wait on the trail for our pursuers. Perhaps we can ambush the advance guard and drive them off."

Salamander placed her hands on her hips. "No, thank you. I'm not sitting in some bug-infested bushes."

"You can stay here and regain some mana with me." Amara brushed her hair back with one hand. "Are you sure you don't want to wait until we're past the monster, Jonas?"

The rogue seemed to waver for a moment, but then shook his head. "No, we'll ambush our pursuers to give you more time."

Amara didn't like the idea, but she realized it was folly to face a monstrous creature without any mana. So, she settled down and opened her soul to the surrounding energy. She would refill her mana as quickly as possible, then they'd face the giant tree monster.

As she cleared her mind, an idea of how to deal with their pursuers took shape. She'd have to talk to the others, but if her plan worked, they might kill two birds with one stone.

# CHAPTER 38

The sound of shouts and the clash of steel jolted Amara out of her meditation. She opened her eyes and was glad to see that Borim had been right—the monstrous creature Jonas had called a treant remained in the center of the space. Inert. As the dwarf had said, it remained passive as long as it wasn't attacked.

She pushed herself to her feet and peered down the trail leading toward the glade. The muted noises of battle implied Borim and Jonas had sprung their ambush, but the leaf-laden branches and bushes growing along the edges obscured her vision.

A moment later, Borim barreled down the path, pumping his arms with his axe struck through his belt. Jonas followed quickly, pursued by angry hisses and clicks.

"I take it the ambush didn't go well?" Amara said as they neared her position.

"The size of the force was far larger than expected," Jonas replied, breathing hard. "However, the dungeon has attacked them with what appear to be toadstool men, so we have some time before they reach us."

She frowned at hearing there were more kobolds than expected. She'd planned to let them catch up and then pincer them between the treant and her *Divine Weapon*. But if there were a lot of them as Jonas said, then she couldn't risk it.

Borim gasped as he bent over to place his hands on his knees. "Those scaly bastards took more effort than I thought they would to put down. Best we attack the Challenge Monster straight away. Just give me a moment to catch my breath."

"Can't we just go around it?" Salamander asked as she twirled her hair.

Jonas pointed to the edges of the clearing, where thick brambles grew. "The dungeon will have created barriers to prevent that. And should we manage to squeeze through somehow, I imagine the monster will chase us down."

"Great." Salamander let out a long sigh. "I guess I'll just fight the walking shrubbery."

As the others talked, Amara took a moment to check her mana and was pleased to see she'd nearly refilled three quarters of her soul. It should be enough to allow her to cast *Divine Weapon*, with mana left over for a few healing or support spells. The situation wasn't ideal, but she had a feeling she wouldn't have time to refill her mana after each fight.

The dwarf straightened up and pulled out his axe. "Ready when you are, lass."

Salamander stood up and stretched. "Are we really going to fight a tree? I don't suppose you can cast a big floaty axe, can you?"

Amara paused at the girl's suggestion. Could she alter the shape of her *Divine Weapon?* She'd never tried before, and an axe would be more effective against the treant. But then she remembered it mirrored the blade the goddess Melischar wielded, so she doubted it could be altered.

As she wove the spell, she pictured a giant lumberjack's axe in her mind. When the familiar flaming sword appeared, she felt vaguely disappointed.

"I'll attack first with my spectral weapon," Amara said. "If that doesn't work, Salamander will use her fire spells. I don't want anyone to get too close to that tree monster."

"Agreed," Borim said. "If I get killed by a walking tree, tell the people at the castle I died from literally anything else."

"No one is going to die," Amara said firmly. She glanced over her shoulder where the sounds of battle still raged. The toadstool men, as Jonas had called them, sounded like they were putting up a good fight against the kobolds. She hoped her group didn't encounter them.

Amara confirmed everyone was ready and then sent her sword soaring toward the treant. The creature ignored the spectral blade until it slammed tip first into the monster's trunk; the weapon's momentum buried the blade all the way to the hilt. Thick red liquid oozed out of the wound and dripped down the bark like sap. The treant let loose a groaning roar—the sound like branches creaking in the wind—before it sagged forward.

Borim slapped her on the back as he guffawed. "What a pushover! I guess you could say its bark was worse than its bite."

The treant violently shook its leafy head, sending dozens of round pods raining down on the clearing. When they struck the ground, the cases split open, and a miniature copy of the monster sprouted from the soil. The seedlings immediately tore themselves free from the dirt and scurried back toward the treant that had birthed them.

Jonas sprinted forward as he hurled a throwing knife at the nearest seedling. "We must kill them before they reach the treant!"

Amara ordered her *Divine Weapon* to attack the seedlings. Though its hilt vibrated as it tried to obey, the blade was wedged within in the treant. She looked on in shock. Nothing she had seen previously had been able to constrain her weapon. *Is the sap-like substance magical?* Amara wondered.

With her spectral weapon stuck, she chased after the closest sprouted creature. She'd just have to kill them with her staff. She cursed as she brought down her wooden staff and struck nothing but an empty patch of grass. The little seedlings were surprisingly agile.

She continued to pursue the tiny plant creature toward the tree, and her weapon finally struck it with a glancing blow a few paces from the treant. The seedling was knocked onto its side, and she brought down the end of her staff to squish it. Sticky green liquid burst out, spraying across her legs.

"Well, that's disgusting," she commented as she shook her foot. "I didn't think they'd be filled with sap or whatever."

She looked around to check on the progress of her group and saw they had killed about half of the seedlings. But the rest of the tiny tree-like creatures had clambered up the trunk of the treant. As she watched, the seedlings burst open, and the sticky liquid inside sealed the wound shut.

The treant let out another groan as it tore the spectral sword free and tossed it aside. Then it fixated its beady eyes on Amara. The creature let loose an enraged roar and plodded in her direction.

Amara stared up in horror at the enormous treant bearing down on her. She tried to dodge a ponderous swing of its arm, but she couldn't escape its massive reach. With a flash of light, her *Divine Weapon* zipped into view and took the treant's punch. The force of the blow sent glistening cracks spider-webbing down the ghostly weapon.

As Amara sprinted away. Behind her, she heard the *thunk* of a throwing knife striking the treant. A blow from behind struck her and sent her tumbling across the clearing. She came to a stop in a soft patch of grass, stars dancing in her vision.

When she tried to push herself up, her arms gave out, and she collapsed back to the ground. She hurriedly cast *Heal Wounds* on herself as the treant charged nearer. Before the monster could reach her, Borim appeared in its path.

The dwarf launched himself forward and buried his axe deep into the treant's leg. Then he ripped his weapon free in a torrent of red sap. He slammed it back against the same spot, hacking off a chunk of the bark-like skin. But it was like a mouse trying to cut down a human with a needle. Borim managed to dodge a powerful kick before falling back.

Jonas appeared at Amara's side and offered his hand. "This Challenge Monster is not suited to my talents. I feel rather . . . ineffectual at the moment."

Amara gripped his hand as she pulled herself to her feet. She gasped as pain exploded from her back—the hit must have injured her spine. But as motes of light splashed against her armor, the wounds beneath mended, and the pain quickly faded.

"Salamander," Amara called out as she hobbled away from the monster. "Burn the tree!"

Salamander had remained back from the fighting, but now she stepped forward. Her face pinched with concentration as she summoned a swirling ball of fire between her palms. With a cry, she released a stream of liquid fire at the treant, the flames splattering against its trunk before she adjusted her aim to engulf its leafy crown. The foliage ignited, quickly spreading through the branches. It transformed into an inferno as the creature staggered about, groaning in pain.

Thrashing its burning head, the thing desperately sent another wave of pods loose upon the clearing. While Amara couldn't be sure, there seemed to be fewer than last time.

Jonas raced to the nearest seed. As the pod split open, he kicked the seedling into the air before impaling it on his dagger. "We must kill them all!"

She sent her *Divine Weapon* through the clearing, the flaming blade mowing down many of the seedlings. Her companions followed; hacking, stabbing, and stomping on any of the creatures they could catch.

Despite their efforts, a handful of the tiny saplings managed to reach the burning treant. These clambered up the parent's legs and torso before bursting open and smothering the fire with sap. Bellowing, the treant reared once more and spread its arms wide. It tromped toward Jonas, who rapidly retreated.

Amara's spectral sword sailed on a course for the treant, but the spectral blade broke apart before it could meet its target. The timer on her spell had finished. She swore under her breath as she reached into her quiver. Then she glanced over at Salamander. "Do you have any mana left?"

"I have a bit," the girl called back. A ball of fire still swirled in her hands.

"Cast your spell again," Amara shouted. As she did, she launched a dart at the treant. With her *Dart Deadeye* on cooldown, she knew it wouldn't do much damage. But hopefully they could wear down the monster bit by bit.

A jet of fire struck the treant, engulfing its arm. The creature swung its flaming limb around as it staggered about.

Amara took the opportunity to hurl a dart, and the missile buried itself above the creature's eye. Red sap dripped from the wound and the treant turned its attention toward her.

She skirted the edge of the clearing—giving the prickly brambles a wide berth—while trying to keep ahead of the pursuing treant. She wracked her brain, trying to think of a spell to use. If she used *Cloak of Shadows,* then the monster would just attack her group members. And she didn't want to partially blind her own group with *Holy Light,* in case it didn't work on the walking tree.

But her *Holy Light* spell and the dart imbedded in the creature's forehead gave her an idea. She slowed to let the treant catch up. When the monster was only a few paces away, she hurled a dart at its eye. The missile plunged into the dark orb and clear fluid burst out like a popped grape.

As the monster creaked and staggered, she readied another dart. This one missed and struck just above its remaining eye. She had to sprint away as she readied another missile. Amara once again slowed to allow the treant close the distance. When it stomped near to her, she threw the missile with a grunt and let out a cry of triumph as it plunged into the monster's remaining eye.

Flames creeping toward its crown, crimson sap dripping from a dozen wounds, the treant lurched to a halt.

Her quiver spent, Amara had no weapons that could hurt the treant, so she let Jonas and Borim go to work. Together, they hacked and stabbed at the blinded monster until it at last collapsed to the ground. When it shook this time, Amara was ready. She squashed the handful of seedlings that fell around the clearing.

As she crushed the last one under her boot with a squelching sound, the treant dissolved, leaving nothing behind.

"Did . . . did we win?" Amara asked breathlessly. "Is it over?"

Jonas nodded as he ran a hand through his hair. "The challenge monster is defeated."

She glanced over at where the monster had been a moment earlier, shocked something so massive could just dissolve into nothing. But then she realized it *had* left something behind. She stalked forward to see a single fruit in the shape of a pear, the skin sparkling as though it contained a constellation within.

As she picked it up, she frowned. "What is this thing?"

Borim laughed and slapped his knee. "You must be the luckiest girl around. That right there is a spirit fruit. And one bite of that will change your life."

"Should we eat it then?"

"I would advise against it." Jonas stepped forward and shook his head. "A spirit fruit contains an immense amount of power. In order to properly consume it, you must prepare for weeks, and then only do so in a controlled environment."

"I see," she said, a bit disappointed she couldn't use it right away. It probably would have helped in the quest to complete the dungeon.

"We must leave this place," Jonas said as he pointed at the center of the clearing, where a sapling had appeared. The tree's shape closely resembled the treant and was climbing toward the sky at a rapid pace. "The monster will soon reappear to guard the clearing."

Amara waved at her mimic on the far side, and her pet scuttled over, the priestess still stuck on top of it. Harold, the pig farmer, followed closely behind.

Harold rubbed a hand down his face when he reached them, looking pale. "That thing was terrifying. I can't believe you fought against it and *won*."

Salamander gave him a broad grin. "You should hear about all the other stuff she's done."

"*She's* done?" Borim grunted. "I think my axe played a pretty important role in most of our kills."

Amara gave the dwarf a grin. "I softened them up for you."

"Bah!" Borim threw up his hands. "That's the problem with Trickster Clerics—they always steal the glory."

Jonas regarded the dwarf with a bemused expression. "When have you ever encountered another Trickster Cleric?"

The dwarf ignored him and then tramped off to the far side of the clearing, muttering and shaking his head as he went.

"We should make haste," Jonas urged, pointing at the tree.

Amara raised her brow in alarm at how fast the sapling was growing. She hurried across the clearing with the others to reach the far side. They'd barely reached the trail when the treant tore itself free from the ground and retook its position.

A thought she'd had when they'd first arrived returned to her. "It seems like it won't attack anything outside of the clearing. Is that right?"

Jonas nodded. "I believe so. Most dungeons present fair challenges to all who attempt them. Unless, of course, you enter with a large or overpowered group."

"Then if I don't directly attack it, the monster will ignore me," she mused before a smile spread across her lips. "I have an idea to get rid of our pursuers, and for once, there won't be any danger for us."

Jonas frowned. "If true, it would be your first plan which didn't put you in extreme peril."

She grinned at Jonas's reaction and then began to explain a modified version of her earlier plan. By the time she finished, even the staid rogue was smiling.

# CHAPTER 39

Amara roused herself from meditation as someone tapped her on the shoulder lightly. She opened her eyes to see Jonas, and then wearily rose to her feet. After stretching her back, she walked over to the edge of the clearing to peek through a bough heavy with pine needles. On the trail leading to the treant, she spotted a seething mass of kobolds approaching.

Many of the lizard-like creatures sported wounds, though she couldn't be sure if they'd received them from her group's ambush or the toadstool men. A fight broke out among them. As she watched, the kobolds shoved and clawed at each other as they tried to avoid being the first one to enter the clearing.

Finally, one of the smaller creatures was pushed forward, and when it failed to regain its place on the path, it turned to face the treant. With wide eyes, it skirted around the brambles at the edge of the glade.

At first, Amara feared the challenge monster wouldn't react, perhaps having a cooldown on its aggression after having fought her group. But when the kobold reached the midpoint of the clearing, the leafy monster sprang to life and stomped in the intruder's direction.

The kobold let out a squeak before it turned and fled. But it found no safety with its companions on the path, and they refused to let it escape. The lizardman let out a panicked hiss as the treant grabbed its legs, and then swung it around, slamming it against the ground.

Though Amara grimaced, she kept her gaze trained on the monster as it smashed the kobold to a bloody pulp. The small intruder dead, the treant tossed the corpse aside before stomping back to the center of the clearing.

After a few more minutes spent jostling for position, the kobolds finally found their courage. While the reptilian warriors readied their weapons for combat, Amara could feel power emanating from their mages as they prepared to cast their spells.

*Did they push the first kobold forward just to test the monster?*

She didn't have long to dwell on her thoughts. The kobolds surged forward. A barrage of ice shards pelted the tree, followed by a gale of wind forcing it back. Nearly a score of kobolds swarmed into the clearing, stabbing and hacking at the treant.

"If you plan to act, now is the time," Jonas whispered to Amara.

She hurriedly wove together her mana to cast *Divine Weapon*. She prayed Jonas was right, and the treant wouldn't turn hostile toward them if she didn't attack it directly. After a moment, her spectral sword formed in front of her, the blade blazing with an ethereal fire which gave off no heat. She immediately sent the blade skimming around the edge of the clearing.

The *Divine Weapon* struck the kobolds from the flank and cleaved through two of them before they could even react. As the blade slashed and stabbed, three more fell as they tried to reform their lines. The kobolds faced the impossible task of a battle on two fronts.

"Ha," Borim called out. "Take that, you scaly bastards!"

Jonas pointed at the casters clustered at the rear of the kobolds. "It would be advisable to deal with the magic users first."

Amara nodded then directed her floating weapon to concentrate on the mages; they represented the only real threat to her group. The spectral blade deflected a flurry of frozen lances before descending on a kobold with swirls of frost encircling its hands.

At the sight of the *Divine Weapon* flying toward it, the caster hastily conjured up a wall of ice. But it did little to stop her spell. The blade shattered the glacial barrier, slicing through to sever the kobold's head.

The treant had used the distraction she'd created to wade into the kobolds, crushing the diminutive creatures under its massive feet. A groan escaped its woody lips as its eyes bulged with madness. It grabbed a pair of kobolds and hurled them into the brambles. The lizardmen loosed terrible screams as they landed wetly on the spiked bushes.

Amara sent her *Divine Weapon* angling toward the other spellcaster in the group. Before her spectral sword could strike, a blast of wind sent the blade tumbling back. She recovered quickly, and tried another path, only to have a gale stop her weapon cold.

After two more attempts to attack the kobold mage, she grimaced in frustration and turned her attention to easier prey. Her weapon carved through the lizardmen battling the treant. Two more quickly fell to her flaming sword, the last of which fell to the ground in two pieces. As their comrade's remains oozed, the rest of the kobolds fled from the clearing. The magic user conjured a wall of air before sprinting away.

It would have been easy to cut down the fleeing kobolds, but she pulled her spectral weapon back. In the confusion of their retreat, she didn't want to accidentally strike the treant. The last thing she needed was to provoke another battle with the incredibly tough tree monster.

Once her *Divine Weapon* had reached their position, she released the spell, and the blade disintegrated into shards of light. "I think that will buy us some time. If you could watch over me while I meditate, we'll leave once I've replenished my mana."

Jonas pointed toward the far side of the clearing. "I don't believe we'll have time for that. It appears the dungeon thinks we've dawdled here for too long."

Amara followed his gesture to see horrors staggering in their direction. After a second, she realized they must be the toadstool men Jonas had described. But she'd expected something cute, like in a video game. These creatures looked completely inhuman—like some eldritch nightmare conjured into existence by a twisted mind.

Their heads were bulbous, with pulsating veins stretching the length, and nearly one hundred red unblinking eyes stared out in every direction. The creature's bodies were misshapen, as though a malevolent god had twisted them into caricatures of humans. Some only had a single limb, while others had dozens, with flaps of grey skin hanging down loosely.

"Are these what you called toadstool men? She couldn't tear her eyes away from the monstrosities. "Why didn't you tell me they were so . . . terrifying?"

Salamander took a step back. "I'm with Amara. I'm going to have bad dreams about those things. What's wrong with their *heads*?"

"They die the same as anything else," Borim said gruffly. "If the kobolds could fight their way through them then we can, too."

Jonas motioned at the trail leading away from the clearing. "Still, caution is warranted. We should continue to the next challenge."

Amara hesitated for a moment. She barely had a quarter of her mana remaining, and she hated the idea of continuing without meditating. But then the sight of dozens more of the toadstool men boiling out of the forest spurred her on. "Alright. Let's get going."

Jonas once again took the lead. The others formed a star around Harold and Mimi. As they started to move again, the toadstool men slowed their pursuit.

She continued to glance over her shoulder until the disturbing creatures at last disappeared from view. After a few more minutes of walking, peace returned to the forest. Once again, birds sang, and insects buzzed. But this time she knew it was an illusion, and death lurked behind every tree.

Salamander shook her head. "I mean, seriously, what was wrong with their heads? They looked so gross. Why is no one talking about it?"

"They're gone for now," Amara replied. "We should just keep an eye out for the next monster, or whatever the dungeon has in store for us."

Ahead, Jonas slowed and then held out his hands to stop them. "It appears the next challenge has to do with a puzzle."

Amara looked past the rogue to see a clearing filled with patches of wildflowers. Statues lined the edge of the forest, each standing at least six feet tall, their features worn smooth by the passage of time. Each of the monuments had a gaping mouth, as though the sculpture was silently screaming.

Borim reached up to clap the rogue on the shoulder. "I guess this is your time to shine, Sneaky."

Jonas shook off the dwarf's hand. "I am not *sneaky.*"

"Now don't go getting your small clothes in a bunch. I didn't mean anything by it," Borim replied. "We're just lucky to have a rogue in our group for this encounter."

Jonas nodded, looking distracted. "If no one objects, I'll examine the clearing."

"Just be careful," Amara said. "I don't have much mana left to cast healing spells, and I'd like to save it in case those horrible toadstool men catch up with us."

The rogue set out slowly into the clearing. Only a few feet in, he pointed at a patch of red flowers growing close to the ground. "Those mask a pit beneath."

She stared intently at where he'd pointed, but she couldn't see anything different from the surroundings. If Jonas hadn't warned her, then she could have easily blundered into the pit trap. And she doubted her spells would be much use if she lay broken at the bottom of a hole.

The rogue continued through the wildflowers until he reached the first of the statues. He stopped there and examined the carving until he turned around and returned to the group. He looked troubled as he trotted up to them.

"I believe those statues are part of some trap. However, I cannot locate any trip wires or other mechanisms to trigger it."

Borim hefted his axe. "I say we just push through. How bad could the trap be?"

Salamander pointed at Emmaline, still tied up on the mimic's back. The priestess hadn't said a word since they'd entered the dungeon. "What if we use her to test it?"

Borim tugged on his beard. "The girl's got a good idea. At least we'd find out if there were any traps. And it's not like we're going to let her live any way."

Amara shook her head. "I'm not a fan of her, but we can't use her as a living shield."

"Why not?" Borim continued. "The baroness is probably going to chop off her head when we get back. And while we're on the topic, I'm starting to think that lady is as crazy as a bag of moles. She's got an unhealthy obsession with you."

Jonas frowned. "I agree with the dwarf. The recent events seem to have taken their toll on the lady. And her orders have been nothing short of disastrous. I think you may need to re-examine your relationship with her when we return."

"We'll talk about it when we get back," Amara said. "There's no point worrying about it until we're safely out of the dungeon."

But truth be told, she'd been thinking along similar lines. Everything the baroness had been involved with had turned into a complete disaster. Lady Ingrid had announced her publicly as an avatar for everyone in her fief, which had led to her being betrayed to the Forces of Chaos. And after denying her request to attempt the dungeon with her group, the baroness had sent her with a party of traitors who'd tried to kill her.

*How do I cut ties with the most powerful person in the North?*

She pushed down her thoughts as she focused on the clearing in front of her.

Jonas regarded her as he spun a dagger in his palm. "I believe the only way forward is for someone from our group to trigger the hidden trap. And as the group's only rogue, I'm the logical choice."

"What?" Amara said, her voice rising slightly. "I'm not going to let you just blunder into some trap. What if it's immediately fatal? What if a giant log swings down and crushes you?"

Borim tugged on his beard. "She's got a point. You won't be much to help our group if you get squashed as thin as flatbread."

"I'm afraid we don't have time to discuss the options."

Jonas pointed back down the trail with his dagger. When Amara turned, she spotted the toadstool men creeping forward. The dungeon was once again pushing them forward.

"I don't like this," she said. "But you're right—someone has to go." And she'd already decided that someone should be her. She took a step forward, only to let out a cry of surprise as Jonas sprinted past. She heard a *whoosh*, and then the air ignited as the trap triggered.

# CHAPTER 40

At the sound of the trap triggering, Jonas activated his skill, *Evasion.* Leaping into the air, he twisted around the gouts of flames issuing forth from the statue's mouth. But even with his ability, he still felt fire licking at his arms, and the intense heat made him grimace with pain.

Jonas landed lightly and then spun away as the firestorm behind him weakened then flickered out. He found himself standing in a patch of yellow flowers, and he took a minute to glance around to check on his companions.

He sought out Amara first and breathed a sigh of relief to see she was unscathed from the trap. The moment she'd agreed with him, he'd known she was about to do something rash. She relied far too much on her Luck to get herself through encounters.

The fact she had such a high Luck stat still boggled his mind. Outside of emperors and adventurers of the highest rank, Jonas had never read of anyone having more than one or two points in that attribute. And while he'd suspected there was something different about her from the moment they'd met, he'd never dreamed she'd turn out to be an avatar.

To Jonas, the idea of living incarnations of gods still seemed like nothing more than a myth from a lost era. After all, among the scholars of the South, few believed in the existence of the gods—and those who did assumed they had abandoned humankind long ago.

He'd spent much of his youth reading books arguing against the existence of the gods. The greatest philosophers had all claimed everything in the world could be explained by magic, and magic alone. Even the Area Quests—those given by mysterious forces and offering impressive rewards—were thought to be a remnant of a long-buried core, perhaps put in place by the First Emperor of Man.

But since meeting Amara, he'd seen things he couldn't explain. And the Forces of Chaos seemed convinced she was an avatar. The longer he was around her, the more he solidified his belief she *was* the incarnation of Melischar.

The existence of a flesh and blood avatar came with troubling implications. If the gods of Order existed, then it stood to reason the gods of Chaos did as well. And after touring many of the southern kingdoms during his youth, he knew their leaders were woefully unprepared for another Age of Strife. If the Forces of Chaos marched south, and the Harbingers rose from their barrows, then they would sweep the human kingdoms and republics aside with little trouble.

*No matter what,* Jonas thought, *Galoth's Wall must hold.*

He shook his head to focus on the task at hand. His mother had often scolded him for letting his mind wander. And standing in the middle of a trap laden glade was no place to lose your concentration.

Amara raised her foot to take a step forward, but then seemed to think better of it. She shook her hand at him. "How could you be so reckless?"

He simply shrugged in reply. "As the group's rogue, I was perfectly suited to trigger the trap. And we didn't have time to consider other options."

"But you could have been killed!"

"I was completely safe with my ability," Jonas answered as he eyed the ground. "And I believe I have deciphered the puzzle to this area." He pointed at the patch of red flowers growing in an irregular shape in front of the statue. "The colors indicate safe areas and traps."

Amara chewed on her lower lip. "I don't think the dungeon would make it that easy."

Jonas searched the clearing as he examined the different blossoms. Clusters of red and blue flowers grew in front of the worn statues, and yellow blooms created narrow pathways leading to the far side. "Yes, I do believe I'm correct. However, I'll have to test my theory."

His *Evasion* ability was on cooldown for the next ten minutes, but he didn't need to tell Amara that. If he triggered another trap, his high Dexterity stat should help him to evade it. Regardless, Jonas felt confident in his assessment.

Borim lifted his helmet and scratched his head. "Be careful out there, lad."

Jonas nodded then crept forward. He kept his *Detect Traps* skill active as he moved, spotting several more pits hiding under the red flowers. However, as he passed a growth of the same blossoms near the second statue, he didn't detect anything.

He suspected it had something to do with the statue itself, as he could not discern any tripwires or pressure plates under the plants. *Perhaps the carvings have some magical ability to observe certain areas?*

While he wanted to examine the stone heads to learn more about the traps, the imminent arrival of the toadstool men necessitated a safe path across the clearing for his companions.

He continued to snake his way through the glade, always keeping his feet inside the boundaries of the yellow flowers. After a few minutes, he reached the other side safely. As he turned, he wondered what the blue flowers represented. Maybe a frost or lightning spell? If it was lightning, he was grateful he hadn't triggered that one. His *Evasion* skill could only do so much.

"I can't believe that worked," Amara called out from across the clearing. "So, just follow the yellow flowers?"

Jonas nodded and watched as Amara led the others through the narrow lanes of blossoms. Several times she had to stop to ensure her pet mimic didn't step off the path. While the monster listened to her orders, it still wasn't the most intelligent creature around. And it was struggling with the weight of Emmaline on its back.

"No reward?" Borim asked as he reached Jonas's side.

Jonas shook his head. "It appears we've angered the core in some way."

"Bloody stingy dungeon," Borim snorted. "I was hoping for a replacement shield."

Jonas had to step back to give the others room as they reached him. He smiled at Amara, but she gave him a chilly look in reply. He could see by her pinched brow she was furious at him for triggering the trap.

Amara opened her mouth as if to say something, but then scowled and knelt in the grass. She closed her eyes and folded her hands in her lap. "I need some time to meditate."

Jonas examined the far side of the clearing where the toadstool men had begun to mill about. As he observed them, they formed into loose ranks and marched across the clearing. He watched intently as the creatures tromped across areas with red and blue flowers, but no traps triggered.

*The dungeon monsters must be immune to the traps.*

"I'm afraid there is no time to meditate," he said to Amara. "The toadstool men are once again giving chase."

Amara let out an annoyed little huff and then blew a strand of red hair out of her face. "So, I'm just supposed to go through the rest of the dungeon with no mana? What if we defeat the toadstool men?"

It was a risky gamble to face the strange creatures pursuing them. There was no guarantee the dungeon would grant them time to recover if they vanquished the toadstool men. And if a second wave arrived immediately afterwards to drive them onwards, they'd be in no shape to fight the upcoming challenge monster.

Jonas rubbed his chin. "I believe we should keep moving. There is the possibility the dungeon core thinks we're part of the kobold group, which is why we're receiving this treatment. Perhaps if we put some additional distance between our parties, it will allow us more time to rest between encounters."

Emmaline raised her head from atop the mimic. "Please, release me. I don't want to die on the back of this . . . pet." As Emmaline spoke, Mimi licked the priestess with her long tongue, making her shudder.

Borim poked Emmaline with the butt of his axe. "Maybe you should have thought of that before trying to murder our friend. You're lucky we don't feed you to the mimic, and just end the matter."

"I think you should listen to him," Amara added. "I'm getting pretty tired of you Church types trying to kill me everywhere I go. And I'm close to losing what little mercy I have left for you."

"I didn't do it for the Church," Emmaline cried out. "Do you honestly think I didn't know Lady Ingrid was a Gnostic? I did it for her. She's going to die for a hopeless cause here. If it wasn't for you and your false hope, she'd leave with me for the South. I . . . I care for her deeply."

Borim prodded her harder with the butt of his axe. "Shut your mouth, already."

Jonas stepped forward. "I will gag her for the remainder of the dungeon."

"Wait!" Emmaline screamed out. "Please, I'm begging you—don't let me die blindfolded and gagged on the back of this mimic. I deserve a better fate than that. I'll . . . I'll take a binding oath to serve you."

Amara laughed. "What good would that do? Didn't you take an oath to serve Lady Ingrid?"

"No. I never took a binding oath with Lady Ingrid," the priestess replied, the words tumbling from her mouth. "If you release me, I'll promise anything you want. Just please, don't let the dungeon slaughter me like a trussed-up hog."

"Like I would trust your word," Amara scoffed.

"It is no small thing to offer," Jonas said, shocked anyone would enter such a contract. Very few were willing to take a binding oath, as the consequences for breaking it were severe. "Her words will bind your very souls. Such oaths are rarely ever used as they're unbreakable."

"I just want to get back to Lady Ingrid," Emmaline pleaded. "Please, give me one last chance to see her."

Amara shook her head. "Gag her and tighten her blindfold. I don't trust anything she says."

"As you wish." Jonas walked forward and fished a piece of cloth out of a pouch. When he reached the bound priestess, he tore it in half. Then he forced open her mouth and stuffed a piece inside before tying it in place with the other strip.

"Let's keep going," Amara said, her eyes darting over to the far side of the clearing. "I *really* don't want to fight those things."

Jonas followed her gaze to see the toadstool men continued to advance. At their current pace, they would reach them in mere seconds.

He spun his knives around on his palms—a nervous tick he'd had since he'd received his class—and took point for the group. So far, the dungeon hadn't placed any traps on the trails leading to the challenge areas, but he didn't dare grow complacent. If he missed a trap and someone died, he'd carry the weight of his failure for the rest of his life.

The forest closed in around him as he forged ahead, the path little more than a game trail. The environment was claustrophobic, and his nerves felt frayed after only a few minutes. As he stalked forward, he kept a keen eye for movement among the trees or any sign of traps.

But he reached the next clearing without incident. While Jonas had heard of many dungeons attacking parties moving between challenges with low level monsters, this one didn't engage in such behavior. *Or at least it hasn't done so yet,* he corrected himself.

He didn't dare let down his guard.

As he stepped free of the overgrown path, he felt like he could finally breathe again. But his relief lasted only for a moment. In the center of the clearing stood their doom.

Three enormous wolves—far larger than any he'd seen in his life—bared their teeth and snarled at the sight of him. As this dungeon was nearly a thousand years old, they may even be conjurations of the legendary dire wolves that once infested these lands.

Behind them stood a striking woman with soft features and green skin. She had flower blossoms interwoven through her dark hair, and what little clothing she wore was crafted from leaves. But while she was coldly beautiful, power radiated off her in a suffocating aura, and she carried a simple bow

Behind the strange woman and the trio of wolves, nearly a hundred toadstool men had been arrayed in battle formation. These carried an assortment of weapons, from carefully crafted clubs to swords that gleamed in the sunlight.

The green-skinned woman stepped forward and nocked an arrow. "I am Fen, servant of this dungeon. I have been sent to inform you this core will not be destroyed by your pathetic invasion. Your corpses will feed the soil and help the dungeon grow stronger than ever."

Borim appeared beside Jonas and shouldered his axe. "Oh, this is bad. Very bad."

*The dungeon thinks we're invading to destroy the core,* Jonas thought grimly. *Which means it will no longer try to present a fair challenge and will instead attempt to kill us.*

He suspected this area normally held an easier monster, but it had been replaced with the most powerful minions at the dungeon's command. He recoiled as the wolves released a suffocating aura of power, the killing intent unmistakable. One of the beasts would most likely be more than a match for the party.

Jonas sheathed his daggers and opened his hands in a non-threatening gesture. He knew if given the chance, he could explain the situation to Fen, who he recognized as a dryad. But before he could take a step forward, Amara strode past him with a determined look on her face.

He let out a sigh and re-equipped his weapons with a deft motion. While he enjoyed Amara's company, Jonas had noted she had little gift for diplomacy.

Though he didn't have much hope they could win against the assembled might of the dungeon, he would do whatever it took to get her through this alive—even if he had to resort to previously unthinkable things.

No matter what, Jonas would ensure that Amara lived to see another day.

# CHAPTER 41

Amara knew from the bleak expressions on her companions' faces they were in serious trouble. Only Borim had a glint of glee in his eyes, probably expecting to make a glorious last stand here. But Jonas had sheathed his weapons—never a good sign—which meant he thought they stood no chance against the dungeon monsters arrayed against them. Meanwhile, Salamander was as white as a sheet, while Harold cowered behind the mimic.

As Amara walked forward, and the wolves grew larger, she understood their feelings. The aura radiating off the creatures nearly drove her to her knees. And while the karaxi they'd fought had felt dangerous, the giant insect paled in comparison to these beasts. Amara had no doubt these were the final Challenge Monsters of the dungeon.

But she could see by the trail on the far side they were nowhere close to finishing the dungeon. Had these monsters all been gathered here to meet them? And what had the strange green woman meant when she accused them of invading the dungeon?

Amara hoped she could find some way to explain that her group wasn't attacking the dungeon—they were seeking refuge.

Amara stopped suddenly as the woman who had named herself Fen raised her bow and pointed the arrow in her direction. She held up her hands and took a step back. "Only the five of us came to challenge your dungeon." Amara glanced over at the struggling figure of Emmaline. "I mean, the six of us. We were chased in here by an army of Chaos, and we certainly don't plan on destroying anything."

"Lies!" Fen replied, rage twisting her face. "The ones who entered behind you are burning and despoiling my beautiful forest as we speak."

Amara raised her brow at the woman's words. Apparently, the Issurians and kobolds had given up on being subtle and settled on razing the dungeon.

"What part of *I'm being chased by the Forces of Chaos* don't you understand?" Amara asked, her patience growing thin. "Do you have leaves stuck in your ears or something?"

"Amara!" Jonas said sharply.

But Amara waved him off. She was tired of being pushed around by those more powerful than her. She hadn't wanted to announce herself as an avatar to the castle, or wear the stupid green dress to the feast, or leave for the dungeon without her group. No matter what happened, she wasn't going to let anyone push her around again.

"How dare you speak to me in such a way?" Fen cried out. "I will slay you myself!"

"Do I *look* like I'm here to destroy your dungeon core, or whatever you call it?" Amara shot back. "I'm trying to stop the Forces of Chaos. I serve the goddess Melischar—in fact, I'm her avatar, and I'm not having a great day. So, I recommend you let me through before I get angry."

"*Amara!*" Jonas hissed. "This must be dealt with diplomatically."

"Have you noticed none of the other intruders are human?" Amara asked, her voice rising. "I know you probably have roots growing through your skull, but is it *that* hard to tell the difference between us and the kobolds?"

"There is a group of humans only a short distance behind you," the dryad said thornily. "And it is clear you cannot be trusted."

Amara started. *Ackley's group.* They must have been drafted into the fight after the loss of so many kobolds. The pale Issurian woman was probably testing their loyalty—or simply didn't care if they died.

Fen waved the toadstool men forward with one green hand. "The gods long ago abandoned this world, and you sully their name by claiming to be an avatar. You will die here, and your bodies will fertilize the dungeon to give rebirth to what you destroyed."

Borim fished around in his pouch for his empty flask and unscrewed the lid. He upended it into his mouth. When not a single drop drained out, he sighed. "I was hoping there was at least a bit left. But you all best get going. I'll hold off this plant lady and her overgrown mongrels for as long as possible. There's a chance you might be able to slip around those bastards chasing us and reach the entrance."

"This isn't a hopeless situation," Amara said, though her words rang hollow in her ears. Her party was trapped between the proverbial rock and a hard place. They couldn't retreat on the narrow trails without running into the kobolds chasing them, and they couldn't move forward through the assembled might of the dungeon. And cutting through the forest was out of the question. The growth was so thick it would take hours to hack a path through it. "There must be something we can do."

Jonas stepped forward, wisps of ghostly power swirling around him. "Please stand back, as this spell may be dangerous if you approach too closely."

"What are you doing?" she asked, alarmed at the power eddying through the air. She'd never seen anything like it before.

"I am surrendering myself to the darkness." Jonas raised his weapons, letting out an uncharacteristic war cry. The guttural words rang across the clearing as he charged toward the toadstool men.

Despite his warning, Amara couldn't let Jonas fight the dungeon monsters alone. She spun around to face Salamander. "Do you have any mana left?"

The girl shook her head. "I'm sorry. I used the last of it against the treant."

Amara looked over her shoulder at Jonas, pressing her lips together; he had nearly reached the mass of toadstool men converging on him from all sides. She faced Borim. "Do you have any way to help him?"

The dwarf shook his shaggy head. "I can't do much outside of axe range." Then he brightened and patted the mimic. "But we can make sure they don't flank him, can't we? Come on, you little gluttonous walking box—we've got a rogue to help."

Mimi angled herself toward Amara and peered up at her with puppy-like eyes. As she did, she waggled her behind slightly.

"Drop the priestess here and go with him," Amara said, glancing worriedly in the direction of Jonas, who had disappeared into the horde of toadstool men. "But do it fast!"

Amara's pet shook herself to dislodge Emmaline, and the priestess dropped to the ground with a cry of pain. Then the mimic uncoiled her tongue, pressed it against the ground, and sprung off it to launch herself toward the fungal horrors.

Borim followed right behind, storming into the horde of toadstool men and hacking at any who came into range. His strikes appeared to do little damage to them—their skin was hard, like wood—but the force of his blows sent them reeling back and kept the creatures off balance.

Amara hefted her staff and moved to follow the dwarf. She didn't have enough mana left for her *Divine Weapon* spell, and even *Holy Light* was out of the question. If she was going to fight, it would have to be with her staff.

*I swear, if I get out of this alive, I'm never neglecting my Weapon Proficiencies again.*

Before she could take a step forward, something caught at her arm. She glanced down to see Salamander holding onto her for dear life.

"Please, don't leave us alone," Salamander whispered. "If . . . if this is it, I want to be with you."

Amara's heart broke at the girl's forlorn expression. She knew Salamander fully expected to die here. And when she looked at Harold, he had the same hopeless expression on his face.

The pig farmer took off his hat and wrung it between his hands. "Should I fall here, tell my family I love them. And if you can, I'd appreciate if you could check in on them. My wife has been . . . struggling since her brother was killed by the ogres."

*This is my fault,* she thought to herself. *I'm the reason they're here.*

But with no mana, there was little she could do. Frustration welled up in her soul as she turned her head to watch the battle.

Strange wraithlike trails of power swirled around Jonas as he battled the toadstools like a man possessed. His daggers flashed through the air, carving a path through the creatures. Each unlucky fungus that caught the edge of his blade withered and died, leaving little more than a dried-out husk when it dropped to the ground. And with each kill, another ghostly line of power appeared in the surrounding air.

Amara gasped as Jonas turned in her direction. His eyes were completely black. He didn't even seem to register the sight of her as he tore mercilessly through the ranks of toadstool men. She realized with a start he'd used his Wraith Rogue spells—something he'd sworn to never do.

*He's giving up everything he believes in to keep me safe.*

Borim and the mimic were having a more difficult time against the onrushing mob of toadstool men. Mimi didn't even seem to enjoy the taste of her prey, spitting out every limb she tore off with her sharp teeth. Borim hacked relentlessly at the creatures like a deadly lumberjack. It took a half dozen strikes to fell a single attacker, but still he pushed onward.

Amara turned her gaze back to Jonas, only to let out a cry as a fungal horror ran him through with its spear. Before the creature had even pulled its weapon free, she was already weaving together the strands of mana to cast *Heal Wounds.*

The glade brightened with a soft glow as motes of light descended on Jonas like softly falling snow, circling the wound before disappearing through his armor. As the spell finished mending his wounds, he staggered forward, the ghostly power eddying around him like a hurricane. He drove his blades into the nearest creature, the power ripping it apart into wet chunks. A savage kick tore another toadstool in half at the waist, but despite all the carnage, the hideous creatures still pressed on with no regard for their own lives.

As a wave of toadstool men rushed in her direction, Amara spotted Salamander out of the corner of her eye. The girl was bent over the bound form of Emmaline, making sawing motions with her tiny knife.

"What are you doing?" Amara called out, swinging her staff at the creatures charging her. "If you untie her, she'll just attack us."

"She promised she wouldn't," Salamander shouted over the sounds of the battle, struggling to cut through the ropes around Emmaline's arms. "And no one deserves to die like this."

Harold grabbed Salamander's wrist to stop her. "Take off her gag first," he said. "And make her swear a binding oath before you release her."

Salamander frowned, but then pulled off the priestess's gag. "Do you swear to never harm Amara in any way?"

"Yes," Emmaline gasped. "I swear it on my soul."

The moment the words left the priestess's mouth, writing appeared in Amara's vision.

**Do You Accept Emmaline Kohn's Binding Oath? (Yes/No)**

Amara hurriedly selected "Yes" as she swung her staff at the nearest toadstool man. The weapon cracked against the creature's head and sent it reeling. A moment later, she felt a tendril of mana stretch between her and Emmaline. The string of energy tightened and grew taut.

"Did it work?" Salamander asked, her blade pressed against the rope that bound Emmaline's ankles.

"I think so." Amara ducked under a clumsy swing from a toadstool man. As she did, she thrust the end of the staff into the creature's gut, making it crumple around her weapon. She shoved it back, putting some distance between them.

Amara swung her weapon around desperately as more of the horrors swarmed in her direction. She couldn't hold them off long with her weapon and soon they would reach Salamander and Harold. In front of them, Borim had fallen to his knees, bleeding from a dozen wounds, while Mimi had a spear sticking out of her head. Thankfully, her pet's wound didn't appear overly serious, as only a tiny bit of clear fluid was leaking out.

*I have to do something*, Amara thought, gritting her teeth.

At her thoughts, the word "Avatar" appeared in her vision as it had when she'd been trapped in her room at the Dancing Gnome Inn. But she keenly recalled Melischar's warning about being reduced to a burned-out husk if she used the spell too soon.

As she pushed another toadstool man back with her staff, Amara felt a lump in her pouch press against her thigh. Inside was the spirit fruit the dungeon had rewarded them with for defeating the treant. Jonas had said it contained an immense amount of power. She looked over at the rogue, who was still slashing his way through the seemingly endless waves of toadstool men. Would the spirit fruit be enough to fuel her *Avatar of Melischar* spell?

She fumbled for her pouch and ripped the fruit free to stare at it. The skin sparkled like it contained the essence of a thousand stars. And it felt warm to the touch, as if it had been sitting in the sun for hours.

"What are you doing?" Salamander cried out. "Even I know it's dangerous to eat that thing."

"I have no choice." Without pausing to think about it, Amara bit into the fruit. As the sweet flesh touched her tongue, a jolt of electricity arced through her mouth. The power scorched her veins and made her shudder, but she forced herself to chew and swallow. She quickly downed the rest of the spirit fruit, swallowing the soft chunks whole.

As she finished the last morsel, Amara felt mana overflowing into her soul, powered by an endless well of energy from her stomach. It coursed through her veins like she was burning alive from the inside. She knew she had to use the power before it consumed her.

Amara wove together the pattern to cast her *Avatar of Melischar* spell, praying that the mana from the spirit fruit would be enough to avoid the fate Melischar had warned her about. But even if she didn't survive the transformation, at least she'd have a chance to save her friends.

# CHAPTER 42

As Amara finished weaving together the last strand of mana to cast *Avatar of Melischar*, a shockwave of pure light burst forth from her body. The concussion knocked the closest toadstool men to their knees, and a howling wind buffeted her companions. But somehow, they kept their footing.

Her feet rose off the ground as a white liquid spread across her body before hardening into the shape of shining white armor. A gilded longsword appeared on her belt, the blade thrumming with unimaginable destructive power. She knew instinctively a single swing from the sword could level mountains. As her armor solidified, brilliant golden wings erupted from her back, the tendrils glowing with divine power.

Even with the infusion granted to her by the spirit fruit, Amara felt the transformation draining her mana at an alarming rate. She knew she would only have seconds to accomplish what she planned to do here before she'd have to relinquish her avatar form.

Amara gazed around the clearing, the world taking on new meaning. Wherever she looked, she could see the strands of fate binding together every living thing. When a toadstool man rose to its feet and charged at Jonas, she gave the slightest tug to alter the creature's destiny.

The hundred-eyed creature tripped on a slight rise in the ground and then tumbled forward to impale itself on its spear; its bloated head hit the spear and erupted in a fountain of gelatinous fluid.

Amara turned her attention to the other dungeon monsters regaining their footing. She deftly wove the threads of fate to ensure all manner of calamity befell the toadstool men. Weapons snapped, feet tripped, and eyes suddenly went blind. Within seconds, her power had reduced the attackers to a confused mob.

Her hand strayed toward the gilded longsword on her belt, but when her fingers curled around the hilt, the force of the mana that surged from her nearly made her topple over. Any additional draw on her mana would likely shatter the tenuous grip she had on the spell.

Amara released the weapon with a sharp exhaled. Her vision darkened for an instant, and a jolt of burning agony wracked her chest. She tried to soothe her overstrained soul between spasms of pain,. Untamed primal energy continued to pour into her from the spirit fruit, but *Avatar of Melischar* withdrew it even faster. The burden on her soul was quickly becoming too much.

*I have to defeat the dungeon before my body gives out.*

Amara floated forward, heading toward the Challenge Monsters at the center of the clearing. The rest of the group could handle the now catastrophically unlucky toadstool men, but Amara needed to destroy the dryad and wolves herself.

"Slay them all," she commanded her group, her voice booming across the clearing.

Another wave of agony wracked her body, like she was being dipped headfirst into lava. She felt something tighten and then crack around her soul. But she pushed down the pain and continued forward, strengthened by the determination to give her friends a chance to escape.

Behind her, she heard the sounds of her party going to work on the blundering toadstools. Each time the dungeon creatures tried to mount a defense, she would tug gently to alter the strands of fate again. No weapons touched her friends as they moved through their attackers with impunity.

As she floated toward the dryad, Amara flared her newly sprouted wings in a blaze of golden light. She glared down at the woman, now cowering underneath her, and lifted her hand in preparation to bring destruction down upon the monsters. But before she could weave the next strings of fate, Fen knelt and bowed her head.

Amara raised her brow slightly as the wolves followed suit, laying down before her. The sounds of battle faded from the clearing. When she glanced over her shoulder, Amara saw that the toadstool men had taken the same position of submission.

Another wave of agony washed over her body, and her wings failed, dropping her unceremoniously to the ground. Her knee twisted beneath her weight, but she stifled a cry and straightened up quickly. She didn't dare show any weakness here.

*I'm burning alive,* Amara thought, her mind becoming fuzzy. *But I can't give up the power. Not yet.*

She staggered forward and stopped a few paces away from the dryad. Then she placed her hand on the hilt of her sword. "Do you . . . surrender?" The pain had grown almost too much to bear, but she tried to keep it from showing on her face.

The dryad, with skin the color of verdant foliage, glanced up with an expression of awe. "Please accept my apology, Avatar. I didn't recognize you after so long."

"Will you let us leave this dungeon?" she asked, her voice faltering.

"Nothing under this dungeon's control will lay a hand upon you," Fen intoned. "The core swears you shall not be harmed. However . . . as this is clearly a dispute among the gods, we are bound by our oaths to let the Forces of Chaos proceed unhindered. I hope you understand, as dungeon cores are forbidden from taking sides in the eternal conflict."

Amara nodded, unable to speak. Her soul convulsed, and a blackness spread across her skin like a creeping ichor. She bit down on her lower lip to keep from screaming until she tasted blood.

*I'm not going to survive,* she thought, *but at least I saved my friends.*

The last of her mana had been exhausted, and the avatar spell had begun to draw upon her very life force. She waved her companions forward, only staying on her feet through sheer willpower.

As the rest of the party approached, her spell faltered, and her pristine white armor blew away like dust in the wind. The sword disappeared a moment later, and finally, the threads of fate blinked out.

She was Amara once more.

Her strength failed her, and she fell to her knees, gasping for air. Her ribs felt broken, and each time she tried to draw in a breath, the movement sent sharp pains stabbing into her chest. Unable to stay upright, she toppled face first into the soft grass.

From around her, she heard the concerned cries of her friends. Her eyes listlessly flicked to her hand—the skin was scorched and flaking like it had been roasted over a fire. But more concerningly, she couldn't feel any pain from it. In fact, she couldn't feel anything at all below her neck.

Something was forced into her mouth, and she heard Jonas shouting as if from a great distance. Why couldn't he just let her sleep? She was so tired, and all she wanted to do was close her eyes.

But when her lids drooped, she felt a rough hand grab her cheeks. Against her will, someone worked her jaw to make her chew the object, and once she swallowed, a rush of energy surged through her limbs.

The renewed energy came with a price. The moment the haze blanketing her mind lessened, excruciating agony came rushing back. Her eyes opened wide, and she screamed as the pain overwhelmed her senses; she couldn't stop screaming, and she flailed wildly when someone grabbed her forearm.

She heard Borim curse as her skin sloughed off under his grip. And the pain intensified tenfold where he'd grabbed her.

Another round object was shoved into her mouth—she belatedly recognized it as one of the healing pills she'd crafted—but this time, she chewed it on her own. As she swallowed, another wave of healing energy passed through her body, but it barely did anything to numb her suffering.

More than anything, she knew she needed to cast *Heal Wounds* on herself. However, she didn't have any mana remaining, and when she tried to draw upon her soul, it felt *damaged* somehow. Amara wondered if by pushing herself too far, she had injured herself permanently.

After swallowing two healing pills, the pain had abated slightly, and she took a second to inspect her wounds. Her arms were blackened up to the elbows, and she suspected her legs would look the same. But more worryingly, her fingers wouldn't obey when she willed them to move.

*What have I done to myself?*

Her panic grew by the second, spurred on by the fact the Issurians and kobolds would soon catch up to them. And she couldn't even move. How would her group deal with their pursuers without her at their side?

A wet tongue lashing her face interrupted her worries, and she angled her head slightly to see Mimi standing over her. Her pet let out a whine as she licked Amara's face again.

"I'm . . . I'm . . ." Amara's voice trailed off as her head flopped to the ground. She'd meant to tell her pet she was fine, but she couldn't even manage that. All she wanted was for the pain to end.

"We must place her on the mimic," Jonas said. "And why is that traitorous priestess free?"

Amara faded briefly out of consciousness, lulled by the drone of conversation. But a moment later, she cried out in pain again as she was hefted from the ground and placed on top of Mimi. Her pet's wood-like skin softened and conformed to her body, lessening the pain slightly.

Borim let out a grunt as he released Amara and stepped back. "What do we do if she dies?"

"Amara's not going to die," Salamander said sharply, her eyes glistening. "She's the avatar and she'll be fine. I just know it."

Amara grimaced as her pet trotted forward with an uneven gait. She wished she had the same faith in her recovery as Salamander did. To defeat the dungeon monsters, she'd injured herself far more severely than she'd thought possible.

And the only consolation was she had gained another level. Though her eyesight was blurry, she could see the little notification blinking in the corner of her vision. Maybe if she improved her Vitality stat, it might aid in her recovery.

But try as she might, she couldn't pull up her character sheet. And the relentless pain made her feel exhausted. All she wanted to do was sleep. She blinked her eyes slowly, and as the world faded, she watched Emmaline approach her side with a thoughtful expression on her face. Then everything turned black.

She awoke to cries and the clash of weapons. All around her, she could see kobolds trying to break through her companions to reach her on the mimic's back. But then she felt herself losing consciousness again. Once more, the darkness took her.

Amara jerked back to consciousness after what felt like a long time. In a panic, she scanned for any sign of the lizard men, but they were nowhere to be seen. Had her group defeated them?

From her position on the mimic, she could only see Borim, Emmaline, and Salamander, and they all sported fresh wounds. The battle against the kobolds must have been a difficult one. She craned her head to try to see Jonas, but there was no sign of him. And she couldn't see Harold, the pig farmer, either.

*Had they fallen in battle?*

The thought of Jonas dying filled her with despair. But she couldn't summon the energy to ask about him. She stared at Borim pleadingly until the dwarf finally noticed she was awake.

He must have sensed her question, because he only shook his head. "I'm sorry, lass. He stayed behind with Harold to give us a chance to escape. The kobolds . . . they . . . well, you know what those scaly bastards do to people. He was a hero."

Amara stifled a sob at the dwarf's words. But then she blinked away the tears. No, she refused to believe Jonas was dead. The dwarf had said Jonas had stayed behind with the farmer to buy them some time. Which meant Borim hadn't seen him fall.

The dwarf smiled at her stiffly, though it was plain to see the expression was forced. "At least the dungeon gave us all parting gifts. I think the stupid glowing gem felt bad about stiffing us after we stumbled our way through those traps." He hefted a round shield and knocked on its metal surface. "I finally got myself a shield again. And the dungeon even gave you two presents." He opened a pouch on his belt and withdrew a softly glowing spirit fruit along with a strange, featureless gray cube. "Don't ask me what this box thing does. Maybe it's another mimic?"

She opened her mouth to ask about Jonas, fighting to move her parched lips, but again her body betrayed her. All she could muster was an pitiful croak.

Instead of talking, she turned her attention back to her limbs. The blackness had retreated on her arms, and while she couldn't see her legs, they felt moderately better. Apparently, the healing pills had done their work. And when she concentrated, she could make her fingers twitch.

Salamander approached her side. "We'll get the kobolds back, right?" she asked, her voice cracking. "I . . . want to hurt them for what they did."

Amara could only nod. No matter what, she'd find a way to recover. And with the spirit fruit and the strange gift from the dungeon, she hoped it wouldn't take too long. Then she'd find Jonas—and if the kobolds had hurt him in any way, she would slay every Chaos-worshiping creature she could find in the North. And then she'd cross the Wall to wipe the rest of them from existence.

# CHAPTER 43

Selena wrinkled her nose as she stepped over a steaming pile of horse dung. Everything about Oksberg grated on her nerves, and she couldn't wait until they left this cesspool of humanity behind. If her orders had been obeyed, then Arturo should have the horses saddled and ready to depart upon her return.

The sky above the city was streaked with red, and she knew it wouldn't be long until nightfall. And though her subordinates had protested about leaving so close to dark, she refused to spend another day in this disgusting town. Three days of searching Oksberg for the false prophet was more than enough for her. She would scour the rest of the North until she found the woman who'd murdered her Frederick, and then she'd return to Bishop Krause with her head.

As she approached the stables behind the inn where they were staying, she noted approvingly that the paladin Arturo had carried out her orders. Five saddled horses had been gathered, along with their loaded pack animals. She was honestly surprised the paladin had obeyed her. He'd grown more rebellious on the trip north—especially after the incident a few days earlier.

They'd stopped at a small hamlet, whose name she hadn't bothered to learn. Once there, she'd sought out the mayor to demand shelter for her group. She'd known immediately the portly man had something to hide by his evasive attitude. And while he'd provided a house for them to sleep in, she'd suspected there was heresy to root out in the community.

As her companions had settled in, she'd set out to discover the hamlet's secret. And it hadn't taken her long. In a nearby barn, she found a spacious Gnostic shrine. The sight of the pagan symbol—a cluster of stars—had sent her into a rage. The twisted and evil heretics hiding in the village were no different than the false prophet she hunted.

But she bided her time, waiting until after the sun had set to punish the unbelievers. Once the last light had been extinguished in the village, she raised her veil and set out to purge them. Her people believed by hiding their faces from those they slew, they could prevent vengeful spirits from identifying them. And she planned to create many new spirits before the night was out.

Selena had stood in the middle of the community, feeling *dirty* from being surrounding by so many heretics. Their evil clung to her like a viscous oil, and she knew only a purifying fire could wash away the disgusting feeling. After another wave of revulsion washed over her, she'd carefully gathered her mana and called down a storm of fire on the hamlet. A vast column of hellfire descended from the sky, turning night into blinding orange day. The simple wooden houses ignited like dry tinder, and the screams of those burning inside had been like music to her ears.

Selena had listened to the heretics burn, even as her foolish companions desperately tried to save the people trapped inside. Why they wasted their time, she couldn't guess. But they hadn't been able to save a single soul.

She'd purged every last heretic from the hamlet.

By the next morning, ten of those who had accompanied her north had disappeared. Only Arturo and four others remained. Anger at their betrayal had flared inside her, but only briefly. She realized quickly that the deserters had lacked the proper faith for their mission. She was better off without them.

As she took the reins from Arturo, Selena examined the paladin closely. Though he had remained with her after the purging, he'd grown rebellious over the last few days. Perhaps she would have to deal with him, as well.

"It's dangerous to set out so close to dusk," Arturo said, his hand resting easily on the pommel of his sheathed sword. "There are things more dangerous than goblins out there."

Selena waved her hand dismissively. "There is no evil that will not fall before the power of the Church."

"While what you say is true, our numbers are greatly diminished. There are only four of us remaining."

Selena arched one eyebrow. "Only four? There were five of us when we entered the city."

"Carianne wasn't in her room," Arturo replied with a frown. "And her belongings were also gone."

"Another deserter?" Selena shook her head. "I didn't think the brothers and sisters recommended by the bishop would have such brittle faith. At the first sign of adversity, their belief in our holy mission shatters. I'm sorely disappointed."

"You burned an entire village," Arturo said between clenched teeth. "I'm only remaining with you to restrain your madness. The bishop will judge you when we return to Leissen."

"Judge me?" Selena laughed. "The bishop would have applauded the death of the heretics. My only regret is that I can't purge *all* those unfaithful to the Church."

Arturo took off his helmet, his long blond hair tumbling out in waves. Then he angrily scrubbed his bushy mustache with his hand. "If you believe such things, then you don't know the bishop. He would never approve of the murder of innocent women and children."

"How are your burns?" Selena asked him in a sickly sweet tone.

Arturo only glared at her in return, his lips twitching up into a snarl. His fingers opened and closed around the hilt of his sword before he yanked them away. Without another word, he spun around and began to tend to his horse.

She smirked at his reaction. The fool had hurled himself into a house engulfed in flames and dragged out a young girl and boy. Both the toddlers had expired shortly afterwards, and for his effort, the paladin had received burns to most of his body. The man had sat in front of their tiny bodies and wept for almost an hour.

At first, she'd thought he cried from the pain. But no amount of healing had calmed the inconsolable paladin. Selena could not understand his anguish. Didn't Arturo realize those children had been destined to grow up into heretics like their parents? Through their deaths, they would strengthen the Forces of Order.

*Why did the bishop provide me with such an emotional weakling for my party?*

After a shrug of her shoulders, Selena strode over to her own horse. She placed one foot in the stirrup and then swung her leg over. Once she was seated in her saddle, she glanced at the others. Not one of them would meet her gaze.

Selena didn't care if they feared her, as long as they obeyed her orders. She kicked her horse's side and then pushed the beast into a trot. She quickly passed the side of the inn and entered the street.

Oksberg was a dirty and rundown city, nothing like her beautiful home to the south. The buildings here had been painted with drab colors, and half of the wooden structures looked like a mouse's sneeze could fell them.

She wouldn't miss this place one bit.

Selena navigated through the streets, ignoring the glares of those passing her. She suspected many in Oksberg were heretics, but she couldn't burn down a city of this size. Though if she had the ability, she might consider it.

The sound of a voice calling cut through her reverie and made her tug on her reins. She could have sworn she heard "avatar." A moment later, she heard it again. She whipped her head around. On the far side of the street, a youth stood on a crate, shouting something about an avatar.

Selena guided her horse through the throngs of people lining the street until she reached the young man. Once there, she glared down at him imperiously. "Did I hear you mention something about an avatar?"

The youth looked relieved at the sight of her. "Thank Holy Birgitta. Someone finally wants to listen to me."

Selena suppressed her surprise at the man's reaction. Surely, he must know by her robes she belonged to the Church. And any heretical talk about avatars was enough to get you burned at the stake. Was this youth a fool?

"No one here will listen to me," he continued. "I tried to meet with the king, but I couldn't get an audience. And then I tried to meet with the Adventurer's Guild. They wouldn't even let me inside because I'm not an adventurer."

Arturo cantered up beside her. "Leave the boy alone," he warned.

"My name is Uwe," the young man said, his face brightening at seeing a paladin approach. "Lady Ingrid sent me here to find help. My home, Stout Oak Keep, is under siege by a huge army of Chaos. And an avatar has shown up to help us. But we need more people to man the fortress."

"The castle is under siege?" Arturo said sharply. "And no relief army marches to help them?"

Selena's lips curled up into a wicked smile at the mention of an avatar. Apparently, the bishop had been right. The false avatar *had* traveled north. And now her vengeance for Frederick was almost at hand. "Where is Stout Oak Keep?"

"It's only about three days ride north," Uwe replied, still blissfully unaware of the doom hanging over his head. "I made it quicker, though. Of course, I almost killed my horse. Will you all help me?"

Arturo stroked his drooping mustache. "We must inform the local bishop immediately. I campaigned in the North many years ago, and Stout Oak Keep was a linchpin in the defenses. Aid must be sent to them straight away."

"No, the avatar is there." Selena tried to keep her excitement in check. "There is no time to waste. We must ride for Stout Oak Keep without any delay."

"Oh, thank Holy Birgitta." Uwe seemed to almost sag. "I was so afraid I was going to fail Lady Ingrid. She will be so happy with me."

"And what makes you think you'll ever see her again?" Selena raised her hand, and blue flames blanketed her palm. "You stand here, spreading heresy for all to hear. Do you believe an avatar has truly returned? They are nothing but myths created to weaken the Forces of Order."

A rough hand grabbed her wrist and wrenched her to the side.

"I told you to leave the boy alone," Arturo snarled. "There's no way to know if this is the woman we seek. False avatars are as common as leaves in the forest."

Selena shook him off. "I know in my heart she is the one who murdered Frederick. And I will burn this boy for serving her."

"You're going to burn me?" Uwe yelped as he backed away. "I was only following my noble's orders . . ."

The flames rose higher in her hand and illuminated the rapidly darkening street. Already, the sun was sinking beneath the horizon, and the first stars had appeared overhead. The fire sent shadows dancing and then flickered across the faces of the townsfolk who had gathered to watch the heated exchange.

Selena raised her voice so all could hear. "I know many in the North have strayed from the true path. But know this—if you are a heretic, the Church will punish you. Let this boy's execution bring you back to the true faith!"

"Have you gone mad?" Arturo shouted. "They'll hang us if we start murdering people in the streets."

"I am a servant of the Church," she replied. "And I am above their petty laws."

"Wait!" Uwe screamed, gesturing wildly at the sky. "See, I wasn't lying. It was all true!"

"Your pathetic attempts at distraction won't work on me." She raised her hand again but stopped when Arturo gasped, and a murmur of surprise rippled through the crowd. With a sigh, she leaned back to see where the young man was pointing. It was obviously a pathetic attempt to cling to a few more seconds of life, but she would humor him for a second.

But as she craned her head back, her eyes widened with surprise. In the sky, it was as though a new sun had been born. Where only a patch of empty blackness had been the night before, a star burned brightly. The star that legend said would represent the goddess Melischar.

From the crowd, a man emerged wearing the garb of the town watch. He raised his spear and pointed at the star. "The boy speaks the truth! The gods have returned. And they have need of us!"

"Lies!" Selena screamed. "This is all the work of the Trickster Cleric." She stabbed a finger at Uwe as flames wreathed her body. "How did you cast this illusion? Is she here with you?"

"I . . . I don't know what you're talking about." Uwe pointed weakly the brightly burning star. "But that's proof, right?"

"I will burn you—" Her words cut out as a rock struck her back. She wheeled her horse around to see who had thrown it, only to find a growing mob. "The Church will destroy any who stand against it. Do not allow yourself to be fooled by this simple trickery."

Arturo grabbed her reins. "We have to get out of here!"

"No!" Selena wove together her mana, preparing to cast her *Firestorm* spell. If she let these onlookers live, they would spread the Trickster Cleric's idolatrous lies. There was no other way. For herself, for the Church, for the memory of Frederick. "I will purge this heresy!"

As the firestorm descended from the sky, she shaped it into a swirling tempest, one that could incinerate every last heretic surrounding her. And when Uwe turned to bolt, she brought down the entire burning column down upon him. Flames engulfed the young man, and his screams filled the street. Soon, the cries of the other heathens joined Uwe's in a divine chorus. The smoke from their burning corpses blotted out the star, and Selena smiled at the devastation she'd wrought.

The Trickster Cleric wouldn't win with simple parlor tricks. No, Selena wouldn't allow herself to be fooled into believing some mythical goddess had returned. And now she knew where the false prophet was located.

It was only a matter of time until she would have her vengeance.

# CHAPTER 44

Amara groggily opened her eyes and took in her surroundings. She was lying prone on a canopy bed, her head propped up with a fluffy pillow and a blanket pulled up to her chin. The closed drapes obscured her view of the room, but from the finery, she suspected she was back in the castle. Which meant they'd escaped the kobolds—but it also meant she'd have to deal with the baroness after disobeying her orders.

*I think I'd rather face the kobolds again.*

The memory of the previous day came rushing back, and her heart ached as she remembered Jonas's bravery. The thought of her missing friend drove her to push herself into a sitting position. As she did, the blanket tumbled off her chest, revealing a fresh nightgown. Someone had taken the time to clean and change her. Had they also dealt with her wounds?

Amara was almost afraid to see what had become of the injuries she'd sustained by overtaxing her soul. After a moment, she took a deep breath, and then lifted her hands to examine them. She let out a sigh of relief at the sight of her hands—the blackened skin had retreated, leaving dark brown bruises in their wake. Her burn scars, though, remained unchanged.

It took her several minutes, but she managed to push back the thick blankets and swing her legs over the side of the bed. She felt like she was moving in slow motion. Everything on her body ached, and her stomach twisted with hunger. But more than anything, she needed something for her parched throat.

Without warning, the hanging drapes were thrown open, and Salamander appeared from behind them. The girl almost squealed with glee at seeing Amara.

"You're up!" Salamander exclaimed, clapping her hands. "I'm so glad you're alright. I thought for sure you were going to sleep forever. Well, not *forever.* I didn't think you were going to die. But it's been such a long time."

"It's only been a day." Amara ran a hand through her hair. She froze when she found carefully parted locks instead of the usual untamed mess. Someone had been brushing her hair while she slept.

*Well, that's a bit creepy*, she thought to herself. *I hope it wasn't Ingrid.*

Amara had been putting it off, fearing what she'd discover, but she needed to inspect her soul. As she probed it with her mind, she was surprised at how normal it felt. There seemed to be fault lines running the length of her soul, but they appeared to be healing. How was that possible?

"How do you feel?" Salamander asked with a mischievous grin. "Is your soul all better, by any chance?"

"It does feel a bit better," Amara said slowly. "What did you do to me?"

"We spent days using that weird cube thing the dungeon gave us," Salamander replied. "Baroness Stick-Up-Her-Bum said it was a rare treasure used to heal damaged souls. I think the dungeon felt bad for you. Or maybe the dungeon liked us more than those lizard men? Can a big glowing gem lie to you?"

"Wait . . ." Amara swung her gaze back to Salamander. "You said I was out for days?"

Salamander nodded and grinned at Amara like a cat who had swallowed a canary.

"I need to get dressed." Amara pushed herself to her feet and swayed unsteadily. "Do you know where my armor is?" If Ingrid was to be believed, the magic in her armor should have repaired the damage it had sustained. "I need to find Jonas."

She couldn't believe she'd wasted days in bed while her friend was most likely being tortured by the Forces of Chaos somewhere. Why hadn't someone woken her earlier? Had she been unconscious all this time?

As she tried to remain upright, the aches and pains returned tenfold, and she gritted her teeth until it passed. She gingerly reached out to draw upon her mana—a *Heal Wounds* spell should cure most of her injuries—but then jerked away as though bitten. As she touched her soul, it felt like she was trying to use a pulled muscle. Even with the treasure, it would take a while before she was fully restored.

But with or without magic, she still needed to find Jonas. She tottered over to a wall and grabbed her cloak from a peg. As she swung it around her shoulders, she inspected the room.

While her new quarters were nowhere near as luxurious as Lady Ingrid's, they were still impressive. A canopy bed dominated the middle of the room, and finely crafted furniture cluttered the walls. There was a door on the far wall she suspected led to a bathroom.

After a few seconds of searching, she spotted her armor mounted on a rack in the corner of the room. Beside it was a new staff with runes carved along its length, which gave off the impression of great power.

"Get your gear," she called out to Salamander. "We're going to Malcheron's camp to rescue the others."

"You want to go out there in your shape?" Salamander asked, her smile fading. "You'd probably lose to a giant rat."

"What are you waiting for?" Amara demanded, her brow descending. "Every second we waste is another second Jonas has to endure torture at the hands of Malcheron."

*If he's even still alive.*

She ruthlessly pushed down her worries and focused on getting dressed. But as she did, Salamander walked over to the heavy ironbound door and swung it open.

"Amara's awake," the girl called out into the hall.

Borim strode through the entrance with a big grin on his face. "Typical Trickster Cleric—sleeping away the day while the rest of us protect the fief. You know, I'm pretty sure you were faking it the whole time."

"Do you know where Malcheron's camp is?" she asked, struggling to lift her leather chestpiece over her head. She felt as weak as a newborn, but hopefully her strength would return the longer she was on her feet.

Borim frowned. "Why would you want to walk into that viper's nest? Was the dungeon not dangerous enough for you?"

"Why do you think?" Amara snapped at the dwarf, her frustration with her companions building. "Did both of you lose your hearts out there? Jonas is probably being tortured as we speak."

Borim rounded on Salamander. "Did you not tell her, lass? That's not right."

"Tell me what," Amara demanded, lowering her armor. She hated to admit it, but she was going to need help to get dressed.

"The rumours of my demise were greatly exaggerated," a voice called out from the hallway. A moment later, Jonas strode into the room with Mimi bounding along at his side. He was covered in half healed cuts and bruises, but beyond that, he didn't look any worse for wear.

Amara let out a gasp and dropped her breastplate. Then she wobbled over to him and threw her arms around his neck. "I . . . thought I lost you." As she held him, she felt the worry drain out of her.

Jonas returned the hug, but then gently disentangled himself as Mimi forced herself between them. "There are perks to having a wyvern on your side in a conflict."

"Then the baroness . . ."

"She saved them," Borim said, as he nodded his shaggy head. "Ingrid found us about halfway back to the castle. Apparently, she'd seen the smoke from the burning dungeon, and had flown out on Nyrax to find out what was going on. Once we told her about Jonas and Harold, she located them a few leagues behind us. The kobolds didn't stand a chance against her and the wyvern."

"What of the Issurian leader?" Amara asked.

"We didn't see her again," Borim replied with a shrug. "Which was probably a lucky thing. Maybe Noah injured her in their battle. Or maybe she had better things to do. Who knows why those cold-addled Issurians do anything? After all, they're dumb enough to serve the Chaos Gods. Anyone who does that isn't quite right in the head."

"And what of Ingrid?" Amara asked, worried how the baroness had reacted to her actions.

"Ah . . ." Borim replied slowly. "Now that's another matter. Things aren't . . . good here."

Jonas frowned and nodded. "Our dwarf friend speaks the truth. She has imprisoned anyone who may have had the chance to betray you, and she plans to hang them upon your awakening. Moreover, she's rather unhappy about you disobeying her orders."

"Great. Just great," Amara replied. "What do you think we should do? Should we leave the castle?"

"I believe that might be an overreaction," Jonas replied. "Especially since there were several arrivals while you lay unconscious. The Broken Brotherhood, the Gnostics, and King Jakob of Oksberg have all sent representatives."

"How did they get here so fast?" she asked, frowning. "And what do they want?"

"Most likely, they used teleportation scrolls—no small outlay of gold, even for nobility." Jonas grinned before he continued. "Though they had good reason to do so. After your little display of divine power in the dungeon, you have officially proven me and all the other skeptics wrong. I suppose I'll have to rethink everything I learned over the years. So many books need to be rewritten."

"What are you talking about?" She crossed her arms. "Is everyone being purposefully vague today? I'm still strong enough to toss you all into the river if you don't start making some sense."

Salamander interrupted before Jonas could continue. "There's a star in the sky! The gods are back!"

"There's a . . . star?" Amara asked slowly, not sure what her friend meant.

Jonas nodded. "Once night falls, you can see for yourself. A new celestial body is quite the event. I imagine the Church-aligned astronomers will be falling all over themselves to explain such an event in the South. But to all the Gnostics, it's a clear sign the gods have returned."

"So what does that mean for us here?"

"I have no idea." Jonas replied. "Lady Ingrid hasn't granted any of the representatives entry into the castle. I imagine they will want to meet you, now that you've awakened—"

Before Jonas could finish, Ingrid flew into the room like a tempest and held up her hand to silence him. "I will speak with Amara alone."

Salamander raised her chin, a defiant glint in her eyes. "I'm not leaving my friend."

Borim spread his feet and stared up at the baroness. "Same goes for me."

Jonas's hand twitched imperceptibly toward his dagger before he placed it on his belt. "I wish to stay as well, Lady Ingrid."

The baroness's eyes narrowed. "What I plan to say is not for your ears."

"Try to get rid of me," Borim growled.

"It's alright," Amara said, trying to cool the tension. "I'll be fine. I promise."

Jonas hesitated, but then motioned at the door. "We shall remain just outside. If you have any need of us, just call."

Ingrid waited until the door had shut behind the group, before she turned to stare at Amara. Her face was unreadable. "Firstly, I am glad you emerged from the dungeon unscathed. In hindsight, there may have been a few flaws with my plan."

"Do you think?" Amara retorted. "I told you I should have gone with my group."

"Be that as it may," Ingrid said, her brow lowering slightly, "I must also apologize for the actions of my priestess. Her betrayal was done out of a misplaced sense of loyalty to me. However, I will not tolerate such actions, and I plan to hang her with the other traitors this afternoon. Assuming you are well enough to attend, of course."

"Who wouldn't want to attend a mass hanging after waking up from a coma?" Amara replied sarcastically.

"I am doing this for your sake." Ingrid walked over to a table and poured herself a cup of wine. She took a sip and stared at Amara. "You were sent here by the gods to save me, and I don't take that lightly. And a strong message must be sent to any who would betray us."

"I don't want a bunch of innocent people to die for me." Amara walked haltingly over and poured herself a cup of wine. She lifted it to her lips and then gulped it down. The liquid burned her throat but gave her a pleasant warm feeling once it reached her stomach. "I think I have a plan to find out who betrayed me. Which means you may not have to hang anyone."

"I am all ears, if that's the case," Ingrid said, taking another sip of her wine. "There are many skilled servants languishing in my dungeon whose services I'd prefer not to lose."

"Once my soul is fully healed, I can cast *Holy Light*. The spell description says it should make anyone who serves Chaos flee. If you bring them out, then I can cast the spell and see who it affects."

"That is an interesting proposal," Ingrid mused. "However, I still must insist that Emmaline is hanged today. And I wish for you to attend."

Amara grimaced at what she planned to say next. Very few defenders remained at Stout Oak Keep, and they needed anyone who could hold a weapon or cast a spell. Even if they were a traitorous priestess. "I think you should give her a reprieve and let her prove herself. And she swore a binding oath to never harm me, so I should be safe around her. Plus, she seems . . . fanatically loyal to you."

"To be honest, I was shocked she swore a binding oath." Ingrid placed her cup down on the table. "And it seems it came with some surprising side effects. She has been clawing at the walls of her cell, trying to reach you. The oath appears to compel her to ensure no harm comes to you as well."

"It really did that to her?" Amara asked, surprised at the news. She hadn't truly believed the binding oath would work, let alone push Emmaline to try to reach her.

"Yes." Ingrid replied with a sigh. "And I will consider your words on the matter of the traitors, though I promise nothing at this time. I cannot allow treachery against the avatar to stand." She took a sip of her wine. "Now to the matter of you disobeying my orders. While I understand it worked out for the best this time, I must insist you heed my commands in the future."

Amara took a deep breath. She wasn't looking forward to the next part of their conversation. "I will help you defend your home, but I am not your subject. Do you understand me? I'm the avatar, and you swore to serve me."

Ingrid's eyes narrowed, but she didn't reply. As the silence stretched out between them, the baroness crossed her arms and tapped her foot against the reed mat on the floor. "All I want to do is keep the messenger of the gods safe. Would you rather I throw you to the wolves?"

"And yet while you claim you want to keep me safe, everything you've done so far has put me in danger." Amara ignored the baroness's darkening expression and continued without a pause. "I know you didn't mean me any harm, but after you exposed me as the avatar to the entire fief, I was *immediately* betrayed to Malcheron. Not to mention that the group you sent with me to the dungeon was going to murder me for gold."

"I have plans for Ackley and his group when I get my hands on them." Ingrid's jaw tightened and her eyes blazed with anger. "A hanging is far too good for those scoundrels."

"I need to level up so I can fight Malcheron," Amara said. "And no matter what you say, I'm not going to stay in the castle like a bird in a gilded cage. But I'd rather have you at my side than against me."

The baroness didn't reply for a long while as her eyes bored into Amara's. Finally, she stepped forward and took Amara's hand in her own. "I suppose I have no choice but to accept. There is little hope of holding my home without your aid. I will do whatever it takes to keep you safe. You have my word. However, do not forget you were sent here to save me. No matter what the emissaries offer you, remember that Stout Oak Keep must be saved first and foremost. And promise to at least heed my council."

*Is she afraid of the diplomats stealing me away?*

Amara didn't bother contradicting the baroness's claim that she'd been sent here to save her and instead just nodded. She'd expected more of a fight and was relieved Ingrid had given in so easily.

"I'd like to go meet the emissaries, actually," Amara said. "Will you give me a minute to get dressed?"

Ingrid raised the cup of wine to her ruby lips and drained it. "Firstly, I must warn you the Knights Tarsillan are untrustworthy." She placed the cup sternly on the nearby table. "No messenger was sent to them asking for aid, and yet they somehow learned of our predicament. The Knights have long been a thorn in the side of the Northern lords, and my family helped to oust them from these lands many generations ago."

"If anyone wants to help us, then it's not like we can afford to turn them away."

"Do not trust them," Ingrid repeated, eyes narrowing as she strode over to the door. "And I will not surrender a single acre of my land to them. Now it is time for *you* to understand *me*."

Amara nodded. She'd hoped things would be easier once help arrived, but it sounded like there would be discord between the baroness and the Knights Tarsillan. Still, maybe she could smooth things over as the avatar. At the very least, she could always use *Charm Person* on someone if things got ugly.

Without another word, Ingrid opened the door and strode out into the hallway. Her cloak billowed out behind her as she disappeared through the opening.

Jonas poked his head in a moment later. "Is everything alright?"

"I think the lady and I have reached a truce, for the moment," she replied. "At the very least, she agreed to not send me on any further suicidal missions while surrounded by traitors. That has to be an improvement, right?"

"That *is* good news."

Amara pointed at her armor on the stand. "I'm going to get dressed and then we can go meet with the emissaries." When Jonas didn't move, she raised her eyebrow. "If you could give me a bit of privacy?"

"Of course," he replied hurriedly. "My apologies."

"There's no need to apologize," she said, but he'd already closed the door after him. It was doubtful Jonas had heard her words.

With a shake of her head, Amara returned to her armor. But then she remembered the weight of it. She was still too weak to lift the heavy leather breastplate, never mind wear it. Instead, she walked over to her bag and retrieved one of the simple peasant dresses from inside. She shed the nightgown, laying it out carefully on the bed, and slid the dress over her head.

Once she'd finished dressing, she gathered up her meager supplies from the room. She placed her spare, slightly singed dress in her pack, followed by her alchemy equipment, and then her knife. Finally, she walked over to the wall and picked up the new staff. The power coursing through it thrummed in her hand. She'd have to ask Ingrid later what it did.

Amara glanced around the room one last time to ensure she hadn't forgotten anything and then headed over to the door. She grasped the heavy iron handle before heaving it open. Her group was waiting patiently for her in the hallway. But there was no sign of the baroness.

"Where's Lady Ingrid?" she asked. "I thought she was coming with us to meet the emissaries."

Borim shrugged his broad shoulders. "She just stalked off without saying anything to us lowly adventurers. And she had some crazy eyes."

"That's probably a bad sign," Amara said, biting down on her lower lip. "Hopefully, she just plans to meet us there. Now that I think of it, where are the emissaries staying?"

"They've set up a camp just outside of Fusson," Jonas replied. "From what I've gleaned by listening to the guards, they weren't granted access to the village."

Amara slung her backpack over her shoulder before hurrying down the hallway. After Ingrid's remarks about the knights, she didn't trust the baroness to meet with them alone. She wanted to try to catch up with Ingrid before she reached their camp.

But when she staggered out into the inner courtyard, there was still no sign of the baroness. She slowed slightly to catch her breath. Her body was exhausted from her ordeal in the dungeon and mutinied against her in pain with every step. At a slower pace, she headed back through the castle toward the outer walls.

Once she reached the emissaries' encampment, she would craft a plan to defeat Malcheron and save the fief once and for all. And then she could see about restoring the Wall.

# CHAPTER 45

Amara continued through the narrow hallways of the castle, managing impressive speed despite her weakened state. With her party hot on her heels, she swept past throngs of surprised servants and then entered the outer courtyard, certain she would find the baroness there. But there was still no sign of Ingrid. Amara was growing more worried about the baroness by the moment.

"Where did Ingrid *go*?" she asked as she scanned the outer walls.

"What'd you say to make her so upset?" Borim said in his gravelly voice. "No offense, but you have all the diplomatic grace of a trogg drunk on mushroom wine."

"I didn't do anything to her," Amara retorted. "And for once, I think I was actually pretty restrained. Maybe she just doesn't like dwarves."

"I doubt that's possible," Borim said coolly. "We're such an agreeable people."

Jonas snorted at the dwarf's comment but didn't say anything.

Borim shot the rogue a glowering look, then bowed his head as he tried to keep up. "Dwarves have short legs, you know."

Amara gathered up her skirt in both hands, so she didn't trip over the hem. "If you want, I'm sure Jonas could carry you."

"I'd rather chew rocks," Borim replied with a frown. "I'm just saying we don't need to run."

"The last thing I want is for the baroness to talk to the emissaries alone." Amara glanced up as they strode past the tower where Nyrax roosted. There was no sign of movement up there, either. "Ingrid said her family has a history with the Knights, and I want to be there for the first meeting."

As Amara continued, she noticed Mimi was having a hard time keeping up as well, so she slowed her pace slightly. Once her pet had caught up, the mimic rubbed her rough wooden body against Amara, and then let out a muted growl.

"I'm fine," she said, scratching Mimi's head. "Were you worried about me?"

Mimi bobbed her body up and down, her long tongue flopping out of her mouth. Then she licked Amara, leaving a trail of slime behind.

Amara laughed as she shook the saliva off her hand. It was nice to have her pet back without a traitorous priestess stuck to her.

As Amara continued through the castle, she kept glancing over her shoulder, expecting the baroness to appear at any moment. But they reached the outer gates without a trace of her. And the young man standing guard, an underfed peasant stuffed into a suit of armor, simply waved at them.

"Did the baroness pass by here?" Amara asked as she neared the youth.

The guard shook his head, his helmet falling over his eyes.

"Thanks," she replied to the guard as he struggled to right his helmet.

*Should we wait for Ingrid?* Amara considered her options for a moment. They had nothing to gain by waiting around in the castle. She might as well continue on to the emissaries with her party. Maybe the baroness was already there.

She crossed the bridge, water burbling underneath, and then stopped when they reached the far side. "Where are the emissaries staying?" She glanced over in Jonas's direction. "Have you seen their camp?"

"While I am not certain," Jonas said with a smile, "I can hazard a guess." He thrust his hand in the direction of a group of tents which had sprouted in a field beyond the village. The shelters, which were nothing like the simple ones erected by the refugees in Fusson, looked like they had each cost a king's ransom.

Amara mentally kicked herself for not seeing the tents and made a note to stop and look the next time before opening her mouth. In the afternoon sun's glow, one tent stood apart from the rest. Festooned with brightly colored flags bearing the emblem of a golden hippogriff astride a wall, it towered over the rest of the lodgings. Was that the symbol of the Knights Tarsillan?

As the ramshackle party crossed the field and approached the grouping of tents, Amara realized she should have probably worn something more impressive than a simple dress. If only she'd been strong enough to wear her armor.

*I guess I'm going to present myself as the peasant avatar.*

For some reason, that thought made her giggle. And when her companions shot her worried glances, she simply waved them down. "I'm fine. It's just that I didn't expect to be wearing a worn dress and muddy boots when I met the knights."

Borim guffawed. "Nothing wrong with being a bit eccentric. It makes people walk lightly around you."

Jonas found it less funny, and his features tightened with worry. "Perhaps you should have worn something more regal for the first meeting."

Salamander rose up on her tippy toes to pat Amara on the shoulder. "I think you look nice. My mother had a dress like that." At the mention of her imprisoned parent, her expression fell.

"Don't worry," Amara said hurriedly. "Once we're done here, we'll find a way to get your parents out of debtor's prison. You have my word."

"It's not that . . ." Salamander trailed off. "We can talk about it later."

"Alright, if you're sure," Amara replied, surprised at Salamander's reaction. Was something else troubling the girl?

Before she could push the matter further, they arrived at the cluster of tents. A fire built in a circle of rocks burned merrily in the center of the camp, and a weapon rack holding spears and lances sat next to the tent with the hippogriff emblazoned on it. As she approached at the head of her group, a man in golden armor stepped out with a lowered halberd.

"State your business," he commanded. As he did, he pushed up a visor to reveal a deeply lined face and a chin of gray stubble. But his eyes still shone with determination, belying his age.

"I'm the avatar of Melischar, and I'm here to see the emissaries."

"Sure you are," he replied, looking her up and down. "Get out of here before I give you a kick on the backside."

Jonas stepped forward and rose to his full height. "I am Jonas of House Stein, seventeenth in the line of succession. And I demand to speak to your commander."

The old warrior scowled. "You state your title like we accept the authority of the heretic houses in the South. The Knights Tarsillan remembers your betrayal."

Salamander bounced forward. "She really is the avatar. For real. I promise."

"I *am* the avatar," Amara said, more sternly. "And I doubt your commander would appreciate you sending me away."

The old man reached up to rub his chin, but then shook his head. "I'm no seer, but I doubt the avatar of the gods would show up looking like a farmer's wife with this rag-tag bunch. Begone before I get too annoyed with you and forget myself."

Borim stepped forward with a raised finger. "Now listen here, you tin-can-wearing fossil. She's the avatar and deserves your respect."

The knight tightened his grip on the halberd, and the lines forming his frown deepened. He opened his mouth to say something but shut it as an even more ancient man strode out of the tent.

"What's all the racket out here, Edmund?" the newcomer said. He wore fine golden robes, with numerous trinkets hanging from the belt cinched at his waist. A gray beard hung down past his chest, and his face was a maze of wrinkles. His bleary eyes peered out at them. "And who do we have here?"

"I'm the avatar of Melischar," Amara said, sidestepping Edmund. "And I wish to speak with you."

"Oh-ho, so you're the avatar," the man in the robes said. "My name is Frederick, and I'm a chaplain to the knights. I suppose you could say I'm in charge of this little expedition."

Edmund's bushy gray eyebrows rose. "You don't believe her, do you?"

Frederick pointed at the blue sky above them, with only the wisps of clouds marring it. "Haven't you seen the star? The gods have finally returned. And the seers told us she was located here."

"But . . . but . . ." Edmund spluttered. "There are false avatars everywhere. And we still don't know what the star means."

"I suppose I should do *some* due diligence." Frederick leaned forward to peer at Amara. His eyes widened slightly. "Are you . . . a serf?"

"No, I'm not a serf," she replied sharply. "I just like dressing for comfort. Alright?"

"I can hardly blame you for that. I'm often guilty of the same thing back home." Frederick lifted a case from his belt. Then he spent a minute making a show of opening it. From inside, he pulled out what looked like a golden monocle. "If you wouldn't mind letting me examine you?"

"Is it going to hurt?"

"Oh my, no." Frederick screwed up his face. "At least I don't think so. Is this the one that hurts? Or is that the other one back at Caer Caithon? Was that the one my dog stole? No matter, we'll find out in a moment, won't we?"

Amara stared blankly at the old man. Clearly, he wasn't all there.

As the wizened man raised the monocle to his eye, she braced herself for the coming pain. When Ingrid had examined her, it had felt like her soul was getting wracked by fire. And when Tecala, the leader of the Issurians, had done so, Amara's soul had been buffeted by freezing winds. But she relaxed slightly as Frederick removed the monocle from in front of his eye and smiled. "Is . . . that it?" she asked.

"Incontrovertible proof she is the avatar," Frederick exclaimed. "The sliver of divinity is unmistakable. Please, come into my tent and we'll see about getting you some new clothes. Are you hungry or thirsty? We brought many provisions with us."

Edmund stepped forward and raised his halberd. "Did you even use that thing right?" he asked. "Are you sure she's not some charlatan looking to rob us blind?"

"Oh, I'm very certain." Frederick blinked a few times. "Unless, of course, I forgot to activate it. Did you feel anything, my dear?"

Amara briefly considered lying, but then shook her head. She didn't want to begin her relationship with the knights by deceiving them. Even if it meant she'd have to endure some pain.

"Oh drat." He raised the monocle again. "I'm always so forgetful."

This time, it was like a combination of flames and freezing winds assailed her soul. She shut her eyes, telling herself this was the only way to prove herself to the knights. After a moment, it was over, and she sucked in a breath. Her soul ached, the fault lines from the overuse sending ribbons of pain slicing through her chest.

"Oh my," Frederick muttered. "Something terrible has happened to your soul, avatar of Melischar. You must not cast anything for quite some time, or you may damage it permanently. Yes, it will take many weeks to heal properly."

*More good news,* she thought to herself glumly. *I thought I'd be able to use my spells to retake this fief.*

Edmund's weapon dropped from suddenly limp fingers as he gaped at her. Then he dropped to his knees and bowed his head. "My apologies, Avatar. I offer my life for my impudence."

"It's . . . fine?" Amara said, uncomfortable. "I really don't want your life."

"Thank you for your mercy," Edmund said, still keeping his head bowed.

Frederick waved his hands at his companion. "Oh, get up, you old fool. She's an avatar, not one of our gods." Then he turned back to Amara. "Now, let's see about getting you some food. Where did you hide those crates, Edmund?"

Amara pointed her hand at the pile sitting not five feet away. "Those ones?"

"Thank you, my dear." Frederick laughed, his ancient voice making it almost sound like a cackle. "I'd lose my head if it wasn't attached to my neck."

Jonas stepped forward. "Where are the rest of the knights?" he asked. "Surely, it's not just the pair of you."

"Hmm? The knights, you say?" Frederick said. "They only sent us graybeards in case it was a trap. Our duty is nearly completed, so it would be no great loss if something happened to us. And it wouldn't be the first time the lords of the North tried to lure us out to destroy our holy order once and for all."

"It's just the two of you?" Amara asked, incredulously. "Are your armies coming?"

"They are assembling, but they will not come until we send word."

"How far away are they from here?"

Frederick shrugged his shoulders. "I suppose a few weeks by land, and maybe half of that by sea? However, Stout Oak Keep is one of the most powerful fortresses in the North. I'm sure there's no rush to bring our forces here. Now that I think of it, where are the lord and his armies? And where are the forces of the other Northern kings? The snooty emissary from Oksberg won't even talk to us. Can you imagine that?"

"They're all gone," Amara said. "There is no one left to hold the castle."

The stooped chaplain paused in the process of opening a crate. "All gone, you say? That's impossible. If that was true, then the castle would fall within days. And with it, Galoth's Wall. Such a thing would bring calamity to all the lands to the south."

Jonas nodded. "It's true. No one remains to defend the castle aside from the baroness and a handful of guards."

"I see, I see," Frederick muttered. Then he fished a scroll out of his pocket and handed it to Edmund. "Return to Caer Caithon immediately. Muster all of our forces and march north with all haste. Scrape up every man and woman who can hold a weapon. Tell them the fall of the Wall is imminent."

"I can't leave you here alone unprotected," Edmund protested.

"Go." The chaplain shooed him away with gnarled hands. "The fate of every-thing may rest on your shoulders. Now hurry up already."

Edmund nodded and then turned to Amara, his face deadly serious. "Please watch over him, Avatar. He is my dear friend." Then he retrieved the scroll and unrolled it. As he spoke the words of power, bright lines swirled around him, and the world almost seemed to fold in on itself. A moment later, the old knight was gone.

"Now," Frederick said, before he descended into a coughing fit. "Sorry. The perils of growing old. I never recommend it to anyone. As I was saying, let's go talk to the Gnostics and the fellow from Oksberg. With you here, they may be more amenable to discussion."

Amara nodded, shocked at the news: help was weeks, perhaps even months away. With only Ingrid and her party at her side, and with no immediate relief forthcoming, could they even hold the castle? She didn't know the answer, and that troubled her deeply. Maybe the Gnostics and the diplomat from Oksberg would bring better news. Amara sighed. For someone with a high Luck stat, she certainly didn't seem to have much of it lately.

# CHAPTER 46

As she waited for the others to arrive, Amara plucked at the robes that Frederick had graciously provided her. The garments felt itchy against her skin and the faint odor of wood smoke clung to them. But Jonas and the others had insisted that she not wear her comfortable dress to greet the emissary from Oksberg.

In front of her, Borim dropped a wooden chair on the ground and then wiped his brow. The dwarf and Jonas had been setting up the seating area. A semicircle of chairs surrounded the place where she was supposed to preside over the meeting. Frederick had claimed the setup would give her an air of authority. And while he seemed a bit eccentric, Amara trusted the old man's opinion.

Jonas placed the last chair and then took up a position behind it. He smiled and motioned at the rickety wooden piece of furniture, most likely retrieved from the nearby village of Fusson. "I have arrived with your throne, divine avatar." His words had a joking air, though from his pinched expression, she could see his mirth was forced. It was clear that what had happened in the dungeon still hung over him.

"Does it come in gold?" She touched a finger to her chin and peered at it. "Or maybe something with a bunch of swords on the back?"

Jonas raised his eyebrow. "Swords?"

"Never mind," she replied. "It's just something from my world."

Borim combed his fingers through his beard. "A sword chair doesn't sound too comfortable. You'd probably be pricking your ass every time you sat down. What sort of lunatics live in your world?"

"It was just a joke." Amara let out a sigh. Sometimes, she missed being around people who would get her references.

"Here they come," Borim said, jerking his head toward the tents. "Try to look regal and divine."

"How am I supposed to look regal?" She was still just a skinny girl who had grown up in a household where hotdogs had been a fancy meal. Sometimes, she wondered why Melischar hadn't chosen someone else.

"There's no need to worry," Jonas said. "They will see you the same way we do—as a leader, and as the servant of Melischar."

Amara gave him a half smile. "I hope you're right."

As she waited for the others to arrive, she decided to take the time to level up. In her hurried flight from the castle, she still hadn't advanced her class. She pulled up her character sheet and inspected it.

| Amara Solace (Pewter Rank Adventurer) | Trickster Cleric, Level 6 |
| --- | --- |
| Stats | |
| Strength | 7 |
| Dexterity | 3 |
| Constitution | 9 |
| Intelligence | 4 |
| Wisdom | 12 |
| Charisma | 1 |
| Vitality | 6 |
| Luck | 14 |
| New Stat Points | 3 |
| | |
| Titles | Titan Slayer (Rank 1) |
| | |
| Weapon Proficiencies | |
| Staff | Novice |
| Darts | Novice |
| | |
| Skills | |
| *First Aid* | Apprentice |
| *Herbalism* | Apprentice |
| *Alchemy* | Apprentice |
| | |
| Martial Abilities | |
| *Dart Dead Eye* | Novice |
| | |

| Spells | |
|---|---|
| *Cloak of Shadows* | 1st Circle |
| *Charm Person* | 1st Circle |
| *Heal Wounds* | 2nd Circle |
| *Divine Weapon* | 1St Circle |
| *Holy Light* | 1St Circle |
| *Avatar of Melischar* | Inactive |
| | |
| **New Expertise Points** | 1 |

With all of her lingering injuries, she quickly decided to add two points to Vitality. According to Jonas, the skill increased your healing rate. Apparently, some legendary adventurers could heal wounds almost as quickly as they received them. But they had all been over Level 100, so she had a ways to go before she reached anything close to that threshold. Next, she placed a single point in Luck. It had kept her alive countless times so far, and she wanted to continually increase her most important stat.

Amara turned her attention to her Expertise Point next. She didn't want to use it on a new spell, as she couldn't summon even a trickle of mana from her battered soul. But as she looked over her Weapon Proficiencies and Martial Abilities, she didn't see anywhere she wanted to place the point either. Instead, she decided to save it.

When she next leveled up, she would use the two points to increase her Staff Proficiency. And she doubted she'd have to wait long, as she already felt close to the next level threshold. How many kobolds had her group slain after she'd fallen unconscious? She'd have to ask them for more details about their battle when she had a chance.

Her leveling up complete, Amara returned to fidgeting with her robes as she waited. After a few minutes, she watched people emerge from the tents and follow Frederick in her direction. She took in a deep breath and lifted her chin slightly in an attempt to look haughty. In total, five emissaries had arrived at Stout Oak Keep, excluding Edmund from the Knights Tarsillan, who had already left to gather their forces.

Oksberg had sent a single representative, a man who moved with the dangerous grace of a skilled warrior. He had short, dark hair parted to the side, a youthful face with a sharp jaw, and a scar that stretched from his cheek down to his mouth. He wore well-tailored black clothing that showed off his impressive physique, and a sword hung from his belt. His face was impassive as he approached Amara.

Meanwhile, the Gnostics had sent three representatives, all of them women. None of them appeared to be much older than Amara, and they all looked related. All three had silky, black hair hanging down to their waists, and oval faces with dark eyes. In unison, they curtsied to Amara and then took their seats.

The man from Oksberg remained standing as he looked her up and down. "This is the supposed avatar? I find her lacking."

Frederick plopped down in a chair with a grunt. "Already forming opinions when you haven't even talked to the poor girl yet, Walter?"

"Hold your tongue, knight," the warrior, Walter, said sharply. "I have no idea why you've been granted entry to this fief, which I remind you has sworn vassalage to my father."

"Oh, is that so?" Frederick replied, leaning forward to peer at the man. "Then where are Oksberg's armies? I see no stout men of your city here to repel the armies of Chaos. Though I must admit my eyesight isn't what it used to be. Perhaps I just missed them?"

"Be silent, or I will silence you," Walter snarled, his hand going to his sword hilt.

"Stop your nonsense," Frederick said. "You're like a little dog yapping with your idle threats."

Walter's eyes nearly bulged out of his head. Amara stepped forward and crossed her arms before rapidly uncrossing them. She didn't want to show them how nervous she felt. "If we're going to defeat Malcheron, then we all need to work together."

"And who is this Malcheron?" Walter asked, turning his attention to Amara.

"Who's *Malcheron?*" Amara frowned. "You don't know?"

Frederick leaned back in his chair, and with great difficulty crossed his legs. "Malcheron is the leader of the Issurians, you fool. Didn't your father fill you in on anything before sending you up here?"

"I have no time to read endless reams of parchment," Walter replied with a dismissive wave of his hand. "My father sent me to determine if we needed to intervene and nothing more. This is a job for a warrior, not a weakling scribe."

"Enough," Amara said, her voice rising. "I am the avatar, and you all must listen to me." She was mildly surprised when everyone fell silent. She hadn't expected them to follow her orders. After she'd cleared her throat, she continued. "The castle will soon fall to the Forces of Chaos, and I have to assume that's bad."

"*Bad?*" Frederick snorted. "Try end of the world bad."

Amara opened her mouth to reply, but stopped when a draconic shape detached itself from the walls of Stout Oak Keep. The wyvern, Nyrax, sailed in their direction on leathery wings before circling their position and landing nearby. Ingrid stepped off the beast's back. In shining armor with a sword on her belt, she looked the very image of a noble lady.

She strode over to the assembly and then bowed to Walter. "My apologies for being late, my prince."

Walter grunted in reply. "It's about time you showed up. My father will hear how you kept me waiting for days before granting me an audience."

"I was otherwise disposed tending to the avatar," Ingrid said, her features tight. "She was seriously injured battling the Forces of Chaos."

Amara turned back to Frederick. "You were implying something would happen if the castle fell?"

"It will bring about an apocalypse to all the southlands," the old knight replied.

"What are you talking about?" Amara asked. "Why is it apocalyptic?"

Frederick peered at each of them in turn. "Do you truly not know? Has the church deadened your minds to the point none of you remember the past? Or have the Chaos-aligned traitors scrubbed your history clean of any mention of the Wall?"

"Get to the point," Walter snapped. "What do you know about the castle we don't?"

"Yes," Amara said, peering at the old man intently. "Please tell us everything."

Frederick rubbed a hand down his lined face. "I suppose I have time for a brief history lesson. When Galoth, the first emperor of man, constructed the wall, he built fifteen fortresses along its length. A core was placed in the depths of each fortress to power the shield holding back Chaos."

"The forts maintain Galoth's Wall?" Walter asked, suddenly looking unsure of himself. "If that's true, then . . ."

"Yes," Frederick said with a sigh. "Fourteen of the forts have fallen to the Forces of Chaos. If Stout Oak Keep falls, then the magic protecting the wall will come down. And nothing will keep the full might of Chaos out of the South."

Ingrid stepped forward, her armor clinking. "Why should we believe you?"

"Why would I bother lying?" Frederick shrugged. "I'm too old to waste my time with such frivolities."

"To regain control of my lands," Ingrid said fiercely. "I know you knights sit around in your drafty castle plotting revenge against my family. And I will not let it happen."

"I'm perfectly happy living in the mountains," Frederick said, leaning back in his chair. "Far less Issurians around to ruin your day."

Jonas looked stricken as he stepped forward to stand beside Amara. "Is what you say true?"

Frederick nodded.

Amara was still confused by the discussion. "Aren't the armies of Chaos already able to travel over the Wall? What does it matter if it fails?"

Frederick cupped a hand to his ear. "Could you speak up a bit?"

She repeated her question in a louder voice.

"What does it matter? What does it *matter*?" Frederick asked incredulously as his eyes widened. "Don't they teach the youth anything today? Oh wait, you're from another world, so I imagine they wouldn't. But the walls keep out all but the weakest Chaos creatures. There are ancient and powerful things you couldn't imagine dwelling in the North. The knights will survive in our fortress, but the rest of you would be in trouble."

"Does my father know this?" Walter demanded as he took a step forward.

"Hmm . . . ?" the wizened chaplain replied. "How should I know? Never met the man. At least I don't think so, but my memory isn't what it used to be."

Walter seemed to recover slightly. "If the Chaos armies come, then we shall defeat them."

"Ha, I'd like to see that." Frederick slapped his knee. "Our most recent scouting reports state there are at least 150,000 Issurians, kobolds, ogres, goblins, and dark dwarves just beyond the wall here. That old bat Abiloch has gathered half the Forces of Chaos for when Stout Oak Keep falls."

Ingrid gasped and turned pale at the revelation.

Amara felt stunned at the news. She'd thought facing Malcheron and his thousands of soldiers was bad enough. But there was another, much larger army waiting just beyond the wall? How could they stand against so many? As it was, defeating Malcheron's army felt like an insurmountable task.

"One hundred and fifty thousand Chaos creatures?" Walter breathed. "I must take my leave. My father must be informed immediately." He started to turn, but then stopped. "Where are your armies, baroness?"

"They fell in battle," Ingrid replied tersely. "Along with my . . . brave husband. I sent numerous messengers to your father, pleading for help."

"No such messages reached us," Walter said, his jaw set. "However, there may have been some interference from the Church. But regardless, these lands must not fall. Lady Ingrid of House Vogel, I order you to hold this keep until relief arrives."

"I will do my duty," Ingrid replied stiffly. "And I swear my family's ancestral lands will not fall."

Walter paused and turned his attention to Amara. His eyes looked her up and down as he scrutinized her. "I'm afraid I must ask. Are you truly the avatar? Have you come to save us in our hour of need? Or do you only provide false hope?"

Amara straightened up to her full height, though she still stood nearly a head shorter than Walter. "The goddess Melischar sent me to gather the Forces of Order, and to restore Galoth's Wall."

"I find all of this hard to believe," Walter admitted. "Yet I have seen the star in the sky myself. And the Church burned many innocents to suppress the news of your arrival."

"The Church burned people?" she gasped. "When did that happen?"

"The night the star—your star—appeared in the night sky, the Church attacked a gathering listening to a young man from Stout Oak Keep. The handful of survivors all told the same tale of a messenger claiming an avatar had arrived in the North. My father never would have believed something so far-fetched had the Church not acted so quickly to suppress the news. After the star appeared, and the heinous slaughter of our citizens, he suspected there might be a grain of truth to it. Now, with the news of the Chaos army gathering, I find myself believing it as well."

"What happened to the messenger?" Lady Ingrid asked, her lips pressed together to form a line. "And do you know his name?"

"The boy, Uwe, perished from his wounds," Walter said. "I'm sorry for your loss."

Lady Ingrid nodded expressionlessly, but her hand tightened on the hilt of her sword until the leather creaked.

Amara felt a lump form in her throat at hearing the name. Now she'd never have a chance to make up for the way she treated Uwe. She still felt bad about making him think her pet mimic was going to eat him.

"A mob tore down the church and strung up the local priests afterwards," Walter continued. "There is no longer any Church presence in Oksberg. Though the perpetrators have eluded capture so far. I would have liked to see them hanged myself."

Walter hitched up his belt, and then, after a brief hesitation, bowed to Amara. "I will put my faith in you—please do not make me regret my decision. My father had already begun to call his barons to deal with the undead threat on our western border. But I will convince him to bring them north instead with this news. If I am successful, look for a relief army from the South in three weeks' time." With his final words, he strode off toward his tent.

"Oh-ho, a relief army from Oksberg," Frederick said, slapping his knee. "Will the wonders never cease?"

Amara turned to face the three Gnostic women who still hadn't spoken. "Can we expect any help from your sect?"

The woman to the right nodded her head. "My name is Emilia, and these are my sisters Lena and Ida. The sackcloth prophet told of your arrival, and a fleet set out for the North many weeks ago. However, they will need a port when they arrive. Otherwise, our army will have to land far to the south and march overland. And time appears to be of the essence."

"The sackcloth prophet?" Amara asked. "Who in the world is that?"

"The man who heralded your arrival into this world," Emilia intoned. "The one who spread news of you throughout the South, giving hope to the down-trodden Gnostics. You may know him as Brother Otto."

"Brother Otto?" she gasped. "He made it out of Leissen alright?"

"Yes," Emilia said, her lips curling up into a smile. "And he is raising a force to oppose the Church throughout the South. The gods have returned, and the Forces of Order must be made whole to fight against the foul armies of Chaos. He speaks very highly of you, I might add."

Amara pushed down her surprise at hearing about Brother Otto. She'd have to learn more information about him when they were done here. But the Gnostics' requirements for a port had given her an idea.

"The Forces of Chaos are waiting for their quest to complete before they attack, right?"

Jonas nodded his head. "Most likely, they will have to hold all the objectives for several weeks to earn the quest reward. However, I cannot say with certainty, and at best I'm offering you an educated guess. This is obviously no normal location, based on the strategic importance of the castle, which may alter the quest."

"Then what happens if they lose one of the objectives?"

"The timer for the quest would reset," Jonas replied, realization dawning on his face.

"We need to attack the port," she said. "Once we retake Ahrenshoop, we'll kill two birds with one stone." She returned to face Emilia. "How long until your fleet arrives?"

"Perhaps a week," the Gnostic woman replied, folding her hands primly in her lap.

"Then we have a week to prepare." Amara said. "And I'll need all your help." As she spoke, she could only hope her soul would recover sufficiently by then. Because otherwise, she didn't know if her plan could work.

# CHAPTER 47

The newly born star blazed in the night sky, almost like a second sun, its mere presence mocking Malcheron. He had executed his plan to perfection in order to secure victory in the South. He'd bribed corrupt churchmen to prevent reinforcements from arriving and had carefully cultivated spies throughout Stout Oak Keep. With methodical precision, he'd eliminated the troops garrisoned at the fortress and then finally the lord himself. But when victory had nearly been in his grasp, the long-absent gods had intervened to thwart his ambitions.

He curled his hand into a fist and took a deep breath to calm himself. Even if the reports were true and an avatar had arrived at Stout Oak Keep, not all was lost. If he held the quest areas for another fourteen days, then he would complete the quest given to him by the augur board. Once he had the rewards, he would order his forces to storm the castle. While an avatar was a powerful opponent, no soldiers manned the walls of the keep.

The baroness and the avatar stood alone.

And should the representative of the gods prove impossible to defeat, he still had a magical item from Abiloch, his mother, to use in case of emergencies. He reached down and ran his claws along the case containing the *Scroll of Banishment.* It had been gifted to him in case a high-level adventurer had come to the fortress's aid. Anyone he cast it upon would find themselves hurled into the pit of a volcano. Not even an avatar could survive such a thing.

A gruff voiced emerged from the darkness. "Best not be wandering off from the camp alone."

He turned to see the commander of the dark dwarves, Storgom, standing behind him. The dwarf had a two-handed axe resting on his shoulder and wore the dark armor of his people.

"I just needed a moment to think," Malcheron said quietly. "The fates seemed to have turned against us."

"Aye, the bit with the dungeon was a bloody disaster," Storgom grunted. "But at least Tecala still lives. It was a near thing with her wounds."

"Yes, I am grateful for that," Malcheron replied. "However, between the adventurers and the dungeon, we lost nearly forty kobolds."

"And double that number of goblins," Storgom added with a grimace. "Not that we'll miss them much."

"Over one hundred injured and dead, and they only managed to capture a single knight." Malcheron's lips curled up in a snarl, exposing his sharp teeth. "I should have sent Brap'toc and his ogres instead."

"You couldn't have known," Storgom replied, his voice falling slightly. "Everyone thought the Gods of Order had long ago abandoned this world."

"I doubt my mother will be so understanding."

"We just need to take the castle before the messenger reaches her," Storgom said. "If you present her with the avatar's head, I bet she'll be pretty happy. We might even get ourselves a nice little duchy."

Malcheron nodded at his friend's words. "When this world falls, I want you and Tecala to ascend with me to join the Chaos Gods."

"I think I have a bit more leveling to do first." Storgom laughed as he shifted the axe on his shoulder slightly. "What do you suppose the Chaos Gods do all day? Do you think they have anything like fishing up there? I'd sure miss sitting on the rocky shore of an underground lake and drinking a pint of mushroom beer."

"I have no idea," Malcheron admitted. "Though the idea of ruling a world sounds enticing."

"We should head back to camp," the dark dwarf said. "Tecala will probably be worried about you."

Malcheron arched his eyebrow. "I had assumed she sent you out to fetch me."

"Ha," Storgom replied. "Not likely. She's been too busy moping around the camp since she failed you." When Malcheron glared at him, he hastily added, "Her words, not mine."

*I'll have to rectify that notion,* he thought to himself. *It was my failure for not facing the avatar myself.*

Malcheron spun on his heel and set a course back to the camp. He had responsibilities, and he couldn't while away the night stargazing. If things went as planned, he'd soon snuff out the star that tormented him so.

He marched through the camp, Storgom at his heels as they passed by the kobold burrows and entered the field containing the yurts of Malcheron's people. The nearly festive mood of the previous week had evaporated like frost under a bright morning sun. And the few Issurians who glanced up from their fires had worry etched onto their features. The defeat inflicted by the avatar had shattered their morale.

As he continued to walk toward his command tent, Malcheron glanced over at his friend. "I believe I have some work for you."

"It's about time," Storgom replied with enthusiasm. "Do you want me to test myself against the avatar? I always thought the stories about them were exaggerated."

"No," Malcheron replied. "Unless I state otherwise, no one is to confront the avatar except for myself. If you encounter her, I want you to retreat. Understood?"

"Dark dwarves aren't known for running away from a fight." Storgom glared at him. "Are you asking me to be a coward?"

"I'm asking you to exercise caution," Malcheron replied. "We still don't know the extent of her powers. However, she managed to cut her way through a high-level dungeon and defeat our forces. She has clearly been building her power in secret for many years."

"Bah," Storgom said. "She's mortal, which means she'll fall to my axe. Not much she could do against being cleaved in half."

"The God of War's avatar, Birgitta, slew a Harbinger in single combat. Do not underestimate their power."

"I still say I could take her out," Storgom grumbled.

"As I was saying," Malcheron continued, "I want to move the timetable forward."

"You do? But what about the quest?"

"If the army continues to sit in camp and stew over the defeat, morale will only continue to fall," Malcheron said. "And I can't risk sitting around waiting for the quest to complete while an avatar is out there working against us. I want to be in a position to lay siege to the castle the moment we complete the quest."

"Ah, so I'll finally get to assemble my war machines?" Storgom's eyes glittered with excitement as he rubbed his meaty hands together. "I have some amazing new things to show you. Should I go get started now?"

"Yes," Malcheron inclined his head. "Tell your people to begin their preparations immediately. I want the war machines assembled and at the gates of Stout Oak Keep before the fourteen days are up."

"I'll knock down the walls faster than you can say the avatar's name." With that, Storgom turned and strode off into the darkness.

Malcheron watched as the dark dwarf hurried off toward his camp. The mountain dweller's kin had brought all manner of strange mechanical contraptions over the wall with them. While he recognized some of them as catapults and ballista, the long metal tubes proved impossible to decipher. Hopefully, the war machines would be up to the task of breaching the ancient—and magical—walls of Stout Oak Keep.

"There you are," the throaty voice of Tecala cut through the darkness as she strode up to his side. "I must speak with you."

"Is there word from my mother?" he asked sharply. The messenger bearing news of the avatar had only departed earlier in the morning and shouldn't have crossed the Wall yet. Still, Abiloch often had ways of learning things before word reached her.

"No." Tecala shook her head, and strands of dark hair fell over her flawless features. "I believe we should speak in private."

"As you wish." Malcheron felt a pit growing in his stomach. If Tecala wanted to speak to him away from the prying ears of his people, then the news must be dire indeed. And he fully understood the price of failure here. His sister's fate of eternal suffering within a volcano would pale in comparison to what his mother would do to him.

Tecala fell in beside him as they walked across the camp. But before they reached the tent at the center, she slowed and stopped at a man who had been crucified. Nailed to the boards was a knight with too many wounds to count; whips had lashed his body, bruises had been bludgeoned into his limbs, and goblins had stabbed him with spears. And yet somehow, he still clung to life.

"This isn't right," Tecala said, frowning. "He fought bravely against me in battle."

"And he nearly killed you," Malcheron replied with steel in his tone. "This filthy human deserves a far worse fate." When the kobolds had carried Tecala back into camp, a deep wound had been cleaved across her chest. Only through the liberal use of healing pills had they stabilized her long enough for the camp healers to repair the damage.

"This isn't how you treat your enemies," Tecala continued. "He should be given a swift and painless death."

"His crucifixion stands." Malcheron gestured in the direction of his tent. "And I won't speak any further on the subject."

He strode forward without waiting for her reply. The human would die on the cross as punishment for daring to harm Tecala. But as he walked past the crucified knight, he couldn't help but glance up at the man's swollen face. While the human didn't appear long for this world, his eyes still blazed with hatred. If the Forces of Order had had a hundred men such as him, Malcheron wasn't sure if his invasion would have succeeded. Thankfully, the South had more than its share of cowards, fools, and traitors.

*And now, an avatar,* he reminded himself darkly.

Upon reaching his tent, he nodded at the guards, and then pushed aside the tent flap to stride inside. He moved over to the table containing the maps of the area, examining them while he waited for Tecala to join him. His camp was clearly marked near the mountain valley leading north, and Stout Oak Keep was shown to the south.

Tecala entered the tent a minute after him, most likely lingering by the knight nailed to the cross. Without a word, she strode over to the table holding the wine and poured some of the rich red liquid into a goblet. Then she walked over and handed it to him.

Malcheron held the cup without drinking. If she felt he needed a drink, then the news had to be catastrophic. "Out with it already," he growled.

"A relief army assembles to march on the fortress."

"Impossible," he said, waving his hand dismissively at her. "There is no such army."

Tecala inhaled deeply before continuing. "The king of Oksberg has called upon his barons after burning down a church and executing every last priest within the city's walls."

Malcheron's grip tightened on the cup until the gold crumpled in his hand. The liquid inside sloshed over his fingers, but he barely noticed. Had the king discovered the priests were working for him? They'd been paid an exorbitant sum of gold to turn the people against Stout Oak Keep. "How many will march in the relief army?"

"The messenger said five hundred knights and perhaps five thousand infantry. And a significant number of casters as well, though those numbers are harder to pin down."

"With so many, their numbers will nearly match our own force," Malcheron snarled. "How did this happen?"

Tecala frowned. "Apparently, some of the local church officials burned an entire crowd of people when the star appeared in the sky."

"Those fools. How could they have been so stupid?" He could tell from Tecala's expression she hadn't finished with the bad news yet. "There's more?"

"The Knights Tarsillan are stirring in their mountain fortress."

"The Knights?" Malcheron tossed his ruined cup aside. "They haven't interfered in the North for centuries. Are they called by the star?"

Tecala shrugged and crossed her arms. "At least six thousand knights and an equal number of infantry are gathering."

"If they link up with Oksberg, then they will have more than three times our number." He looked disbelieving at Tecala as she chewed on her lower lip. There was obviously *still* more bad news. "What else?" he snapped. "Have the Gods of Order themselves descended to defeat me?"

"A fleet of Gnostic ships departed from the South and are on the way with an additional two thousand infantry. Thankfully, there are no knights among them, but they boast many powerful casters."

"So, the Kingdom of Oksberg, the Knights Tarsillan, and the Gnostics all march to relieve the castle?"

Tecala walked over to his side and placed a hand on his shoulder. "I will stand by your side when you defeat them."

Malcheron gently pushed her off and then stormed over to the tent flap. He hurled it open and faced his guard outside. Events were rapidly conspiring to doom him to a fate worse than death. He had to move quickly if he wanted to stay ahead of them.

"Assemble the army!" he shouted to his nearby commanders. "We march for Stout Oak Keep tonight!"

# CHAPTER 48

The sun rose angrily over the walls of Stout Oak Keep and dyed the low-hanging clouds a bloody crimson. Amara glanced up at the dawn sky, hoping Borim was wrong about red mornings being a dire omen. She shook the thought away and focused on gathering up her meager possessions, which were scattered around the knight's tent.

She'd slept fitfully on a cot provided to her by Frederick the previous evening. The discussions about the coming battle had gone late into the night, and with the freely flowing wine, none of them had wanted to make the long trek back to the castle. The Knight's Tarsillan tent had been too small to fit anyone but the old chaplain and herself. But the others from her group had found shelter in a tent provided by the Gnostics, while a tipsy Ingrid had returned to the castle atop Nyrax.

Amara stretched as she felt every ache and pain from the injuries she'd received in the dungeon. Her soul still felt battered from overuse. Hesitantly, she reached out for her mana, and let out a sigh of relief as she was able to tease out a thread of the strange energy. At the rate her soul was healing, she suspected she might be able to cast normally in another week or so. But she doubted she'd have the luxury of waiting that long.

She was planning a scouting mission as soon as they took Ahrenshoop.

Tossing and turning on her cot the night before, Amara had been unable to keep her thoughts from returning to Noah. She still didn't know his fate, but if he'd been captured by the Forces of Chaos, she could only imagine the appalling treatment he was receiving at their hands. The more she thought about it, the more she realized she had to find out if he still lived. After all, she owed him her life.

Now all she had to do was convince the others to launch a dangerous mission into the heart of the Chaos army. If they refused to help, she might have to go off alone with her pet mimic. But she doubted Jonas would ever forgive her if she did something so reckless on her own. And she didn't want to even think about how Ingrid would respond to such a plan.

Amara decided to discuss it with her group later. Right now, she needed to pack up her few things. She opened her backpack and then stuffed her night-gown inside. Next, she carefully added the provisions graciously given to her by the Gnostics. And finally, she placed a sheathed knife on top.

Once she'd fully woken up, she planned to retrieve her armor from the castle. Then she wanted to head into the nearby forest to gather some herbs. She'd exhausted nearly all the healing pills she'd created using her Alchemy Skill. And she wanted more of the pills before she faced the armies of Chaos again.

Amara lifted her new staff and examined the softly glowing runes. While it was obviously magical, she'd forgotten to ask Ingrid about it. Regardless of what the enchantments engraved in the wood did, it would likely be far superior to the glorified stick she'd been using since Leissen.

Now that she'd packed up all her belongings, it was time to set out for Ahren-shoop. They'd hammered out a rough plan the night before. The eight of them—the three Gnostic women, the elderly knight Frederick, and her group—would travel to the port village. It had taken over an hour, but she'd finally managed to convince Ingrid to stay behind to guard the castle. Even after relenting, the baroness had been visibly unhappy with the plan.

Once Amara arrived at Ahrenshoop, she would use her *Cloak of Shadows* to scout the enemy's defenses. As Stout Oak Keep's lord and army had already been defeated, the village was likely only lightly garrisoned.

If all went to plan, Amara and her party would attack the night before the Gnostic fleet arrived. Emilia claimed to have a device that allowed her to communicate with the admiral of the flotilla. With this device they could coordinate to take the village and hold it with the Gnostic reinforcements. But if they attacked before help arrived, Malcheron could just send a force to retake it immediately.

The sound of beating drums interrupted her thoughts, and she glanced out of the tent questioningly. Had one of the relief armies arrived already?

But when Jonas ducked into the tent with his daggers drawn, she knew the opposite was true—Malcheron's army had appeared at the castle, weeks early.

"We must leave immediately," Jonas said as he pulled back the tent flap to glance outside. "A force of Issurians are rushing toward the bridge, and kobolds are encircling the village."

"What are they doing here already?" Amara hastily tied her backpack shut. "I thought they wouldn't attack until they completed their quest?"

"Perhaps Malcheron received word of the relief armies gathering," Jonas replied. "He has been surprisingly knowledgeable about the goings on to the south."

"What should we do?" she asked, biting her lower lip. Would Lady Ingrid and the few remaining guards be able to hold the castle? Should she attempt to cut through the Issurians to help defend the fortress?

But if they couldn't break through, then they'd be trapped between the river and the Chaos army. And she didn't doubt that would result in a swift death.

"I believe we should continue with our original plan." Jonas motioned for her to hurry up. "The fortress is strong enough that even a force of peasants led by Lady Ingrid should manage to hold it for a short period of time. And our skills will be more useful for harrying the attackers from outside the walls."

Amara frowned and then slung her backpack over her shoulder. Next, she picked up her quiver of darts—cleaned and repaired by Salamander—and then hurried outside. Frederick stood just beyond the entryway, a strange, pulsating orb in his palm.

"Ah, it's about time," the old man grumbled. "You wouldn't want to be inside when I closed the tent. No, you certainly wouldn't." As he spoke, he held up the device, and then with a hissing sound, the tent, cots, and supplies disappeared into the glowing orb. Within seconds, the only trace of where the camp had been was a patch of flattened grass.

She couldn't help but gasp at the display of magical power. "Where do I get one of those things?"

Frederick chuckled as he stuffed the magical device into a pouch on his belt. "I'm sure one of our runesmiths can whip you up something similar in the future. Mind you, in order to do so, you'd have to be alive, which means we can't stay here. No, we certainly can't. Not with that horned demon Malcheron on his way. I'd never hear the end of it if I lost an avatar to him."

"So, you think we should leave as well?"

"No point getting penned inside the walls like cattle." Frederick hefted a halberd in his gnarled hands with surprising ease. "Not while we have so much work to do. After all, if we were stuck inside, who would complete all the quests out here?"

Amara glanced over to see her other companions and the Gnostic sisters hurrying in their direction. Borim arrived first, followed closely by Salamander, and finally the three dark-haired women. There was no trace of the sister's expansive camp either—they must have a magical item like Frederick.

*I really want an instant tent like that,* she thought to herself. *It would have made the trip north far more bearable.*

But now wasn't the time for such thoughts. She could see ranks of Issurians and kobolds issuing forth from the trees like a plague of locusts. In front of them, peasants fled their homes with what little they could carry, all streaming in a frantic swarm toward the castle.

When she turned her gaze toward Fusson, it seemed like everyone was abandoning the village as well. The gates had been flung open, and people were streaming toward the bridge leading to the fortress. A few of them dragged carts behind them, but as the Chaos army neared, these were hastily abandoned on the side of the road.

Amara watched as a flurry of activity unfolded on the bridge leading to Stout Oak Keep. Clusters of men worked feverishly near the supports, then sprinted back across the river toward the gates of the castle.

"What are they doing?" she asked Jonas.

"It appears they are about to use magical crystals to destroy the bridge." He frowned deeply. "There likely won't be time to take the peasants inside."

"Ingrid wouldn't do that, would she?" Amara said, a note of alarm creeping into her voice. "If she does, then everyone outside will be slaughtered!"

"Lady Ingrid must destroy the bridge before Malcheron's forces can seize it," Jonas continued. "If they manage to secure the crossing, then this siege may be over in a matter of days."

Borim strode up beside them. "My people never leave a dwarf behind," he said gruffly. "I didn't think even ol' crazy eyes would do something so cruel to her own subjects."

Before the dwarf had finished speaking, something ignited on the bridge, followed by a flash of light, and then a deafening concussion. Three more explosions followed in short order, the magic erupting from within them brighter than the sun, and with a groan, the bridge collapsed into the river. The rushing water quickly swept away the timbers, leaving only the jagged supports protruding above the surface.

The inhabitants of Fusson stopped on the bank, many of them falling to their knees in despair. And with every moment that passed, more arrived to join their ranks. There were well over one hundred people trapped outside of the castle.

*How could Lady Ingrid leave them trapped outside?*

Amara opened her mouth to speak, but Jonas cut her off.

"I know what you are planning," the rogue said. "However, nothing can be done for them without sacrificing our own lives."

Frederick nodded his head. "This fine young man speaks the truth. Trying to save a panicked mass of peasants would be like a shepherd trying to guide his flock through a karaxi-infested forest. Most likely, the shepherd would end up in the monster's belly, along with his sheep. No, I think it's better to depart with all haste."

"I won't leave them," she said flatly. "I've left too many people behind already."

Borim tugged on his beard and squinted his eyes as he stared at the Issurians. "I'm with Amara. Best to go down doing something noble. What's the point of being a hoity-toity avatar's companion if you can't save a few peasants? Plus, I wouldn't mind going another round against those horned bastards."

"We should go," Salamander said in her reedy voice. "I need to get back to my parents."

Amara brushed back a strand of her hair absently with one hand. She didn't know what to do. She couldn't just leave the people of Stout Oak Keep to die on the riverbank. But her group was split on the matter.

"I'll stay here with Borim and Mimi," she said, gazing at her companions one by one. "We'll save as many as we can and then meet you at Ahrenshoop."

"And how will you fight?" Jonas asked sharply. "Will you hurl yourself at the Issurians with nothing more than your staff? Or will you instead risk permanent damage to your soul in a hopeless bid to hold back a horde of Chaos creatures? What you are planning is madness."

Amara didn't reply for a moment, stung by Jonas's uncharacteristic rebuke. "I have to do something," she replied, finally finding her voice. "If they die, then it's on me."

"If they die, then it is on their lady who abandoned them," Jonas shot back. "While you are powerful, you cannot defeat a Chaos army alone. Sometimes people are lost in war, and nothing, not even an avatar of the gods can change that fact. We must withdraw to fight another day."

Amara glared at him. She couldn't believe Jonas, out of everyone, wanted to abandon the peasants of Stout Oak Keep to their fate. "I'm going to save them, with or without you."

"I gave up everything I believed in to keep you alive," he said, his tone suddenly flat. "And you would throw your life away at the first chance presented to you?"

"I . . . I have to do something," she said, some of her anger draining away. Obviously, Jonas's use of his wraith rogue abilities had left some lasting scars on his psyche.

Emilia, the Gnostic woman, who had remained silent until this point, stepped forward and curtsied. "If I may speak, divine avatar?"

"What do you want?" Amara snapped before catching herself. After a deep breath, she continued in a calmer tone. "I'm sorry. And yes, you may speak."

"My sisters and I can stay behind to create a diversion," Emilia said, curtsying again. "Our magic will give the people of this land time to escape. And through our actions, we shall instill renewed faith in the gods."

Jonas spun his daggers around in his hands as he peered at the girl. "Do you think you can handle the Issurians alone?"

Emilia nodded. "My family has always had an affinity for earth magic. And while the Issurians are powerful, there is little chance they can stand against an elemental conjured by all three of us."

"If you can delay them for a bit, then we'll hold the road for any who manage to get away." Amara pointed at the wagon trail leading toward the coastal village of Ahrenshoop.

When Jonas opened his mouth to speak, she shook her head. "I won't seek out a fight with the Issurians, but I need to give the people a chance to escape. No matter what you say, you won't convince me to leave."

Jonas hesitated for a moment before replying, seemingly torn. "If you fall, then all hope is lost," he said. "I want nothing more to protect the people of the land, but the relief armies from the South march for the avatar. And while I may as well ask a tiger to give up its stripes, I must ask you to not do anything to needlessly endanger yourself during the battle."

"I'll be fine," she said with a forced smile. For the first time since she'd arrived in this world, she was facing a fight with no spells. And it made her nervous.

Frederick rubbed his chin. "Since you seem intent on staying, I'll stand by your side like the knights of old. However, it's a bit alarming to have an avatar with such reckless impulses. I see I'm going to have my work cut out for me keeping you alive." He turned to face Jonas. "Is she always like this?"

"You have no idea," Jonas said darkly. "If we bumped into a Harbinger, she'd probably challenge it to a fist fight."

"I think I'd like to see such a thing before the gods take me." Frederick guffawed before he turned to survey the ranks of kobolds closing in on Fusson. "How about this, Avatar? We'll act as your rear guard, keeping you safe while holding the road open. Does that work for you?"

Amara considered the knight's plan and then finally gave him a terse nod. She gestured at the three Gnostic sisters. "We need to slow the Chaos army before they reach the peasants. So, how does your magic work?"

# CHAPTER 49

Amara ducked as her Luck blared a warning of impending danger, and a second later a crossbow bolt sailed over her head. She straightened up and tapped Salamander on the shoulder. Once she had the girl's attention, she pointed at the clump of nearby Issurian crossbowmen.

Salamander nodded with a determined look on her narrow face and then sent a jet of flames in the direction Amara was pointing. A shield flared to life around the Issurians and the magical barrier deflected the fiery spell where it ignited the surrounding grass.

"That's not fair!" Salamander cried out. "How do they have—"

The girl's words cut out as Amara grabbed her collar and yanked her to the side. Immediately afterward, a volley of bolts slammed into the ground where Salamander had been standing.

"We must retreat!" Jonas shouted. He bled from half a dozen superficial wounds on his face and arms, but no Issurian could land a serious blow on him. Bodies of the demonic creatures lay scattered around at his feet.

Borim and Mimi had taken their toll on the attackers as well, and after the initial clash, the Issurians had retreated out of melee range. Once they had fallen back, they equipped an assortment of bows and crossbows and began to pepper Amara's group with missiles.

She dodged another crossbow bolt but winced as it thudded into Mimi behind her. Thankfully, it didn't penetrate far into her pet's wooden shell. She reached over and plucked it free before tossing it aside. In return, she received a slimy lick from the mimic.

Amara fought down the temptation to call upon her magic and scanned the valley for any more refugees. But aside from the handful of stubborn ones who remained clustered on the shore of the river, everyone else had either fled into the forest or reached their position.

It was time to leave.

"Cover our retreat!" she shouted at Jonas and Borim. "I'll lead the villagers into the forest."

Borim nodded as he batted another arrow aside with his new shield. The missile clanged against the steel surface and then dropped to the ground. It seemed like nothing could get past the dwarf's defenses when he had a shield. And he was grinning from ear to ear like a maniac.

"I . . . I will deal with them." Jonas said as he took in a ragged breath. A moment later, wraith-like wisps began to swirl around him. As he took a step forward, the ghostly storm grew more intense until it resembled a hurricane. The remaining Issurians took one look at his magic before breaking and fleeing.

"Good job, Sneaky!" Borim roared as he clapped Jonas on the shoulder. "That magic of yours is impressive. And to think you were holding out on us all this time."

Jonas frowned and pushed the dwarf's hand off his shoulder. "I'd hardly say threatening them with the loss of their souls should qualify as impressive. Monstrous and vile perhaps, but certainly not impressive."

As the Issurians retreated, Amara received a notification that she'd gained another level. Now she could improve her Staff Weapon Proficiency. She hoped it didn't function the same way as her spells, where she was granted a vision and had to spend weeks figuring it out. She needed to become a better fighter, and fast.

Amara walked over to Jonas. "I understand you don't like your class, but we're fighting to save everyone. Sometimes you have to do things that you don't want to." As she spoke, she inspected the huddled mass of civilians on the road behind them. Around fifty of them had reached their position on the road. Hopefully, the rest had found safety in the dense forest.

To her credit, Ingrid had emerged from the castle riding her wyvern. And while she'd managed to pluck many of the peasants from the banks and ferry them to safety, the approaching Issurians had eventually driven her back with spells and missiles. The wyvern had finally withdrawn and a small knot of peasants had been left to their fate.

Amara took one look across the valley, now swarming with kobolds, Issurians, and the towering forms of ogres she had previously mistaken as giants. Many of the peasant buildings had ignited, and black smoke billowed toward the sky as frightened farm animals fled in front of the advancing army.

As she watched, an ogre caught a goat in one of its meaty fists. The creature lifted the struggling animal and started to eat it alive. Amara tore her gaze away, unable to watch anymore.

Instead, she inspected the rubble outside the walls of Fusson, which only seconds ago had been a towering earth golem. The Gnostic sisters had used their magic to conjure a minion composed of earth and rock. The golem had smashed through the lines of the advancing army before a trio of powerful Issurian spell-casters had managed to bring it down. But the diversion had given time for the peasants to escape.

Frederick walked up beside her as he combed his fingers through his long beard. "Oh-ho, what a battle. It invigorates the blood and strengthens the spirit to fight against the foul creatures of Chaos. Did I ever tell you about the time I went north of the wall? No, I don't imagine I did. Well, I'll have to tell you someday. In the meantime, it's best we take our leave. Eventually, someone will realize we're a real threat."

Amara nodded. She hadn't seen the old knight do much in the fight, but she didn't bother contradicting him. After all, he'd been nothing but supportive of her so far. And that alone made him a better ally than most of the people she'd met in this world.

Borim trotted over, letting his shield hang from the strap on his shoulder. "Stop flapping your lips, old man. It's time to get out of this place."

Frederick lifted his hand up to shield his eyes and then made a point of peering over the dwarf's head. "Do you hear something, Amara? I thought I heard something make a noise. Was it an ant? Or perhaps another diminutive creature like a gopher?"

"Knock it off," Borim roared. "I'm above average height for a dwarf, and you know it."

"Yes, you are most stout for a dwarf." Frederick chuckled and lowered his hand. "And I was just saying to the avatar we should depart immediately. However, before we go, I must first find my halberd." He glanced around the road, but then started with surprise when he noticed it in his hand. "Ah, there it is. It appears some fiend had cast invisibility on it while I was holding it."

Borim shook his head and then stalked away, mumbling something about senile old men.

Amara couldn't tell how much of Frederick's behavior was for theatre, and how much was real. She hoped most of what he did was for his own amusement. Otherwise, she might have another problem to deal with in the near future.

With one last look at the despoiled valley, she turned and headed down the road. The Chaos army seemed more intent on encircling the fortress than chasing those fleeing. She was just lucky they hadn't realized she was outside of the walls.

She quickly reached the position of the cowering villagers and raised her hand to get their attention. "My group is heading toward Ahrenshoop," she called out in a loud voice. "You're all welcome to come with us, but I can't promise your safety. We're going to try to retake it from the Chaos army."

Harold, the pig farmer, pushed his way to the front of the crowd. He held a thick cudgel in one hand. "I think I speak for all of us when I say we'll defend our home. Those bastards burned my house, and I want a little payback."

A murmur of agreement spread through the crowd. Though most of the adults were graybeards, there were a few men and women of Harold's age. She didn't think any of them would last long in an open battle, but she had no plans to fight fairly.

Without another word, she proceeded down the road, and she was happy to see the majority of refugees fall in behind her. Only a handful forged off in another direction into the forest. She hoped they would find safety far from the battle.

After a few minutes of walking, Jonas joined her side. They hiked in silence for nearly a league before he finally spoke.

"I think you should consider allowing me to lead the attack on Ahrenshoop," he said, spinning one dagger around in his palm.

"I'm not going to let you fight in my place."

"Why must you always hurl yourself into danger without any thought to your own safety?" he said sharply.

She didn't answer for a moment, pondering the question. "I don't know, to be honest," she admitted. "But maybe it has something to do with my father. I . . . felt so powerless to help him when he was dying. And I guess I don't want to ever feel that way again. No one should have to die because I can't help them."

"There is a thin line between bravery and foolhardiness," Jonas said, his tone softening. "I admire the fact you want to help people. However, I must ask you to be more cautious in the future. Even holding open the road could have ended in tragedy had their forces not been focused on encircling the keep. And, as Frederick said, your soul has undergone significant trauma. It is important you don't strain yourself until it is completely healed."

As Jonas continued to walk, he fished out the nondescript silver cube they'd received from the dungeon. "However, I will continue to use this on your soul in the meantime."

"What exactly is that thing, anyway?" she asked, changing the subject. The last thing she wanted to do right now was argue with Jonas.

"This is an extremely rare treasure used to treat damaged souls," he replied, hefting it slightly so the dappled sunlight reflected off of the metal. "Such a thing is only ever granted by defeating a final challenge monster in a dungeon. And even then, I've only heard of a handful being received in my lifetime. It requires two people to operate, and it's activated by feeding mana directly into it. In fact, with the way you overtax yourself, you should hang on to this device. I suspect this won't be the last time you strain your soul."

A ghost of a smile twitched up on Amara's lips. "I'm not totally *reckless*, you know. Don't tell me your decision to fight the flying snakes on your own wasn't dangerous."

"There's a difference—I was desperate to increase my level."

"And things aren't desperate now?"

"I'm expendable and tainted by Chaos," he replied, his mood souring. "You are not."

The smile faded from Amara's face. "You're not *tainted by Chaos* just because of your class," she said, softly. "After all, Frederick didn't seem to care. And he should know more than anyone whether your class makes you a servant of Chaos. I bet there are lots of people like you in the knights."

"I . . . I have lived with the shame of my class for many years," he said. "It is a stigma that cannot be shed in a single day. However, I promise to be useful to you."

"I don't want you to just be *useful*," she continued. "You're my friend and I care about you. I don't want to see you suffering from something that wasn't your fault. You didn't choose your class."

He turned his head to stare at her intently with his sharp hazel eyes. "I was awarded my class based on my past deeds. While you may deny it, that is how classes are assigned here. You were a thief and thus became a Trickster Cleric. While you may no longer follow that path, you still earned your class through your actions. I . . . I committed a terrible deed in my childhood."

"What happened to you?" she asked hesitantly.

Jonas peered around as if to see if anyone else was listening. But the group had become staggered across the road, and no one except for Mimi was within earshot.

"I am responsible for the deaths of everyone in my household," he said, his shoulders slumping forward. His voice took on a tortured tone as he continued. "The maids, the butlers, the cooks, my mother, and . . . even my own sister."

Amara reached out and took his hand. "I'm sure whatever happened wasn't your fault."

Jonas pulled away from her grasp and took a step back. "I cannot absolve myself of the guilt." He took in a deep breath before continuing. "They died because I was too weak to protect them. And my sister died at my hands."

"Tell me what happened."

Jonas gazed off into the distance before continuing. "Assassins arrived at our manor while my father was away with our household retinue. Someone must have let them in, but I never learned who. They methodically worked their way through the lower levels, dispatching anyone who attempted to stop them. My mother fled upstairs with my sister and I, and once we reached the master bedroom, she barred the door. However, it did little to slow our pursuers."

"I was only ten at the time. But my father had always told me I must protect my family at all costs. Mounted above the fireplace in the room was the sword Foe Reaper, said to take its power from the souls of those it slayed. My father believed it to be a relic of a time before the First Empire, but whatever the truth of its origin, the sword was powerful beyond comprehension. I had always been cautioned never to touch the Foe Reaper, as it was protected by a magical spell. My mother, in her desperation, removed the ward protecting the weapon as the door came down. Before she could draw the blade, an assassin slew her with a crossbow bolt."

"I took up the fallen sword and drew it from its sheath. However, I couldn't handle the raw power it possessed. I unleashed it without understanding or caution. The magic destroyed everything around me, leaving nothing untouched."

"Everything?" Amara asked as comprehension slowly dawned on her.

Jonas nodded. "Including my own sister, who was cowering in the corner. Afterwards, only I remained standing in the once opulent room, which had been reduced to rubble. When my father returned, he blamed me for their deaths. He remarried soon afterwards, and while he didn't want to publicly disinherit me, I was moved down the line of succession behind his new children and my uncles. And when I received a class with abilities so similar to the power which had slain his daughter, he banished me from my family's lands."

"I'm so sorry," she said, unsure of what else she could say. "You were only a child at the time. There was no way you could have known what would happen."

"Perhaps," he replied. "And yet my sister's blood still stains my hands. The power I bear is evil. I will use it to defend you and these lands, but you will never convince me otherwise."

Amara pressed her lips together. For once, she was at a loss for words, but as the silence stretched out between them, she knew she'd missed her window to comfort Jonas. Instead, they continued on to Ahrenshoop in uncomfortable silence.

*I'll find a way to make him see the truth about his class someday.*

As they continued to walk, she turned her attention to her soul. She practiced drawing out strands of mana, each effort becoming easier than the last. Once they reached the coastal village, she'd most likely need to cast her spells—otherwise people might die. She could only hope her soul was up to the task by the time they arrived.

# CHAPTER 50

Amara brushed aside the stray petals on the rough-hewn slab of wood that served as her workstation and held up the final healing pill she'd created. Unlike her previous attempts, this one was perfectly spherical and compact. Even though she hadn't increased her Alchemy skill, she was still improving with each attempt.

She placed the pill next to the other dozen she'd created and then leaned back against the rough cave wall. She'd placed her meagre possessions around her in the narrow alcove. And just outside her small room, the refugees from the village huddled together in the dim light of the cave where they'd taken shelter. A wood cutter from the village had guided them to this place, and the extensive caverns had proven the perfect refuge from Malcheron's forces.

The sound of footsteps crunching on the gravel made her look up, and she spotted Jonas approaching with more flowers in his hand. Along with several others who possessed the herbalism skill, he'd been collecting the silverbells and karo root needed to create healing pills. But she didn't recognize the flowers he held.

Jonas stopped in front of her and then shifted his feet slightly. "These are for you," he said, as he thrust the white flowers out for her to take.

"Are these for another type of pill?" She took the bouquet and examined them. Apparently, Jonas's mother had been a noted alchemist. So, he knew many of the plants required to craft potions and pills.

"Not exactly." He coughed into his hand. "It is my thanks to you for listening to the story of my past. I know it must not have been easy to hear all the dark acts I've committed."

"Oh," she said, her eyes widening as she realized the flowers had nothing to do with alchemy. "But you didn't need to do this for me. Everyone has a past."

"And yet you don't go on about yours."

"Trust me," Amara said. "No one would want to listen to mine. I had a sick father, and a mother who abandoned us the moment he fell ill. And then, after a few hard years, I ended up in this world."

"What is your world like?" He pushed over a piece of wood with his foot and then sat down on it. He leaned forward slightly, resting his elbows on his knees, and peered intently at her.

Amara shrugged. "It's a lot more advanced than this place in a lot of ways. But we don't have any magic."

"No magic?" Jonas's brow rose. "I imagine that would make mundane tasks far more difficult."

"Not really. There's a lot of technology to do the things you use magic for here. Though I wish we'd had healing spells in my world."

"For your father?"

"Yes," she said quietly. "I couldn't do anything to help him in his final days. But at least I'm not as useless in this world." She turned away and blinked her eyes rapidly.

Jonas reached out and touched her hand. "I can't imagine you being useless in any world. And what you have done here is nothing short of miraculous. I have faith you will save this world."

She patted his hand as she scrubbed at her cheek. Their eyes locked for a moment, but then she averted her gaze as Salamander hurried over to them. She quickly withdrew her hand before the girl reached her.

Salamander stopped short and gave them a confused look. After a second, she shook her head and pointed toward the mouth of the cave. "There's someone outside for you."

"There's someone here for *me*?" They'd only reached the cave the previous evening. And no one aside from the people here should know their location. "Who is it?"

"It's a surprise." Salamander gave her a mischievous grin. Without a further word, she turned and skipped back the way she'd come.

"That's not funny!" Amara called after her. Then she gestured at Jonas. "I guess we should go see who it is."

Amara picked up three of the healing pills she'd created and handed them to Jonas. Once he'd taken them, she stuffed the rest into the pouch on her belt. She would hand them out to the others when she had a chance. Finally, she pushed herself to her feet and grabbed her staff, which was leaning against the wall.

With Jonas at her side, she navigated her way through the crowded interior of the cave. Most of the peasants had little more than the clothes on their back, but not a single one complained. They simply seemed happy to be alive. And many of them had thanked Amara personally for keeping the road open to allow them to escape.

As she walked, Harold rose to his feet and joined her side. The man had been like her shadow since they'd arrived here, and he'd made the other peasants keep their distance. She slowed and handed the pig farmer one of the healing pills she'd created. When he raised his brow questioningly, she explained, "It's the least I can do after that dungeon fiasco."

Harold smiled, showing a gap where his front teeth should be. "I'd hardly call anything a fiasco where an avatar comes down from the heavens and saves my life. And once we rebuild, my wife is going to bake you a few pies."

"I'd like that," Amara said.

When they reached the entrance to the cave, she stopped short, and Harold and Jonas nearly collided with her. Standing at the edge of the forest—flanked by two men holding leveled spears, and one hunter with an arrow nocked on his bow—stood the priestess Emmaline.

"You have to be kidding me," Amara muttered under her breath. Emmaline was the last person in the world she wanted to deal with right now. Without thinking, she drew mana from her soul. While she doubted she could cast more than a single spell, she trusted the priestess about as far as she could throw a dragon.

As she inspected the priestess, she realized the woman must have fought her way through the lines of the Chaos army. Emmaline's face was pale and drawn. And blood seeped out from a deep wound on her leg.

"What did you do to Ingrid?" Amara asked flatly. "If you've hurt her, then you're about to have a bad day." Though she didn't particularly like the baroness, Ingrid was one of their most powerful assets in the fight against Chaos.

"I . . . I swear I didn't hurt Ingrid," Emmaline said, casting her gaze on the ground. "And I had to find you. I had to make sure you were alright."

Jonas stepped forward and placed himself between Amara and Emmaline. It was obvious he still didn't trust the woman. "Because of the vow you took?"

"What?" Emmaline said, blinking her eyes. She swayed slightly, like a tree in a heavy breeze. "No. At least not completely. She's the avatar, and I had to make amends for what I did. Don't you see? I almost killed her and doomed the world. I . . . I came to apologize. And to ask for your help."

"My help?" Amara laughed harshly. "Why in the world would I help you?"

"It's not for me!" Emmaline swayed again, this time sagging to her knees. No one moved to help her. "Lady Ingrid said she granted me leniency because you asked her to do so. She claimed you wanted to use me against the Forces of Chaos. Well, there is another who could help sway the battle far more than me."

"And who is that?"

"Noah," Emmaline replied as her eyes became glassy. "When . . . when the baroness released me yesterday to help with the defense of the castle, I was taken to the outer walls. From my vantage point, I could see Noah nailed to a cross. He's still alive."

The mention of Noah startled Amara. Before the arrival of the Chaos army at Stout Oak Keep, she'd been planning to scout the enemy camp for any sign of him. He'd saved her life back in the dungeon, and if she had a chance to return the favor, she had to try.

Jonas rounded on Amara. "To even consider such a thing would be folly."

"I owe him for saving my life," she said quietly. "I can't leave him nailed to a cross."

"And will you simply stroll into the Chaos army's camp and pull him down?"

"I'm a Trickster Cleric," she replied. "And I still have two unused Expertise Points. Maybe the gods will give me what I need." She'd been planning to use the points to increase her staff ability, but new spells might be just what she needed.

"What of your soul?" Jonas asked. "Will you damage it again? Eventually, even the use of the treasure will not be able to repair it."

"It honestly feels much better," she lied. It still hurt when she drew mana from her soul, but it *was* continually improving. A few more treatments from the strange gray box and she should be able to cast most of her spells.

"Where is Noah located?" she asked Emmaline.

The priestess opened her mouth to reply, but before a single word emerged, she tumbled forward onto the rocky ground. Her head struck a stone with a loud cracking sound. She lay there without moving, a pool of crimson blood spreading out beneath her face.

Amara crossed her arms. "There's no way I'm healing another person who betrayed me!"

Harold walked over and prodded Emmaline with the end of his cudgel. "You might not have much of a choice. At least if you want her to survive the night."

Amara frowned as the memory resurfaced of her healing Ackley and his group moments before they betrayed her. But if she didn't heal Emmaline, then she might be consigning her to death. The priestess still wasn't stirring after her fall.

*I guess it's a good test of my abilities,* she thought, without much conviction.

With a barely suppressed curse, she marched over to Emmaline's side. She stopped in front of the prone woman and then wove together the strands of mana to cast *Heal Wounds.* Only a dull ache emanated from her soul this time, and the pattern quickly took shape. A moment later, a soft white light flooded the clearing around the cave's mouth.

The peasants looked on in wonder as motes of light swirled around Emmaline. One by one, the lights splashed against the woman and her wounds healed shut. The blood pooling around her head drained back into the cut on her scalp.

After a minute had passed, Emmaline pushed herself into a sitting position. She placed a hand against her forehead and her fingers came away sticky with blood. Then she snapped her gaze over to Amara in horror. "I'm so sorry you had to heal me."

"Oh knock it off," Amara snapped. "I know you don't like me, so don't pretend like you're sorry."

"I only did what I did in the service of Lady Ingrid," Emmaline replied as she wrung her hands. "There are so many false avatars in this world. I thought you had arrived to take advantage of her. And then when I saw her showering you with gifts . . ."

Amara frowned as she listened to the priestess. The woman's attitude toward her *had* completely shifted. Maybe there was a grain of truth to her story. But regardless of the reason for the change in the priestess's manner, she wouldn't let down her guard again. "As I was saying before you so gracefully face-planted, where are they holding Noah?"

"He's in an easily reachable spot," Emmaline replied. "And there are only a few guards stationed around him. With your magic, we could easily slip in, heal him, and then escape without being seen."

"I didn't ask for your plan," Amara said, her voice growing dangerously low. "I asked where he was located."

"Why don't I show you myself?" Emmaline pushed herself to her feet. Once standing, she massaged her thigh where she'd been injured. No trace of the deep wound remained.

"I'm not going with you," Amara retorted. "Haven't you ever heard of the frog and the scorpion?"

"I don't think so." Emmaline wrinkled her brow. "But I'm not going to stay behind while you go save Noah on your own. I . . . I betrayed him as well. And I need to make things right."

Amara ran a hand through her hair. "What do you think, Jonas? Could we infiltrate the camp and save him?"

"It's foolhardy to even consider it," he replied stiffly. "All of our efforts should be focused on retaking Ahrenshoop. Emilia has said the fleet is only two days away with good winds. If something happens to you, it could dash our only hope of relieving the castle."

Amara mulled it over for a minute, while no one said anything. "I owe Noah my life," she said. "If there's any chance of saving him, I want to take it."

"And if you fall?"

"I'll just have to make sure no one sees me." She gave him a half smile. "I have two unused Expertise Points, which should give me some interesting Trickster Cleric spells. Let's see what I get, and then we can form a plan."

Jonas didn't argue, but she could tell by the look on his face he would have words for her later in private. And while it was dangerous placing herself in the middle of the Chaos army, she knew it was time to live up to her class's name. Hopefully, they would never see a Trickster Cleric coming.

# CHAPTER 51

Amara stood with her hands on her hips as she gazed angrily at Jonas. They stood a short distance away from the cave, surrounded by ancient trees with moss draped limbs. The air was as silent as a cathedral and lent the place a vaguely holy feeling.

Jonas pounded his fist against his palm. "Why must you always engage in such reckless behavior?"

"With the spells I have, it's hardly reckless," she replied. "I can slip in and out before anyone knows that I'm there. Why don't you want to help Noah after he saved all of our lives?"

"I honor his sacrifice by staying alive." Jonas rubbed the bridge of his nose. "As you should do, as well."

She was about to give him a stinging retort when she heard movement in the bushes. She glanced over her shoulder to see Borim and Frederick approaching, with Salamander trailing behind them. She'd sent the girl to gather the others for this meeting.

"Oh-ho," Frederick said as he approached. "What's this I hear about a plan to attack the Chaos army?"

Jonas rounded on the old knight. "Please tell her this is a rash idea that will only end in tragedy."

"Oh, I don't know," Frederick replied. "There might be good cause to stir up the hornet's nest a little bit."

"Thank you!" Amara said, giving Jonas a knowing smile. He only scowled in return. "Finally, someone understands that we need to keep hitting Malcheron to keep him off balance. And if we can free Noah, then he'll be a powerful asset in our campaign against the Forces of Chaos."

Frederick shook his head, his long beard swaying. "You misunderstand me, Avatar. A single soldier would never be worth risking someone of your importance for. But we can't let the siege proceed without challenge. No, we must do something. I suggest we attack after nightfall and destroy as many siege engines as possible."

Jonas frowned and drew one of his daggers. He spun it around absently in his palm. "And I believe we should wait for reinforcements to arrive before attacking. The Gnostics are only a few days away."

Borim stroked his beard and narrowed his eyes. "I never thought I'd say it, but I agree with Sneaky over there. It's too dangerous to barrel headlong into the enemy. Mind you, I wouldn't object to nipping at their heels a bit. But charging right into an army's camp? No, thank you."

Salamander twirled a strand of hair around her finger. "I'm with Borim. It's way too dangerous, even for you."

"So, you're all against my plan except for Frederick?" Amara looked at them each in turn, surprised they didn't want to attack the camp. She'd expected at least Borim would agree with her idea. Normally, the dwarf would hurl himself headlong at any enemy without worrying about the consequences. "May I remind you Noah is in this position because he sacrificed himself to give us time to escape?"

"We all appreciated him beating the snot out of that horned woman," Borim said. "And in thanks, I haven't said a single bad word about that insufferable prick. Not that I haven't had the occasional urge."

"If none of you want to go with me, then I'm going with Mimi," Amara said firmly. "With my pet, I can slip in and out unseen."

"What if it's a trap?" Salamander asked. "Do we all really trust that slimy priestess now? She tried to have Amara killed!"

Jonas shook his head. "The priestess's loyalty is the only thing I'm not concerned about. Her oath will compel her to ensure no harm comes to Amara. Which means she honestly believes her plan has a good chance of succeeding. And if she travels with Amara, then she will do her utmost to keep her safe."

Frederick strode forward and rapped the butt of his halberd against the hard ground. "Do you all plan to hide in the depths of that damp cave until the relief armies arrive? Not the best plan if you want to win against the Forces of Chaos. Not the best plan at all."

"What if we combine our plans?" Amara asked. "While you all create a diversion by destroying the catapults or whatever they use in this world, I'll free Noah. That way, we'll kill two birds with one stone."

Borim stroked his beard. "We'll paint a huge target on our backs, but if we bring a few of the locals who know the forest, we might manage to slip away afterwards unseen. I don't like it, but this old graybeard might be right. If we let Malcheron work unhindered, the fortress might fall before anyone gets here to help."

She turned her gaze to Salamander next.

"I'll always go with you," the girl said. "You know that."

She shifted her gaze to Jonas, the lone holdout.

He scowled and slammed his dagger back into its sheath. "If you're going to hurl yourself into the maw of a dragon once more, then I suppose I'll have to keep you safe. However, I must say this is reckless beyond reason. If we want to disrupt the siege, then we should attack the supply lines and foraging parties. Our numbers are far too small to attack the army directly."

"I promise we'll come up with a plan that keeps us all safe."

"I hope you're right," Jonas replied. "Because I don't want to lose any of you." With that, he stalked off into the forest.

"He'll come around, lass," Borim said. "Don't you worry about it."

Amara stared in the direction he'd gone, but she wasn't sure if the dwarf was right. Jonas had been growing more protective since the incident at the dungeon. And it was rapidly becoming a problem.

*What if I am being too reckless?*

So far, she'd survived nearly impossible odds thanks to her high Luck stat and her overpowered skills. But now she was facing enemies far more dangerous than the ones she'd encountered in the South. Maybe she *should* take some time to hammer out an effective plan.

With that thought, she turned toward Frederick. "What do you think we should do?"

Frederick smiled, his face wrinkling like ancient papyrus. "Oh-ho," he exclaimed, "do I have a good one for you." Then he set about explaining his plan to free Noah and destroy the siege weapons.

Amara shivered in the freezing water of the river, cursing Frederick for his plan through chattering teeth. She clung to the edge of the log they'd launched down the river just before sunset. To the pickets around the camp, it would look like nothing more than a fallen tree drifting downstream. But hidden on the other side was the raiding party they'd assembled, made up of Jonas, Harold, Emmaline, and herself.

In the distance, she could make out the island and the dark, looming shape of Stout Oak Keep on the shore. On the far bank burned the endless campfires of the Chaos army. They seemed as numerous as the stars above, and she felt her chest tighten with worry.

*I hope this isn't a bad idea.*

But it was too late to turn back now. She'd committed to the plan, and Frederick, along with Salamander and many hunters from the village, would attack shortly. Once the others had the Chaos army's attention, her party would slip ashore and free Noah.

According to Emmaline, the cross bearing the warrior had been relocated to a spot where the bridge to Stout Oak Keep had once stood. If all went as planned, they could quickly dispatch the guards and then get Noah to the water. Then they'd float him further downstream.

She felt optimistic about the plan working. After meeting with her group, she'd finally finished leveling up. She absently pulled up her character sheet to inspect it.

| Amara Solace (Pewter Rank Adventurer) | Trickster Cleric, Level 7 |
|---|---|
| **Stats** | |
| **Strength** | 7 |
| **Dexterity** | 3 |
| **Constitution** | 9 |
| **Intelligence** | 4 |
| **Wisdom** | 14 |
| **Charisma** | 1 |
| **Vitality** | 8 |
| **Luck** | 16 |
| **New Stat Points** | 0 |
| | |
| **Titles** | **Titan Slayer (Rank 1)** |
| | |
| **Weapon Proficiencies** | |
| **Staff** | Novice |
| **Darts** | Novice |
| | |
| **Skills** | |
| *First Aid* | Apprentice |
| *Herbalism* | Apprentice |
| *Alchemy* | Apprentice |
| | |
| **Martial Abilities** | |
| *Dart Dead Eye* | Novice |
| | |
| **Spells** | |
| *Cloak of Shadows* | 1$^{st}$ Circle |
| *Charm Person* | 1$^{st}$ Circle |

| *Heal Wounds* | 2$^{nd}$ **Circle** |
|---|---|
| *Divine Weapon* | 1$^{St}$ **Circle** |
| *Holy Light* | 1$^{St}$ **Circle** |
| *Illusory Disguise* | 1$^{st}$ **Circle** |
| *Duplicate Self* | 1$^{st}$ **Circle** |
| *Avatar of Melischar* | |
| | |
| **New Expertise Points** | **0** |

Upon leveling up, Amara had added two points to Wisdom, and one additional point to Luck. And then she'd used her Expertise Points to gain two new spells. Both had been allocated to her speciality Trickster Cleric school of magic.

The first point had granted her the spell *Illusory Disguise*. According to the description, the spell would allow her to turn into any humanoid close to her approximate height and weight. She could alter her features and even her voice to match any race she wanted. While possibly useful, she felt it was redundant compared to her *Cloak of Shadows* spell.

The second spell seemed far more impressive. When she allocated the last Expertise Point, she had been granted a critical luck success and received a spell titled *Duplicate Self*. With this new spell, Amara could create a perfect illusion of herself to control. According to the description, though her duplicate had no physical form, it could perform any actions she commanded.

Amara pointed toward the shore and began to kick her feet. Once all four of them were swimming in the same direction, the log angled toward the muddy bank. The shore quickly grew closer and before long, she could make out the outline of the cross. And she also spotted several humanoid shapes guarding it.

Thankfully, they didn't appear to be any Issurians guarding the crucified warrior. Any of those would have complicated the rescue effort. And had they seen ogres, Amara might have considered calling it off completely.

The branches of the log scraped against the bottom and the party came to a stop about ten paces away from the shore. In the dim light, Amara could make out three kobolds clustered around the base of the cross. Now all she had to do was wait for the signal.

Amara didn't have to wait long. In the distance, a jet of flame erupted from the forest, striking a half-constructed wooden tower. The timbers of the siege engine quickly ignited, creating a burning pyre.

Another stream of liquid fire doused a second tower and a mountain of barrels. A moment later, a deafening explosion shook the world and sent fire soaring high into the sky. A blast wave coursed across the camp, knocking down tents and striking Amara with surprising fury.

She was stunned for a moment at the scale of the destruction. What in the world had Salamander struck with her fire? But she didn't have long to ponder it, as the kobolds guarding Noah sprinted in the direction of the flames.

With a gentle shove, Amara pushed herself off the log and swam toward the bank. Her feet soon touched the muddy bottom, and she winced audibly as she splashed forward. It was hard to stay quiet while emerging from the water.

But there was no one nearby to hear her. And a moment later, she was joined by Jonas. His daggers had been glinted in the light, and he moved with his usual grace. Unlike her, he didn't make a sound as he rose out of the river.

Harold blundered out of the water next, trying in vain to suppress a cough. Next came Emmaline, who seemed like she was part otter with her powerful strokes and slick, wet hair.

"After we get Noah down," Amara whispered, "bring him to the river. Remember, we need to get away as quickly as possible."

Without waiting for the others to acknowledge her, she bent down and crept in the direction of the cross. She felt terribly exposed in the open, but it seemed like the attention of everyone in the camp was fixated on the raging fires.

As she neared the cross, she finally understood the source of the explosion. Positioned in a nearby trench was a long bronze tube mounted on a wooden cart. She immediately recognized the primitive device—the Forces of Chaos had cannons. Which meant they must have gunpowder as well. Or whatever the magical equivalent of it was. Salamander must have hit one of the explosive stockpiles with her fire spell.

Amara returned to the task at hand and sprinted the final distance to the cross. She stopped in front of Noah and looked up in horror. His body was so mangled, she couldn't understand how he was still alive. He looked like he'd lost at least twenty pounds. And several of his wounds had turned black and were weeping puss.

While she wanted nothing more to heal him, the white light that accompanied her spell would act like a beacon. For now, all she could offer him was a healing pill.

"I still don't like you," Noah whispered through cracked lips.

She jumped at the sound, shocked to find him conscious. Then she gave him a lopsided grin. "Right back at you."

At her words, Noah slumped forward again. She hoped he'd only lost consciousness. Otherwise, all of her efforts had been for nothing.

Harold ran forward with a pair of pliers and grabbed the nail protruding from Noah's foot. He tugged at it, but it didn't budge. Then he twisted the tool to the side and placed his entire weight against it. Still, nothing happened.

"We need to hurry!" Amara hissed. "What's wrong?"

"I think it's stuck in his heel bone," Harold grunted. "I guess we could cut off his foot."

Emmaline stepped forward and crossed her arms. "I'm not going to let some pig farmer cut off his better's foot!"

Harold shrugged. "It wouldn't be the first time I cut off someone's limb. Better to lose a foot than end up dead."

Amara shook her head. "We're not cutting off anything. Just get the nail out!"

Jonas moved over to help the pig farmer, and together they managed to wrench the nail free. Their efforts were rewarded with a tortured groan from Noah.

Jonas gave Harold a boost to grab the nail impaling Noah's wrist. Harold started to work the metal spike free, ignoring the crucified warrior's weak protests.

Amara glanced around nervously, and her heart skipped a beat as she spotted the three kobolds returning to their post. Luckily, they were engrossed in their conversation and hadn't yet spotted her group in the darkness.

But as soon as they noticed Jonas and Harold working on the cross, the kobolds would raise the alarm. And then the entire fury of the Chaos army would descend upon them. No matter what, she could not allow the kobolds to reach their position.

She stalked forward, intent on stopping the guards. With the new spells at her disposal, she would make sure the kobolds didn't live long enough to give them away.

# CHAPTER 52

Amara steeled herself as she prepared to call upon her mana to deal with the approaching kobolds. While she'd drawn progressively more energy from her soul over the last few days, casting a spell still caused her discomfort. But she needed to give Jonas and Harold more time to get Noah down from the cross.

She winced as she wove together the strands of mana to cast *Divine Weapon*, but then stopped and let her spell fizzle out. If she didn't want to draw attention to their position, then she should probably avoid summoning a six-foot-tall flaming sword.

Her hand instead went to the quiver of darts on her waist, which she'd kept covered in the river by an oilskin. But even with the critical success chance her skill gave her, she didn't know if she could take out all three of the lizard-like creatures before they raised the alarm.

As the kobolds neared her position, still engrossed in their conversation, she wracked her mind for some way to deal with them. She was quickly running out of time. For a second, she considered using her *Cloak of Shadows* to sneak up behind the kobolds and dispatch them with her staff, but she discarded the idea. Once again, there was no way to be sure she could kill them without announcing her presence.

*Maybe it's time I start acting like a Trickster Cleric.*

Shortly after meeting Jonas for the first time, he had advised her to allocate the majority of the Expertise Points she received to her class specialty spells. But she'd ignored his advice up until now. Perhaps, instead of trying to bull her way through battles, she should try to use her illusions to defeat her enemies.

Amara wove her mana into a tapestry of energy as she called upon her *Illusory Disguise* spell. As she did so, she pictured Tecala—the leader of the Issurians—and attempted to recreate the horned woman as closely as possible.

Thankfully, the spell didn't conjure any ambient light like *Heal Wounds*. She wasn't even sure if it had worked until she lifted her hand and was greeted by the sight of pale skin and clawed fingers. When she glanced down, she saw her dress had been transformed into dark plate armor that clung to her body. And, somehow, she *felt* taller.

The kobolds stopped short a few paces away and stared up at her with wide eyes. Then their gaze snapped over to Jonas and the others working to free Noah from the cross. An alarmed hiss issued out of their toothy maws, and they lowered their spears threateningly.

But Amara simply pointed in the other direction. She couldn't speak their language, so she'd have to rely on hand gestures.

The kobolds hissed again, and the largest stepped forward. It spoke in a guttural tongue and gestured wildly at her party. Then the creature tried to push its way past her toward the cross.

She held out her arm to stop it. The kobold stumbled to a halt and looked up at her with shock. Once more, she pointed back in the direction it had come. But this time, she furrowed her brow and tapped her foot against the ground. Her illusion spell was so impressive it sounded like a hoof striking the hard-packed earth instead of her boot.

The kobold let loose a few more hisses and then retreated a few paces. The others repeated their companion's unintelligible words before they raised their spears. While it was hard to read their reptilian features, they appeared puzzled at her orders.

Amara gestured more insistently at the camp, in an attempt to convince them to leave. She didn't dare let them linger and witness her return to human form. And while the spell only took a trickle of mana to maintain, it was quickly becoming unbearable with the exhausted state of her soul.

The kobolds lowered their heads and slunk away. One of them glanced back over its shoulder and hissed something at her. Then it scurried after its companions, and they disappeared back into the sea of tents.

Amara let out a sigh of relief before turning her attention back to the raid on the far side of the camp. She hadn't seen any more of Salamander's fire spells, and she suspected the raiding party had already retreated into the woods. Which meant she was running out of time.

She turned and sprinted over to the cross. When Harold lifted his head and spotted her coming, he cried out and nearly lost his grip on the wooden beam. She quickly let her disguise dissolve and returned to her normal form.

Harold clutched at his chest and gasped for air. "By Holy Birgitta, don't do that to me again! I thought that horned woman had come to claim me this time."

Emmaline smirked at the pig farmer. "Are you so easily deceived?"

"Don't pretend you didn't see me cast my spell," Amara replied, with an eye roll. "I saw you looking over in my direction when I was dealing with the kobolds."

The priestess frowned, but didn't reply.

Amara looked up at where Jonas was yanking free the final nail that held Noah to the cross. She waited as he tore out the metal spike and then tossed it aside. As Noah sagged, she stepped forward with Harold, and they caught the battered warrior in their arms.

She struggled under the knight's weight, even as emaciated as he was, but with the farmer's help, the two managed to lower Noah to the ground. Once he was flat on his back, Amara placed a healing pill in his mouth. She was about to help him chew it, but he swallowed it without any prompting. The fact she didn't see any noticeable improvement showed the extent of his injuries.

"How are you still drawing breath?" Harold asked, scratching his head.

"*Fortify,*" Noah replied in a weak voice. "I kept using my skill over and over. Malcheron wasn't too impressed that I was taking so long to die."

Jonas pointed in the direction of the log they'd floated down the river on. "If we are going to make our escape, we should move with all haste." He hopped off his perch on the cross and then leaned down to grab one of the knight's arms. "Once we are in the river, I will lash him to the branches."

Harold took Noah's other arm, and together with Jonas, they began the laborious process of dragging the knight toward the river. The man was far larger than either of those pulling him, and it made for slow going. After a few paces, the farmer started letting loose colorful curses.

Amara hurried over and took one of Noah's legs. She gestured at Emmaline to do the same, who only sighed in response. But after a brief hesitation, the priestess grabbed the knight's other foot.

"What is the traitor doing here?" Noah whispered in a scratchy voice. "I thought Lady Ingrid would have hanged her for her actions."

"It's a long story . . ." Amara trailed off as she heard noises behind them. She glanced over her shoulder and froze when she spotted a seething mass of goblins and kobolds charging in their direction. And behind them followed the unmistakable looming shapes of ogres.

*I guess I wasn't as convincing as I thought.*

She dropped Noah and spun around to face the approaching army. "Get him to the river!" she cried out. "I'll give you time to get the log free." The darkness should cloak their escape, and the fast-flowing current would quickly take them beyond Malcheron's reach.

"I'm not leaving you behind," Jonas said with an edge to his voice. He dropped Noah's arm and then took a step in her direction.

"Nor am I," Emmaline said, then she frowned. "I don't know why I said that."

"I promise I have a plan." Amara gave him a pleading look. "Please, just trust me this time."

The rogue looked torn, and his gaze darted between the mass of approaching Chaos soldiers and her face. Then he exhaled and spun around on his heel. He grabbed Noah's arm, and with renewed urgency, helped Harold drag the knight into the water.

But Emmaline didn't budge. "I have to stay to protect you," she said. "As much as I hate that fact."

She didn't have time to deal with trying to convince the priestess to leave, and her plan wouldn't work with any others around. Instead, she hastily cast *Charm Person* on Emmaline. As the priestess's face twisted with confusion, she pointed at the river. "Help them get Noah to safety."

Emmaline smiled dumbly and bobbed her head. "Anything you wish, Avatar."

Amara turned her attention back toward the charging Chaos creatures as she prepared to cast her spell. For her plan to succeed, she needed the Chaos creatures to be afraid of an avatar of the gods. She could only hope kobold and goblin mothers told tales of her predecessors to frighten their children.

She raised her hand to the sky and then cast *Holy Light*. The spell detonated like a starburst, sending dazzling waves of illumination bursting outwards. She continued to channel trickles of mana into it, creating a miniature sun in her palm.

The waves of light crashed over the charging Chaos creatures and wreaked havoc among their ranks. Many stumbled around blindly, causing them to collide with those behind them. Others reeled away, desperately clawing at their own comrades to escape. And the few who managed to resist the effect couldn't get through the confused mob.

Amara blinked her eyes as she tried to clear the afterimages burned in her retinas. Then she prepared to cast her next spell. For once, she wasn't going to blunder around with a giant flaming sword. She was going to earn her class name.

As she finished weaving her mana to cast *Illusory Disguise*, she had the sensation of rising off the ground. In one hand, a flaming sword took shape that thrummed with barely constrained power. And while she knew it was only an illusion, she could somehow *feel* its destructive aura. As she floated forward, white armor formed around her body and golden wings burst free of her back to cast a warm glow over her surroundings.

Those not blinded by her spell skidded to a stop. The goblins stared at her with looks of sheer terror, and as a group, they broke and fled back into the camp. Then the kobolds began to stream away from her position. After a few seconds, only a handful of confused-looking ogres remained. The towering creatures gaped at her, though she wasn't sure if they were shocked by the sudden appearance of an avatar or the fact their companions had fled.

Amara glanced back at the river to see that Jonas and the others had disappeared. She swept her gaze over the water, but there was no sign of her party anywhere. They must have successfully escaped downstream on the log. Which meant her job here was complete.

The sounds of cheers and bells ringing made her look up at the fortress in surprise. On the walls of Stout Oak Keep, she could make out the shapes of men and women standing on the battlements. Many of them had their fists raised in celebration.

*I really hope that I'm not about to disappoint them by disappearing.*

She tore her gaze away from those cheering on the walls as she let her illusion spell drop. Her wings blinked out, and her armor disappeared into a puff of light. She wanted to be far away from this place when the ogres finally decided to resume their attack.

In the sudden darkness, she cast *Cloak of Shadows.* The world around her changed to muted tones of gray, and once she was completely hidden from view, she set a course down the riverbank. *And not a minute too soon,* she thought as she watched the real Tecala push her way through the ogres with a contingent of Issurians.

Amara broke into a jog, her wet clothes chaffing uncomfortably against her skin, and headed downriver. She wasn't sure if any of the creatures in the Chaos army had the ability to detect invisibility. But if they did, then it would be a good idea to put as much distance between herself and them as possible.

She stopped every few kilometers to listen for any sounds of pursuit, but heard nothing except her own pounding heartbeat. Which was lucky for her, as a cold sweat was beading on her forehead from the strain of holding her spell. She was glad she hadn't needed to cast her *Divine Weapon,* as she didn't know if her soul could have handled it.

She released *Cloak of Shadows* and continued down the riverbank. After a few miles, she slowed when she heard someone call out. She pressed her lips together as she searched the reeds for where the voice had originated.

A moment later, Jonas stepped out with his daggers drawn. He glanced back the way she'd come. "Did anyone follow you?"

"I didn't see anyone pursuing me," she replied with a shrug. "And it's good to see you, too."

Jonas relaxed slightly. "Believe me, I'm practically ecstatic to see you uninjured. And I nearly climbed out of the water to stop you when I saw you assuming your avatar form again. However, I quickly realized it was only your disguise spell."

"It was pretty impressive, wasn't it?" She grinned at Jonas, though she wasn't sure if he could see it in the dim light. As she'd run, the stars had appeared overhead in the sky, including the one representing the goddess she served. The celestial bodies had given her enough light to navigate by without breaking an ankle.

"How is Noah?" she asked.

"He's recovering, though I believe he will need several of your healing spells."

"I'm glad we managed to save him."

"I hope the risk was worth it," Jonas replied. "The raid on the siege engine seemed to end abruptly. When Salamander struck that unstable magic, it must have thrown off their plans. I hope no one was injured in the blast."

"I don't think it was magic," she said, remembering the cannon she'd seen. "And we can't wait for the relief armies to arrive. If what I saw works like it does in my world, then this siege might be over in a matter of days. We need to get back and talk to the others immediately."

"I see," Jonas said. "That sounds dire indeed."

Amara nodded. While Stout Oak Keep might have magical walls, she wasn't sure if they could survive a pounding by cannons. They might have to move before the relief armies arrived or all would be lost. Hopefully, the old knight Frederick would have some ideas. Because otherwise, she didn't like their odds of success.

# CHAPTER 53

By the time Amara limped back into camp, she was exhausted, cold, and in a foul mood. All she wanted to do was find her bedroll and collapse. On their way back, her group had given the Chaos army a wide berth, but their caution had added several hours to their journey. And even after being healed, Noah had required help for much of the way.

She examined the knot of people who gathered at her arrival, and she felt a surge of relief upon seeing Salamander standing with Borim at her side. And behind them were Mimi and Frederick. She was grateful none of them appeared to have suffered any injuries in the raid.

"I'm so glad you're back." Salamander ran over and flung her arms around Amara's waist. "I was worried about you."

Borim crossed his thick arms. "Good to see you in one piece, lass."

Amara patted the girl's shoulder as she tried to disentangle herself. Then she looked over at Frederick standing nearby. The knight was using his halberd to prop himself up, and he had dark circles under his eyes. "How did the raid go?"

"The raid?" Frederick frowned. "Not as well as I had hoped. Some cursed magic exploded before we could get to the bridge-building supplies. And the ensuing blast sent us all for a hard tumble. Let me tell you, at my age, a fall is hard to recover from. But at least I didn't break anything."

"They had bridge supplies?"

The elderly knight nodded. "They must have gathered wood before attacking in case the bridge was destroyed. Once they're done rebuilding the span, they'll use rams and ladders to storm the castle. I don't think it's likely the castle will last too much longer, even with our brave efforts."

"I have worse news," Amara said, running a hand through her hair. "Have you ever heard of cannons?"

Frederick nodded solemnly. "Our scouts witnessed them being deployed against a rebel kobold fortress in the North. We had to torture a few dark dwarves to learn their secrets, but they spilled everything in the end. If the engineers are to be believed, they can bring down walls in a matter of days."

"They had numerous cannons in the camp along the shore," she said. "I think we need to defeat them before the relief forces arrive."

"Oh-ho," Frederick laughed gruffly. "And how would you do that? Stealing away a knight and causing some mischief is hardly the same as routing an army."

"I don't know yet." She scowled. "But right now, I can't even think straight. I'm going to get some sleep and then we can talk about it later."

"No time for sleep," Frederick replied. "I need to help you improve your soul."

"Later," she said firmly. "I'm not going to have you flay my soul for fun right now. And if anyone tries to stop me from reaching my bedroll, then they're going to see what an angry avatar looks like."

Frederick guffawed. "I've stared down an ancient Issurian caster in a frozen mountain pass. You'll have to do better than that to scare me off. Now, I have some important work for you nearby."

Amara sighed and looked at her friends for help. But Borim appeared almost asleep on his feet, his lids drooping, and the others seemed content to let Frederick steal her away. She suspected they would be asleep within minutes of her departing with the knight.

*Bunch of traitors,* she thought, sourly.

"Come with me," Frederick said. Without waiting to see if she followed, he turned and strode off into the forest.

With another drawn-out sigh, she waved at her pet to follow, and together they traipsed after the ancient knight. The others immediately headed into the dark cave. From inside, she could hear the villagers and peasants rousing. The cry of a baby broke the still air.

*Maybe I wouldn't have gotten much sleep after all.*

Amara trudged deeper into the forest, with Mimi rollicking along at her side. After a few paces, she caught sight of the old man standing by a tree.

"We haven't got all morning, you know!" he called out. "Now, put a little *oomph* into your stride."

Amara wondered if she could throttle the old man without souring relations with the Knights Tarsillan. But she quickly dismissed her fantasy. If Frederick thought this was important enough to put off sleep, then she should probably listen to him.

After a few more minutes of walking, they reached a clearing in the forest. In the distance, the first rays of the sun peaked over the canopy, turning the leaves a golden color. Already, the air was warming up, and she felt slightly better than she had on the trip back.

"Would you just tell me what you want?" she asked wearily. "Otherwise, I'm going to fall asleep against the nearest tree."

Frederick stabbed a crooked finger in her direction. "You've been holding out on me."

"I have?"

"Oh yes, you certainly have." Frederick placed his hands on his hips and leaned forward. He very much looked like a wizened bird in his current pose. "Your dwarven friend tells me you have a spirit fruit."

"I got it as a reward from the dungeon."

"Well, it's time to use it."

Amara shook her head. "I almost died the last time I ate one."

"Because you didn't have me at your side to guide you." As Frederick spoke, he pulled out five glowing crystals from a pouch on his belt and placed them in a circle. "And you didn't have any treasures."

"What are those things?" The crystals had been expertly cut, and if they hadn't been the size of her fist, she'd suspect they were diamonds.

"Hmmm? These things?" Frederick scratched his head. "Don't tell me you haven't seen these before."

"I haven't exactly been exposed to many rare gems in this world," she retorted. "Most of my time has been spent trying to scrounge up enough food to avoid starving."

Frederick puffed up his cheeks and then exhaled. "Those stupid churchmen. The Beacon of Khaneri isn't something to be ignored. The moment it was lit, they should have found you and begun your training. Somewhere in the heavens, the gods are weeping at your treatment."

"So, are you going to explain what those do?"

"Sorry, I went off on a bit of a tangent there," Frederick said. "These little beauties are mana crystals. Not too bad in a pinch when you need to refill your soul. Of course, these are empty. But they will help with any overflow during the process. I want you to purify your soul and cast off your old self. It's the first stage in spiritual alchemy."

"Oh, is that all?" she replied sarcastically. "Why not change my hair color while I'm at it, too?"

"Take this seriously," Frederick barked. "Do you think you can win against an entire army of Chaos when you're only Level 6?"

"Level 7," she corrected him.

"Hmph . . . Level 7, then." Frederick glowered at her for interrupting. "As I was saying, you need to get past the first bottleneck. A spirit fruit can improve your soul and even give you a few levels if you're lucky."

Amara perked up at the mention of levels. Anything to do with improving her soul was academic to her, but the Expertise Points that came with levelling up would be a real boon. Especially since she'd been forced to use the points she was saving up for her *Staff Proficiency*. "So, how does it work?"

"Normally, someone spends years preparing to advance," the old knight continued. "But you don't have years, do you? And those people didn't have a spirit fruit."

A thought suddenly occurred to her. "Shouldn't I share it with my friends?"

"Hmm? Your friends?" Frederick shook his head, his long beard waggling. "They already agreed to give it to you. Except I didn't have a chance to talk to that rogue fellow, but he doesn't seem to be the type to object. Not with the way he looks at you. Oh my, no."

Amara furrowed her brow. "What do you mean by that?"

"Never mind." Frederick waved his hands at her as if to banish her thoughts. "Not the thing to focus on right now. No, definitely not." He paused and then rubbed his chin. "What was I saying again?"

"Something about advancing?"

"Oh yes. Now, you need to discard your old self. And when you feel your soul shifting, you need to eat the fruit."

"Showing off?" Amara exclaimed. "I used it to save my friends."

"Yes, yes," he continued. "Whatever you say. So, who are you right at this moment?"

"Who am I?" she asked. "I'm Amara. A girl from Earth."

"And who was she?"

Amara shrugged. She'd never really considered who she was before. "I was just a girl who grew up poor."

"Oh really?" Frederick examined her with rheumy eyes. "And that's all there was to you?"

"I mean, there's more." She looked down and scuffed the dirt with the tip of her boot. "But to be honest, I don't want to talk about it with someone I barely know."

"It's rare for one to know themselves," Frederick continued. "My tutor practically had to hit me over the head to jar loose my old attachments when I hit my first bottleneck. Come to think of it, I seem to recall being hit with a thick book of his a few times. Needless to say, I wasn't too broken up when he died. So, back on the subject at hand, I need to know who you *think* you are."

"I don't know." She longed for her bedroll, and she didn't particularly want to do any deep thinking after the night she'd had. "I guess I'm just someone who never got close to anyone besides my dad. My mom abandoned us when I was young, and I don't have many friends—"

"Really now?" Frederick interrupted as he raised a single bushy gray eyebrow. "I know at least three people who would happily lay down their lives for you."

Amara paused before continuing. The old knight was right—she had more friends currently than she'd had in her whole life. Why hadn't she thought of it that way?

"And you won't be poor much longer," Frederick said without waiting for her answer. "Kings, doges, and princes will lavish gifts upon you once they realize the gods have returned. And I promise—no one will abandon you again."

*Have I become a completely different person here?*

She'd never really stopped to think about it, but maybe she wasn't the old Amara from Earth. She had a loyal group of friends, and everyone in this world was counting on her—something no one besides her father would have ever imagined back home.

*Is Earth even my home anymore?*

The realization that this place was her home hit her like a lightning bolt. And as it did, she felt a tickle in her soul. She wasn't any of the things she'd said. She was an avatar for the goddess Melischar.

"Oh-ho, that certainly did something." Frederick pointed at the circle. "I think it's time to eat the spirit fruit. But this time, don't use the energy for casting. Instead, use it to purify your soul. And if it becomes too much, direct some into the crystals surrounding you."

"How am I supposed to know how to purify my soul?"

"You simply burn away all the parts of yourself that are no longer necessary," Frederick said. "And then expand your soul. If you ever want to cast your avatar spell again, you're going to need to reach the second stage of advancement. Oh, and by the way, this is called the calcination of the soul."

Amara listened to his words as she walked to the center of the crystals. Once she was roughly in the center, she sank down on her knees. Then she took out the spirit fruit from her pouch. Like the previous one, the fruit's skin shone like stars burned beneath it. "Do I eat the whole thing?"

Frederick nodded.

Amara raised the fruit and bit into it. This time, there was no rush to gulp it down, and she savoured the tangy juice that sprayed into her mouth. It was like nothing she'd ever eaten on Earth, and she felt energy surging back into her soul. She chewed slowly before swallowing. Within a few minutes, she was done, and her soul was brimming with mana.

The sensation of the restless energy quickly became uncomfortable, like trying to squeeze into a pair of pants that were too tight. She had to use the mana before it overwhelmed her abused soul.

Amara let her instincts guide her as she used the energy to expand and reshape her soul. She sculpted new flows to allow the mana to move more easily, and as she did, images of her old life appeared in her mind.

She witnessed her mother leaving again, but this time, the pain and hurt faded away. More bad memories followed, but the sting of them lessened with each one.

After what felt like an eternity, the raging mana in her soul was circulating along new channels, and the cracks had healed without leaving a trace behind.

For the first time in what felt like weeks, Amara's soul was strong and healthy. And an ocean of mana sloshed around inside.

She cracked her eyes open and blinked a few times at the blinding light. The sun hung high in the sky above her. How long had she been focused on her soul?

"Oh-ho," Frederick said. "You're done already?"

"Already?" she croaked. "How long was I out?"

"No more than half a day or so."

"Half a day!" But as she spoke the words, the rumble in her stomach proved the knight wasn't lying. And she also noted she had a level up notification in the corner of her vision. "I'm starving," she said simply.

"Then let's fetch you a nice big meal," he said. "And then we'll see about testing your purified soul. Hopefully, it will have expanded enough to allow you to cast your avatar spell. But we'll see, won't we?"

Amara nodded as she staggered to her feet. If she could cast her avatar spell without burning out her soul, then everything would change. She could throw the Chaos army out of Ahrenshoop and then march on the castle with the Gnostics.

*Maybe Malcheron will be running from me with his tail between his legs before the week is out.*

With that pleasant thought, she followed Frederick on the path back to the camp. And while she would never admit it to him, she couldn't wait to test out her improved soul.

# CHAPTER 54

Amara pushed aside the leaves of the bush she hid behind to peer down at the village of Ahrenshoop. In the distance, the setting sun's crimson rays reflected off of the roiling sea, while dark clouds gathered on the horizon. And scattered across the waves was a vast approaching fleet.

She stifled a yawn as she glanced around at her companions sheltered in a thicket on the hill overlooking the village. After advancing her soul, she'd slept for nearly an entire day. Normally, she would have been mad at the others for letting her slumber for so long, but this time, she let it go. She'd needed the rest.

Harold appeared at her side, his feet crunching on the carpet of pine needles underfoot. He held a rough club loosely in one hand as he gazed down at the village. The farmer didn't speak for a moment as he took in the sight of the kobolds gathered near the docks. Finally, he whispered, "The others are ready when you are."

Amara nodded. A significant force of peasants and townsfolk were gathered behind the hill. While only a handful of them had armor or proper weapons, their resolve to push out the invaders was strong. She knew they wanted to retake their homes from the Chaos army more than anything else in this world.

But before they could launch their attack, she had to complete her leveling up. Amara been procrastinating the entire journey to the village. When she'd awoken from her long sleep after eating the spirit fruit, she'd checked out her level status and was startled to learn she'd gained three levels. It was a shocking amount to advance in a single day, even for her.

Frederick had advised her to focus on improving her current spells. But she didn't have time to space out with some long vision. Instead, she was tempted to increase one of her Martial Abilities.

*I don't have any more time to waste thinking about this,* she thought, as she watched the kobolds form up into disciplined ranks.

At the sight of the ships, the kobolds had rushed about, struggling into their armor and arming themselves. Now, well over two hundred of the creatures stood in battle formation awaiting the Gnostic fleet. While the village was surrounded by a palisade, there was no such protection at the collection of rickety docks projecting out into the water. The kobolds would have to hold the Gnostics back without any fortifications.

Shortly after the fleet had appeared, several riders had been dispatched from the village. The kobolds rode what appeared to be oversized lizards that moved with an ungainly gait. While the mounts looked unpleasant to ride on, they moved surprisingly fast.

Amara and Salamander had intercepted the kobolds on the road to the keep. A blast of fire from the young mage had taken them down with ease, and the unpleasant smell of burnt lizard flesh still lingered in Amara's nostrils. She'd originally wanted to capture at least one of the creatures, but had decided they couldn't risk one of them getting through to warn Malcheron.

By the time the leader of the Chaos army learned of the village falling, she planned to have transformed it into a fortress. And it would cost Malcheron dearly if he tried to retake it.

"I believe that's our cue," Jonas said as he watched a galley approach the dock. The men on board rowed hard, the prow cutting through the foamy water.

With a frustrated sigh, Amara decided on a compromise. She would use two Expertise Points to increase her staff ability—Jonas had told her advancing Weapon Proficiencies didn't provoke visions—and then save the remaining point to upgrade a spell later. She was fairly certain this upcoming battle would give her enough experience to grant another level.

Amara pulled up her character sheet in front of her.

| Amara Solace (Bronze Rank Adventurer) | Trickster Cleric, Level 10 |
| --- | --- |
| **Stats** | |
| **Strength** | 7 |
| **Dexterity** | 3 |
| **Constitution** | 9 |
| **Intelligence** | 4 |
| **Wisdom** | 14 |
| **Charisma** | 1 |
| **Vitality** | 8 |
| **Luck** | 16 |
| **New Stat Points** | 9 |
| | |
| **Titles** | **Titan Slayer (Rank 1)** |

| | |
|---|---|
| **Weapon Proficiencies** | |
| **Staff** | **Novice** |
| **Darts** | **Novice** |
| | |
| **Skills** | |
| *First Aid* | **Apprentice** |
| *Herbalism* | **Apprentice** |
| *Alchemy* | **Apprentice** |
| | |
| **Martial Abilities** | |
| *Dart Dead Eye* | **Novice** |
| | |
| **Spells** | |
| *Cloak of Shadows* | 1$^{st}$ **Circle** |
| *Charm Person* | 1$^{st}$ **Circle** |
| *Heal Wounds* | 2$^{nd}$ **Circle** |
| *Divine Weapon* | 1$^{st}$ **Circle** |
| *Holy Light* | 1$^{st}$ **Circle** |
| *Illusory Disguise* | 1$^{st}$ **Circle** |
| *Duplicate Self* | 1$^{st}$ **Circle** |
| *Avatar of Melischar* | |
| | |
| **New Expertise Points** | **3** |

She quickly chose *Staff* from *Weapon Proficiencies*, and the word "Novice" switched to "Apprentice." She also felt a subtle shift in her muscles and her balance. Next, she dumped all nine Stat Points into Luck. The next few days would most likely see her fight some dire battles, and she needed all the Luck she could get.

Her leveling up complete, she turned her attention back to the village. "I wish we could have attacked while they were sleeping," Amara said. "I don't like the fact they're ready for us."

"No competent captain would sail at night in these waters," Jonas said. "There are far too many sunken rocks and reefs to be wary of."

Amara watched as the Gnostic ship slowed a short distance from the dock, releasing a hail of arrows that peppered the gathered kobolds. The lizard men replied in kind with javelins and crossbow bolts, and both sides exploded into an exchange of missile fire.

She glanced over at Frederick and whispered, "Are you sure you can handle the gates?"

"Oh-ho, are you doubting me now? I promise they'll come down faster than you can blink." The old man chuckled as he stretched. "Although it's been a long time since I fought in a real battle. Don't blame me if I'm a bit rusty with my casting."

Amara thought back to the battle with the Issurians on the road. There, the old knight had done little more than watch from the sidelines. But he'd been adamant that he could take down the gates on his own. He claimed to be a Bolster Mage, which no one in her group had ever heard of before. And he hadn't been willing to provide any details on his spells. She just prayed the old knight could live up to his boasts.

Amara rose to her feet and prepared to call upon her mana. Once they breached the wooden gates of the town, they could attack the kobolds from the rear. If all went according to plan, her party, combined with the thirty or so armed peasants, would act like an anvil for the Gnostics' hammer strike.

She paused as Salamander tugged on her arm. "What is it?" she asked.

"I need to talk to you," the girl whispered, shuffling her feet.

Amara glanced back at the sea, where the Gnostics were lowering skiffs into the water. She didn't dare delay too much longer, or many of her allies would be easy targets as they struggled out of the water. "Alright, be quick."

Salamander led her aside and then glanced around to make sure no one was listening. Then she swung her backpack off her shoulder. With another furtive glance at their nearby group, she flipped opened the flap. From inside, several gold coins glinted in the sunlight. The girl quickly shut it again before anyone else could see.

"Where did you get those?" Amara gasped.

The girl shrugged, but her drawn face betrayed her nonchalance. "Ackley did say they were ours. I guess, I mean, I just took them before we all started running."

"Is this why you've been wanting to talk to me?"

Salamander nodded. "I want to send it back with someone to Leissen so they can free my parents. But I wasn't sure if I should split it with you first." She moved to open the flap of her backpack again.

Amara reached out to stop her. "I think I speak for everyone in the group when I say they're yours. Is this why you've been so worried lately?"

"I can finally save my parents." Salamander chewed on her lower lip. "If something bad happens to me—"

"Don't even think such a thing," Amara said, interrupting her. "But no matter what, I'll make sure your parents are freed."

"Thank you." Salamander gave her a big, lopsided smile, her face lighting up. "I was just worried about getting stabbed or something before I told you."

"I guess I have been a little busy lately," Amara admitted. "And I'm sorry I took so long to talk to you." Amara leaned forward and gave her a hug. She could feel the girl's shoulders relax.

"Be careful today," Salamander said.

"I will." Amara gave one last squeeze and then disentangled herself. "And the same goes for you."

When they rejoined their party, the situation at the port had changed little, aside from another ship nearing the docks. Amara watched as the new arrival added its own missile fire to the attack, forcing the kobolds back from the water's edge. She swept her gaze over the walls. Luckily, the handful of kobolds posted there had their attention fixed on the growing battle at the docks.

Frederick stepped forward and shed his robe. He stood there in his small-clothes, his wizened body little more than a collection of age spots and gray hairs. He was so skinny that his muscles were in perfect relief under his leathery skin. "No time like the present, I suppose. Time to bring down a gate."

Borim peered at the knight with a raised brow. "Have you finally lost your mind, old man? Or is this your version of your blinding spell? Let me guess—anyone who looks at you claws out their eyes?"

"Just watch and learn, my little friend." The almost completely naked knight strode forward and headed down the hill toward the heavy wooden village gates.

Amara exchanged a look with Jonas, but it was too late to stop Frederick now. Instead, she rose to her feet and raced down the hill after the knight. She couldn't let an unarmed old man face the kobolds alone. The thick vegetation tore at her clothing, and several times she almost stumbled when her foot twisted on the uneven ground. But she finally caught up with the knight in front of the gates. For an old man, he moved surprisingly fast.

The others joined them shortly, and they gathered into loose knots outside of the walls. One very surprised kobold appeared in the tower overlooking the gate, but an arrow from one of their hunters quickly felled it. No more appeared to take its place.

"If you have a plan, now is the time to do it," Amara said urgently. "Otherwise, I'm going to have to try something else before they spot us. We're sitting ducks out here." She didn't want to conjure her *Divine Weapon* yet, but it might be the only way to cut through the thick timbers of the gate.

"They say patience is a virtue." Frederick stretched and then swung his arms around. "And one you'd do well to learn."

Amara bit down a retort and then crossed her arms. "Anytime you're ready, then."

Emmaline appeared, seemingly out of thin air. Amara suppressed a yelp. Lately, the priestess always seemed to be hovering near Amara. "If this fossil can't handle it, then my spells will make short work of the gate."

Amara opened her mouth to respond, but an immense surge of mana made her fall silent. The gathering energy dwarfed any spell she had encountered, except perhaps her *Avatar of Melischar*. She took a step back in confusion as she tried to figure out where the power was coming from. But then she realized the knight was quickly swelling in size.

She watched as Frederick grew taller until he stood nearly double her height. Then his muscles began to swell until they rippled under his skin. She took another step back as the knight let out a deep, baritone roar.

Frederick gripped the gates with his fists, and his muscles bulged as he strained against it. A creaking sound filled the air, and then, with a loud crack, the gate snapped off from its metal hinges. He tossed it aside like it weighed nothing and then charged into the village.

Amara watched the knight with wide eyes. She'd expected a lot of things, but she'd hadn't been prepared for the ancient knight to turn into some musclebound hulk. She was eternally grateful his smallclothes had survived the transformation.

Before they entered, she called out to the mass of peasants and townsfolk. "Remember, Jonas is leading the attack, so stay behind us." She'd made the concession the previous evening that her group members would lead the way. While she'd rather be at the forefront of the battle, she'd been forced to admit her healing spells would be needed more than her offensive abilities.

With Jonas in the lead, her party moved into the village and crept past rows of eerily silent houses. Not a soul stirred on any of the filthy streets. The remains of the humans who had dwelt here were evident everywhere she looked. In front of one house, a ragged doll sat propped up on a barrel, and nearby, tools lay scattered in front of a door. And in more than a few places, what appeared to be dried blood was splattered on the walls of the buildings.

The sight of the blood hardened her resolve. It was clear the Forces of Chaos hadn't left many survivors when they took this village. The kobolds who had committed the slaughter here deserved no mercy.

Ahrenshoop was surprisingly large, and there must have been several hundred people living in the village before it had fallen. But Amara wasn't worried about getting lost, as according to those who knew the village, all the winding streets led toward the port.

Amara stopped when she spotted a flash of movement down a side street. She peered around the corner of the building to see a kobold staring at them with hourglass eyes. The creature immediately bolted in the other direction.

Borim moved to chase after the kobold, but she held out a hand to stop him. They didn't want to split up in the claustrophobic confines of the village. More than anything, they needed to stick together.

"Come on!" Harold shouted, showing newfound bravado. "They know we're here now, so let's make them pay!" Without waiting for Amara and the others, the farmer charged forward. The other peasants gave a cheer and then raced after him down the street.

"Wait!" she called out. But none of them acknowledged her as they continued their headlong charge.

"And I thought *you* were reckless," Jonas said, the irony heavy in his voice. "I suppose we should follow them to ensure they don't get into trouble."

Amara nodded before sprinting after the peasants. "They're going to get themselves slaughtered," she panted as she ran. "Didn't I tell them to all stay back?"

"You did," Jonas replied dryly, keeping pace with her. "However, I think they may have become slightly excitable in the presence of the avatar."

Amara let out a sigh and willed her legs to move faster. The one thing she was learning about battles was that they never went according to plan.

The street abruptly opened up into a square around the docks. The mob of peasants had stopped short of the well-armed kobolds, suddenly rethinking their boldness. A section of the Chaos army was already wheeling around to face them. As Amara watched, a wall of spears and shields marched in their direction.

A spear soared out from the ranks of the kobolds, and impaled an older townsman holding a pitchfork. The gruesome weapon burst out of his back in a spray of gore before it soared back to a kobold in gold armor. The creature directed the floating spear with a flick of its hand. After letting the weapon hover above its head for a moment, the kobold sent it hurtling toward the group of peasants again.

"That must be the commander," Amara said through tight lips. "We need to take him out first."

"Agreed," Jonas said, as ghostly wisps began to swirl around him. "Please, as we agreed, let me handle him."

Amara fought down the urge to charge into battle and instead moved to help her downed allies. She quickly cast *Heal Wounds* on the peasant who had been first impaled by the spear, and then began to weave her mana to repeat her spell on the injured woman. Amara was shocked by how little mana her spell consumed. Her soul felt like it contained a vast ocean of power after expanding it with the spirit fruit.

The man rose to his feet. He groped at his chest, amazed, and then reached down to scoop up his pitchfork. As she watched the second injured peasant rouse from her position on the ground, Amara pulled out a dart from her quiver. Just because she'd agreed to stay back didn't mean she wasn't going to fight.

After all, Jonas would need help if he was going to bring down the commander.

# CHAPTER 55

*M*ove, the voice of Luck echoed in Amara's mind. She dodged to the side and felt a rush of air as a javelin sped past her face not half a second later. The missile struck the hard pack street behind her, skittering along until it came to rest against a building's foundation. Amara grabbed a dart from the quiver on her waist and hurled it back at the kobold who had thrown the javelin. The barbed projectile slammed into the creature's face with a sickening crunch.

She didn't bother to wait to see if she'd slain the kobold. Already, she was weaving together the mana to cast her *Heal Wounds* spell. While she'd been occupied healing the injured peasants, Harold had taken a grievous wound from a kobold's blade. She watched as the farmer staggered away from the fighting, trying to stem the bleeding with both hands.

Amara finished casting her spell, and the street brightened as motes of light encircled the pig farmer. But before she could see the result of her handiwork, Borim grabbed her and yanked her to the side.

The dwarf lifted his shield, blocking a kobold's spear thrust meant for Amara and sending the creature flying. While the kobold struggled to recover from its attack, the dwarf brought down his axe with a roar. The weapon cleaved through the kobold's forehead, spraying blood and gore across the ground.

As the mortally wounded kobold staggered back like a drunken chicken, Amara's pet charged forward and clamped its jaws shut on the creature. With a jerk of her body, Mimi tossed the kobold up into the air and then caught the lizard man in her open mouth. A collection of loud cracks and popping sounds followed.

"Thank you," she said to Borim as she tried to catch her breath. "I don't know why my Luck didn't warn me that was coming."

"You're doing too much," the dwarf replied. "Best to keep an eye on your own hide instead of worrying about everyone else."

Amara nodded, but already she was drawing upon her mana to cast another spell. There were too many injured peasants to count. After their initial charge, her ragtag force had been pushed back down the street by the better trained and better armed kobolds. If not for the narrow road, which let only a handful of the lizard men attack at once, they likely would have been completely overrun.

And to make matters worse, the Gnostic ships hadn't been able to force a landing yet. They were still struggling to gain a beachhead near the docks. After being thrown back several times, they'd started landing skiffs full of troops outside the walls. And while they were blocked from view by the palisade, she assumed they were circling around to enter through the breached gates.

She glanced over at Jonas, who was keeping a dozen kobolds at bay. His face was deathly pale, and his eyes looked like spheres of obsidian. The swirling tendrils of power surrounding him emitted a deathly glow.

No kobold wanted to face the rogue in battle, and their lines shied away when he approached. Those he did manage to strike with his weapons were reduced to shriveled husks. And with each of the creatures he slew, he seemed to grow stronger.

Her gaze met his pitch-black eyes for a moment, and a shiver traveled up her spine. She felt a terrible power emanating from him. He no longer looked human.

Amara fought down the urge to call upon her *Divine Weapon*. While her mana reserves had increased significantly after using the spirit fruit, there were still limits to the energy she could draw upon. And she was quickly reaching it that limit with how much she had needed to heal the townspeople.

The ground heaved under her feet, and she nearly stumbled. As she did, the golden spear of the commander narrowly missed her head and then zipped back into the air before returning to its master.

*Why didn't my Luck warn me about that?* she wondered.

Another tremor made many of her allies lose their footing. And then the earth under the kobolds split open with a rumbling sound. From the rift in the earth, a monster born of stone and earth emerged with a deafening cry.

She glanced over to see the Gnostic women, Emilia and her sisters, chanting while they held out their hands. They must have called forth another golem.

Almost immediately after it had emerged from the ground, the commander's golden spear struck the monster's shoulder and tore off a chunk of dirt. The golem roared with pain and clasped a hand over its injured body part. Then it stormed forward, furiously seeking out the source of its pain.

Amara tore her gaze away from the golem and then let out a sigh as she watched a kobold drive a spear through a fallen peasant. She grabbed a dart from her quiver and lobbed it at the kobold. The missile merely bounced off the creature's armor—the timer of her *Dart Deadeye* ability must have ended. But the kobold turned its attention away from the wounded peasant and lifted its shield to block her next throw. Her dart had at least done its job of preventing the creature from finishing off the man.

She hurriedly wove her mana to craft the pattern for *Heal Wounds*. Once again, the air brightened as the spell repaired the damage done to the peasant by the spear. Her mana was rapidly dwindling, and she was worried she would run out before the battle ended.

The golem, standing taller than a house now, rampaged through the kobold's lines. A handful of the creatures cried out as they were crushed under the monster's massive stone feet. But as it took a ponderous swing with its stony fist at the commander, a golden spear smashed into its chest. The golem waved its fists around wildly as it tried to keep its balance; then with a long groan, it toppled backward, crushing several more kobolds as it struck the ground with a shuddering boom.

Amara shifted her feet anxiously, briefly considered casting her *Avatar of Melischar* spell. But a single prod at her mana reserves forced her to reckon with how dangerous that would be. Still, she hesitated for a moment. She hated standing back while others fought her battles, but destroying herself by pulling too hard on her depleted mana reserves would help nobody, least of all herself. For once, however unwillingly, she would stay in the rear without putting herself in undue danger.

She spotted a break in the kobolds' shield wall created by the falling golem and gave her young companion an encouraging pat on the shoulder. "Now, Salamander!

The girl stepped forward and unleashed a stream of fire at the unprotected ranks of lizard men. The flames splashed against their armor and seeped into the openings. Many of the burning creatures tried to flee toward the water, but the missiles from the growing number of Gnostic ships cut them down before they reached the shore.

Amara glanced around quickly to ensure there were no more injured and then began to cast *Divine Weapon*. The mana in her soul reached a dangerously low level as the enormous blade slowly formed in front of her. But it was nothing compared to the drain of *Avatar of Melischar*, and it was well worth the risk to finish off the disorganized kobolds.

She sent the burning spectral weapon hurtling toward the commander, whose flying spear reappeared from nowhere and knocked it aside. The two weapons exchanged blows, their movements almost too fast to follow. With the commander's attention elsewhere, the golem finally regained its footing and waded back into the tightly packed ranks of kobolds.

The air was soon filled with the cries of dying lizard men. The edges of the kobold's lines frayed as some broke in the hope of escaping. But there was nowhere to go for them. Death dwelt in every direction, and dozens of the shrieking creatures fell to the reinvigorated peasants and the Gnostic soldiers wading ashore.

Jonas appeared at her side, his weapons and armor splattered with green blood. "We must defeat the commander, or this battle may still be lost."

"He only has this stupid golden spear," Amara replied without looking at him. If she dropped her focus from the spectral blade for even a moment, it would lose the duel with the commander's weapon. "I doubt he's a real threat."

Jonas shook his head. When he continued, his voice sounded hollow, as if it was coming from a great distance. "Any commander of the Chaos army will possess terrible magic. Now that the battle has turned against them, he will most likely call upon his most powerful spell."

Amara opened her mouth to reply but then froze as she felt an impossibly powerful swell of mana. The river of energy flowing into the kobold ranks dwarfed anything she had felt in the past, and it filled her with trepidation. Had Jonas been right?

The surrounding battle slowed as the sky tore open and the tip of an enormous golden spear emerged from the rift. The weapon radiated with such immense power that it almost drove her to her knees.

Many of the kobolds fled at the sight of the weapon, while a handful of peasants sagged to the ground. Even the Golem slowed and turned its rocky face toward the skies, though she couldn't be sure it was because the Gnostic sister's attention was fixated there or if the magical creature somehow felt the doom descending upon them.

Jonas grabbed her arm and pointed at the kobold leader. "The commander must die before the spell completes. Otherwise, everyone here will perish."

She tore her gaze away from the otherworldly rift and then nodded at Jonas. Then she turned and gestured at Borim, who was busy yanking his axe free from a fallen kobold's face. "We need to stop that caster, now!"

"Sounds like fun!" Borim hollered. "Out of my way, you scaly bastards!" The dwarf leveled his shield and barreled into the kobolds. The distracted creatures were easily bowled over by Borim, and a path to the commander quickly took shape.

Amara spun her staff around, the weight feeling *right* in her hands. She followed in the dwarf's wake and lashed out as a kobold lunged in her direction. The staff cracked against the kobold's head and blasted the creature away like a rag doll. Her eyes widened with shock as the runes flared to life on the wooden stave. The kobold she'd struck had been hurled nearly twenty paces away.

*I guess the baroness didn't skimp on my magical weapon.*

But she didn't have time to dwell on it as they struggled toward the commander. She kept herself behind Borim as the dwarf bulldozed his way through the kobolds, and Jonas lashed out with his daggers at any who got in their way.

Another kobold slipped past her companions and lunged at her with a short sword raised. She slammed her staff into it and sent the creature cartwheeling away through its companions.

As they drew closer to the commander, their doom drew ever closer from the sky. The spear tip bore down with impossible pressure, driving many more around them to their knees. The golem—standing taller than them—crumbled under the weight and stones clattered against the ground as it disintegrated.

At the sight of the golem collapsing, she doubled her pace. She may only have seconds to slay the commander before the spell killed them all. Was the kobold caster planning to die as well, or did he have a way to survive?

When her group reached the commander, she had her answer to the question. She watched as Borim leapt into the air and brought down his axe with both hands. But the steel head bounced off an energy shield as it flared to life, encasing the kobold in a golden shell.

The lizard man let out a barking laugh and then crossed its arms. It must know it was safe inside of its shield and planned to wait until they had all been slain by its spell.

She glanced up at the sky to see more of the spear emerging from the rift. The wooden shaft was covered in enormous runes that pulsated with power. Jonas had said that none of them would survive once it struck the ground, and with the immense pressure it was giving off, they might be dead long before then.

*What should I do?* she thought. *I don't have enough mana for my avatar spell.*

A huge shape trampling through the kobolds interrupted her thoughts, and she was knocked aside as it charged past. She struck the ground hard and rolled a few times before coming to a stop. When she pushed herself up to see what had struck her, she saw the musclebound form of Frederick lifting the kobold commander—energy shield and all—and then, with a grunt, hurling it far into the distance.

The golden sphere soared over the village rooftops and then disappeared into the forest beyond the palisade with a crash. The snapping of branches continued for a while. A flock of disturbed birds took flight from the forest canopy.

The golden spear dueling with Amara's spectral weapon suddenly dropped to the ground, lifeless. But the weapon descending from the rift didn't slow. And the pressure grew more intense with every passing second.

Frederick scratched his head and then pressed his lips together until they formed a line. "Well, that's a tad disappointing," he said in a booming voice. "I thought incapacitating, or at least stunning the caster would work. But it appears the spell is too far advanced to stop. I could destroy the weapon myself if I hadn't lost my halberd. Now where did I put that darn thing . . . ?"

"What do we do now?" Amara asked frantically, her gaze fixated on the spear emerging from the rift. It was like the weapon of a god was descending upon them.

Frederick gestured her forward. "I'm going to throw you beyond the Wall as well. With your spells and luck, you should survive the landing. At least I think so. What do I know, though? Still, it's better than staying here."

"There's no way I'm going to do that!" she exclaimed. "I'm not some sack of potatoes to be thrown around. And how will you all escape?"

The huge man stepped forward and cracked his knuckles. "My apologies, but our fate is already sealed. That spell will destroy the village and everything around it. And I certainly won't be known as the knight who let you die. No, I can't have that."

She crossed her arms and took a step back. "I said I'm not leaving."

Frederick slowed, and his frown deepened. "Oh-ho, so you're not amenable to being tossed? Well, if you plan to stay, then you'd best come up with a plan. And if I were you, I'd do it fast."

A thought suddenly occurred to her. "Do you have any more of those mana crystals? Full ones, I mean."

Frederick reached into the depths his smallclothes and pulled out a gem, pulsating with power. "I have this one."

"Umm . . ." Amara scrunched up her face. "Do you have any others?"

But before the old knight could reply, a group of kobolds charged their position. She snatched the gem from his massive palm and then held it up to peer into its depths. How did these things work?

She turned to look for someone from her party to ask, but each of her friends had their hands full as they fought desperately to hold the kobolds at bay. Their weapons rose and fell as more of the creatures recovered from the intense aura and hurled themselves against them, heedless of their own safety.

Amara focused her thoughts and attempted to draw the mana out from the crystal. But after a few seconds of trying, nothing had happened. She glanced back up at the sky and saw the spear had nearly reached the rooftops. She felt something wet dripping from her nose and when she reached up to touch it, her hand came away red with blood.

*I need to figure this out, and fast.*

She closed her eyes and tried to meditate. But instead of drawing the energy out of the air, she focused on the crystal. Almost immediately, a river of power poured into her soul.

Before she drained the crystal, she hurriedly wove together her mana to cast *Avatar of Melischar.* She focused on forging the wings and sword first, completely ignoring the armor. A powerful weapon in a sheath took shape on her belt, and glowing wings sprouted from her back.

Without hesitating, she launched herself into the air and drew the sword. The power of the blade thrummed with destructive power, and she focused on feeding her mana into the weapon. Already, her soul had nearly run dry, but she only needed this form to last for another few seconds.

She gripped the sword's hilt in both hands as the flames wreathing the blade crackled with heat. Then she angled back and swung it with all her might against the descending spear. The weapons collided, and an explosion of power ripped the sky asunder.

The force of the detonation hurled her away like a rocket and the sword in her hand shattered into shards of light. She struck the nearby water and then skipped across it like a stone. Each impact sent pain lancing through her body, and she cried out as she felt bones snap.

Finally, she tumbled to a stop and then sank into the freezing sea. She struggled to kick her way to the surface, but the agony from the attempt nearly overwhelmed her. As she descended deeper into the inky blackness, she felt herself losing consciousness. And then the darkness took her, and she felt nothing.

# CHAPTER 56

Amara jerked awake in the freezing water and fought against the desperate urge to suck in a breath. As she tried to orient herself in the darkness, she caught a glimpse of light shimmering far above her. She knew immediately that if she wanted to survive, she'd have to force her battered body to swim toward the surface.

*This will not be my final resting place,* she thought to herself.

She summoned up all the strength she could muster and then began to claw her way upward through the murky water. Her lungs screamed for air, but she pushed down the urge to breathe. When she tried to kick with her legs, a jolt of agony nearly made her pass out again.

Once the pain had faded, she continued the long climb out of the darkness. Just when it felt like she was about to black out, her head broke through the surface and into dazzling sunlight. But she was weak and badly injured, and she struggled to stay afloat.

A wave crested over her face and filled her mouth with water, which made her descend into a coughing fit. As her splashing grew more desperate, she scanned the surrounding waters, hoping to spot a Gnostic ship.

*I must have landed close to their fleet.*

But truthfully, she didn't know how she'd been carried by the force of the blast. And worse, the high waves prevented her from seeing the shore. Finally, when she was losing hope, she spotted a Gnostic boat crest a nearby swell. She frantically gestured at them before dipping beneath the surface again.

Amara didn't know if they'd noticed her, and she didn't have the energy left to care. As she sank into the depths, she heard a splash, and then felt strong arms encircle her waist.

When she resurfaced, she could barely hold up her head. Her savior used powerful strokes to carry her in the direction of the boat. And then rough hands grabbed her to pull her on board.

She cried out as her mangled legs struck the edge of the gunwales. The pain nearly overwhelmed her, and the corners of her vision darkened for a moment. When she recovered, she could make out several men and women peering at her with wide eyes.

"Are . . . are you the avatar?" a young man asked. He had dark hair and facial features similar to the Gnostics' sisters. He wore simple robes with a curved dagger on his belt.

Amara opened her mouth to ask about her party, but then slumped back in the bottom of the boat. She didn't even have the strength to speak. Instead, she fumbled for the pouch on her belt. With trembling hands, she opened the flap and grasped for a healing pill. But all she found inside was slime—the pills had dissolved in the water.

"What should we do?" the young man asked one of his companions behind Amara.

"Get her to the shore," a gruff voice replied. "Maybe they can help her there." As the man finished talking, the others took up their oars again.

With a groan, Amara gingerly reached out to touch her soul. She expected to find it damaged again, but surprisingly, this time, it was only drained of mana.

*I guess I should be grateful for small mercies.*

Amara shut her eyes and began to meditate. Her soul refilled slowly, as the excruciating pain from her injuries kept interrupting her thoughts.

By the time the boat neared the shore, she'd refilled nearly a quarter of her mana. She had trouble judging how much energy her upgraded soul could hold, but she should have more than enough to cast a healing spell.

She carefully wove her mana together—worried her muddled mind would make a mistake—and then let out a sigh as the surrounding air brightened.

A blizzard of motes swarmed around her, most of them splashing against her legs. But a surprising number also found her chest and her arms. She'd barely noticed the wounds on her upper body with the mangled state of her legs.

She grimaced with discomfort as her thigh bones straightened and fused back together. After a few seconds, the pain faded to a dull roar in the back of her mind. She'd probably have to cast the healing spell again later. But at least for now, she mended the worst of the damage.

With a supreme effort, she pushed herself up into a sitting position. Those around her gasped, but she ignored them. She scanned the shore and felt a surge of relief at seeing her party and Mimi standing near the docks. None of them appeared to be injured and there was no sign of the ominous spear which had been descending from the rift.

Amara had feared the detonation had injured them after the magical weapons clashed. But it seemed she'd taken the brunt of the damage. She must have stopped it high enough in the sky to prevent any of the others from being wounded.

As the boat scraped against the rocky bottom, everyone placed their oars inside and then jumped out into the shallow water. She was left alone while Gnostics dragged their vessel up onto the shore. She heard voices calling out, and then Borim's head appeared over the side of the gunwale.

"Oh, thank Glonin Goldhand you're not twisted up into a pretzel, lass," the dwarf said, the relief palpable in his voice. Then he turned and called out, "She's alright!"

Salamander appeared next and clapped her hands. "They fished you out like a pearltail!"

Jonas popped into view next. His eyes no longer shone like obsidian, though his skin still looked waxen. He inspected her before speaking. "How do you always manage to emerge unscathed after facing such deadly threats?"

"Unscathed?" she gave him a lopsided grin. "You wouldn't be saying that if you had seen me a few minutes ago."

"Still," he continued, "many lesser casters would have been killed by the impact. However, I am happy to see you are unhurt."

Mimi's eyes peeped over the side of the boat where Amara was sitting. And a second later, a long, sinuous tongue wormed its way over the edge to lick her.

Jonas offered Amara his hand and then helped her climb out of the boat. He stood there wordlessly as she found her balance.

"I think I can stand on my own," she said. But as he released her grip, she tottered like a drunk. Without thinking, she grabbed onto his shoulder. "Is everyone else alright?"

"We suffered shockingly few casualties," Jonas replied. "However, right now we must deal with the Gnostics . . ." He trailed off as he looked past her.

Amara turned to see where he was looking, and she was startled to see rank upon rank of Gnostics kneeling along the shore. Waves lapped at the feet of many of them, but they paid no heed to the cold water. They remained unmoving where they had knelt, with their heads bowed.

Finally, the young man she'd met in the boat walked up to her hesitantly. He placed his hand against his chest before he inclined his head. "My name is Anthon, and I wish to offer you all our lives in service."

Amara recoiled. She didn't want their lives. She didn't want *anyone's* lives.

"Remember, be regal," Jonas whispered under his breath.

The rogue's words made her pause. She needed to act like an avatar—whatever that meant. Channeling her best impression of Ingrid, Amara straightened up to her full height. Her wet dress clung to her in rags, and her hair hung in damp, tangled strands around her head. She did her best to ignore her appearance. "I am pleased to accept your service, Anthon. And I appreciate your efforts in subduing the kobolds."

At the mention of the lizard-like men, she peered around the docks until she spotted a group of the creatures surrounded by the peasants from Fusson. They must have surrendered, as none of them were armed. There was no sign of the rest of the garrison who had been stationed here—they must have either been slain or fled. Which meant the village was theirs.

*Malcheron's going to be pissed when he can't complete his quest,* she thought with a hint of glee. But then she remembered those who had lost their lives here, and her excitement dampened.

She pulled up her quest to see if it had been updated. And as the text floated in her vision, she was pleased to see it had.


**Defend Stout Oak Keep (Divine Quest)**
**The ancient fortress of Stout Oak Keep has been attacked by five armies of Chaos. As the last remaining fortress of Galoth's Wall held by the Forces of Order, it must be protected at any cost. Should this bastion fall, then all may be lost.**
**Objectives (0/6 Completed)**
- **Kill, Capture, or Drive off the Invasion Leader Malcheron**
- **Defeat the Issurian Army**
- **Defeat the Ogre Army**
- **Defeat the Dark Dwarven Army**
- **Defeat the Kobold Army**
- **Defeat the Goblin Army**

**Reward: Epic Chest**
**Bonus Objectives**
- **Control the 4 Villages of Stout Oak Keep (1/4)**
- **Control the Mills (0/2)**
- **Control the Mine (0/1)**

**Reward: Rare Chest**


The sound of Anthon clearing his throat made her look up. "Sorry," she said. "I was just checking out the quest to retake this village."

"Ah, I see, Divine One." Anthon bowed low from the waist again. "I am pleased we were able to help with the quest to retake these lands from the foul agents of Chaos. What would you have us do now?"

Amara chewed on her lower lip. While she'd been the de facto leader of her group for a while and had gotten used to commanding the refugees from Fusson, she had no idea what to do with an army. She looked over at Jonas helplessly.

The rogue grasped her dilemma instantly and stepped forward. "The avatar wishes for you to commence fortifying this village. A deep ditch must be excavated around the palisade, and platforms must be erected behind the walls. Anyone not working should start unloading provisions from the ship."

Anthon looked at her questioningly.

"He's noble-born and my closest advisor," she said, keeping her chin high despite the wet tendrils of hair falling into her eyes. "Heed anything he tells you to do."

Anthon bowed one final time and then headed in the direction of the dock jutting out into the water. The nearest ship had pulled up to the pier, and a swarm of sailors were leaping off with huge ropes in hand to tie their vessel in place. Beyond the harbor, dozens of ships bobbed in the water as they waited their turn.

"You made Sneaky your advisor?" Borim groused. "I thought you'd want some good, solid dwarven advice. Especially when it comes to building. I doubt old Moneybags there has done a single day of hard labor in his life."

"Would you have said anything different?" she asked.

"Well, not really," Borim admitted, his frown deepening. "Except maybe find a few runesmiths to enchant the walls. That way, they could deflect any spells directed at them."

"Why don't you go find someone to do that, then?" she smiled at the dwarf. "That does sound like a good idea."

"Now you're just humoring me," the dwarf replied hotly. "I don't need pity tasks."

"I said it was a good idea, didn't I?"

Borim narrowed one eye as he stared at her. "I guess you wouldn't lie to me. Come on, Salamander. Let's go find someone to turn these into proper dwarven walls."

Amara watched bemusedly as the dwarf dragged the girl off to find a runesmith. After they had disappeared into the crowd, she turned to Jonas. He was still uncharacteristically quiet. "Are you alright?" she asked, softly. "I know you don't like using your class skills."

"That's the problem," he replied. "I . . . enjoyed it this time. I'm worried that my class is changing me. With every kobold I slew, I felt a rush of power. And to be honest, I thoroughly enjoyed the sensation." He looked down, ashamed. "Since you have far more powerful adventurers to draw upon now, you may want to replace me in your group."

"I could never replace you," she said. "And if you don't like using your class abilities, then just stick with your other ones. Regardless, you're a part of my party, and that's never going to change."

His face seemed to brighten at her words, almost like a ray of sunshine poking through the clouds. "I appreciate your kindness, even if you spoke some untruths."

"I meant every word I said." Amara reached out to touch his forearm. For once, he didn't pull away. "There's no one I trust more than you."

He patted her hand and returned her smile. "Perhaps I will take you up on your advice and stick to my core skills and Weapon Proficiencies for a while. The presence of so many Gnostics will likely take some of the pressure off me the next time you hurl yourself into the maw of a dragon. Still, it was impressive the way you shattered that kobold commander's spell."

"I was pretty awesome, wasn't I?"

"And you are so modest about it," he continued, without missing a beat. "That is what's truly inspiring."

"Knock it off," she said, slapping his arm playfully. "I'm pretty sure I've earned the right to think my avatar spell is awesome. And how many girls do you know with wings and a magic sword?"

Jonas stroked his chin before replying. "I suppose I've never counted before."

"You're lying," she replied. "You don't know anyone else who can do that. Wait, do you?"

Jonas only smiled knowingly and then strolled off into the village.

Amara followed after him, wondering if he was pulling her leg. But he stubbornly refused to reply, and after a few minutes, she swore to learn more about the abilities of the nobles of this world. For all she knew, maybe they did possess ancient relics that rivaled her own goddess-granted skills.

Her attempts to drag an answer out of Jonas were interrupted by Harold, who wanted to know what to do with the kobold prisoners. As Amara tried to think of an answer, many others formed a line behind the pig farmer, all waiting for a moment of her time.

With a drawn-out sigh, she set about governing the newly conquered village of Ahrenshoop.

# CHAPTER 57

Malcheron stood next to the table where the body of his lifelong friend, Storgom, was laid out in quiet repose. The dwarf had been caught in the explosion of the powder he'd been so eager to show off in the siege. His friend's face was almost unrecognizable, his features misshapen and his bushy beard burned off completely by the intense flames.

As he gazed at Storgom, Malcheron swore the cowardly avatar would pay for what she'd done. Now, the dark dwarf would never have a chance to ascend and join the Chaos Gods. The only consolation was that his friend had died in battle, so his spirit would spend eternity in the afterlife.

"I wish you could have shown me your new weapons," Malcheron whispered as he reached out to touch his friend's arm. "And I swear upon my life, I will have vengeance on those who murdered you."

The rustling fabric of the tent flap opening made him turn. He saw Tecala framed in the entryway, the light from the bonfire beyond making the shadows dance. He didn't move as she walked over to stand next to him. They contemplated the body of their slain friend in silence for several minutes.

Finally, he turned and spoke. "How much damage did they do?"

"The situation isn't good," she replied in a strained voice. "We lost most of the gunpowder, and at least twenty dwarven engineers were slain. It will . . . put back our plans quite a bit."

"And what of the knight who injured you?" he asked, his voice growing cold. A small party led by the avatar herself had rescued the knight during the attack. In the harsh dawn light, the cross had sat empty, as though it was mocking him. No matter what, he would make the human pay for what he had done to Tecala.

"The scouts haven't located him yet," Tecala replied. "However, when we learn of his position, we shall inform you."

"I assume the kobolds guarding him have been dealt with?" Malcheron leaned forward and ground his fists into the table. He'd assigned twoscore of the kobolds to lie in wait in case anyone attempted to free the human from the cross. And yet, when the attack had come, the soldiers had been insensate from consuming dak leaf. Even being prodded by the point of Issurian spears hadn't been enough to rouse several of them.

"They have been flayed alive and put on display for all in the camp to see, as you commanded," she replied. "No one else will dare consume any of the leaf on sentry duty again."

"And Ahrenshoop?" As if the other disasters weren't enough, earlier in the day, his quest to take the area surrounding Stout Oak Keep had updated to indicate his forces had lost control of one of the villages. Hours later, the unconscious form of the commander from Ahrenshoop had been carried into camp on a litter.

"Our scouts report a large force of Gnostics has landed at the port," Tecala said quietly. "They are busy fortifying the village, and it would be . . . costly to retake it."

"I see." He straightened up and gripped his hands behind his back as he marched over to the map. "And what of the Northmen and the knights?"

"They are still at least a few days away." She was silent for a moment before she continued. "Without the engineers, we may need to retreat. The walls of the fortress are strong, and there may not be enough gunpowder for the cannons."

"Then we won't bring down the walls," he snarled. "Summon the ice mage to my tent. I will have her freeze the waters of the river, and then we'll storm the castle. No matter how much blood it takes, we will seize Stout Oak Keep before the relief forces arrive. And once we do, our armies will pour over Galoth's Wall and drive these pathetic humans before us like the vermin they are."

Tecala frowned. "It will be exceedingly costly to storm the fortress. Are you sure it wouldn't be prudent to retreat instead? If we are caught between the walls and a relief army— "

"Retreat and go where?" Malcheron asked heatedly. "There is nowhere I can hide from my mother's wrath." He refused to share his sister's eternal anguish in the depths of a volcano. His only options were victory or death.

Tecala was silent for a long moment. "Then let me lead the first assault. I won't ask my soldiers to do anything I wouldn't do."

"I can't risk losing you." After Storgom's death, he couldn't let anything happen to Tecala. They were facing a cowardly avatar with no honor, who struck in the middle of the night. He needed to keep Tecala close and safe.

"I must insist." She straightened up and lifted her chin. "My position is commander of the Issurians, and they must see me fighting at their side."

Malcheron fought down a scowl. She spoke the truth, and if he held her back from the battle, her troops would lose faith in her. All the commanders in the Chaos army led from the front, and anything else was considered an act of grave cowardice. When the time came, he himself would have to join the battle, too. "As you wish." He waved his hand at her. "Is there anything else?"

"I do have some good news," she continued, relaxing slightly. "The healers managed to save Servath."

"The kobold commander?"

Tecala nodded. "Our healers mended his most serious wounds. But his soul may take a day or two to recover."

"I still find it hard to conceive how anyone could survive his *Spear of Fate* spell," Malcheron mused. "The avatar must have been growing in power for many years before she revealed herself."

"Perhaps," Tecala replied. "Are you sure your *Scroll of Banishment* will work on her?"

"Yes," he nodded. "I spoke with several of our sages here, and they inspected the magic bound in the vellum. It will transport her to a volcano—possibly the same one where my sister resides—and a spell will continually heal her as she roasts over the lava. It's a fitting fate for someone who murders honorable warriors under the veil of darkness."

Tecala's brow lowered slightly. "I will rest easy once she is dealt with. And you're sure there's no chance of her resisting the scroll?"

"The sages couldn't say for sure . . ." As his words trailed off, he tried to dismiss his lingering worries. There was still much they didn't know about the avatar, and the records from the last Chaos War were incomplete at best. Until he faced her directly, he couldn't know her power. "However, I have faith in my mother's magic."

"I hope you're right," Tecala replied. "If only we had someone loyal to us in her camp, then we could slay her in her sleep."

"Unfortunately, we've never been able to infiltrate the Gnostics," Malcheron said. "But perhaps the gods will yet bless us." He took one last look at the map. The wooden pieces representing the relief armies drew ever nearer. "Order the attack to commence at dawn. And I expect the outer walls to fall before nightfall. There is to be no quarter given—slay everyone you find inside the castle."

Tecala curtsied to him and then strolled out of the tent.

He was left alone in the dim light of his command tent, with only his thoughts and the still body of his oldest friend for company. Tomorrow would mark the beginning of the end for Stout Oak Keep, and with it, the last bastion keeping the Chaos armies at bay.

# CHAPTER 58

Arturo hated himself. More than anything, he wanted to die. But to kill yourself was the greatest of sins for anyone who served Order, and he couldn't bring himself to commit an act that fueled Chaos. Still, he found himself praying daily for Holy Birgitta to grant him a swift and merciful death at the hands of the goblin army infesting this land.

On their flight northward, pursued doggedly by cavalry from Oksberg, they had narrowly avoided several bands of goblins and kobolds. Evidence of a full-scale invasion was clear everywhere they looked, from the burned-out farmsteads to the streams of panicked refugees fleeing southward.

He'd nearly come to blows with Selena when they'd encountered a bedraggled refugee family on the road leading from the castle. The crazed sister had immediately accused the cowering peasants of being heretics and threatened to purge them. Only through convincing her that casting a fire spell would give away their position had he managed to talk her down.

Thankfully, they hadn't encountered anyone else after the family, and as they stood on the crest of a hill overlooking the valley, he finally understood why. Spread out below them was an immense Chaos army. He hadn't heard of such a large force invading the northlands in centuries.

*And instead of fighting them, we're here to murder a simple Trickster Cleric.*

"We must find a way into the fortress," Selena said, snapping Arturo out of his thoughts. "That wretched heretic must be cowering behind those walls. She probably thinks she's safe, but I will dispel that notion."

Arturo's eyes widened at the sister's suggestion. He nearly asked her if she'd lost her mind, but he already knew the answer to that question. Much of their time together on the road had consisted of him listening to her ramblings about heretics. And once the others had deserted after the fiasco in Oksberg, she'd only descended deeper into madness. When she looked at him now, her eyes shone with a strange light and darted around constantly.

*I wish I was powerful enough to slay her.*

The day after they'd fled Oksberg, he'd waited until she'd fallen asleep, and then had drawn his sword with the intention of driving it through her foul heart. But as he'd crept forward to commit the deed, he'd tripped a magical ward she'd set around herself. She'd jerked awake, a fiery spell already half-formed. And while she'd accepted his claim that he'd been investigating a noise, she hadn't let down her guard since. He wasn't even sure if she'd slept in the past few days. With her eyes growing more crazed by the hour, he suspected she hadn't.

And his weak spells and Weapon Proficiencies would have no chance of harming her while she was alert and ready. Before he could land a single blow, she would reduce him to a pile of ash.

Selena tossed back her cloak and raised her hand. As she did, a swell of mana flowed through the air toward her. "Stay behind me as I fight my way through those tainted creatures. And remember, Holy Birgitta will keep you safe if your faith is pure."

For a moment, he considered allowing her to plunge into the mass of Issurians and kobolds beneath them in the valley. At least if he met his end fighting the foul Chaos creatures, it might wash away some of the innocent blood on his hands.

But more than anything, he was a coward. And he wasn't ready to die yet. "And what will you do after you burn your way through thousands of Chaos creatures?" he asked wearily. "Will you swim across the river and then climb the fortress's walls?"

"You don't understand," she muttered as she wrung her hands. "She must never feel safe again. Not for a moment after what she did to Frederick."

"And how will you complete your mission if you're dead?" he asked without a trace of emotion in his voice. Maybe he should just allow her to commit a suicide charge against the army below. The sweet release of death would be infinitely better than seeing the charred bodies of the young children every time he closed his eyes.

*Why did you choose her, Bishop Krause?* he wondered. *Did you know she was mad?*

"I suppose you're right," Selena mumbled. "And there may be more heretics lurking in the shadows here. We must purge them all. Only you understand, since you alone had the faith to stay at my side on our holy crusade." As she spoke, the words spilled out of her mouth and became jumbled together. "You must see now that those children would have grown into heretics like their parents. They had to be burned. Otherwise, their beliefs would have spread like a cancer. You see, don't you?" She looked almost feverish as she stared at him with unblinking eyes. "If we find more heretic children, they must be purged!"

At the mention of the children, he dropped his hand to the hilt of his longsword. He had no illusions about surviving a confrontation with her, but he couldn't allow her to murder any more innocents. He swore he would never witness such a horrifying sight again.

But a voice emerging from a nearby thicket stayed his hand. As he watched Selena's gaze snap over in the direction of the sound, he released his grip on the sword hilt. For a moment, he couldn't breathe, and his chest felt like a snake was constricting around it. What was wrong with him?

A young man emerged from the forest. He had dark hair, a narrow face, and wore the simple robes common to the Far South. "What are you doing out in the open?" he called out in a low voice. "These woods are swarming with goblins. Are you refugees from the village?"

Selena glared at the man coldly. "Are you a heretic?"

The man's brow wrinkled. "A heretic? What are you talking about?"

Arturo placed himself in front of Selena. He was grateful they had ditched their Church robes while fleeing from the mounted troops of Oksberg. "She wants to know if you're with the Church."

"Hardly," the man laughed. "I landed with the Gnostics yesterday. I'm supposed to be scouting the Chaos army, but I stumbled upon you two. It's a miracle you're still alive."

"We heard news of the Chaos invasion," Arturo said quickly. He grabbed his hand to hide the shakes. His adrenaline was still pumping after he'd nearly attacked Selena. "And we came to help."

"We're happy to have anyone who knows how to wield a sword," the man said. "I'll take you back to Ahrenshoop to meet Frederick. He's in charge there."

"How dare you speak his name!" Selena cried out.

"Whose name?" The young man looked confused and turned to Arturo. "Is she alright?"

"The church killed someone close to her named Frederick," Arturo said smoothly. He didn't know why he was covering for Selena. If he exposed her as a sister sent to hunt down the avatar, then they would most likely execute her immediately. But how many would she kill in the process?

*No,* he thought. *I won't let anyone else die at her hands.*

"Are you coming or not?" the man said, clearly exasperated. "I'm not going to die for you two. And before long, someone down there is going to spot us standing in the middle of this hill."

"Yes," Arturo replied. "We're coming. Take us to . . . your leader." For a moment, he'd almost said Frederick. But he knew Selena would react poorly upon hearing that name again.

The man disappeared back into the thicket, and after a brief hesitation, Arturo plunged in after him. Selena followed him, and they headed down a narrow trail leading toward the sea. Once there, he would find a way to deal with Selena. And he swore no one else would die at her hands.

# CHAPTER 59

A candle guttered on the table, sending shadows dancing across the cavernous room. Amara had been told this place had once been used as a church, though apparently, it had been many generations since a priest resided here. And many more since it had been used for its original purpose to worship the gods.

The plaster coating the stone walls bore the faded images of heroes battling against the Forces of Chaos. She immediately recognized the familiar face of Birgitta as the hero struggled against what must be a Harbinger in one painting. The artist had portrayed the monster as some sort of eldritch horror, with a mass of writhing tentacles snaking toward the armor-clad woman. But it was the creature's heads that unnerved her the most—they looked vaguely human, but with gaping eye sockets and mouths locked in perpetual screams. Since she'd likely have to face the Harbinger someday, she prayed the painter had taken artistic license with the creature.

She didn't recognize any of the other scenes painted on the walls. Though she suspected one of them portrayed the dwarven hero, Glonin Goldhand. In the painting, a diminutive warrior faced off against a dragon that blotted out the sun. When she had a chance, she'd have to ask Borim about the battle depicted on the wall. She needed to learn more about the dragons of this world, as one of her quests involved awakening them from their long slumber.

Amara glanced over at Jonas, who was sitting in the corner on a stool sharpening his blade. Beside him was her pet mimic, who had taken on the form of a wooden bench. Earlier, one of the Gnostics had attempted to take a seat on Mimi. She'd yelled in unison with Jonas and nearly scared the man witless. But the last thing she wanted was for her pet to accidentally eat one of their allies.

Amara glanced over at the door, watching for some sign of her companions and tapping her foot restlessly against the stone floor. Neither Borim nor Salamander had returned from inspecting the fortifications yet. They'd been at it for what felt like hours, and if she knew the dwarf, he was probably giving an earful to anyone who would listen about how to *properly* fortify the village.

She let out a sigh and leaned back in the chair. "What exactly do they expect me to do here?"

"I believe they expect you to act like the avatar," Jonas said without looking up. He drew the whetstone across his dagger's blade with a soft scraping noise. "Which means you must remain here until you're needed."

Amara stood up and pushed back her chair. Then she strode over to the entrance and peered outside. The village was a hive of activity, with people carrying supplies off the ships, while others worked feverishly on the palisade walls.

Everyone seemed to be busy except for her. "They could have at least let me heal the injured."

"They have healers of their own," Jonas replied. "And it's best to preserve your mana in case Malcheron decides to launch a counterattack."

"You know he's not going to do that," she replied sourly. "All the scouts have said that he's busy attacking the castle. We should be there fighting him right now, not sitting around twiddling our thumbs."

"As you know, his forces outnumber ours at least three to one." He placed his dagger aside and looked at her earnestly. "While I understand your distaste for sitting around while the residents of the castle fight for their lives, we must wait to face Malcheron until reinforcements arrive."

"Yes, I know." She sighed again as she paced across the room. "But I hate waiting here while people are dying. What if he destroys the core before we reach them? What if the keep falls quickly once the outer walls are taken?"

"I wish I had answers to your questions," Jonas replied. "However, in this case, we must have faith in Lady Ingrid and the defenders. Fortresses like Stout Oak Keep are designed to last for many months under siege. It is highly unlikely that it will fall before we come to its aid, unless the baroness does something foolish."

"I don't exactly have a lot of confidence in her," she replied darkly. "Knowing her, she'll sacrifice everyone else to save herself, just like when she blew the bridge. I never would have done that."

Jonas was silent for a moment as he looked troubled. Finally, he spoke. "I hope you haven't taken the wrong lessons from your recent victories. This upcoming battle will be unlike any we have faced in the past. From the accounts I've heard, the Chaos army has some truly powerful individuals. While you defeated a single commander in combat, their combined might will be fearsome. No matter what happens, you must not charge headlong into their ranks."

"Do I really have another option?" She frowned at Jonas. "If I don't fight as the avatar, then people are going to die."

"People are going to die regardless of what you do," he said. "This is war, and war always exacts a terrible toll. However, if you act rashly, then many more might die trying to save you. Please," he implored, "no matter what you do, remain with the reserves until you're needed."

"You know I can't do that." She glanced outside as the armored men tromped by. Then she turned back to face Jonas. "Only I can defeat Malcheron and the other commanders."

"If you'll allow us," Jonas continued, "I believe Frederick and I can handle Malcheron."

Amara shook her head. "I'll just destroy him with my avatar sword. It shouldn't take more than a few swings, and then you won't have to put yourself in danger."

"I believe you're underestimating the leader of the Chaos army," he replied with a gentle shake of his head. "And that is something you should not do."

"I doubt he'll be much of a challenge . . ." She cocked her head to the side and trailed off as she heard noise outside. A moment later, Anthon, the Gnostic who'd fished her out of the sea, appeared in the doorway. After he'd saved her, he'd been appointed as the informal liaison between the avatar and the Gnostic leaders.

"Riders in the distance," he said breathlessly as he leaned against the door-frame. "We're gathering our forces at the walls."

She turned to look at Jonas. "Riders must mean they're from a friendly force, right?" Aside from the lizards the kobolds rode on, she hadn't seen any horses among the Chaos army.

Jonas shook his head. "The Issurians ride a demonic breed of horse called Kartalians. They are far larger than normal warhorses and are rumoured to have endless stamina. They are said to breed vast herds of them in the northern steppes."

Amara gave Jonas a half smile. "Well, if it *is* an attack, at least I won't be so bored."

Jonas gave her a stern look but didn't say anything.

She ignored his disapproval at her half-hearted joke, checked the quiver of darts on her hip, and hefted her staff. Once she'd gather her meager belongings, she hurried over to the doorway. The sound of wood striking the stone floor made her turn, and she watched the wooden bench awkwardly trot after her. Eyes had sprouted from the backrest, and the bench bent in the middle with each step. Her pet looked truly horrifying.

Without waiting for Jonas, she hurried outside into the bright sunshine. Almost immediately, four Gnostics, each of them radiating an aura of immense power, took up positions around her. She'd argued against being appointed bodyguards, but Gnostic leaders had insisted. And now, everywhere she went, she always had a contingent of Gnostics watching her every step.

*It's not like anyone is going to attack me here.*

Amara did her best to ignore her chaperones as she hurried toward the palisade. About halfway down the street, Jonas finally caught up with her and shot her an annoyed glare. She simply shrugged, and they continued on in silence until they reached the village gates. Once there, she finally spotted Borim and Salamander. The dwarf and the girl stood on a platform placed behind the tall wooden spikes that made up the palisade.

Amara waved up at the dwarf, who grinned broadly upon seeing her. She walked over to the crude ladder leading up to the platform and then clambered up to join her friends. Once she reached the top rung, Borim offered her his hand and heaved her up. She stood up and brushed off her dress before gazing out across the surrounding countryside.

Just outside the walls was the half-finished ditch surrounding the village that the Gnostics had been digging. If anyone had been working on it when the riders had appeared, then they must have retreated inside the village, because there was no one out there now.

Her eyes scanned the hills until she spotted a cloud of frenzied dust emerging from a valley. She could barely make out the riders in the lead—all of whom appeared to be wearing black armor. Which probably wasn't a good sign.

"Those appear to be Issurians," Jonas said softly. "It seems we misjudged Malcheron's determination to take the keep. He likely seeks to wipe us out before reducing the fortress's outer walls."

Borim tugged on his beard. "A bold move, and it might work with the state of these fortifications. I built a better stronghold when I was a child. Of course, we had nests of karaxi and constant troglodyte invasions to deal with back then. Still, it was an impressive fort. My brother could shape stone, and when he—"

"Focus," Amara said, interrupting the dwarf. "We can hear about how you and your brother built a pillow fort later."

"Pillow fort!" Borim roared as a vein nearly bulged out of his head. "I'll have you know my fort held off a tribe of troglodytes for a week." He lowered his tone as he continued. "And it's not like we have anything better to do while we wait."

Amara pressed her lips together but had to admit the dwarf was right. There was nothing any of them could do until the approaching army arrived. As they drew closer, she found her grip tightening on her staff.

"They're humans," Jonas said, the relief evident in his voice.

Amara squinted at the distant figures. "How can you tell?"

"The Issurians don't normally wear helms with their horns," he replied. "And all of them are wearing full helmets."

Borim exhaled and placed the butt of his axe against the platform. "That's a bit of relief. I have an awful lot of work to do before this place could be called a true dwarven fortress. Of course, then it would need some cats, a few crazy relatives, and a sprinkling of ghosts. But it would be an embarrassment to all of dwarven kind if something I worked on fell to those Chaos bastards. That's not something I'd want my relatives to hear about."

"Who do you think they are?" Amara asked Jonas, ignoring the dwarf's ramblings.

"They're definitely not the knights," Jonas replied. "Even the lowliest foot-man of the Knights Tarsillan is said to wear their iconic golden armor."

"Then maybe someone from Oksberg?"

"That seems the likeliest explanation. Though we will have to wait and see."

As she continued to watch the approaching riders—numbering at least several hundred and riding in perfect formation—more Gnostics continued to stream toward the wall. Soon, the platforms and towers were bristling with armed men and women. And more than a few of them radiated with powerful auras as they drew upon their mana.

The mounted soldiers formed up in front of the village and then one cantered forward. He stopped a short distance from the gates and then removed his helm. An angular and scarred face peered up at the assembled Gnostic warriors on the walls.

Amara instantly recognized the man as Walter, the prince of Oksberg. He seemed to spot her at the same time and saluted her with a raised hand.

"I bring reinforcements, Avatar!" he shouted. "If you would open the gate, I'd like to converse."

She nodded and then turned to begin the descent down the ladder toward the ground below. It was awkward going with her staff, and she fought down the urge to simply drop it. But she didn't know how delicate magical items were in this world, and she didn't want to break her only weapon. Plus, she was sure the others would judge her if she just started tossing expensive things around.

Amara leapt the final distance to the ground and then jogged over to the gates. She nodded at the Gnostics manning it, and the three of them lifted the immense bar. After struggling to prop it up against the wall, they opened the gates a crack to allow her to slip through.

As she emerged on the other side, she smoothed down her dress, and then walked the short distance to where Walter waited. When she reached him, she smiled. "I didn't expect to see you for at least another week."

"I grew tired of waiting around for my father's barons to gather," he said as he dismounted. "So, I hired this mercenary group to accompany me north. They are the Black Company, and they are champing at the bit to fight against the Forces of Chaos. Of course, that might have something to do with the vast sum of gold I paid them."

"And what of your father?" she asked.

"He will still take at least a week to reach the keep, maybe longer." Wal-ter frowned. "Some of the barons are hesitant about marching northward after hearing about the Chaos army gathering beyond the walls. They'd rather defend their own lands when the horde marches south. But the fools don't understand. We can prevent the invasion if we save the Stout Oak Keep."

Amara tried to hide her disappointment at the news of Oksberg taking at least another week to reach them. Frederick and the Gnostic commanders all expected the outer walls to fall long before then. Though maybe the defenders of Stout Oak Keep would surprise them all.

The appearance of another rider galloping down the hill made them turn. "Is that one of yours?" Amara asked.

Walter shook his head.

They both stood there wordlessly as the rider approached. The horse staggered to a halt a few paces away from them as a young man wearing the robes of the Gnostics sawed on his reins. "Malcheron's banner flies above the walls of Stout Oak Keep!" the rider shouted. "The outer walls have fallen!"

Walter placed his helmet back on his head. "It seems I have arrived at a fortuitous time."

Amara pressed her lips together. With the outer wall fallen to Malcheron, they would need to march on the keep immediately—even if they were badly outnumbered.

And in that case, everything would rely on her avatar powers. She could only hope she was up to the task.

# CHAPTER 60

Amara gazed at the faces of those sitting in a loose circle around the main room of the abandoned church. The Gnostics had sent Anthon to lead their contingent, though several people with powerful auras stood silently behind them. The knights were represented by Frederick, and the freshly arrived Prince Walter spoke for Oksberg. Her companions had also been granted seats, though Salamander had pointedly refused one and insisted on standing at Amara's shoulder.

Frederick cleared his throat. "As I was saying, it would be best to march on Stout Oak Keep with all haste. The inner walls and the keep likely won't last long. No, they certainly won't. Not with the losses the defenders will have already taken."

"So you say," Anthon replied in a measured tone. The young man paused as one of the Gnostics behind him whispered into his ear. Then he turned and looked at Amara. "What do you believe we should do, Avatar? Our lives are yours."

She blanched under the stares of everyone in the room. Most of these men and women were hardened warriors. And while she'd gained some experience in fighting in this world, she had no idea about tactics or strategy. She wasn't ready to make a decision that could consign hundreds to their deaths.

Amara crossed her legs and leaned back slightly on the wooden chair. She took in a deep breath and glanced over at Frederick. "Do we have any chance of winning? I'm not about to order a suicide charge."

The old knight frowned, deep creases forming on his face. "I suppose it depends on the disposition of Malcheron's forces. If we catch him with his pants down and most of his troops inside the castle, then we can smash him like an oyster against a rock. But if he's prepared for our attack, then it will be a bloody affair."

She turned her gaze to Walter, who hadn't spoken yet. "And what do you think we should do?"

Walter rubbed a hand down his scarred chin. "While I'd prefer to launch a charge and drive those fiends out of my father's lands, I've fought enough of them to know such an attack would be folly. I suggest we march at nightfall and set up fortified positions near the keep before dawn. Malcheron will either have to give battle on our terms or withdraw from the siege."

Jonas nodded. "There is a hill overlooking the valley that will make a perfect spot to array our forces. And there's also a nearby forest where we can conceal your cavalry force."

"I expect to fight in the battle," Walter said, stiffly. "A prince of Oksberg does not hide like some common brigand."

Frederick shook his head at Walter. "You'd do well to listen to him—that young man speaks words of wisdom. A well-timed charge from a hidden force could turn the battle in our direction. And you might be the one to win the battle for us. Think of the glory and accolades you'd gain from that." When Walter nodded hesitantly at his words, Frederick continued, "Oh-ho, that got your attention, didn't it?"

A scowl spread across the prince's face. "Your addled mind will probably forget we're in the forest."

"There is always the chance of that." Frederick guffawed. "Yes, there certainly is."

Amara pressed her lips together. "But what about Malcheron? What if, while we're fighting his forces, he reaches the core powering the wall?"

"Destroying a core is no easy thing," Frederick mused. "However, if it appears the keep is on the verge of falling when we arrive, then we'll change our tactics. Best laid plans of gods and men and all that. I'm sure you have a similar expression on your world."

"I think our expression involves mice," Amara replied. "Though I understand what you're saying." She looked at all those assembled in the room. "Is everyone in agreement on the plan? We'll take up a position on the hill overlooking the keep and try to lure them into attacking us?"

Everyone nodded except for Anthon, who was busy listening to an older Gnostic woman whispering in his ear. Finally, he nodded his agreement. "Our lives are yours, Avatar. We will do our utmost to carry out your wishes."

"Good," Amara said uncertainly, still not comfortable holding so much power over the Gnostics. "Then we'll march before nightfall. Everyone should try to get some rest if they can."

"Rest?" Frederick grinned. "Oh-ho, with everything that has to be done? I'll rest when I'm dead."

"Let's hope that's a long way off," Amara said. "I don't want to lose anyone if we can avoid it."

"I must see to my horse before the battle," Walter said as he rose from his chair. "There is little rest in my future, either." He strode out of the room with his hand on the pommel of his sword.

The others took the prince's cue and filtered out of the room. After a few minutes, she was left alone with just the members of her party. The sensation of someone tugging on her sleeve made her look down to see Salamander staring up at her with big eyes. "What is it?"

"Did you find anyone to take the money to my parents?"

Amara shook her head. "No, since you're going to be taking it yourself. One of the merchant ships with the Gnostic fleet is carrying some refugees south, and they agreed to drop you off with an escort not far from Leissen. There's a risk they might be uncovered as a Gnostic ship, but it's safer than keeping you here for the battle."

"You're . . . you're sending me away?" Tears welled up in the girl's eyes. "Did I do something wrong?"

"No, of course not," Amara said hurriedly. "You just need to take care of your parents."

Borim strode forward and patted Salamander on the shoulder. "I've never met a fiercer warrior than you, and that's coming from a dwarf. Hurry back to rejoin us when you're done. You'll always have a spot fighting at my side."

Salamander dried her tears with the back of her hand. "I'm not leaving. What if you need me? How many times have I saved you?" She paused to count. "It feels like a lot."

"I'll be fine," Amara said in a soothing tone. "This is best for everyone."

"I'm not going," Salamander replied stubbornly. It was clear from the look on her face she was digging her heels in. "They said everyone is doomed if you die. Remember? So, I need to keep my parents safe by keeping you alive. And that's final. Find someone else to bring the gold to them. That's what you promised."

"Wait." Borim perked up. "Did I hear something about gold?"

Amara winced at the mention of the money they'd taken from Ackley. She hadn't found the time to broach the subject with the group yet. And she hoped they wouldn't get upset she'd hidden so much money from them. "Salamander took the gold Ackley offered us at the dungeon. She's going to use it to pay off her parents' debts."

"I see," Borim said, tugging on his beard. "Then that's money well spent, in my opinion."

Amara raised her brow at the dwarf's reaction. She thought he would put up more of a fuss about wanting his share of the gold. Clearly, she'd underestimated him.

"I agree," Jonas added. "There's no better use for gold than helping out a group member's family."

Salamander crossed her arms and glared up at Amara. "Well? Are you going to let me stay?"

Amara looked at Jonas, who simply shrugged. She hated bringing Salamander into a battle, but she also didn't want to force the girl to leave. She had a feeling that Salamander would never forgive her if she did that. "Fine, you can stay with us. My position is in the rearguard anyway, so you should be safe there."

"And I'll be watching over you as well," a voice said from across the room.

Amara turned to see Emmaline standing in the doorway, with Noah looming over her shoulder. As usual, the priestess had a sour look on her face. Behind them stood Harold, the pig farmer, looking decidedly uncomfortable in the company of the other two.

"I'm only doing it to save Lady Ingrid." Emmaline scowled before she continued. "Plus, the fact you made me take this stupid oath. And I'll have you know you can't keep avoiding me. Don't you know I have to make sure you're alright or it drives me insane?" Her expression hardened. "Unless you like doing that to me, that is."

Before Amara could reply, Noah took a step forward and crossed his arms. "I would like to pledge myself to you as well, Avatar. Lady Ingrid must be saved, and I wish to offer my blade for the task."

"Are you fully recovered?" she asked Noah. The last time she'd seen him, he'd been lying in bed trying to recover his strength.

"I am fit to fight," the knight replied. "And I will make those foul Issurians pay for what they did."

Harold ran a hand through his thinning hair. "I can't offer as much as these two, but I'll stand with you. And the others from the village want to help as well. We'll all keep you safe."

"Thank you, Harold," she replied with a smile. She felt touched that he still wanted to protect her after everything they had been through. "When we march later, I'd like you at my side. And you as well, Noah." She raised her brow at the priestess. "Emmaline, I suppose I don't have much choice with you."

"You're the one who made me take the cursed oath," Emmaline replied with a toss of her hair. "Perhaps you should have just trusted me instead and then we wouldn't be stuck together."

"After you tried to have me murdered?"

"Are you really still going on about that?" Emmaline rolled her eyes. "Don't you think it's time to move past those trifles?"

Amara sighed. The priestess had been much more agreeable when she first arrived in the camp. But Emmaline was right. There was more important business to attend to than Emmaline's murderous impulses. Instead, she turned back to face Harold. "Go and get everyone ready to march. And try to get some sleep if you can."

"As you wish, Avatar." Harold started to bend at the waist in an awkward attempt at a bow before she held up her hand to stop him.

"Don't you start doing that, too."

"Whatever you say." Harold gave her a broad grin before he turned on his heel and hurried out the door.

Noah gave a stiff bow next, and then shepherded Emmaline out of the room, leaving Amara alone with her group once more.

"I suppose we should all try to eat and get some sleep before nightfall," Amara said as she tugged on a lock of her hair. "It's probably going to be a long night."

"Come on, Salamander." Borim lightly touched the girl's arm. "Let's go grab some grub. And then maybe we can find somewhere quiet to hole up until it's time to leave."

The promise of food was all it took to entice Salamander to go with him, and the dwarf traipsed out of the main room of the church with the girl hot on his heels. When Borim reached the door, he ushered Salamander outside before he leaned his head back in to wink at them.

As Amara watched the dwarf leave, she found herself wondering what he'd meant by the wink. But the question faded from her mind as she found her gaze once again drawn to the ancient heroes depicted on the walls. When she faced the Forces of Chaos, would she measure up to the feats of the heroes in the past? Or would she fail everyone in this world who she cared about?

"I believe in you," Jonas said simply, as if he could read her thoughts. "And by this time tomorrow, Malcheron and his host will have been banished from the North."

"I wish I had your confidence," she replied as she pressed her lips together. "Every time I use my avatar form, it nearly kills me."

"The advancement of your soul should allow you to use the spell more effectively now." Jonas drew a dagger and spun it in his palm. "And trust in those under your command. Some of the most powerful Gnostics casters in existence have arrived from the South."

Amara opened her mouth to reply, but then froze as she felt Jonas's fingers brush the back of her hand. She glanced up in surprise to see his eyes peering deeply into her own.

"This may be the last night we have together," he said haltingly. "I . . . I would be remiss if I didn't say I had developed feelings for you."

The memory of him bringing the flowers immediately flashed through her mind. Obviously, he'd been trying to work up the courage to say something to her for quite some time now.

Without thinking, she intertwined her fingers through his and smiled shyly at him. She hadn't had much experience with this sort of thing back home. And certainly less than a noble like him would have had. But during their time together, she'd felt a growing fondness for him. And judging by the way her heart was beating excitedly in her chest, it had recently blossomed into something more.

Amara inched closer to Jonas, unsure of what she should do. His hand felt warm and rough in her grip. But it also just felt *right*.

When he stepped forward as well, she stood on her tippytoes and angled her head back to peer up into his eyes. As she did, Jonas leaned down, his lips inching closer to her own.

The sound of the door banging open made her flinch away from Jonas. She stepped back and glanced over to see Salamander standing in the entryway with a surprised look on her face.

"I . . . uhh . . . found some food for you," Salamander muttered, shuffling her feet. She held a few links of sausages in her hands.

Borim appeared a moment later, huffing, as he skidded to a stop behind the girl. "Sorry. This wee lass got away from me." He glowered at Salamander, his eyes dark beneath his bushy brow. "What did I tell you about them wanting to be alone? I swear you're more hard-headed than a dwarf."

Borim escorted Salamander back out of the room—the girl protesting the entire way—leaving them alone once more. But the spell had been broken, and neither of them spoke for a long time.

"I suppose we should go get some dinner," Amara said without meeting Jonas's gaze.

"As you wish," he replied, taking a step back from her.

Together, they walked out of the room, the silence stretching out between them. She desperately wanted to recapture what she'd felt only a few moments earlier, but she had no idea how to do so. After hesitating for a moment outside of the dilapidated church, she set out at a brisk walk in the direction of the Gnostic camp.

As she moved through the throngs of soldiers and peasants preparing for the march, her thoughts of Jonas faded away, replaced with worries for the coming day. Even if she had a chance to rest, she doubted she would be able to get any sleep.

It was going to be a very long night.

# CHAPTER 61

The dawn broke cold and gray over the forested hills surrounding Stout Oak Keep, and the clouds, which had been threatening to storm for several days, hung low and dark in the sky. The forces of the Gnostics had split into three columns and formed up overlooking the ancient fortress. Below them, the Chaos army stirred from within their fortified camp, which they had constructed just outside the village of Fusson.

Amara stared blearily down at Stout Oak Keep and assessed the damage that had been done to the walls. In several places, great gouges had been carved into the gray stone, and gaping holes had been blasted in more than a few sections. The shattered remains of ladders and other siege equipment littered the ground leading up to the fortress, and a makeshift bridge stretched across the rushing waters of the river.

According to the scouts, the assaulting force had frozen the river to allow them to cross and attack the castle. And once the outer walls had been taken, the kobolds had started rebuilding the destroyed bridge. Lady Ingrid's act of blowing the span and abandoning the peasants to their fate had only bought the keep a few additional days.

*What a waste,* Amara thought angrily. *She never should have left her people outside of the walls.*

Frederick stamped his feet beside her and rubbed his hands together. "Oh-ho, what a sight to behold," he said. "I never thought I'd face a Chaos army in battle before my watch with the knights ended."

"I should be fighting at the front," Amara replied, before adding, "as should you with your abilities."

"Now, now," Frederick replied, squinting at the army forming up in the valley below. "The reserve is an important part of the army. They're often thrown into the thickest fighting and regularly decide the battle. Before the day is done, we'll have spilled some blood. I promise you that."

Amara frowned, but didn't reply. She, along with her party and several hundred others, were positioned behind the center column of their force. When the Chaos army attacked, they would be well back from the fighting. Which seemed like a foolish decision, since her avatar abilities could easily sweep most of the army from the field.

"I'm with Amara," Borim tugged on his beard. "The rear of an army is only fit for washerwomen and blacksmiths, not warriors like us. I swear, if my axe doesn't taste blood today . . ." His threats devolved into grumbles.

Jonas spun a dagger around on his palm before shoving it back into the sheath on his belt. "I believe there will be more than enough blood to go around for everyone here. The Gnostics are heavily outnumbered, and even our favorable position may not be enough to counter the Chaos army's numbers."

"Well, aren't you a cheerful one," Borim rumbled. "And no stinking kobolds are going to beat them. Not with a dwarf on their side."

Upon hearing Jonas's words, Amara inspected the hasty defenses the Gnostics had erected under the cover of darkness. Thanks to Walter and his riders, they'd intercepted several Chaos scouts and had arrived undetected on the hill above the fortress. Working quickly, the Gnostics had dug shallow pits on the slope to break up any charge, and sharpened stakes had been cut and placed in front of their lines. It probably wouldn't do much to stop an ogre, but it might help.

*At least I hope it will.*

Amara nervously checked the darts in her quiver for what felt like the hundredth time. Then she inspected her staff to make sure it was in working order. But like the previous ninety-nine times, both were fine.

"It's the waiting that gets you," Borim grumbled. "The battle itself is fine, but even the stoutest dwarf gets the jitters beforehand. Did I ever tell you about the time I faced off against a karaxi queen?"

Amara shook her head and then tried to concentrate on the dwarf's story as his gravelly voice droned on. But her attention kept wavering as she watched the Chaos army form up below. And more concerningly, she spotted a force of Issurians streaming across the bridge toward the fortress.

The dwarf's words suddenly trailed off and he hefted his axe. "Here they come."

Amara glanced back to see that a band of ogres—numbering at least one hundred—had formed up in front of the ranks of the Chaos army. After a brief struggle, which saw one ogre lose its head, the remaining charged in their direction.

"What was that about?" she asked, stunned. "Why did they just kill one of their own?"

Borim shrugged. "That one probably challenged the battle plan. Ogres are always fighting for dominance in their bands. It would be more of a surprise if one of them *didn't* get their head lopped off beforehand. At least it means Mal-cheron doesn't have too much control over them. It's good news for us."

Amara pulled out a dart from her quiver as the ogres stampeded up the hill. Even from this distance, she could feel the soft vibrations of the earth from their heavy footfalls. And as they drew nearer, she realized the sheer size of them. The creatures stood at least twice the height of a man and appeared far heavier.

The ogres' bellowing made her flinch, and she saw the same reaction from the Gnostics bracing for the charge. Most of those in the front ranks wielded oversized spears, which Jonas had called pikes. Even with the new weapons, she still didn't see how the townspeople could stand against the ogres.

She took a step forward, preparing to call upon her avatar spell. If she didn't act now, then the Gnostics would be ground to a paste under the ogres' heavy boots. She had to help them.

"Have faith," Frederick said, putting a hand on her shoulder to stop her. "The ogres' charge is only effective if the opposing force breaks in fear. Not even an ogre is stupid enough to impale itself on a pike. At least I don't think so. Hmmm . . . now, where did I put my halberd?"

Amara didn't bother telling the knight his weapon was in his hand. He'd fig-ure it out soon enough. She stood transfixed as the ogres drew closer and closer to the Gnostic center. An unsettling, throaty chant emerged from the creatures as they broke into a trot, the sound resonating across the valley.

She held her breath as the ogres reached the army, but then exhaled with relief as the front ranks of the huge creatures skidded to a stop. Then the Gnostics let out a war cry, and advanced with lowered pikes, forcing the creatures to give ground. A few of the ogres swatted at them with primitive clubs, but it seemed that Frederick was right—they couldn't break the line as long as the Gnostics stood firm.

But it wasn't long before the cries of the injured and dying echoed across the hilltop. The ogres in the rear hurled heavy rocks into the ranks of the pike-men. And the Gnostic archers responded with a shower of arrows. Both sides suffered casualties, but the Gnostics had the worst of it. The rocks tore through the tightly packed pikemen, but even in the face of terrible losses, they didn't waver. Once again, she had to resist the temptation to leap forward and help with the healing.

"I hate being stuck in the rear," she grated. "I need to do something to help."

"This is just the first phase of the battle," Frederick said. "Oh-ho, you will certainly be needed before long. Just be patient, Avatar."

Another hail of arrows struck the ogres, and one of the smaller ones turned and fled. One fleeing creature triggered a flight from those nearest it, which quickly devolved into a complete rout. The ogres left behind half a dozen of their wounded in their haste to escape.

At the sight of the incapacitated creatures, Gnostic swordsmen and spellcasters rushed forward and mercilessly dispatched the injured trying to crawl after their fleeing companions.

"Not a bad start," Borim mused aloud. "About thirty of ours for a dozen ogres."

Frederick nodded. "It's definitely promising that they didn't break. Not up to the standard of the knights, mind you, but there's something to be said about religious fanatics."

"There are people dying out there!" Amara exclaimed. "I'd hardly call it a *good* start. And they're dying for me."

Jonas shook his head. "They're giving their lives to protect their families and friends to the south. If we don't win here, then all is lost. None of their deaths are on you."

"But I can do more," she protested. "I could have probably defeated those ogres on my own."

Frederick raised a shaggy eyebrow. "And when the commanders arrive, and you've expended all of your mana fighting their foot soldiers? What then?" He patted her shoulder comfortingly. "Have no fear. Your talents will be needed soon enough."

Amara grumbled in reply and crossed her arms. While she knew Frederick spoke the truth, she still didn't like letting anyone die.

As they spoke, the fleeing ogres reached the bottom of the hill, and one of their kind—far larger than the others—stomped forward. Without hesitation, it disemboweled the first ogre to run away. As the fatally wounded creature collapsed, the commander thrust back up the hill.

"That must be the ogres' commander," Frederick muttered. "Oh-ho, I'll surely need my halberd for that beast of a creature. Now, which of you rapscallions hid my weapon?"

Borim scowled at the ancient knight. "It's in your hand, you senile old fool."

Frederick's eyes opened wide with surprise. "So it is. But no need to be rude. Otherwise, I might be tempted to call you a foul tempered, pint-sized, hairy goblin."

"Why, you . . ." Borim sputtered, stabbing his finger in the knight's direction. "You take that back right now!"

"Enough," Jonas said harshly. "Save your aggression for the Chaos army."

After another disemboweling by their commander, the ogres turned and reluctantly trudged back up the hill. This time, they were pelted with arrows, javelins, and spells. The front line almost seemed to melt from the attacks as more Gnostics targeted the creatures. After another dozen had fallen, the ogres seemed to have had enough. They turned and fled before even reaching the Gnostic lines. But they didn't head back toward the Chaos army and instead sprinted in the direction of the forest.

A ragged cheer went up from the Gnostics at the sight of the ogres retreating. However, it quickly petered out as the main force of the Chaos army started tromping forward. A screen of goblins moved in front, while the center was composed of heavily armored Issurians. And the two wings on either side were made up of kobolds. To the rear, several hundred mounted Issurians, along with what looked like dwarves, stood in reserve.

The Chaos army looked insurmountably large, and Amara once again felt nervous about their chances. "How far away did you say the knights were?" she asked Frederick.

"The last I spoke to them, they were at least twenty leagues away," he replied. "And I don't know the location of the fleet. But they know of our situation, and knowing them, they'll probably be doing forced marches."

"Is there any chance of them reaching us in time?"

The old knight shrugged. "Only the gods know."

"Great," she muttered. "And Oksberg probably isn't even coming to help." At least the Black Company that Walter had hired was hidden in the nearby forest. For a moment, she feared the ogres would stumble into their concealed force, but thankfully the ogres angled away from the horsemen's position as she watched.

Amara turned back to view the Chaos army surging up the hill. The Issurians took the lead, with the wings of the kobolds lagging slightly behind. As they drew ever closer, she found herself holding her breath again. The long climb up the hill should tire them out, which might give the Gnostics a better chance at victory. But there just seem to be *so* many of them.

And she realized with a start that she wasn't the only one filled with trepidation at the sight of the enormous army. Several of the Gnostic pikemen had taken a step back, and others cast fearful looks around.

"I have to do something," she said, lowering her staff slightly.

"Wait," Jonas called out as he reached toward her.

Before anyone could stop her, she raced forward, moving past several of the Gnostics who had already turned to flee. She pushed her way through the ranks of men and women until she reached the front of the army and then slowed. From behind her, she could hear her companions shouting her name. But she couldn't hide in the rear while her army fell apart.

At her appearance, a deathly silence fell over the Gnostics. She had planned to give an epic speech to stir bravery in their hearts, but with had hundreds of eyes upon her, she couldn't think of any words.

She cleared her throat and looked around. Then she raised her voice so all could hear. "The fate of the world is on our shoulders. If we fail here, then everything is lost!" The Gnostics merely blinked up at her, but at least they had stopped retreating.

Amara struggled to think of anything further to say. Her mind was blank with fear and adrenaline. With words failing her, she reached for the mana to cast *Illusory Disguise.* Golden wings sprouted from her back and a flaming sword appeared on her belt. As the pure white armor formed over her body, she heard a full-throated cheer go up from the Gnostics. Only a handful had seen her transformation in the village, and her appearance seemed to have done what her words couldn't to bolster their spirits.

She turned and planted her feet as she waited for the advancing Issurians. While she didn't want to cast her avatar spell yet, she could at least boost her army's morale. No matter what Jonas and Frederick said, the Gnostics had to know the gods had returned to help them.

# CHAPTER 62

Borim raced after Amara, cuxrsing her for being so reckless. Jonas sprinted past him, and he lowered his head and pumped his arms in an effort to catch up with the rogue. But the dwarf couldn't match the man's long stride, and he was quickly left in the dust. He'd never understand why the gods had seen fit to make humans so unnaturally tall and gangly. They were like large, flightless birds that had been stretched out by one of the ancient gnome machines deep beneath the Dragonspine Mountains.

He let out a grunt as Emmaline passed him as well. The priestess looked panicked as she careened toward Amara, who was standing out in front of the army in avatar form. Most likely, every enemy caster would be targeting the Trickster Cleric right now. And if the party didn't reach her in time to throw up some defenses, then Amara was about to be obliterated.

The air tearing asunder made Borim skid to a surprised stop, along with the others. He shielded his eyes as a dozen spells—a blinding collection of lightning, shadows, and ice—slammed into Amara. The Trickster Cleric disappeared under the assault, and when the air cleared, only a crater remained where she'd been standing.

"No," Borim murmured, stricken at seeing his friend reduced to ashes. "Why did she do that?"

Beside him, Emmaline fell to her knees, and Jonas took a wobbly step forward before placing both hands on his head. A deathly silence fell over the army as everyone stared at the smoking crater which seconds early had been the avatar of Melischar.

Borim frowned as a handful of Gnostics cheered from behind him. He spun around, ready to hurl a few choice invectives at the fools applauding their own imminent demise. How could they not realize they were doomed without the avatar?

Then he spotted Amara standing in front of the column, completely unscathed. Not even a single hair on her head was out of place. As he watched, several Gnostics spellcasters hurried over to erect shields around the Trickster Cleric. How in the world had she survived?

*Just how powerful is that avatar spell of hers?*

By all rights, she should have been obliterated by the number of spells hammering her position. And yet, she'd shrugged it off as if it was nothing.

Borim pushed back his helmet to scratch his head and then jogged back toward Amara. He was joined by Emmaline and Jonas, who seemed to be in a fierce competition with each other to see who could look more relieved. If he had to choose, he'd say that Jonas was winning handily. But then again, only a blind man could miss the way the rogue looked at the Trickster Cleric.

When he reached Amara, he tugged on his beard. "How in the name of Glonin Goldhand did you survive that, lass? I thought you were a goner for sure."

Amara gave an awkward shrug before lowering her voice to a whisper so no one else nearby could hear. "I may not have really been standing there."

"Then . . ." Borim continued, the truth dawning on him.

"Yes," she replied with a mischievous twinkle in her eye. "I used my new spell, *Duplicate Self,* and then *Cloak of Shadows* to slip away. It worked surprisingly well."

Borim guffawed as he slapped his knee. "And you made a bunch of their spellcasters waste a barrel-load of mana. Nicely done."

Emmaline trotted up beside him, obviously trying to maintain a more dignified pace than her headlong dash when she'd thought Amara was in danger. "Don't ever do that again!" she scolded the cleric. "I nearly ruined my dress running through the mud like a common peasant."

"Oh no," Amara said, feigning horror. "Is your garment alright?"

"Yes," Emmaline sniffed, ignoring the sarcasm. "It's nothing a good washerwoman can't fix. But no thanks to you!"

Jonas moved through the Gnostics to stand beside the priestess. "I never thought I would agree with Emmaline. However, exposing yourself to the enemy was reckless beyond comprehension."

"I had to do something," Amara said, waving her hand at the Gnostics. "They looked like they were ready to break. And I was never in any real danger."

Amara continued in a low voice so the nearby Gnostics couldn't hear. "As I was telling Borim, I was never actually there. It was my *Duplicate Self* the spellcasters were targeting. And now they'll think their powers can't hurt me. Plus, after seeing my little display, it doesn't look like any of the Gnostics want to run now."

Borim chuckled as Jonas relaxed slightly, while Emmaline looked even more annoyed. "Don't feel bad, lad. I thought she was a goner, too."

Emmaline raised her chin and glared down at Amara. "You made me dash into danger while you weren't even there? I regret this oath more every day."

Jonas gave Amara a wan smile. "I suppose I'm glad to see you using your skills so effectively."

Borim pointed down the hill at the approaching wall of Issurians. "We might not be able to stay out of danger much longer. But you stiffened the Gnostic's spines, at least. Bunch of pansies, all wanting to run away at the first sight of an approaching army . . ."

The arrival of Frederick made him trail off. The old man's expression was like thunder, and he pointed a quivering finger at Amara. "What part of *stay with the reserve* didn't you understand, young lady? If I had my halberd . . ."

"I had no choice," Amara replied quickly. "But I'll come back with you now."

Borim followed Amara and the old knight as they strode back toward the reserve. Every day, he found himself growing more impressed with this girl. Maybe, when this was all over, she could even help him with the problems plaguing his homeland. Now that he knew the Chaos Gods had returned, he suspected there was something sinister about the changes he'd witnessed in his clan.

*Those blasted Chaos Gods must have something to do with the rot spreading through the Dragonspine Mountains.*

The thought sobered him, but he pushed it down ruthlessly. He wouldn't be able to do anything to save his town if he didn't survive this battle first. Once his axe had brought down a few thousand Issurians, then he could bring up the idea of traveling to his homeland to free it from the darkness threatening it.

*And then maybe I can get a proper drink again.*

With that pleasant notion, he hefted his axe and watched the Issurians struggle up the steep side of the hill. After what felt like an eternity, the two armies finally crashed together with war cries and the din of steel striking steel. Before long, the reserve would be needed, and when that time came, Borim would be ready.


"The center column is breaking!" Jonas shouted to Frederick. "We must help them!"

"Not yet," the old man replied in a quiet voice. "The Gnostics must hold for a little longer. Oh-ho, they're made of stronger stuff than you think."

Jonas spun a dagger around in his hand, he alternating between glancing over at the Gnostic's lines bulging from the pressure of the Issurians to Amara standing nearby. While he knew the time to fight was near, he dreaded the thought of her placing herself in danger again.

When she'd disappeared under the barrage of spells, it had felt like a part of him died. The thought of never seeing her again had been too terrible to contemplate. And in his grief, he'd been close to hurling himself against the Chaos army alone, and unleashing his full power—something he'd avoided up until this point.

The air above them was like an endless meteor shower in the night as Chaos spells exploded against the magical shields protecting their position. Most of the Gnostic spellcasters were kept busy throwing up defenses to prevent the lines of soldiers from being swept away by ice and darkness. Still, even with their skills, a handful of enemy spells had slipped through during the course of the battle and had left carnage in their wake.

"We must attack now," Jonas urged the old knight. "The lines will break at any moment."

Amara twirled a strand of hair around her finger as she stared transfixed at the battle. "I think Jonas is right . . ." She trailed off as a horn blast sounded across the valley. Another horn blast joined the first, and then dozens more followed it.

"Oh-ho, there's our cue." Frederick said as he tore off his clothing. Almost immediately, he began to swell in size, until the fragile old man had once again become a musclebound monster towering over the peasants and soldiers in the reserve. "The fate of our world hangs in the balance!" he boomed, all trace of his usual dottering confusion gone. "The Forces of Chaos seek to bring down the Wall and spread destruction across all the lands. Everything will be decided in this moment. The gods will it!" Then he threw his head back, and with a roar that shook the valley, shouted, "Charge!"

Jonas watched as the giant man turned and stomped in the direction of the Issurians. Each footfall shook the earth, and the ancient knight continued to grow until he dwarfed an ogre.

With a deep breath, Jonas drew both of his daggers and activated his *Soul Reaper* spell. As he did, the world subtly shifted around him. His vision darkened slightly, and the ghostly trails binding together all life became visible. With a simple touch, he knew he could steal someone's very life essence and store it away for later use. And after all the battles recently, his reserves were *very* full. The thought of using the stolen souls sickened him, but his skills might be needed in this battle.

As the reserve force charged forward with Frederick in the lead, Prince Walter's cavalry issued forth from the forest. The sounds of hoofbeats filled the air as the riders in front blew on their horns. They galloped across the hillside and crashed into the exposed flank of the kobold wing engaged with the Gnostics pikemen.

Jonas didn't have time to watch how the cavalry charge played out—he needed to focus on the melee in front of him. He drew upon his mana as he raced after the old knight. After a few paces, Amara, Borim, and Salamander appeared on his right. And then Emmaline and Noah took up positions on his other side. From behind him, he could hear the others in the reserve letting loose war cries as they charged after Frederick.

He crashed through the rear of the failing Gnostic line and pushed his way toward the advancing Issurians. When he reached the battlefront, he found himself surrounded by the dead and dying. The Gnostic ranks looked like they were on the verge of collapsing, and the ground was slick with blood.

Off to the right, a huge Issurian was carving through men and women with a shadowy blade. Their eyes met, and Jonas raised his daggers in challenge. This Chaos beast would be the perfect opponent for him.

Jonas stepped forward to face the imposing Issurian, but a blast of searing flames made him recoil. As the air cooled, he shot a glare over at Salamander, who had unleashed the spell uncomfortably close to his head. When she shrank back from his look, he reminded himself that his dark-eyed appearance probably frightened her.

He turned his attention back to the Issurian, and his eyes widened with shock as he saw the dark blade slicing toward him. He barely had time to throw himself to the side to avoid near-certain death. But the tightly packed Gnostic ranks didn't give him enough space to evade cleanly, and he collided with an injured Gnostic; the man stumbled forward, holding onto the bloody stump of his arm.

The Issurian swung again, and his blade cleanly sliced the wounded Gnostic in half. The two pieces of the man collapsed to the ground with a disgustingly wet sound as entrails spilled out.

Jonas cursed bitterly at seeing the Issurian slay the wounded soldier, but before he could avenge the man's death, the swirling battle forced him away from his opponent.

He found himself standing among a line of Gnostic spearmen, and he slashed out at any Issurians who came too close. As the lines surged together again, he dodged an Issurian's clumsy sword swing and drove his dagger into the horned creature's neck. His blade sank deep into the flesh, and a surge of power infused his limbs.

Before he could process the soul energy, he watched with awe as a screaming Issurian flew through the air overhead. He turned to see where it had come from and witnessed Frederick rampaging through the Chaos army's line. There had to be more to the knight's spell than simply growing larger, as the old knight was shrugging off blows from swords and axes that would have felled an ogre. And he was using his fists like clubs to crush any who came within reach.

The chaotic battle lines shifted again, and he found himself once more facing the Issurian with the shadowy blade. This time, he directed a fraction of the soul energy he'd harvested into his leg muscles. With an explosive push, he launched himself at the Issurian.

He angled his body to avoid a hasty sword swing, the Issurian clearly shocked by his aggressive attack, and then landed lightly in front of the creature. As his feet touched the ground, he sprang up and plunged both daggers into his opponent's throat. Barely a sound escaped from its lips before its body shriveled up like an ancient Tohkarian mummy.

Jonas ripped his blades free in a spray of dark ichor, and then searched for Amara. During the fighting, they'd been pushed apart, and he needed to make sure she was alright. He spotted her a short distance away, with Borim shielding her and Salamander spraying fire at any Chaos creature who came too close.

He took a step in her direction but stumbled as the ground shifted underfoot. A moment later, an impossibly loud *boom* filled the air, followed by a shockwave that blasted across the hillside. The fighting slowed as both sides retreated a few paces to peer in the direction of the blast.

In the distance, Jonas could see a mushroom-shaped cloud of smoke rising from inside the castle walls. As the smoke billowed in the strong breeze, he realized a portion of the inner wall had simply disappeared. To make matters worse, the front of the keep had collapsed as well, exposing the interior of the ancient building.

With growing horror, he realized that Malcheron had breached the inner defenses of the castle. And there was no way they could stop him from reaching the core in time. Galoth's Wall would fall, and doom would descend upon the southlands.

They had failed.

# CHAPTER 63

Amara mentally ordered her *Divine Weapon* to take up a defensive position in front of her as the Issurian soldiers retreated down the hill. To her right, Prince Walter's cavalry charge had shattered the kobolds, and the black-armored riders were slashing at the remaining creatures as they fled. But the rest of the Chaos army was withdrawing in good order, moving in formation to block the road to the keep.

She scanned the devastated ranks of the Gnostics, searching for her companions. During the confusion of battle, she'd been separated from her party. She spotted Frederick first, his gigantic form looming above the heads of a group of gnostic soldiers.

She sprinted over in the old knight's direction, intent on pressing him to continue the attack. If they didn't stop the retreating Chaos army, then all would be lost. As she ran, she did her best to ignore the carnage littered around her. Hundreds of Gnostics and nearly twice that number of Issurians had met their end on the hill. It was as if a malicious giant had broken its toys and scattered them across the land.

Although she wanted nothing more than to stop and help the injured, Amara didn't dare slow her pace—not while Malcheron had access to the core that powered Galoth's Wall. Frederick had implied it wasn't easy to destroy, but if the Chaos army succeeded, then all was lost.

And if this world fell, then Earth was next.

Amara glanced over in the direction of the castle again and winced at the sight of the destruction. A thick cloud of dark smoke still hung over the keep. And through the haze, she could make out great gaps in the walls. The Chaos army must have used all the gunpowder they had remaining to destroy the fortifications.

She tore her gaze away from the ruins of Stout Oak Keep and focused on Frederick. The old knight had noticed her barreling in his direction. As she neared him, he began to shrink, until he returned to his normal, stooped self.

"We have to attack," she gasped as she skidded to a halt in front of him. "If we don't stop Malcheron, then he's going to bring down the Wall."

Frederick combed his fingers through his beard. "Oh-ho, I'd like nothing more than to renew our attack. Well, I'd like to find my halberd, but then I'd like to stop Malcheron. Hmm . . . or should I stop that horned fiend first, and then find my halberd?" He stared at her with bleary eyes. "What was I saying? And who are you again?"

She regarded the wrinkled old man with shock. He seemed genuinely confused this time. Did casting his spell somehow alter his mental state? Or had he simply pushed himself too far?

With a sigh, she pushed back a strand of loose hair behind her ear. Then she spotted the Gnostic, Anthon, standing a short distance away. Maybe he could order his people to charge. If they attacked now, then they could cut their way through the Chaos army and reach Malcheron before it was too late.

"Take care of him," she said to a nearby Gnostic spellcaster, gesturing toward Frederick. The girl bobbed her head up and down before moving over to touch Frederick lightly on the shoulder.

Amara jogged over to Anthon, who was standing among a knot of the elder Gnostics. Most of them had been busy maintaining magical shields over the army until a few minutes ago, and their faces were haggard from the effort. The battle had been far too close, and everyone had pushed themselves to their limit. Amara barely had half her mana remaining, and she'd only kept so much in reserve in case she had to use her avatar form.

The young Gnostic man smiled at her approach, the strain clear on his face. "It is good to see you well, Divine—"

She held up a hand to interrupt him. "I want you to order the Gnostics to attack. Or if you can't, point me in the direction of someone who can."

The young man grimaced and rubbed a hand down his face. Stricken, he continued, "The army is heavily depleted, Divine One. Should you order us to charge, then we shall obey. However, there is little chance of victory. The steep hill gave us an advantage in the fight, and yet we were very nearly overrun. And many hundreds died . . ."

Amara hesitated at the man's words. Could she order her followers to launch a suicidal charge against the enemy? She swept her gaze over the hillside as she took in the surrounding carnage. Men and women with terrible injuries cried out for aid from the ground, while the handful of healers staggered around doing what little they could. And those few who weren't wounded stood with hollow expressions on their faces. Anthon was right—the Gnostics were a spent force.

"See to the wounded," she said gently. "And you all fought very bravely today. The gods would be proud of you."

Anthon let out a sigh of relief and then seemed to deflate. "As you wish, Divine One."

Amara spun on her heel and then dashed toward the front line. As she did, she pulled out the mana crystal from her pouch. Where she was headed, she was going to need all the mana she could get.

After a dozen paces, Mimi appeared at her side. The mimic had taken on its favored shape of a treasure chest again, and her pet's hide bristled with arrows. But thankfully, none of the missiles had penetrated Mimi's thick wooden shell.

"You need to stay here," Amara said without looking over at her pet. "Where I'm going, I can't keep you safe."

The mimic eyed her, and then simply averted its gaze. It continued along at her side as if it hadn't heard her. Apparently, her pet wasn't going to obey her orders.

"And where do you think you're going, lass?" a gravelly voice boomed out.

She turned to see Borim trotting in her direction, bloody axe in hand, with Salamander at his side. The dwarf had a wicked gash across his cheek, and blood dripped down from his split nose. His younger companion was untouched, though she looked pale and had dark circles under her eyes.

"I have to do this alone," she replied, continuing on without slowing.

"If you're about to hurl yourself at Malcheron, then you're not leaving me behind," Borim said gruffly. "There's glory to be won today!"

Salamander nodded her head solemnly. "I'm going, too. You're going to need me."

Amara stopped and threw up her hands. "I can't take you with me. And none of you are a match for Malcheron and his commanders. Don't you see I have to do this on my own?"

Borim planted his feet and glowered at her. "Better think up a new plan, then. Where you go, I go. And let me tell you, dwarves aren't easy to get rid of."

She bit down an angry retort when she spotted Jonas headed in their direction. Noah and Emmaline trailed after the rogue, both of them looking relatively unscathed from the battle. She immediately knew from their dark expressions that they suspected what she was planning.

Emmaline stopped a few paces away and put her hands on her hips. "Are you going to attempt to run off without me again?"

"I'm going to stop Malcheron," Amara replied in a low tone. "And I can't take any of you with me."

Jonas raised his eyebrow. "I understand you enjoy throwing yourself in to the maw of the dragon, Amara. But this is madness, even for you. May I remind you Malcheron is the leader of the entire *Chaos army?*"

"Do you have a better plan?" she shot back. "The Gnostics can't fight another battle. And if we don't reach Malcheron, then the core powering the Wall will be destroyed."

"How exactly do you plan on reaching the keep?" the rogue asked. "There are still several thousand Issurians and kobolds between you and its walls."

"I was going to use my *Cloak of Shadows*," she replied. "And then I'll defeat Malcheron in my avatar form."

Borim tugged on his beard and interjected. "Not the worst plan you've come up with. Still, not great. If I were you, I'd probably use a catapult to launch us there, and then some sort of gnomish parachute to float down inside the inner walls. Of course, I'd need some time to build all that . . ."

Amara held up her hand to stop anyone else from speaking. "If no one has a better plan, then I'm leaving. The longer we sit here arguing, the more likely they'll bring down Galoth's Wall."

Jonas unbuckled the pouch on his belt and then pulled out a radiant mana crystal. "Prior to the battle, I borrowed several of these from the Gnostics. And I believe your *Cloak of Shadows* spell can be extended to others, correct?"

"Yes," she replied slowly. "But it takes too much mana." Then her eyes fell to the pulsating gem. Could the crystals provide enough energy to get them through the enemy lines? Finally, she shook her head. "It's too dangerous. If I run out of mana before we reach the keep . . ."

Noah stepped forward. "I would risk anything to save the southlands and my Lady Ingrid. Should your spell fail to carry us to the keep, then I shall hold off the Chaos army. I swear you shall not fail in your task."

Borim tugged on his beard. "Better to have all of us along when you face that bastard Malcheron."

"I agree with our stout friend," Jonas said. "If you plan to face the leader of the army, then you will need our help."

"Don't you see!" she cried, pleading with them. "I can't lose any of you."

Jonas was quiet for a moment. "And do you think I could live without you?"

Borim nodded in agreement. "You're my friend and the leader of our party. I don't care about that hoity-toity avatar stuff, but I would never let a friend fight alone. No true dwarf would."

"You're *my* friend, too." Salamander smiled up at her, some of her exhaustion seeming to lift. "And you gave me the chance to save my parents. I'm not going to let some ugly horned guy hurt you."

Emmaline rolled her eyes and let out a long sigh. "I'm oath-bound to help, and truthfully, I don't really care for you. But I need your help to save Lady Ingrid."

Noah scowled at the priestess's words, but then, after a moment he added, "And you have my sword."

Amara felt a lump grow in her throat at her companion's words. She knew she couldn't speak without her voice cracking, so she simply nodded.

With nothing further to say, she turned and headed down the hill in the direction of the retreating Chaos army. The Issurians and kobolds had begun to reform their ranks near the road leading from Fusson to the fortress. From there, they probably hoped to block access to the keep where Amara could only assume Malcheron was hell-bent on destroying the core.

Amara angled her course slightly to head toward the river. Around them, dozens of Gnostics picked through the fallen. Some of them gathered arrows, while others looted the dead Issurians. More than a few hooted with excitement at finding something valuable. But they fell silent and stared at her with wide eyes as she approached.

She ignored the Gnostics, though some of them dropped to their knees at the sight of her, and picked up her pace. As she walked, she planned out her next steps in her mind. They would head toward the river and then skirt along the shore until they reached the bridge. Then, after crossing, they could slip inside the keep through one of the postern gates. If all went well, they might avoid the enemy army completely.

Noah slowed and drew his sword from the scabbard on his belt. The shining blade hissed as it slipped free. "It appears the enemy has spotted us."

Amara bit back a curse, watching as the Issurian cavalry cantered forth in her direction on their dark steeds. She'd hoped they would look unremarkable enough that the enemy army wouldn't pick them out on the hill. But the Gnostics kneeling as they passed had probably tipped off the Chaos army to her identity.

"Gather up!" she shouted. "I'll hide us with *Cloak of Shadows*."

The others drew closer, with Mimi in the center. "I need you to all hold hands," she said. "It's the only way the spell will work."

Emmaline grumbled, but after a moment, they were all holding hands. Once they had formed up, they looked at her expectantly.

Amara drew in a deep breath and then wove together her mana to cast *Cloak of Shadows*. As she did, she gripped a mana crystal tightly in her hand, the sharp edges digging into her palm. She still wasn't sure how much mana the spell would take if she used it on an entire group.

As the colors of the world shifted to shades of gray, she exhaled with relief. While the drain on her mana was significant, it was manageable. Once again, she was grateful that Frederick had taught her how to upgrade her soul.

With her group concealed, she set out at a brisk pace toward the keep. There she would finally meet Malcheron in battle, and the fate of all the southlands would be decided.

# CHAPTER 64

The strain on Amara's soul was quickly growing too much to bear, as she struggled to keep her group concealed with her *Cloak of Shadows* spell. On their way down the hill, they managed to elude the Issurian cavalry and reach the bank of the river undetected. But she'd already burned through one mana crystal, and her soul was nearly empty again. As she placed the spent crystal in her pouch and replaced it with the full one from Jonas, she searched for a clear path to the keep.

The bridge to Stout Oak Keep was only a short distance away, but the Chaos army was blocking any possible entry. Hundreds of Issurian warriors stood in tight lines on the span. And on the far side, a group of ogres blocked the shattered gates. Amara had no doubt even more powerful opponents awaited her if she made it inside of the keep.

She glanced over at the "Level Up" notification she'd received after the battle. For a second, she considered spending points on a new spell in the hopes of receiving something that would help. But with the safety of her entire party depending on her *Cloak of Shadows*, she didn't dare break her concentration. New spell or not, she needed to find a way inside, and fast.

"I shall handle them," Noah said, as though he had read her thoughts. "Once I have engaged the Issurians, then you will be free to reach the ogres on the far side."

"No one is asking you to sacrifice yourself," Amara whispered. "I'll think of something else."

Noah gave her a sad smile. "I would have died on that cross, but you gave me a second chance at life. It would be an honor to use it to protect the greater good."

"No, that isn't . . ." Amara trailed off in shock as Emmaline slipped out of the party's formation and popped into view in front of the entire Chaos army.

"I am truly sorry for what I did to you, Noah," Emmaline called out, as the air crackled around her with an immense amount of power. "And as for you, Avatar, prove your worth and save Lady Ingrid!" With these final words, the priestess called down a column of swirling light upon the Issurians. The spell hammered their formation and sent broken bodies flying through the air.

The priestess cried out as a javelin pierced her shoulder, but she didn't falter as she brought down another blinding attack on the Issurians.

"Time to move, lass," Borim whispered in an urgent tone. "Don't make her sacrifice for nothing."

Amara shook her head, still shocked at Emmaline's actions. But Borim was right—standing around gawking would help nobody. The priestess's attack had created a breach in the Issurians' lines. And the opportunity wouldn't last long.

She winced as she watched a volley of crossbow bolts tear into Emmaline. Though the priestess was bloodied and pierced by a dozen missiles, she still staggered onward somehow, sending spell after spell smashing into the tightly packed ranks of Chaos creatures.

As Emmaline finally collapsed with a guttural scream, Amara tore her gaze away. There was nothing she could do for the priestess without giving away her own position. She crept forward and threaded her way through the confused mass of Issurians before hurrying across the rickety span. The hastily built bridge seemed ready to collapse at any moment, the boards creaking underfoot and swaying wildly with every footfall.

Halfway across the bridge, a fat drop of rain splattered against Amara's forehead. The clouds had finally broken. The rain pattered against the wood underfoot, escalating into a deluge.

Amara shot one last look back at Emmaline, who had disappeared under a crush of Issurians, and then said a quick prayer under her breath for the priestess. She hadn't particularly liked the woman, but she had sacrificed herself to give them a chance and to make up for her past mistakes.

No one spoke as they lurched across the bridge and neared the massive ogres on the far side. Twelve of the great creatures had been left to guard the destroyed gateway. The sound of war cries made Amara look back, and behind her she could see hundreds of Issurians charging in their direction.

*I guess a priestess popping out of thin air gave away the fact that we were invisible.*

She pulled out another mana crystal from her pouch—leaving only one remaining to deal with Malcheron, if she even made it to the Chaos commander. As she did, the largest ogre snapped his head over in her direction. A ridiculously out-of-place golden monocle was perched on its hairy, brutish face—remarkably similar to the one Frederick had used to examine her soul.

Salamander recoiled as the creature swept its gaze over them. "I . . . I think it can see us."

"That is a magical device to spot mana!" Noah shouted. "To arms!"

Amara released her hold on Mimi and backpedaled away from the ogre. She swung her staff around as the creature let out an earthshaking roar. As she stared at her rune-covered weapon, Amara realized just how inadequate the staff was to fight a monstrous ogre. It would be like using a toothpick to hold off a bear.

She needed a new strategy. Fumbling for a dart from the quiver around her waist, she activated *Dart Deadeye.* She'd hope to save her Martial Ability for her battle with Malcheron, but the now that the ogres had spotted them, there was no option to hold anything back.

From behind her, Amara heard the earth rumble, and when she glanced over her shoulder, she witnessed Noah striking the pommel of his sword against the shore. The sandy ground broke open, and a length of the makeshift bridge collapsed into the river.

As the span disintegrated, the dozens of the Issurians that had been crossing the bridge fell into the water, their heavy armor dragging them beneath the surface. The rest, too far away to reach their drowning compatriots, stopped dumbly across the shore. Many of them shook their weapons at her, while other unlimbered bows and loaded crossbows.

She turned her attention back to the ogres and reared back to launch her first dirt. With a grunt, she hurled the missile at the closest ogre, which had lowered its head and was charging at her like an enraged bull elephant.

Amara held her breath as the projectile flew straight at the creature and then tore through the flesh on the side of its neck. A gush of blood shot out, showering the ground and nearby ogres. With a faltering step, the wounded creature slowed, and then stumbled to a stop. The blood continued to spray out of its neck like a morbid geyser.

She ignored the ogre as it dropped to all fours and tried to crawl toward her. Instead of finishing it off, she picked out her next target and grabbed another dart from her quiver.

Her group had split up to face the ogres. Borim was keeping a trio at bay with wild swings of his axe, while Salamander hurled streams of fire from behind him. One of the ogres was already ablaze, and another had blistering burns across its naked torso.

Jonas had activated his class spell and was moving through the towering creatures like a black-eyed reaper. As Amara watched, two ogres shriveled up into husks before collapsing to the ground. When one of them struck the hard-packed dirt, it burst into a cloud of dust, leaving behind only a collection of dried strips of flesh and diseased bones.

Meanwhile, her pet mimic was gnawing on one of the ogre's legs, hanging on with incredible tenacity despite its attempts to swat her off. The creature let out a roar of furious pain as Mimi ripped a bloody chunk from its calf.

When the ogre raised its wooden club to smash the mimic—the weapon really nothing more than an uprooted tree, with leaves still clinging to the branches—Amara hurled her next dart at its unprotected face. The missile slammed into the ogre's eye and sent it lurching back.

Amara followed up her first dart with another, and the second one struck the ogre's other eye, blinding it. She readied another one, but then paused as the ogre crumpled to the ground. The projectile to the eye had felled the great creature.

The largest ogre—the one with the tiny monocle—lumbered toward her. Unlike the others, which had crude clubs, this one wielded a massive two-handed sword. She hurriedly readied another dart and threw it at the ogre.

The creature simply swatted the dart away with its weapon and continued on toward her with a murderous look on its bestial face.

She let out a surprised gasp as her *Dart Deadeye* skill failed to injure the ogre. As she launched another dart, she watched with alarm as the ogre once again knocked the missile aside.

This was no normal ogre.

Amara had to throw herself to the side to avoid being trampled by the creature. She landed hard on the ground, and her eyes widened as she witnessed the ogre's greatsword descending toward her. Without thinking, she rolled to the side and barely avoided the strike, which would surely have decapitated her.

The ogre roared as its sword carved a deep furrow in the earth. It ripped its weapon free in a shower of dirt and then chased after her.

Amara hastily wove her mana together to cast her *Divine Weapon*. The flaming spectral blade took shape in front of her just in time to catch the ogre's next swing. As she heaved herself to her feet, she cast *Duplicate Self,* leaving a perfect copy of herself behind.

But her illusion didn't fool the ogre for a second, and it stomped in her direction, ignoring her duplicate. It barely slowed as it smacked aside her *Divine Weapon* as though it were a child's plaything.

Amara stumbled back as the ogre pursued her relentlessly. Nothing she had in repertoire seemed capable of hurting this monster. She was granted a brief reprieve as the ground split open underneath the ogre's feet. She glanced to the side to see Noah on his knees, the pommel of his sword resting at the edge of the fissure.

Somehow, the monstrous creature caught itself before it tumbled into the pit which had opened in front of it. Then, with an almost lazy swing, it struck Noah with its sword. The knight blocked the ogre's attack with his blade, but the force of the blow sent him cartwheeling to the side. He hit the ground hard, landing in an unnatural position, and didn't stir.

Amara slammed her *Divine Weapon* against the ogre, this time forcing it to give ground. But her advantage didn't last long. The ogre struck the spectral blade with an almighty swing and shattered it into shards of light. Amara stumbled, dumbfounded. Then it transfixed its beady eyes on her, the orbs shining with deadly intent.

The others from her group had noticed she was in trouble. Borim charged in with his shield raised high, slamming into the back of the ogre's leg with a resounding crash. The force of the impact sent the ogre reeling forward.

While the monster was off balance, Jonas launched himself into the fray, and for the first time fear appeared on the creature's hideous face. Still, it blocked the rogue's thrusts, moving impossibly fast for something of its bulk. Then, with a bone-breaking kick, the ogre slammed its heavy booted foot into Jonas and sent him rolling away.

A spout of fire doused the ogre and prevented it from finishing off the rogue. And as it turned its gaze to glare at Salamander, the girl shrank back. The creature stomped toward the mage as it shook the flames off its arm, leaving no trace of injury behind.

Amara's blood boiled at the sight of Jonas being wounded. Ignoring any thoughts of caution, she grabbed the last mana crystal from her pouch and rapidly drained its energy. As her soul brimmed with power, she called upon her *Avatar of Melischar* spell.

Golden wings sprouted from her back and a pearl-colored liquid pooled across her body before hardening into pure white armor. Finally, a sword that thrummed with impossibly destructive power appeared on her waist.

She'd expected the ogre to retreat upon seeing her avatar form, but instead she felt an enormous swell of mana. The creature was calling upon its own unbelievably powerful magic to meet her attack.

Amara didn't wait for the ogre's spell to complete. She flapped her angelic wings as she shot forward, drawing the sword and bringing it down in a two-handed swing upon the ogre.

The power of the blade made the world warp around her, and she laughed as the ogre brought up its sword in a vain attempt to block her swing. She knew the power contained within the avatar's sword would simply erase the creature from the world.

She brought down her blade with a cry but was met with a gale-force wind. A strange force was preventing her from striking the ogre with all her might. When her blade finally hit the creature's sword, it only made a dull clanging sound instead of shattering the blade.

The power of the blow sent the ogre sliding back a few paces, but it appeared completely unscathed from her attack. It must have used a spell to weaken the power of her strike—what she felt should be able to level mountains and cities.

She stared at the creature dumbly, shocked her attack hadn't slain it. What sort of monster was she facing?

But then she spotted blackening on the ogre's fingers. The same thing had happened to her the first time she'd cast her avatar spell and overtaxed her soul. Whatever spell the ogre had used to counter the force of her sword had drained every ounce of mana it had, and then some. While the beast was more powerful than anything else she'd encountered in this world, she doubted it could resist another hit from her sword.

As the ogre tromped forward with its greatsword raised, Amara lifted her own weapon in reply. There was no question this was the ogre commander, and if she wanted to make it to the core before it was destroyed, she needed to finish the monster off quickly. With another cry, she sprang forward to meet the ogre once more. This time, she would sweep it away with the full power of her avatar form.

# CHAPTER 65

The gossamer strands of fate stretched out across the island, pulsating with an ethereal green color as Amara tugged on the one linked to the ogre commander. As she did, the ogre stumbled slightly, and its parry missed her blade.

She cried out with exultation as she swung her avatar sword with all her might—hoping to decapitate the ogre—but as the weapon neared the creature, some force repelled her strike until she was buffeted by a hurricane force wind.

A cold sweat beaded on her forehead as she tried to finish her swing. If she could just make contact with the creature, she knew she could obliterate it with the power contained in her blade. She gasped with exertion, digging her feet into the ground, but she couldn't force her blade any closer.

The power radiating off her blade flayed the ogre's skin into thin strips, exposing muscle and bone beneath. Yet, some mysterious ability prevented her blade from fully cleaving through the creature.

Another blast of wind sent her sliding back a few paces. As she skidded, her feet kicked up a cloud of dust, and she coughed as it swirled around her. When it finally cleared, she could see the right side of the ogre's body had been pulverized into shreds.

Amara strode forward, intent on finishing the battle with the commander. The more time she wasted out here, the more time Malcheron had to reach the core. As she moved forward, the ogre withdrew a pulsating gem from its pouch. Amara grimaced. The creature lifted up the crystal, and blood-red wisps of energy drained into its palm. After a moment, the skin began to reform on its injured side.

She reached out to manipulate the threads of fate again and tugged on them to make the ogre fumble the crystal. The creature growled with anger as the crimson gem tumbled from its meaty fist before hitting the ground and bouncing away. Thankfully, it hadn't been able to fully heal itself. If it could keep healing the damage she inflicted, then her spell would fail before she could wear down the creature.

The ogre let loose a roar, and spittle flecked the corners of its mouth as it stomped forward. It raised the greatsword with its one good arm and swung it around in a powerful arc.

Amara ducked under the ogre's weapon and leapt into the air with her wings flared. She descended on her opponent like a comet, her sword blazing with an eternal light. But once again, her weapon slammed into an invisible barrier, and a sharp blast of wind sent her spinning backward.

She tried to spread her wings, but they crumpled under the gale and she hit the ground hard. As she pushed herself up and shook her head, she glared at the ogre, who was stomping in her direction. Her soul was already half-empty, and soon she would have to release her avatar form. Amara knew once that happened, she wouldn't stand a chance against the ogre.

*I have to finish this, fast.*

She staggered to her feet and tightened her grip on the hilt of her avatar sword. To preserve her mana, she let her wings blink out, leaving her with only the armor and the sword. This battle wasn't going to be decided by her flapping around the towering creature.

She needed to *hit* it with her sword.

Jonas appeared at her side, his eyes as black as a moonless night. "There is no hope of your attacks succeeding," he panted, holding his side where he'd been kicked. "The ogre is using some type of force nullification magic. The more powerful the attack, the more it resists. But I believe I have a method to defeat it."

"There's no way he's going to survive my next attack," she growled.

Amara pushed Jonas out of the way as the ogre charged at them. She deflected its thrust, her muscles screaming in protest from the force of the creature's swing. Then she knocked aside another thrust as the ogre drove her back. Her mana was rapidly draining, and she knew she had to preserve if she hoped to stop Malcheron.

"Listen to me!" Jonas shouted from a few paces away. "The ogre will outlast you with its inherent healing ability and anima crystals. None of the skills you possess can injure it."

"Then what am I supposed to do?" Amara called back as she ducked under another clumsy swing. The ogre might be powerful, but its size made it slow. Which was probably the only reason any of them were still standing.

"My blades only need to touch it," Jonas said as he hurled a throwing knife at the ogre. But the creature barely flinched as the invisible wall of wind protecting it deflected the weapon. "If you can grant me an opening, then I may be able to finish it off."

Amara pressed her lips together, still uncertain of what to do. Judging by the ogre's flayed skin, there was a cost to it deflecting her attacks. One more massive strike from her avatar sword might finish off the creature. But it might also burn through most of her remaining mana.

She took a step forward, but then hesitated as Jonas spun his dagger around in his palm.

"Please, trust me," he said quietly.

Amara scowled but let her armor shatter into shards of light. The moment she did, she felt the power of the goddess leave her limbs, and she almost collapsed to the ground. Her body and soul felt like she had been beaten by a group of village children with sticks.

"Look out, Amara!" Salamander shouted, pointing at the Issurian missile troops on the bridge, who had leveled their crossbows.

Amara clung on to the last shred of her divine power as she gathered the strands of fate together. She reached up to touch a handful of glowing filaments in the air, and as she did, the fletching on a flight of Issurian crossbow bolts failed, sending the missiles angling down sharply into the ogre.

The hail of bolts met the same resistance she'd experienced, and some of them hung suspended in the air before dropping to the ground. The ogre simply gave a bestial chuckle and tramped in her direction.

She altered the course of the wind to uplift a javelin hurled from another Issurian on the broken bridge. The missile shot toward the ogre but was once again stopped by the creature's ability. Unlike her other attacks, the ogre barely seemed to expend any effort to prevent the javelin from reaching it.

But she hadn't expected simple missile weapons to harm the ogre—she'd only been trying to keep its attention while her pet and Jonas circled around behind it.

At the last moment, the ogre noticed Mimi as the mimic rushed forward. Her pet galloped the final distance between herself and the ogre before clamping down on the creature's leg. Surprisingly, nothing stopped Mimi from biting into the commander. With a ferocious shake, the mimic tore another a bloody chunk from the ogre's calf.

*Does its skill only stop fast-moving attacks? Or deadly ones?*

She didn't have time to dwell on her questions as the ogre roared with fury. She watched with horror as it kicked Mimi free, and her pet tumbled head over heels until it slid to a stop. She desperately searched for any way to help Jonas as the ogre loomed over the rogue. If she used her avatar form again, then she'd have no mana left when she faced Malcheron.

*I have to trust Jonas.*

With no other options remaining, Amara lifted her staff and charged toward the ogre. As she did, a hail of bolts rained down around her, one tearing through her thigh. With a cry, she toppled forward and her staff flew out of her hands. She pushed herself up to see Jonas facing off against the ogre alone.

The rogue must have used his *Evade* ability because he nimbly danced around the ogre's powerful sword slashes. But although the creature was ponderous, it still managed to avoid Jonas's dagger thrusts. Neither one could land a blow on the other, though the swirling eddies of power around Jonas appeared to be growing stronger, like a hurricane gathering strength over the water.

The ogre retreated from Jonas's next attack, and the rogue easily parried the creature's lumbering attacks. The whites of Jonas's eyes had been dark before, but now they leaked inky blackness. He appeared truly inhuman.

She watched with shock as Jonas easily dodged another swing and then rolled forward under the ogre's next attack. With his skills activated, he seemed almost untouchable.

Jonas surged to his feet in front of the ogre, too close for it to strike him with its massive, unwieldy sword. But instead of burying his daggers into the commander's leg as Amara expected him to do, he lightly scratched its thigh with the tip of his weapon.

The ogre howled in pain and furiously backpedaled, though Jonas made no attempt to pursue it. Amara watched as a blackened rot spread across the ogre's leg. The skin around the wound shriveled and darkened until the entire leg was little more than withered skin and bone.

In desperation, the ogre commander pulled out another blood-red crystal, but the infusion of power did little to slow Jonas's class ability. Within seconds, the creature dropped to its knees, and then tumbled face-down on the ground. The decay continued to spread until there was nothing more left than a charred-looking husk.

The ogre commander was dead.

After hovering over the corpse for a moment, Jonas turned and hurried in Amara's direction. The wraithlike storm of power around him slowed and then plunged into his chest. With a shudder, his eyes slowly cleared as he returned to himself.

Jonas reached her side and knocked a bolt out of the air with his dagger. As he stood protectively over Amara, the surrounding air *whooshed*, and a volley of flames exploded over their heads.

Amara turned to see Salamander spraying fire at the Issurians clustered on the bridge with a furious expression on her face. In their tightly packed ranks on the narrow span, none of them could escape the girl's wrath. Dozens of the creatures burst into flames as Salamander sprayed them with fire from her palms. Some of the burning Issurians leapt into the fast-moving river, while others ran screaming back through their own ranks, spreading fire wherever they went.

Amara barely had time to celebrate Salamander's victory before the surrounding air began to cool and crackle. She spotted a kobold spellcaster on the far riverbank holding up a staff, snow swirling around its body. Her eyes widened as the kobold brought down the butt of its weapon and a wave of ice spread across the rushing river.

The frost continued up onto the island, underneath their feet, and then spread under her palms. She tore her hands free as the biting cold sent sharp pains traveling up her arms. Before she could push herself up, Jonas grabbed her arm and dragged her to her feet.

A handful of Issurians clambered down from the bridge to the frozen river below. When it didn't crack under their feet, dozens more jumped onto the icy surface before racing in Amara's direction.

Amara staggered to her feet, the wound on her thigh leaking blood at an alarming rate. She bent forward to pull the bolt out. When it wouldn't budge, she wrenched it back and forth, grimacing from the pain. Finally, she wiggled the missile free and then tossed it aside. As the trickle of blood leaking out from the wound became a steady stream, she hurriedly cast *Heal Wounds,* and the world brightened around her.

Once her injury had sealed shut, she limped in Borim's direction. The dwarf stood by the frozen shore with his shield raised against the Issurian missiles. Salamander sheltered behind him, flames wreathing her hands.

Borim jerked his head toward the castle. "Take care of Malcheron, lass. We'll hold them here."

Jonas took up a position beside the dwarf. "I have consumed a . . . horrifying . . . amount of soul power. It will be an easy task to hold back the Issurians."

Salamander nodded as well, her big eyes fixated on the approaching Issurian horde.

Amara hesitated, knowing no matter what her companions said, they would stand little chance against the approaching horde. The three of them trying to hold back the entire Chaos army would be liked using a pebble to stop a flood— they would disappear under a deluge of the creatures.

While she wracked her brain for a plan, she absently directed a healing spell at Mimi and then another at Noah, who was still prostrate on the ground. As the motes of light swirled around them both, the mimic lurched back to her feet. Noah roused a few seconds afterward, and he pushed himself into a sitting position before lifting his helm to peer around quizzically.

"I'm not leaving any of you behind," Amara finally said, turning her attention back to her companions. "We'll all make a run for the castle. Maybe we can find a way to barricade the gates behind us before they get in."

"That's not much of a plan," Borim grumbled. "And certainly not one to bet the world on."

"I said, *I'm not leaving any of you behind,*" Amara said with steel in her voice.

Borim stabbed a finger in her direction, and he opened his mouth to speak, but his response was drowned out by the beating of drums and the blasting of trumpets.

Amara turned in the direction of the noise to see a wave of riders in black armor charging down the hill. Behind them, the greatly diminished ranks of the Gnostics surged toward the Chaos army.

"What are they doing?" she whispered. "Anthon said they were a spent force—they'll all be slaughtered."

Borim tugged on his beard. "No doubt they saw their avatar in danger, and they're rushing to save you. Still, there's a fine line between bravery and stupidity . . ." The dwarf trailed off as hundreds of flapping banners appeared from behind the hill.

Her party watched, enraptured, as thousands of riders in gleaming golden armor galloped over the crest of the hill, followed by thousands more infantry charging down the slope with pikes held high.

Amara laughed in relief. The Knights Tarsillan had finally arrived.

# CHAPTER 66

The Issurians crossing the frozen river hesitated and then slowed as they glanced nervously toward the golden-armored host that had crested the hill. As the Knights Tarsillan surged down the slope in a cacophony of shouts, drumbeats, and horn blasts, several of the smaller Chaos creatures took a step back.

Amara slowed her casting, the pattern to call forth her *Divine Weapon* already half completed, as she waited to see what the wavering Chaos soldiers would do. Would the reinforcements finally break their resolve?

The kobold spellcaster was the first to flee, tossing away its staff as it scrambled back toward the shore. The sight of their ice mage fleeing seemed to break what little morale remained among the Issurians, and en masse, the horned creatures turned to escape. What started as a retreat quickly turned into a rout, as dozens of Issurians fought one another to escape from the approaching knights. Many slipped on the ice and were trampled underfoot, while others jumped off the edge of the frozen water and flailed about in their heavy armor.

After a few seconds, only a determined knot of Issurians remained on the rickety bridge. But after the two groups eyed each other across the frozen expanse for a long minute, the creatures finally withdrew in the direction of the Chaos army forming up near the village of Fusson.

Amara exhaled with relief as she watched the enemy retreat. She had drained her last mana crystal, and she didn't want to waste what little energy remained in her soul fighting any more Issurians. Not that her group was in any shape for another pitched battle. Jonas winced with pain after every movement, while Borim was a mass of cuts and bruises, and Noah still hadn't regained his feet. Only Salamander had emerged from the battle against the ogres relatively unscathed.

"Thank Birgitta," Jonas breathed. As he spoke, he brought up a hand to his chest and grimaced. "Amara, I would be eternally grateful if you could heal my wounds."

"Oh, right," she said, releasing her *Divine Weapon* spell, and instead forming the pattern for *Heal Wounds*. "I don't suppose any of you have more mana crystals?"

Jonas shook his head. "I only obtained the three from the Gnostics."

Borim wiped his sleeve across his cheek, scowling when it came away covered in blood. "I don't have one either, lass. And I think those damn Chaos bastards are determined to make me as ugly as a troglodyte."

"A lot of women like a face with a bit of character." Amara grinned. "And yours has a *lot* of character."

"You're going to kick a dwarf when he's down?" Borim grumbled. "Ironic, coming from someone who looks like you."

Amara's grin faded. "And what is *that* supposed to mean?"

"I bet you could hide behind a stalagmite without being seen," Borim guffawed. "You're just lucky Sneaky over there likes the scrawny type."

Jonas frowned and stepped forward. "Such words are uncalled for, Borim."

"That's so mean!" Amara exclaimed, before her lips twitched up into a ghost of a smile. "But I guess I started it."

The rogue glanced at both of them and then threw up his hands. "I suppose there's no need to defend your honor, then." After a moment, he turned and gazed at the Black Company charging down the hill. "At least with the arrival of the Knights Tarsillan, there is no need to pursue Malcheron alone. With our combined might, we should easily defeat him."

Amara chewed on her lower lip. "I'm still going inside to find him. Lady Ingrid is in there somewhere, and the knights might not reach the castle before Malcheron destroys the core. If we fail here, then everyone who sacrificed themselves will have done it for nothing. I won't let all those deaths be on my conscience."

Jonas slammed both daggers into their sheaths on his belt. "Do you recall our conversation about *not* hurling yourself into a dragon's maw at every opportunity?"

"We defeated the ogre commander, didn't we?" Amara turned and began to walk toward the gates. "I doubt Malcheron will be much more difficult." But her words rang hollow even to her. The ogre had been a far more challenging opponent than she'd expected. She could only hope Malcheron and the other commanders were easier to defeat.

"This is folly!" Jonas cried out. "I doubt Malcheron will destroy the core before the knights drive off the Chaos army." He thrust his arm in the direction of Fusson. "Look! Already, the kobolds lines are breaking under Prince Walter's assault. And the reserves retreat without even being committed."

Amara turned her attention back toward the battle. True to Jonas's words, the Chaos reserve force was streaming away in a disorganized mass. And the kobold's lines were dangerously bowing as the cavalry pressed home another charge. Still, she didn't dare wait and risk letting Malcheron succeed.

*I have to stop him here and now.*

"I'm going inside," she said, firmly. "I know it's dangerous, so you can all remain here. But I have to stop him before he brings down the wall."

"Scrawny there is right." Borim hitched up his pants. "We need to stop Malcheron before he reaches the core room. But you're crazy if you think you can leave this dwarf behind. Let's go kill that horned bastard and end this once and for all. Then we can get to the important part—finishing the quests and getting some treasure."

"I'm begging you to reconsider," Jonas said as he crossed his arms.

"This is what I have to do," Amara replied simply.

Jonas grimaced and rubbed a hand down his face. "Then, as always, there is no place for me but at your side. I just pray the cost isn't too high for your rashness."

Amara smiled softly at him and then stepped forward to touch his arm. "Don't worry. I've got this."

Jonas's scowl deepened, but he made no reply.

Amara brushed off his reaction and she rechecked her equipment. She had ten darts remaining, her staff was battered but not broken, and her soul was nearly half-full. She hoped it would be enough to defeat Malcheron.

With Jonas in the lead, her group headed toward Stout Oak Keep. They arrived at the broken gates to find them blockaded with debris, but after traveling down the wall a short distance, they discovered a tower with an open door.

"I shall scout inside." Jonas said, as he slipped through the doorway. "Unless you'd like to charge in there, Avatar?" His words dripped with ire.

She frowned and then shook her head curtly. She'd never seen Jonas this mad at her before.

The rogue disappeared inside and then reappeared a moment later. He beckoned them inside with one hand.

Amara crept through the entryway and scanned the room. A table in the center of the main room had been upended violently, and broken pieces of tableware, along with the remnants of a meal, were scattered across the floor. As her eyes traveled upwards, she noted bloodstains covering the walls. The sight only stiffened her resolve.

Jonas pressed himself flat against the wall beside the door that lead to the courtyard beyond. He gingerly opened it a crack and then peered out. He shut it again almost immediately. "The kobold commander you dueled with at Ahrenshoop is lying in wait beyond this door. And he is accompanied by our old companions."

"Our old companions?" Amara scrunched up her face in confusion before she realized who Jonas was talking about. "Not Ackley and his group!"

"The very same." Jonas turned to face Noah. "And you must brace yourself for ill tidings."

"What did you see?" the knight asked stiffly.

"The baroness and her wyvern lie slain near the inner gates," Jonas continued as he eyed Noah warily. "However, you should take solace in the fact she brought down many Issurians and kobolds before falling."

"Those bastards!" Noah muttered, his face twisting with rage. "I'll slay every last one of them myself!" He leapt toward the door leading to the courtyard and tried to shove Jonas aside. "I must kill them all!"

Amara's eyes widened at Noah's reaction. She hurried forward and grabbed one of Noah's arms, Borim joining her a second later on his other side. As they struggled to pull the knight off Jonas, she took an armored elbow to the face. She cried out in pain and reeled back, clutching her mouth. When she pulled her hands away, her palms were covered in blood.

At the sight of her injury, Jonas's expression darkened. His foot snapped out and landed squarely in the middle of Noah's chest; the force sending the knight staggering back. "Control your emotions before you further harm the avatar! I will not forgive a second such outburst."

"I . . . apologize, Avatar." The sight of her blood seemed to have penetrated the haze of Noah's rage, and the knight took a labored breath as his fingers curled around his sword hilt. "But I must ask you to step aside. I am honor-bound to seek vengeance against those who harmed my lady." His voice dropped to a soft growl. "So please, get out of my way before I am forced to move you."

Jonas stepped forward with a dangerous glint in his eyes at the knight's words, but Amara held up her hand to stop him. "He's upset about Lady Ingrid's death, and he needs a minute to cool down." She winced from the pain of speaking. She reached up to rub her jaw and then moved it back and forth. At least it didn't *feel* broken. And when she wiggled her teeth with her tongue, none of them felt loose. Comforted by the fact she wouldn't have to waste mana on another healing spell, she continued. "But you're not going to defeat the kobold commander on your own, Noah."

"I must have vengeance," he whispered through clenched teeth.

"And you're going to have it," Amara replied in a soothing tone. As she spoke, she tried to untangle her own emotions. She'd had a complicated relationship with the baroness, and she didn't quite know how she felt about the woman's death. And she still hadn't begun to process Emmaline's recent sacrifice.

"Then what are we waiting for?" Noah asked harshly.

"Nothing," Amara replied after a moment. "Let's go kill the commander."

She knew from her previous battle with the commander that the kobold was protected by an energy shield of some sort. And if it had time to call down its rift spear, then they were all doomed. They had to defeat the creature quickly.

As Noah took a step in the direction of the door leading to the courtyard, she held up her hand to stop him. "I'm going to disguise myself as an Issurian. If I can get close enough, I should be able to incapacitate or kill the kobold before he realizes he's been tricked."

Jonas glanced through the crack in the door again. "The kobold is wearing a golden monocle, which is very similar to the ogre commander's. Correct me if I'm wrong, but it appeared the other commander could see through your illusions."

Amara hurried over to see for herself. She peeked through the narrow opening to confirm the kobold was indeed wearing a golden monocle. Which meant her illusions were useless. She cursed under her breath as she realized her plans were dashed.

Borim marched over to stand behind the door as he raised his shield. "Frontal assault it is, then. I don't much like skulking around, anyway. That's something a goblin does—not a dwarven warrior. We charge out there, crack its head open like an egg, and then give Ackley and his group a little payback for betraying us."

When Jonas looked over at her questioningly, Amara simply shrugged. With Malcheron nearing the core, there was no time for intricate plans. And if she was being honest, she couldn't think of any other options.

Borim took her shrug as approval for his plan, and he yanked the door open, nearly ripping it off its metal hinges. With his shield held up to protect himself, the dwarf charged out into the courtyard with a guttural war cry.

Amara followed the dwarf through the door, staying in cover behind his wide shield. As she bent low, she started to weave together her mana to cast *Divine Weapon*. She needed something to counter the inevitable flying golden spear the kobold would launch in her direction.

The commander spun around to face them, and the inevitable deadly spear zipped up to hover over its shoulder. The lizard-like creature let loose a series of scraping hissing sounds as it took a step forward. Then it gestured insistently at Ackley and his party.

Noah let loose a roar and raised his shining sword. His long strides quickly outpaced the others, and he took the lead as he charged toward the kobold commander. The air crackled with mana as he summoned vast torrents of power, and the ground trembled with each step he took.

Amara felt a massive surge of energy as Noah skidded to a stop and brought down his sword pommel to strike the hard-packed earth. The ground heaved and cracked, nearly throwing her from her feet. And from where Noah had struck, a chasm raced toward the kobold.

The creature nimbly leapt to safety and swung its spear around into a guard position. Once again, it gestured at Ackley and his group, who were only now preparing for battle—though they appeared reluctant. They formed up behind the kobold, the surrounding air shimmering as they called upon their own magic.

Amara peeked around Borim's shield as she wove together the last strands of energy to summon her spectral blade. The towering weapon took shape in front of her and swung around to point at the kobold. Without hesitation, she sent it speeding forward to deal with the flying spear.

Her weapon flew straight like an arrow, while Jonas raced past her to catch up with Noah, who had resumed his charge. Salamander ducked into the rogue's vacated spot behind Borim's shield, a nimbus of flames burning around her hands.

"Take out the kobold first!" Amara shouted to her group. She increased her pace as a dark void ripped open in the sky above them. She recognized it from Ahrenshoop—the kobold was calling upon its *Rift Spear* spell. But at least there wasn't any sign of its energy shield yet. Maybe the kobold couldn't maintain it for long and was waiting for the spear to fully emerge from the rift before casting it.

Amara tapped Salamander on the shoulder, and then pointed at Eldred, the big warrior. The girl's magic should keep Ackley's group on the back foot and hopefully prevent them from helping the Chaos commander.

As she turned her attention back to the kobold, she gasped in surprise as a narrow sword blade erupted from its scaly neck. Then the weapon withdrew, leaving a gaping wound in its place.

She watched with shock as the creature clawed at its throat, trying in vain to stem the bleeding. It let out a long hiss, then dropped to its knees before crumpling to the ground. The kobold didn't stir as a pool of blood spread out beneath its body.

Ackley stepped forward, and then with a flourish, flicked the dark blood off of his rapier. "At last, our plan has come to fruition, Avatar. We stand ready to aid you in the battle against Malcheron, and I'm proud to say he never suspected our duplicity. This entire time, we have been helping you unseen from the shadows."

She fought down the overpowering urge to roll her eyes at Ackley. Once again, it appeared the traitorous duelist was changing sides. And she was mildly insulted that he thought she was actually dumb enough to believe his lies.

Amara stalked forward with her *Divine Weapon* hovering over her shoulder. She would end the traitorous duelist and his group once and for all.

# CHAPTER 67

Amara hardened her resolve as she marched forward. The idea of killing humans still unnerved her, but Ackley had betrayed her multiple times. And she was fairly certain he'd murdered his group's last healer. The world would be a better place without him.

The duelist must have read her expression as he held up his hands to deter her advance. "I understand our previous relationship was . . . tumultuous, to say the least, but I meant everything I said. My group has worked tirelessly to aid you in achieving your goals."

"Everything you say is a lie," she spat back. "And you obviously helped the Chaos army take the castle."

"True," Ackley conceded. "I may have provided a modicum of information in exchange for our lives. Yet I also left the tower gate open for any who wished to foil Malcheron. And I distracted the guards watching over your sturdy knight friend there with some dak leaf. You must understand we were placed in a difficult situation."

The duelist's words made her slow. Someone *had* left the postern gate open to the tower. Without that, they might not have found a way inside before it was too late. After all, if the gates had been barred from the inside, then even Jonas's lock-picking ability would have been useless.

And when she thought back to Noah's rescue, there had been a surprising lack of guards. But the kobolds might have consumed the dak leaf—whatever that was—on their own, and Ackley was just taking credit. She couldn't trust anything that came out of his lying mouth.

After a few more paces, she slowed and then pointed at the open tower gate. "Leave and help the knights in the battle outside.

Kymber, the bard, raised her brow. "You're just letting us go?"

"And why wouldn't she?" Ackley continued smoothly. "She understands the great danger we placed ourselves in to help the avatar defeat the fiendish Chaos army."

"But after everything that happened?" Kymber said as she lowered her lute slightly.

Eldred, the big warrior, placed a hand on the bard's shoulder. "Don't look a gift horse in the mouth."

Noah took a menacing step forward. "I will not let these traitors depart. They had a hand in Lady Ingrid's death. They must be hanged for what they've done."

"I said they're free to go," Amara repeated with a thread of steel in her tone.

Jonas lowered the throwing knife he'd been holding. "Are you certain?"

She nodded.

"Bloody bad idea," Borim grumbled. "They'll probably just stab us in the back again. At least if we fight them, they can only stab us in the front."

Amara shepherded her group to the side, her spectral weapon positioned between Ackley's party and her own. The duelist strode past her with a smile plastered across his face and an air of nonchalance about his movements, but the others huddled together like frightened sheep surrounded by wolves. It was as though they didn't believe she was letting them go.

"Why are you allowing them to depart?" Jonas asked under his breath as the group reached the tower door. "Others will probably suffer in the future from your decision."

"They deserve to die," she replied in a low tone. "But I don't have the mana for another battle right now. And I can't risk any of you getting hurt before we face Malcheron."

"Ah, I see." Jonas nodded his head. "There is wisdom in your actions."

"Don't act so surprised." Truthfully, she was already regretting her decision to allow them to leave. Still, if it meant she had to fight one less enemy, then it was worth it, in her mind. And if it became necessary, she could always hunt them down in the future.

She waited a few moments to ensure Ackley's group had truly departed, and that this wasn't just some ruse before she continued into the heart of the castle. She walked past Nyrax, the lady's wyvern, whose body bristled with javelins and arrows. And then she arrived at the baroness herself.

Amara slowed at the sight of Lady Ingrid. The woman's face was frozen in a mask of pain, her eyes staring sightlessly up into the sky. She had a ragged wound on her chest, and her left arm was completely blackened.

Noah rushed over to the baroness's side and dropped to his knees. He picked up her hand and pressed it against his chest. Tears streamed down his face. "Forgive me, my lady."

Borim walked over and patted the knight on his back. "There will be time for grieving later. Right now, we need to kick that horned bastard in the backside."

"Yes, you are right." Noah rose to his feet as he scrubbed his cheeks fiercely. "Malcheron will pay for all the evil he has committed. I will slay him myself!"

Amara let Jonas take point as Borim helped Noah to his feet. They continued silently toward the inner gate, their eyes searching for any sign of kobolds or Issurians on the walls above. But they reached the entrance without spotting any movement.

The inner gate had been shattered as though from some massive force, but there were no scorch marks to indicate gunpowder. And someone had built a makeshift barricade behind the broken doors, which was strewn with the bodies of the keep guards. Before the Chaos army had used gunpowder to bring down the inner walls, the defenders had fought desperately to keep them out.

*I should have marched to their aid the moment the Gnostics arrived,* Amara thought. *They're all dead because of me.*

She did her best to dispel her dark thoughts as she kept an eye out for any Chaos creatures skulking in the shadows. But no further challenges presented themselves. Maybe the kobold commander had been the last line of defense.

"I wish Frederick was here," Amara whispered, unnerved by the stillness in the air. She kept expecting Malcheron to spring another trap. "He would know more about the core."

Jonas nodded. From the strain on his face, it was clear that he, too, was waiting for an ambush. "He stated it was located at the base of the tower. That information will have to do."

The inner courtyard was strewn with pieces of rubble from the explosion. Blackened bodies—both human and kobold—were scattered around like rag dolls. She stopped and looked up at the section of the keep where the entire front wall had collapsed. She could see directly into familiar rooms, and in a few places, furniture hung precariously over the edge of the shattered floors.

Jonas stopped short and held up his hand. "Wait. Something is wrong."

"I don't see anything—" Amara's words were cut off as a disc borne of the darkest night hurtled toward her. She tried to throw herself out of the way, but she was a second too slow. The shadowy weapon engulfed her hand holding the staff.

She screamed as she dropped her weapon, and the staff clattered to the ground. The darkness from the spell ate away at her flesh like acid. She hurriedly wove together the mana to cast *Heal Wounds*, but as the surrounding air lightened, the shining motes just drifted around lazily without purpose.

When she glanced down at her hand to see why her spell wasn't healing it, she gasped in horror at the sight of a rotted stump. Her right hand had simply disintegrated from the spell. She grabbed onto her wrist and staggered to the side as waves of agony assailed her mind. The pain was far worse than when she'd been burned in Leissen, and it took all of her willpower not to cry out again.

From the shadows, dozens of Issurians materialized, bearing missile weapons and weaving together mana to cast spells. At the center of the Chaos formation stood Tecala, flanked by a towering horned creature radiating an impossible amount of power.

Amara knew immediately that she was facing Malcheron.

*How did they hide themselves?* she wondered through the fog descending over her mind like a blanket.

Amara lurched to the side as she dodged another spinning disc of darkness. If she let her terrible injury distract her, then there was no doubt she would perish. If there was any hope of her party surviving, she needed to force herself to fight.

Borim appeared at her side, his eyes widening at the sight of her missing hand. His shocked expression quickly transformed into one of rage as he knocked a crossbow bolt out of the sky with his shield. He roared a challenge and thumped his chest. *"I'll murder every last one of you horned bastards for hurting her!"*

Amara shook her head to try to clear the cobwebs from her mind. As she did, she watched Noah charge forward, but he went down in a hail of bolts.

When she turned her gaze to Jonas, she witnessed him being driven back by a barrage of ice and shadow magic. He managed to evade everything thrown at him, though the attacks prevented him from reaching her side.

"Amara!" he called out, his hand outstretched in her direction.

She glanced back to Tecala, who was fighting to control a massive spinning disc between her outstretched fingers. With every second that passed, the shadowy conjured weapon grew larger, vibrating with barely constrained Chaos energy. She knew the Issurian commander meant to finish her with one last devastating blow.

*I won't go down without a fight.*

Amara raised her left hand and called upon her *Holy Light.* A burst of illumination that rivaled the sun exploded in her palm and turned the world white. As it faded, she could see the shapes of the Issurians soldiers staggering about blindly. But as she blinked away her tears, she cursed when she saw Tecala was unphased by her spell.

Amara started to cast *Divine Weapon,* but she fumbled the weaving as a cold sweat broke out on her forehead and her stomach lurched uncomfortably. The pain from her wound was distracting her at the time when she needed to be at her sharpest. And she had no idea why her injury was resisting healing. Maybe her *Heal Wounds* spell wasn't capable of restoring a lost limb. But then why wasn't it doing something about the burning shadows still eating away at her skin?

Tecala's lips twitched up in a smirk as she launched the pulsating disc of pure darkness at Amara. The weapon spun like a saw blade as it tore through the air. The shadows that streamed from it almost seemed to devour the illumination from her *Holy Light* spell.

With no other options remaining, Amara wove together the strands of mana to cast her *Avatar of Melischar* spell. If she hoped to survive this attack, saving any amount of mana for Malcheron was no longer an option.

As she finished interlacing the mana, she stepped forward and shouldered Borim out of the disc's path—the dwarf had selflessly moved to shield her from the spinning disc of darkness. But she knew instinctively if she allowed the disc to strike the dwarf, he would simply be swept away by the foul power of Chaos. The amount of power contained within the roiling darkness of the spell surpassed even the kobold commander's *Rift Spear*.

She focused all of her energy on her avatar armor, and the strange white liquid thickened across her front first. Hopefully, it would be enough to resist the attack.

The sun faded as the shadowy weapon neared her, and the air warped from the power in the strike. She grasped at the sword forming on her hip, but her fingers slipped as she struggled to unsheathed it with her wrong hand. Then she glanced up again to see the impossibly large disc nearly on top of her.

And then the sun blinked out as she was engulfed by an inky blackness, like being swallowed by the depths of a dead galaxy.

# CHAPTER 68

Malcheron watched with bated breath as Tecala's *Shadow Discus* spell crashed against the avatar and exploded into grasping tendrils of darkness. As the air cleared, he snarled at the sight of the girl emerging intact after enduring Tecala's third Circle spell. Though as he peered closer at the avatar, he could see cracks spider webbing across the pure white armor.

*Maybe she's not as powerful as I thought.*

He drew forth a torrent of anima from his soul and wove it together to create a rift into the depths of Chaos. All he needed to do was buy the dark dwarves working in the depths of the castle a little more time. Once they had destroyed the core, then his mother could sweep south with all the Forces of Chaos. And the pathetic army arrayed against them outside the castle would be slaughtered like cattle.

Two swirling rifts tore open the air above him, and unearthly shrieks emanated from the hungering darkness. As the fissure grew larger, a pair of serpents slithered out. Their scales were made of shifting shadows, and their maws dripped ichor blacker than a moonless night. Where the eyes should have been, empty sockets gaped open.

"*Kill*," he commanded, and pointed at the avatar.

The avatar slowed at the sight of the serpents, a look of concern flashing across her face. At the sight of her hesitation, a spark of hope flared to life within him. And the embers only grew brighter as he watched her fumble for the sword on her belt—the loss of her hand appeared to have crippled her fighting ability. He would exploit her weakness to the fullest.

Without hesitating, the two shadowy serpents surged out of the rift. The creatures landed on the ground and glided forward, leaving a trail of foggy gloom in the wake. The very air shimmered with the foul power they possessed.

The avatar finally managed to draw her sword, but her response was slow and clumsy. When she swung at the nearest shadow serpent, her blade sailed above the agile creature's head.

"I will handle the avatar," he said to Tecala, standing next to him. "Take the rest of your soldiers and deal with her companions. The dark dwarves must be given the time they require."

"What of the scroll?" Tecala asked in a low voice. She had used an immense amount of anima in her attack against the avatar, and the effort was showing in her pinched features.

"I will use it should my spells fail," Malcheron replied with a furrowed brow. "It would be better to slay her while she's injured and weakened than attempt to trap her."

"As you wish." Tecala gestured at the Issurians and moved forward to face off against the avatar's allies. Then she struggled to conjure another *Shadow Discus.*

Malcheron knew she was in no condition for a prolonged battle, but now wasn't the time to worry about her. He needed to defeat—or at least delay—the avatar long enough for the dwarves to complete their task. Victory was within reach, and he wouldn't allow it to slip through his fingers.

Around him, the Issurians dropped their crossbows and drew their short-range weapons. With a cry, they surged forward and clashed with the avatar's companions. He doubted these low-level soldiers could defeat them—especially the rogue that radiated an unholy power—but they only needed to keep them busy.

Malcheron returned his attention to the avatar and watched with satisfaction as the first serpent coiled around her legs. While she struggled against the shadowy monster binding her, the second one reared up with a gaping maw.

*Will you be defeated so easily, Avatar?*

As he lifted his hand to form a shadowy spear in his palm, a single droplet of sweat beaded on his forehead. Between keeping the rifts open and conjuring the weapon, his soul was nearly at its limit. Should his next attack fail, he would have no choice but to use the Scroll of Banishment.

He reared back to hurl the spear, when inexplicably, his heel slipped on the blood soak ground. With a grunt, he teetered to the side before regaining his balance. After he'd righted himself, he glanced around to see similar misfortune was befalling all of his men. Sword strikes went wide, crossbow strings snapped, and magic exploded before striking the avatar's companions.

And when he returned his attention back to his shadow serpents, his eyes widened at the sight of the monster missing its strike. It should have been impossible for his magical summons to miss at such close range, but somehow it had.

The realization of what was happening struck him like a bucket of icy water— this avatar had the power to manipulate fate. He'd been a fool to delay using the scroll his mother had given him.

Malcheron reached into the pouch on his belt and drew forth the vellum parchment. But as his hand closed around the item, it slipped from his grasp and tumbled to the ground. He let loose another snarl as he bent down to pick it up, but once again, it slid through his fingers. This time, it bounced on the hard-packed earth and disappeared among the feet of his soldiers.

*How do I fight someone who can control fate itself?*

A nearby detonation nearly deafened him, and then winds buffeted the courtyard like a hurricane. He shielded his eyes and grabbed onto his cloak flapping behind him. As he looked up, he could see the avatar had cleaved one of the serpents in two with her blade. The powerful Chaos energy contained within the summoned creature was streaming out like a geyser.

As she turned her gaze toward him, her blade thrumming with incomprehensible power, he knew his doom had come. He couldn't stand against such immense might. Without the Scroll of Banishment, he would surely die this day.

He dropped to his knees and once again searched for the scroll. But among the stampeding feet of his Issurians battling the dwarf and the rogue, he couldn't spot the cursed thing. He glanced up again to see his last remaining shadow serpent coiling tighter around the avatar in an attempt to crush her.

As she struggled against the monster, her armor shattered before breaking into motes of light. But before his conjured shadow snake could finish her off, she raised her sword with her one good hand and plunged the tip down the serpent's throat. The monster wailed like a damned soul as it exploded into a gale-force wind.

After the final serpent's death, the rifts snapped shut, and anima flooded back into his veins. He gave up on his search for the scroll and instead rose to his feet. The avatar had lost her armor and was vulnerable.

He reversed his spear, wisps of shadows bleeding off the shaft, and leaned back to hurl the projectile at the avatar. Shockingly, no twist of fate made him stumble as he launched the missile at the girl.

The avatar cried out with exertion, her red hair streaming behind her as she parried the thrown spear, and both weapons exploded into a storm of light and dark. When the air cleared, the avatar stood there, any trace of divinity gone. She was nothing more than a girl again.

Malcheron laughed with relief at the sight of her standing there helplessly. The avatar wasn't nearly as powerful as he'd suspected—she'd expended all of her mana.

He raised his hand and conjured another spear of darkness. This time he didn't throw it, and instead strode toward her. He didn't need the Scroll of Banishment. He would slay her with his own two hands.

Many of his Issurian soldiers had been slain, but they had separated her from her protectors. A clear path was open to the avatar. He would end the threat the Gods of Order presented once and for all.

# CHAPTER 69

As her avatar spell faded, Amara felt her strength draining away. The pain from her lost hand returned tenfold, and she felt a heavy weight of exhaustion settle over her body like a cloak. In the past, she'd been able to cast even after draining the last of her mana, but this time, her battered body simply failed.

She was facing Malcheron alone, injured, and with only a few drops of mana remaining.

Amara glanced over to the far side of the courtyard to see Jonas drive both of his daggers into an Issurian's neck; the creature sizzled as its skin blackened and shriveled up like overcooked bacon. The rogue was splattered head-to-toe in dark blood, and his eyes shone with an eerie light. There was something different about him this time—something dangerous. And the power he radiated almost rivaled Malcheron's.

But she knew he couldn't reach her in time to help. Nearly a dozen Issurian soldiers stood between them, and the horned creatures had ranged out to block his path. Even in the face of terrible losses, the Chaos soldiers fought on bravely.

She retreated from Malcheron's advance as she desperately tried to think up a plan. Waves of killing intent radiated off of the towering demon-like creature, and the sensation nearly brought her to her knees.

Nearby, Borim and Mimi protected Salamander as the girl hurled gouts of flames into the Issurian ranks. As the dwarf turned his head in Amara's direction, his eyes widened with alarm at seeing her predicament.

"I'm coming, lass," Borim boomed. "Just let me deal with these bastards!" He buried his axe in an Issurian's face and then knocked aside another with his shield. He weathered another rush of Issurians like an immovable object, hacking and shoving the frenzied creatures back.

Amara wove together the last dregs of her mana, the pain from drawing upon her soul making her wince. The loss of her hand seemed to have done something to prevent the energy from properly circulating through her body. She couldn't overtax it as she had in the past.

She intertwined the mana to cast *Charm Person,* the spell that took the least amount of mana, but as the spell completed, nothing happened to Malcheron except for a flash of light from a sigil on his dark armor.

*He must have protection against charm spells.*

A danger warning blared in her mind, and she ducked as a crossbow bolt sailed over her head. When she straightened up, she let out a gasp of shock at the sight of Malcheron charging at her. She threw herself to the side and barely missed being skewered by his black spear.

She rolled across the ground and didn't stop until she struck a fallen Issurian. The creature was grievously wounded but still alive. It groaned as it clutched at her with bloody hands. She shook off its clawed grip and then scrambled away before the creature could grasp her again.

Amara regained her feet, only to come face-to-face with Malcheron once more. The horned monster loomed over her and laughed harshly as he lifted a spear that seemed to bleed darkness.

Without thinking, she raised her palm and cast *Holy Light.* A sunburst exploded from her outstretched hand, and the world turned white.

For a second, she couldn't see anything through the blinding light. Then the outline of Malcheron appeared right in front of her. Before she could even recoil, she felt a searing pain tear through her ribs.

Amara looked down in shock to see that a spear had been driven through her chest, just above her breastbone. Then she lifted her gaze to see Malcheron staring at her with unblinking red eyes. Somehow, he'd resisted her *Holy Light* spell as well.

*I should have listened to Jonas,* she thought as she weakly clawed at the bloody spear protruding from her chest. *We should have waited for reinforcements.*

Malcheron tore the spear free in a spray of blood and lifted it to strike again. But before he could, Amara's pet mimic slammed into his side and made him stumble forward.

Mimi lurched to a stop, her wooden front covered in blood, and planted herself between Malcheron and Amara. The mimic's eyes shone with rage, and she opened her mouth to reveal rows of sharp teeth.

"You bloody horned devil!" Borim shouted as he reached the mimic's side. "Leave her alone and pick on someone your own size!"

"What he said!" Salamander added as she hurried over to join the dwarf and the mimic. The Issurians they had been fighting pulled back slightly as their commander faced off against them.

Though Borim barely came up to Malcheron's waist, Amara watched with pride as the dwarf glowered unflinchingly at the leader of the Chaos army.

With a roar, Borim leap forward, and swung his axe down at Malcheron. The towering commander brushed aside the blow almost casually and then smashed his gauntleted fist into the dwarf's helmet. The force of the punch sent Borim flying, and he hit the earth before tumbling for a few paces. When he finally stopped rolling, he shook his head with a sputter before he tried to push himself up. But after two failed attempts, he slumped back to the ground before tearing off his dented helmet to reveal matted, bloody hair beneath.

Mimi launched herself at the commander next, and her tongue shot out and splatted against the Issurian's leg. With a jerk of her body, she nearly yanked Malcheron from his feet. But the commander recovered quickly and reached down the wrench the tongue free. Then he met the mimic's charged with a solid kick that knocked the wooden creature over.

As the mimic struggled to right itself like a turtle on its back, Malcheron returned his attention to the prone dwarf and raised his spear to finish him off. But before he could deliver the killing blow, the commander cried out with pain as Salamander raced forward and pressed her burning hands against his side.

"No, Salamander!" Amara shouted. A numbness was spreading through her body, and a warm liquid was dribbling out of her lips. "You can't defeat him!" She feebly tried the stem the blood pouring out from her chest as she took a lurching step toward her friend. No matter what, she couldn't let Malcheron hurt Salamander.

"Jonas!" she cried out, her voice raspy. "Save Salamander."

The rogue paused in the act of slashing an Issurian throat, and his eyes widened at the sight of her wound. He raced in her direction, but a wall of Chaos soldiers closed in around him to block his path. She knew the rogue would never reach their young companion in time.

Amara watched in horror as the Issurian commander spun around, his spear poised to drive through Salamander. However, something made him hesitate.

Malcheron stared down at Salamander with impassive eyes. The girl cowered in front of him, and she raised her arms in a hopeless attempt to ward off the dark spear. After a moment, the commander lowered his weapon. Then he simply backhanded Salamander.

The strike sent the girl tumbling head over heels before she rolled to a stop next to Borim. After a second, she sat up, looking disheveled, and lifted the hair out of her eyes. Then she wobbly rose to all fours and crawled over to check on the injured dwarf.

Amara breathed a sigh of relief at seeing Malcheron spare Salamander. She didn't know why he hadn't killed her—especially after Salamander had wounded him—but she was grateful.

She once again tried to draw upon her mana to cast another spell, but her soul resisted. If she could just heal herself, then she could get back into the fight to help her friends. Already, she felt drowsy, and a comforting darkness beckoned her.

*I'm losing too much blood,* she realized. *If I don't do something, I'm going to die.*

Malcheron stalked over to her and examined her like he was looking at a wounded beast. "You fought bravely, Avatar," he said, his words stilted. "However, your cause is hopeless. And your god's return ends now."

The Issurian commander hefted his weapon, only to let loose a roar of rage as a knife sliced through his cheek. He spun around to face Jonas, who had finally cut his way through the Issurians blocking his path.

"I'll kill you for hurting her," the rogue rasped, his voice almost completely inhuman. His crazed eyes shone like obsidian. As he stepped over the shriveled bodies of the soldiers he'd slain, a storm of wraiths spun around him like a cyclone. And a terrible killing intent that overwhelmed the one Malcheron emitted filled the air like an oppressive miasma.

At the sight of the rogue, Malcheron took a step back. He placed his spear in a defensive position and then gestured with his hand to open a yawning abyss at his feet. A swell of impossible power radiated from the swirling void as it devoured the ground. The remaining Issurians took up positions around their commander, many of them looking uneasily at Jonas.

*I need to find a way to help him.*

Amara closed her eyes and slowed her breathing. As she did, she traced the pathways of her life force with her mind. In the past, she'd always managed to push her mana beyond the limits of her soul, but her injured hand was preventing that somehow.

Amara followed the pathways until they ended in ragged breaks at her missing hand. She focused on the break for a moment, trying to figure out what to do. One of the conduits seemed to lead to her hand, while the other led back to her soul.

With a supreme effort, she focused her mind and willed the pathways to heal. When that failed, she altered her tactics and instead tried to force the energy conduits together to form a loop and bypass her injury.

She nearly wept with relief as the pathways forged together, and she felt a surge in her life force. Though she was completely out of mana, at least she could draw upon what little remained of her life energy for a few more spells. For a second, she considered casting *Heal Wounds* on herself, but she knew what she had to do instead.

As blood poured out of her chest, she wove together the strands of mana to cast a spell. She knew it would probably be the last one she ever cast, but she needed to save her friends. She was the reason they'd charged in here, and she needed to make sure they survived.

Amara finished weaving the energy together, watching with fading vision as Jonas stepped aside to dodge a shadowy spear hurled by Malcheron. Another weapon immediately reappeared in the commander's hand, and horrifying insects born of shadows began to claw their way out of the abyss Malcheron had conjured.

She struggled to focus on the complex pattern of her spell, and then let out a sigh as she finished. In front of her, Jonas and Malcheron continued to lunge and feint, their weapons clashing with explosions of power. And while the commander's complete attention was focused on the rogue, Amara's spectral sword quietly took form behind him.

At the sight of the weapon, Tecala called out a desperate warning to Malcheron from her position near the keep's entrance. But it was too late, and the *Divine Weapon* swung with the force of the gods, cutting deeply into the Chaos commander's neck.

The Issurian toppled to the side, his head nearly severed. The shadowy spear in his hand blinked out of existence. As he fell, he produced a pulsating red crystal in his hand.

Amara dropped to her knees, her vision going dark. Already, her arms had fallen to her sides, and she couldn't feel her legs. But she recognized the crystal—it was the same type of gem the ogre commander had used to heal himself.

"Stop him," she gasped.

Jonas darted forward and agilely kicked the gem from Malcheron's grasp. Then, for good measure, he leaned down and slit the commander's throat with his blade. The withering rot immediately started to spread through the mortally wounded commander's body.

"No!" Tecala screamed, raw pain in her voice as she raced forward.

The other remaining Issurians drew back, many of them throwing down their weapons. More than a few turned to bolt away, though there was nowhere for them to go.

Amara toppled forward, the last of her energy spent. A second later, Jonas appeared at her side to catch her. As the world continued to darken, she felt something being pressed into her mouth. Without thinking, she swallowed and felt a burst of strength.

She glanced down at her chest to see the bleeding slow and then stop. A moment later, Jonas shoved another healing pill into her mouth. As she swallowed, the wound on her chest closed completely. She still felt weak, but at least she didn't feel like she was on the verge of death any longer.

"Stay with me," Jonas pleaded as he took her hand. As he did, he motioned at the dwarf. "Get the cube!"

"What was that, lad?" Borim said groggily. He still hadn't moved from where he'd landed after being struck by Malcheron.

The sound of hoofbeats interrupted Jonas's response, and Amara craned her head to the side to see riders pouring through the gate. Frederick was in the lead, with an armored knight at his side, and a veiled female caster on the other. The woman was hurling blue fireballs with abandon at the fleeing Issurians.

*I defeated Malcheron,* Amara thought to herself, still shocked they had won. *I just hope Frederick brought some healers with him.*

# CHAPTER 70

Amara leaned back in Jonas's arms and gazed up into his eyes. He still had the countenance of his reaper class, but she'd never been so happy to be close to him. His dark eyes met hers, and he brushed back a lock of her hair.

"I thought I lost you," he murmured.

She lifted her hand to touch his face, but then froze when she realized she'd automatically used her right arm, which ended in a ragged stump. It was a strange feeling losing a hand, and it was as though she could still feel it—almost like a phantom limb.

As she inspected the stump, she noted the shadows ringing the edge had grown and were spreading down her arm like an infection. Hopefully, the knights would have a way of curing her and restoring her hand.

*I really don't want to go through life with only one hand.*

Amara tried to push herself up into a sitting position as she scanned the ranks of Issurians clustered at the far end of the courtyard. Her *Divine Weapon* hovered between the two groups, discouraging any of the Chaos creatures from renewing their attack.

And in the center of the courtyard, Malcheron still thrashed around on the ground, clearly in his death throes. Spurts of blood sprayed out from his terrible neck wound, but as she watched, each spray grew weaker. And the rot from Jonas's ability was quickly spreading through the commander's body.

Borim stumbled over to them, his gaze strangely unfocused. His face was caked with blood, and he wobbled slightly as he stood there. In his hand, he held the familiar metallic cube the dungeon had gifted them.

She watched as Jonas snatched the cube from the dwarf's hand and then began to pour mana into it. The metal shifted and swirled, almost like it was made of mercury. The magical artifact began to glow with a pale blue light as he offered it to her.

"Here, hold this in your palm," Jonas instructed. Turning to the dwarf, he snapped, "Help me activate it!"

Borim nodded groggily. But he did as he was told, and added his mana to the cube.

As she took the device from Jonas, she felt a soothing sensation flood her soul, and the blackening of her limbs retreated. She probably wouldn't be able to cast anything for a while, but she doubted she'd need to with the battle against Malcheron won.

A moment later, Mimi appeared at her side. The wooden boards making up her pet's chest had been cracked and splintered by Malcheron's kick, but her pet seemed none the worse for wear. And as if to prove it, Mimi gave her a long, slimy lick.

"Help me up," she whispered to Jonas. Her throat felt parched, and she could barely talk. But she didn't want to remain on the ground with so many Issurians nearby. Now that their only route of escape was blocked by the knights and the Gnostics, they might decide to make a desperate last stand.

Jonas helped her to her feet and then wrapped his arm around her waist to hold her steady. "Are you alright?" He looked at her with concerned eyes. "There is no shame in resting after such severe wounds. After all, the healing pills may not have completely mended your internal wounds. If you'll allow it, I'd like to find you a healer."

"I really am fine," she lied. It felt like her insides had been fed through a blender, and then her soul had been hammered on a dwarf's anvil. But she needed to finish this once and for all.

With Jonas's help, she hobbled over to Frederick. As she crept forward, Harold the pig farmer appeared at the old knight's side. Though battered, he was still in one piece. As she lifted her injured arm, she realized it was more than she could say about herself.

Frederick had halted his mount a few paces away, and though the old knight looked exhausted, he didn't have the same look of confusion as before. The Gnostics and Knights Tarsillan with him had spread out and formed a line between Amara's party and the remaining Issurians. And several of the knights had dismounted to watch Malcheron die.

"Oh-ho, what an epic battle you missed!" Frederick called out with a smile plastered on his face. His gaze darted down to her injured arm and his eyebrows rose slightly. "I had planned to scold you for running off alone, but it seems you've suffered enough. And through the grace of the gods, you even managed to defeat Malcheron. What an impressive feat for one so young as yourself. Though you'll probably be left out in the songs about the battle, seeing as you disappeared like a skulking goblin."

"I didn't disappear," she said indignantly. "Someone had to reach the castle to stop Malcheron."

"And there are no more servants of Chaos about?" the old knight asked, his smile fading. "I assume you checked the core room? What am I saying—of course the avatar and her stalwart companions did."

Amara froze at the old knights' words. She'd thought Malcheron had laid an ambush to catch them unaware. But what if he'd only been delaying them? It would make sense, given how he'd arrayed his forces. The kobold and the ogre commander must have been placed to slow her advance. Otherwise, they would have joined their forces in the hopes of defeating her with their combined might.

"I don't know where the core room is," she said, what little color remaining in her face draining away. Had they come this far, and fought so hard, only for Malcheron to claim victory in the end?

Frederick scrubbed a hand down his lined face. "Well, isn't that dire news? Best you take this, then." He tossed her a glowing mana crystal. "The battle is not yet won. Oh, and let me know if you've seen my halberd. I think I'll have use of it yet."

She barely managed to snag the crystal with her left hand. And she nearly fumbled it several times before tightly clutching it to her body.

Jonas drew one of his daggers. "Do you truly believe others have gone on ahead to attempt to destroy the core, Frederick?"

The old knight opened his mouth to reply, but a maddened screech from nearby interrupted him.

A woman wearing simple Gnostic robes and a veil obscuring her face pointed a quivering finger at the rogue. "Don't you dare say his name!" As she continued to scream, she unleashed a gout of blue flames toward the rogue.

Just before it struck Jonas, he shoved Amara out of the way and took the brunt of the blast on his chest. The flames engulfed him and sent him reeling away.

The veiled woman turned and unleashed a storm of fire at Frederick before he could react. The old knight disappeared into the firestorm and his horse's tortured screams echoed across the courtyard.

Amara found herself too stunned to react for a second. Why was one of the Gnostics attacking them when the fate of the South hung in the balance? Had a traitor somehow infiltrated their ranks undiscovered?

"Do not do this!" shouted a knight from beside the woman. "You swore we would stop the Chaos army before completing our mission." But for his effort, he was rewarded with his own blast of flames.

Amara snapped out of her shock and immediately sent her *Divine Weapon* soaring toward the woman, grateful to feel her renewed mana supporting the spell.

But as she did, the spellcaster held out her hand with a ruby in her palm. Then she calmly brought down the pommel of the dagger on the gem and smashed it to pieces. The ruby shattered and a cloud of energy enveloped the spectral weapon. A moment later, Amara's flaming sword disintegrated into brightly colored dust.

Amara watched the destruction of her *Divine Weapon* with disbelief. At the sight of her spell being so easily dispelled, she redoubled her efforts to drain the mana from the crystal Frederick had tossed her. Her soul ached from forcing it to refill so quickly, but she needed the energy to heal her friends. Jonas had extinguished the flames covering him by rolling around on the ground, but he now laid on the ground, unmoving. And she couldn't even see Frederick through the conflagration enveloping him and his mount.

She paused in the process of weaving together her mana to cast another spell as the woman turned her wild gaze in her direction. As their eyes locked, recognition flashed in her mind—it was Selena, the woman she'd battled and then charmed back at the inn in Leissen.

Somehow, the Church had tracked her down here.

When Selena raised her hand to cast another spell, Amara attempted to throw herself out of the way. But all she managed in her current state was to topple over ungracefully like a felled tree. Still, through sheer Luck, she avoided the jet of flames, and the woman's screeching intensified.

"I'll burn you for what you did, filthy heretic!" the woman screamed, spittle foaming at the sides of her mouth. "I'll roast you alive, and then feed you a healing potion to burn you again! You should suffer a thousand deaths for what you did to Frederick! You filthy, disgusting, monstrous pagan! All of your kind must be purged!"

Amara vaguely recalled that the crossbowman who'd attacked her with this woman had been named Frederick. Had Selena come all this way for vengeance?

Without rising, Amara directed a healing spell at Jonas. Then she cast another toward the old knight, who had been pinned under his smoldering mount. Neither of the men were moving, but at least the motes of light swarmed over them, showing they still drew breath.

Chaos erupted in the courtyard in the wake of the woman's attacks as both the Knights Tarsillan and the Gnostics raced in her direction. With the attention diverted from them, the Issurians swarmed over to pick up their dropped weapons, while Tecala sprinted toward Malcheron. Noah, who had been healed by the Gnostics, belatedly tried to block Tecala's path but was forced to retreat as she hurled a flurry of shadowy discs at him.

"Stop her!" Amara croaked as she pointed at Tecala.

With a flash of purple light, the horned woman plucked a glowing red gem the size of a melon out of thin air and sent healing magic streaming toward Malcheron.

But the knights either didn't hear her order or ignored it. A young knight hurled himself in front of Amara, blocking the next torrent of blue fire. He screamed in agony as the flames consumed him.

Amara finished draining the mana crystal just as Malcheron regained his feet. But instead of resuming his attack, he stumbled away in the direction of the keep. With the commander of the Chaos army withdrawing, she turned her attention back to Selena, who was marching in her direction.

The woman from the Church had already burned three knights who had tried to attack her, and a seething mass of fire was forming in the sky. With every second that passed, the churning inferno grew larger, until it threatened to consume the castle.

Amara hastily cast *Charm Person*, but a pendant around Selena's neck flared with light, and the woman didn't slow her approach.

*Is everyone immune to my spells?* Amara thought with mounting panic.

Instead, she changed tack and cast *Cloak of Shadows*. If the Selena couldn't see her, then she couldn't target her. But as she teetered away, her pursuer followed her path unerringly. She could obviously see through Amara's stealth.

Only one option remained to Amara, but she feared using it. Her soul was already strained to the limit, and she'd barely refilled half of her mana. If she cast her *Avatar of Melischar* spell again, there was no telling what would happen.

Her hesitation allowed Selena to catch up, and the woman stopped only a few paces away, her chest heaving as she drew in excited breaths. As she stared at Amara, her crazed eyes nearly bulged out of their sockets. "At last, I have my vengeance!" Selena cried out.

Amara began to weave together the mana to cast her avatar spell, but it was already too late. Selena would burn her to a crisp long before she could finish.

"I'm not simply going to burn you," Selena babbled. "You will be erased from existence." She raised both hands and called down the seething inferno from the sky. The mass of flames sharpened into a tornado-like spout until a fine point was drilling down on them.

Amara braced herself for the end, but then a fountain of red flames struck Selena a glancing blow.

The veiled woman screamed and stumbled back. Then she turned to see where the flames had originated, and her eyes narrowed as they focused on Salamander standing nearby. With a flick of her wrist, Selena altered the trajectory of the column of flames, and the burning whirlwind smashed down squarely on top of the girl.

"No!" Amara screamed out, her hand outstretched. She watched with horror as Salamander disappeared into the swirling mass of fire. The girl didn't even have time to cry out before she was consumed by the flames. After a second, the spout careened onward to reveal an empty spot where her friend had been standing.

Nothing remained of Salamander—she'd been reduced to ash by the spell.

It felt like something broke inside of Amara as she finished casting her avatar spell. Glowing wings burst out of her back, and even as she felt her soul fracture, she ignored it. She would destroy the woman who had killed Salamander.

She would make her *suffer.*

For the first time, the madness in the woman's gaze faded slightly. She blinked at the sight of the outstretched angelic wings and then blinked again before she shook her head as if to clear her thoughts. "Your pathetic illusions won't fool me! The gods have abandoned us!"

"They have abandoned *you,*" Amara snarled, as the cracks in her soul multiplied.

"I will—" Selena's sentence cut off as the knight who had implored her to stop rose from the ground and plunged his sword into her back. The tip of the weapon erupted from her chest in a spray of blood.

The knight was grievously wounded. Half of his face was burned away, revealing muscle and bone beneath. But held himself steady as he gripped the sword hilt and savagely twisted the blade, impaling Selena. "I know now the avatar is real," he muttered. "And you will be judged for your actions . . . as will I."

Selena grabbed the blade with her bare hand and angled herself to fling a blue fireball at the knight. The detonation shot the man across the courtyard, where he slammed into the stone wall. He crumpled to the ground like a marionette whose strings had been cut.

Amara reached for the avatar sword on her belt to finish off Selena, but before she could grasp the pommel, Harold appeared behind the woman and smashed his cudgel down on her head.

The pig farmer's face was twisted with rage as he continued to hammer his weapon against the woman's skull until he was spattered with blood. Only once Selena had dropped to her knees, her head lolling lifelessly, did he finally stop to suck in a deep breath. "Sorry, Avatar," he gasped. "I was waiting for an opening. And . . . I'm sorry about your friend."

"Thank you," Amara said, her voice cracking. The grief of losing Salamander made it feel like her hearted had shattered in her chest. It was as though all the joy had left the world and everything looked gray and lifeless. And along with the anguish came a tidal wave of guilt for her part in the girl's death.

Before she could find her voice, the surrounding air warped. At first, she feared Selena was casting another spell, but then she spotted Malcheron standing among a knot of his troops. And he was reading from a scroll that pulsated with an astounding amount of power.

In front of her, the air ripped open to reveal a portal—within was a chamber filled with molten rock and dark, twisted monsters. Then she felt an irresistible force drawing her in. She flapped her golden wings desperately, but it was no use.

She was being sucked into the nightmarish world on the other side of the portal.

# CHAPTER 71

Malcheron could feel the rot eating away at his veins. And with every beat of his heart, the rogue's poison inched closer to his soul. Luckily, his enchanted armor was slowing the spread for the moment. But if he didn't find a healer soon, he would lose himself completely and never ascend to join the Chaos horde among the stars.

Still, the threat of death paled in comparison to failing his mother. After Tecala had partially healed him, he'd immediately sought out the Scroll of Banishment. He'd found it scuffed but otherwise undamaged, lying among the bodies of his soldiers. According to his mother, it would work on any hero, regardless of their level.

However, after he'd spoken the words of power emblazoned on the vellum, the avatar had *somehow* managed to resist the banishment spell. Even as he watched, she took a halting step away from the portal, her golden wings flapping mightily. It should be impossible to resist the power contained within the spell, and yet she was not only struggling against it, but she was close to escaping.

Malcheron held out his hand as he conjured another shadowy spear in his palm. If the avatar wouldn't go quietly into her banishment, then he would help her along. The effort of drawing upon his anima made him grimace with pain, the tendrils of the rot threatening to worm their way into his soul.

He raised the spear, intent on impaling the avatar and knocking her through the portal. But as he flung the shadowy weapon, a knight in golden armor hurled herself into the projectile's path. The spear skewered the girl, leaving the avatar untouched.

*Why do these fools sacrifice themselves so readily for this avatar?* he thought to himself furiously.

Malcheron prepared to conjure another *Shadow Spear*, but froze as a knight heaved a horse off of himself. The man who rose from the ground was wizened and stooped, but his face was unmistakeable—it was the former commander of the Knights Tarsillan.

"Oh-ho," Frederick said, his body swelling to impossible proportions. He glanced over at the avatar, who was losing her battle against the portal. "Up to your old tricks, I see, Malcheron."

"Frederick," Malcheron replied in a flat tone. Though the knight was ancient now, he knew he couldn't hope to stand against him in his current condition. And with every minute that passed, more of the cursed knights and Gnostics flooded the courtyard. Yet he could still sacrifice himself to buy more time for the dark dwarves working to destroy the core.

"Leave me," he said wearily to Tecala. There would be no ascension for him, but at least she could still have a future. "This battle is lost, but before I fall, I wish to know you survived."

"I will never leave you," she whispered. Then she reached over to grab his hand as she mumbled something rapidly under her breath.

He raised his brow in surprise, but his expression transformed to one of dismay as he spotted the teleportation scroll in her hand. Before he could stop her, the world folded around him, and he disappeared through to a snow-covered mountain pass.


Amara watched as Malcheron and Tecala disappeared, while she fought a losing battle against the pull of the portal. The fissures in her soul continued to expand, and she could feel the last of her life force ebbing away. Whatever terrible spell Malcheron had cast was about to claim her.

"Give me your hand!" Harold shouted, inching closer to Amara. But he recoiled as an invisible force started to draw him in.

Jonas appeared beside the pig farmer, his shirt burned away completely, and the skin beneath reddened. His eyes had returned to their normal white color, though a tinge of darkness still lurked in the corners.

"No matter what, you must not allow yourself to be transported through the portal!" Jonas shouted, his hair blowing in the wind. "These scrolls are used as punishment by the worshippers of Chaos. If you are drawn in, you will be condemned to an eternity of suffering."

"What should I do?" she called back. Her strength was rapidly failing, and the damage to her soul was growing more severe by the second. If she didn't release her *Avatar of Melischar* soon, her soul would shatter into a thousand pieces.

Jonas turned his gaze toward Selena on her knees. The servant of the Church had blood dripping down her face, and she was slowly slumping forward. He rushed over to Selena and grabbed her by the back of her robes. When her eyes fluttered open and she tried to feebly push him off, he simply slammed his fist into her face, making her go limp once more.

Amara watched as he dragged the nearly unconscious woman toward the portal, and without hesitation, hurled her into the burning, monster-filled world beyond. Selena's screams of terror echoed out a second later.

Jonas ignored the tortured cries as he turned back to Amara. "You only have to stay strong a little while longer. As with a teleportation scroll, the portal will grow more unstable with every person who uses it."

She watched with renewed hope as the edges of the portal frayed and the hellscape on the other side became blurred. But the effort to resist the portal was growing more difficult by the moment. She wouldn't last much longer.

"I can't hold on," she whispered, her eyes widening with fear. Her feet dug deep channels into the ground as she was dragged backward toward the yawning opening.

Jonas looked around with jerky movements as though searching for someone else to throw through. But aside from the pig farmer, there was no one else near them, and the fighting had moved closer to the ruined keep.

"What if we form a human chain?" Harold called out. "Maybe we could reach her that way?"

Jonas simply shook his head. Then a sad smile flickered across his face. "Save the South and unite the Forces of Order, Amara," Jonas said. "I have faith in you."

"Wait!" she screamed, the realization of what he was planning dawning on her. But she couldn't move—not without losing her battle against the force dragging her toward eternal punishment.

With one last lingering look at Amara, Jonas raced past her and threw himself into the portal. He disappeared through as another agonized scream from Selena rang out.

"No . . ." she whispered in disbelief, tears forming at the corner of her eyes. First Salamander and now Jonas? She had failed them all by recklessly chasing after Malcheron instead of waiting for help.

*None of this would have happened if I had simply listened to Jonas.*

The sound of Frederick stomping forward made her blink away the tears. Behind her, the portal continued to fray, and the world beyond rapidly cycled through dozens of horrifying locations. She doubted she could hold on much longer, as the last spark of her mana threatened to flicker out like a lamp in a windstorm.

"Give me your hand, Avatar," Frederick boomed. "I will draw you away from the portal to safety."

She forced herself to take a step forward, her half-healed wounds screaming in protest. Her hand brushed against Frederick's massive fingertips, but before she could grab onto him, her overtaxed soul shattered into two halves. Her life force evaporated, and her avatar spell failed. With her divine strength snuffed out, the force drawing her toward the portal picked her up and effortlessly flung her through.

The last thing she saw was a look of immense sorrow on the old knight's face before the portal blinked shut and she was buffeted by a blast of arctic cold.

Then she knew only darkness.

# EPILOGUE

**B**orim massaged his temples gingerly. The throbbing pain refused to go away, and his vision continued to go blurry at random times. He'd hoped to have his head wound healed, but with the thousands injured during the battle, a dwarf with a lump on his head was hardly high priority.

It still stung him that Malcheron had escaped. What hurt even more was how easily the Issurian had defeated him in personal combat. Even with all his defensive abilities activated, Malcheron had laid him out like he'd been a child.

*The next time I face that monster, things are going to be different,* he thought to himself. *I'll match his level and send him scurrying away like a frightened goblin.*

The thought of leveling brought with it a pang of sadness. He'd lost everyone he cared about in the battle to save the keep. Where would he find a new group?

He let out a sigh as he trudged up the hill. After dealing with the dark dwarves in the core room—an immense and sprawling underground structure they had only begun to explore—the knights had pitched their camp on the hill overlooking Stout Oak Keep.

Borim set a course for the tent housing Frederick. As he walked, more than a few knights shot him curious looks, but none moved to stop him. Which was a smart decision, since he was in the mood to crack a few skulls.

He arrived at his destination and spotted an old man, possibly even older than Frederick, lounging outside of the tent. "Edmund," he said, recognizing the knight as the one he'd met outside of Fusson. "Is your friend available?"

Edmund pressed his weathered lips together. "He's with the avatar inside."

"I see." Borim plopped down on a nearby crate and took out a sausage from the pouch on his belt. He bit into the juicy meat and chewed thoughtfully as he waited for the knight to emerge. He didn't like what the old man was doing, but it wasn't like he had any say in the matter.

After about a quarter of an hour had passed, Frederick emerged with a familiar girl at his side. She had red hair, a far-too-skinny body, and what humans probably considered cute features. Though he would always prefer the rugged and chiseled face of a dwarven woman. At her hip hung a quiver full of darts, and a magical staff glowed with power in her hand.

"Hello, Borim," Amara said with a smile. "How are you doing? I can't wait to adventure with you again."

"I'm good," he grumbled without meeting her gaze. "And I think I'll pass on the adventuring."

Amara's expression fell, but then she nodded.

"I'll talk to you soon, Amara," Frederick said, ushering the woman away. "Remember, keep practicing your spells." Then he turned toward Borim. "Oh-ho, has a small child come to visit me? Or perhaps some kind of intelligent gopher?"

"Knock it off, you senile old goat." Borim leapt down and stuffed the uneaten food in his pocket. "And I'll have you know. I hate what you're doing."

Frederick shrugged. "The war against Chaos has just begun. And the people need an avatar."

"Amara is still alive," he said through gritted teeth. "It's wrong to just replace her with a lookalike. And I'd bet my last pickaxe that someone will catch on."

"The girl they've chosen is a very skilled illusionist, or so I've been told," Frederick continued. "And if Amara still lives, she probably wishes she didn't. Most likely, she's in the lair of a Harbinger or some equally unpleasant place. The Scrolls of Banishment crafted by Abiloch are all but inescapable, even for someone as talented as her."

"I'll find a way to get her out." Borim looked down glumly at his boots. "Just you watch."

"Now that, I would like to see." Frederick walked over and touched the dwarf's shoulder. "I feel her loss keenly, too."

Borim brushed off the old man's hand and bit down a stinging retort. There was no reason to take out his frustration on this old man. No matter how good it would feel.

"Now, where is my halberd?" Frederick said wistfully. "I swear, I just had it earlier."

Edmund stepped forward, a halberd in his hand. "It's right here, you old coot."

"Oh-ho, thank you," Frederick replied. "While you were gone, I kept losing my weapon."

"I know," Edmund sighed. "I know."

The sackcloth felt scratchy against Otto's skin, and he'd been rubbed raw in too many places to count. More than anything, he wanted to take his clothing off and burn it. But after narrowly escaping Leissen dressed only in a sackcloth, the first Gnostics he'd encountered had believed him to be some sort of wild prophet. And they had hung on his every word as he described the avatar.

Word had quickly spread about the "sackcloth prophet," and now, no matter how much he hated his garb, he was stuck with it. At least if he wanted to retain his position as the de facto religious leader of the resistance against the Church.

A young girl running down the corridor interrupted his thoughts. The citadel he was staying in had been carved deep into the living rock of a desert mountain. Not that such construction was unusual in the South, where many of the buildings had been built underground to escape the unbearable heat outside. But at least they had good food here. Which was really all that mattered in life.

"Brother Otto," the girl gasped, as she stumbled to a stop in front of him.

"Yes," he replied, with only passing interest. It seemed like people ran up to him breathlessly half a dozen times a day. Still, he reminded himself that she might have word about the battle in the North. The last he'd heard, the Gnostics had set out to fight the Chaos army in a last-ditch effort to hold the Wall. There had been no word since then, and he was beginning to worry.

*What if the Wall fell to Chaos?*

"The beacon is lit!" she cried out.

"Hmm?" He hated to admit it, but he'd only been half-listening.

"The Beacon of Khaneri!" she repeated with shining eyes. "An avatar has been born into this world."

The mention of an avatar grabbed his attention. "An avatar you say? Are you sure?"

She bobbed her head up and down, a few strands of her brutally straight hair falling over her face. "The brothers claim the avatar of Alodia has been reincarnated."

"The Goddess of Fertility?" Brother Otto absently adjusted his sackcloth. But it did nothing to lessen the itching. When he got back to his room, he would slip into the satin robes he'd smuggled in a few weeks earlier. "Now that *is* interesting. I believe they were always fire mages, were they not?"

"Yes! The new avatar is a fire mage!" The girl bounced up and down on her toes. "And she's downstairs!"

"I see." Brother Otto rubbed his chin, trying to hide his excitement. "Let's go meet her, then."

He followed the woman down the rough-hewn corridor as they descended into the bowels of the ancient citadel. The birth of a new avatar could signal two things: either the first had fallen in battle at Galoth's Wall, or the Gods of Order now believed this world could be saved from Chaos.

Brother Otto could only pray it was the latter. With the growing threats from the wastelands, the horrors rising in the Dragonspine Mountains, and the mysterious sea raiders reported by the coastal cities, they were going to need all the help they could get.

# ABOUT THE AUTHOR

G. B. Scally is the author of the Vularia Reincarnation Cycle, originally released on Royal Road. She lives with her husband—also a writer—her two young children, and a chocolate Labrador Retriever in a small town in Ontario, Canada. When she's not writing, she spends her time keeping active, reading way too much LitRPG, and dreaming of new worlds to write about.

# DISCOVER
# *STORIES UNBOUND*

## PodiumAudio.com